THE NIGHT FERRY

Also by Michael Robotham

SUSPECT

LOST

DOUBLEDAY

New York London Toronto Sydney Auckland

THE NIGHT FERRY

Michael Robotham

A novel

PUBLISHED BY DOUBLEDAY

Published in the United States by Doubleday, an imprint of
The Doubleday Broadway Publishing Group, a division of
Random House, Inc., New York.
www.doubleday.com

Library of Congress Cataloging-in-Publication Data

Robotham, Michael, 1960–
    The night ferry : a novel / Michael Robotham.—1st ed.
        p.   cm.
1. London (England)—Fiction. 2. Amsterdam (Netherlands)—
Fiction. I. Title.
PR6118.O26N54 2007
823'.92—dc22   2006019771

ISBN 978-0-385-51790-4

PRINTED IN THE UNITED STATES OF AMERICA

10 9 8 7 6 5 4 3 2 1
First Edition

This one is for Alpheus "Two Dogs" Williams,
a mentor and a mate

acknowledgments

This is a story that could not have been told without Esther Brandt
and Jacqueline de Jong, who were invaluable in helping my re-
search. Through them I met Sytze van der Zee, Leo Rietveld and the
remarkable Joep de Groot, my guide through Amsterdam's famous
red light district.

Elsewhere I am indebted to Ursula Mackenzie and Mark Lucas
for their friendship, advice and belief that I have something inside
me that is worth writing. For their hospitality I am grateful to
Richard, Emma, Mark and Sara. And I'd be lost without my three
daughters, Alex, Charlotte and Bella, who make me laugh and forget work.

Yet again, however, it is Vivien who deserves most of the credit.
My researcher, plotter, reader, reviewer, lover and wife, she is *my*
love story.

BOOK ONE

When the first baby laughed for the first time, the laugh broke into a thousand pieces and they all went skipping about, and that was the beginning of fairies.

—SIR JAMES BARRIE,
Peter Pan

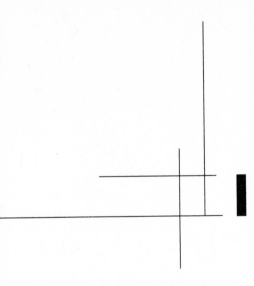

It was Graham Greene who said a story has no beginning or end. The author simply chooses a moment, an arbitrary point, and looks either forward or back. That moment is now—an October morning—when the clang of a metallic letter flap heralds the first post.

There is an envelope on the mat inside my front door. Inside is a small stiff rectangle of paper that says nothing and everything.

Dear Ali,
I'm in trouble. I must see you. Please come to the reunion.
Love, Cate

Sixteen words. Long enough to be a suicide note. Short enough to end an affair. I don't know why Cate has written to me now. She hates me. She told me so the last time we spoke, eight years ago. The past. Given long enough I could tell you the month, the day and the hour but these details are unimportant.

All you need to know is the year—1998. It should have been the summer we finished university; the summer we went backpacking across Europe; the summer I lost my virginity to Brian Rusconi and not to Cate's father. Instead it was the summer she went away and the summer I left home—a summer not big enough for everything that happened.

Now she wants to see me again. Sometimes you know when a story begins . . .

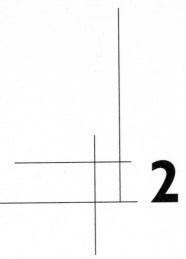

2

When the day comes that I am asked to recalibrate the calendar, I am going to lop a week off January and February and add them to October, which deserves to be forty days long, maybe more.

I love this time of year. The tourists have long gone and the kids are back at school. The TV schedules aren't full of reruns and I can sleep under a duvet again. Mostly I love the sparkle in the air, without the pollen from the plane trees so I can open my lungs and run freely.

I run every morning—three circuits of Victoria Park in Bethnal Green, each one of them more than a mile. Right now I'm just passing Durward Street in Whitechapel. Jack the Ripper territory. I once took a Ripper walking tour, a pub crawl with ghost stories. The victim I remember best was his last one, Mary Kelly, who died on the same date as my birthday, November the ninth.

People forget how small an area Jack roamed. Spitalfields, Shoreditch and Whitechapel cover less than a square mile, yet in 1888 more than a million people were crammed into slums, without decent water and sewerage. It is still overcrowded and poor but that's only compared to places like Hampstead or Chiswick or Holland Park. Poverty is a relative state in a rich country where the wealthiest are the first to cry poor.

It is seven years since I last ran competitively, on a September night in Birmingham, under lights. I wanted to get to the Sydney Olympics but only two of us were going to make it. Four-hundredths of a second separated first from fifth; half a meter, a heartbeat, a broken heart.

I don't run to win anymore. I run because I can and because I'm fast. Fast enough to blur at the edges. That's why I'm here now, flirting with the ground while perspiration leaks between my breasts, plastering my T-shirt to my stomach.

When I run my thoughts become clearer, or at least concentrated. Mostly I think about work and imagine that today someone will call and offer me my old job back.

A year ago I helped solve a kidnapping and find a missing girl. One of the kidnappers dropped me onto a wall, crushing my spine. After six operations and nine months of physiotherapy I am fit again, with more steel in my spine than England's back four. Unfortunately, nobody seems to know what to do with me at the Metropolitan Police. I am a wonky wheel on the machine.

As I pass the playground, I notice a man sitting on a bench reading a newspaper. There is no child on the climbing frame behind him and other benches are in sunshine. Why has he chosen the shade?

In his mid-thirties, dressed in a shirt and tie, he doesn't raise his eyes as I pass. He's studying a crossword. What sort of man does a crossword in a park at this hour of the morning? A man who can't sleep. A man who waits.

Up until a year ago I used to watch people for a living. I guarded diplomats and visiting heads of state, ferrying their wives on shopping trips to Harrods and dropping their children at school. It is probably the most boring job in the Metropolitan Police but I was good at it. During five years with the Diplomatic Protection Group I didn't fire a shot in anger or miss one of the wives' hair appointments. I was like one of those soldiers who sit in the missile silos, praying the phone never rings.

On my second circuit of the park he is still there. His suede jacket is lying across his lap. He has freckles and smooth brown hair, cut symmetrically and parted to the left. A leather briefcase is tucked close to his side.

A gust of wind tears the newspaper from his fingers. Three steps and I reach it first. It wraps around my thigh.

For a moment he wants to retreat, as if he's too close to the edge. His freckles make him look younger. His eyes don't meet mine. Instead he bunches his shoulders shyly and says thank you. The front page is still wrapped around my thigh. For a moment I'm tempted to have some fun. I could make a joke about feeling like tomorrow's fish-and-chips.

The breeze feels cool on my neck. "Sorry, I'm rather sweaty."

He touches his nose nervously, nods and touches his nose again.

"Do you run every day?" he asks suddenly.

"I try to."

"How far?"

"Four miles."

It's an American accent. He doesn't know what else to say.

"I have to keep going. I don't want to cool down."

"Okay. Sure. Have a nice day." It doesn't sound so trite coming from an American.

On my third circuit of the park the bench is empty. I look for him along the street but there are no silhouettes. Normal service has been resumed.

Farther along the street, just visible on the corner, a van is parked at the curb. As I draw nearer, I notice a white plastic tent over missing paving stones. A metal cage is propped open around the hole. They've started work early.

I do this sort of thing—take note of people and vehicles. I look for things that are out of the ordinary; people in the wrong place, or the wrong clothes; cars parked illegally; the same face in different locations. I can't change what I am.

Unlacing my trainers, I pull a key from beneath the insole and unlock my front door. My neighbor, Mr. Mordecai, waves from his window. I once asked him his first name and he said it should be Yo'man.

"Why's that?"

"Because that's what my boys call me: 'Yo man, can I have some money?' 'Yo man, can I borrow the car?'"

His laugh sounded like nuts falling on a roof.

In the kitchen I pour myself a large glass of water and drink it greedily. Then I stretch my quads, balancing one leg on the back of a chair.

The mouse living under my fridge chooses that moment to appear. It is a very ambivalent mouse, scarcely bothering to lift its head to acknowledge me. And it doesn't seem to mind that my youngest brother, Hari, keeps setting mousetraps. Perhaps it knows that I disarm them, taking off the cheese when Hari isn't around.

The mouse finally looks up at me, as though about to complain about the lack of crumbs. Then it sniffs the air and scampers away.

Hari appears in the doorway, bare-chested and barefooted. Opening the fridge, he takes out a carton of orange juice and unscrews the plastic lid. He looks at me, considers his options, and gets a glass from the cupboard. Sometimes I think he is prettier than I am. He has longer lashes and thicker hair.

"Are you going to the reunion tonight?" I ask.

"Nope."

"Why not?"

"Don't tell me *you're* going! You said you wouldn't be caught dead."

"I changed my mind."

There is a voice from upstairs. "Hey, have you seen my knickers?"

Hari looks at me sheepishly.

"I know I had a pair. They're not on the floor."

Hari whispers, "I thought you'd gone out."

"I went for a run. Who is she?"

"An old friend."

"So you must know her name."

"Cheryl."

"Cheryl Taylor!" (She's a bottle blonde who works behind the bar at the White Horse). "She's older than I am."

"No, she's not."

"What on earth do you see in her?"

"What difference does that make?"

"I'm interested."

"Well, she has assets."

"Assets?"

"The best."

"You think so?"

"Absolutely."

"What about Phoebe Griggs?"

"Too small."

"Emma Shipley?"

"Saggy."

"Mine?"

"Very funny."

Cheryl is coming down the stairs. I can hear her rummaging in the sitting room. "Found them," she shouts.

She arrives in the kitchen still adjusting the elastic beneath her skirt.

"Oh, hello," she squeaks.

"Cheryl, this is my sister, Alisha."

"Nice to see you again," she says, not meaning it.

The silence seems to stretch out. I might never talk again. Finally I excuse myself and go upstairs for a shower. With any luck Cheryl will be gone by the time I come down.

Hari has been living with me for the past two months because it's closer to university. He is supposed to be safeguarding my virtue and helping pay the mortgage but he's four weeks behind in his rent and using my spare room as a knocking shop.

My legs are tingling. I love the feeling of lactic acid leaking away. I look in the mirror and pull back my hair. Yellow flecks spark in my irises like goldfish in a pond. There are no wrinkles. Black don't crack.

My "assets" aren't so bad. When I was running competitively I was always pleased they were on the small side and could be tightly bound in a sports bra. Now I wouldn't mind being a size bigger so I could have a cleavage.

Hari yells up the stairs. "Hey, sis, I'm taking twenty from your purse."

"Why?"

"Because when I take it from strangers they get angry."

Very droll. "You still owe me rent."

"Tomorrow."

"You said that yesterday." *And the day before.*

The front door closes. The house is quiet.

Downstairs, I pick up Cate's note again, resting it between my fingertips. Then I prop it on the table against the salt and pepper shakers, staring at it for a while.

Cate Elliot. Her name still makes me smile. One of the strange things about friendship is that time together isn't canceled out by time apart. One doesn't erase the other or balance it on some invisible scale. You can spend a few hours with someone and they will change your life, or you can spend a lifetime with a person and remain unchanged.

We were born at the same hospital and raised in Bethnal Green in London's East End although we managed to more or less avoid each other for the first thirteen years. Fate brought us together, if you believe in such things.

We became inseparable. Almost telepathic. We were partners in crime, stealing beer from her father's fridge, window shopping on the Kings Road, eating chips with vinegar on our way home from school, sneaking out to see bands at the Hammersmith Odeon and movie stars on the red carpet at Leicester Square.

In our gap year we went to France. I crashed a moped, got cautioned for having a fake ID and tried hash for the first time. Cate lost the key to our hostel during a midnight swim and we had to climb a trellis at 2:00 a.m.

There is no breakup worse than that of best friends. Broken love affairs are painful. Broken marriages are messy. Broken homes are sometimes an improvement. Our breakup was the worst.

Now, after eight years, she wants to see me. The thrill of compliance spreads across my skin. Then comes a nagging, unshakable dread. She's in trouble.

My car keys are in the sitting room. As I pick them up, I notice marks on the glass-topped coffee table. Looking closer, I can make out two neat buttock prints and what I imagine to be elbow smudges. I could kill my brother!

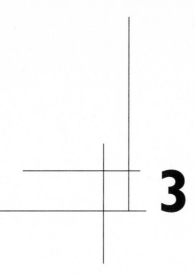

3

Someone has spilled a Bloody Mary mix on my shoes. I wouldn't mind so much, but they're not mine. I borrowed them, just like I borrowed this top, which is too big for me. At least my underwear is my own. "Never borrow money or underwear," my mother always says, in an addendum to her clean-underwear speech which involves graphic descriptions of road accidents and ambulance officers cutting off my tights. No wonder I have nightmares.

Cate isn't here yet. I've been trying to watch the door and avoid talking to anyone.

There should be a law against school reunions. They should come with warning stickers on the invitations. There is never a right time for them. You're either too young or too old or too fat.

This isn't even a proper school reunion. Somebody burned down the science classrooms at Oaklands. A vandal with a can of petrol rather than a rogue Bunsen burner. Now they're opening a brand-new block, with a junior minister of something-or-other doing the honors.

The new building is functional and sturdy, with none of the charm of the Victorian original. The cathedral ceilings and arched windows have been replaced by fibrous cement panels, strip lighting and aluminum frames.

The school hall has been decorated with streamers and balloons hang from the rafters. A school banner is draped across the front of the stage.

There is a queue for the mirror in the girls' toilets. Lindsay Saunders leans past me over the sink and rubs lipstick from her teeth. Satisfied, she turns and appraises me.

"Will you stop acting like a Punjabi princess and loosen up. Have fun."

"Is that what this is?"

I'm wearing Lindsay's top, the bronze one with shoestring straps, which I don't have the bust to carry off. A strap falls off my shoulder. I tug it up again.

"I know you're acting like you don't care. You're just nervous about Cate. Where is she?"

"I don't know."

Lindsay reapplies her lipstick and adjusts her dress. She's been looking forward to the reunion for weeks because of Rocco Manspiezer. She fancied him for six years at school but didn't have the courage to tell him.

"What makes you so sure you'll get him this time?"

"Well I didn't spend two hundred quid on this dress and squeeze into these bloody shoes to be ignored by him again."

Unlike Lindsay, I have no desire to hang around with people I have spent twelve years avoiding. I don't want to hear how much money they make or how big their house is or see photographs of their children who have names that sound like brands of shampoo.

That's the thing about school reunions—people only come to measure their life against others and to see the failures. They want to know which of the beauty queens has put on seventy pounds and seen her husband run off with his secretary, and which teacher got caught taking photographs in the changing rooms.

"Come on, aren't you curious?" Lindsay asks.

"Of course, I'm curious. I *hate* the fact I'm curious. I just wish I was invisible."

"Don't be such a spoilsport." She rubs her finger across my eyebrows. "Did you see Annabelle Trunzo? My God that dress! And what about her hair?"

"Rocco doesn't even have any hair."

"Ah, but he's still looking fit."

"Is he married?"

"Hush your mouth."

"Well, I think you should at least find out before you shag him."

She gives me a wicked grin. "I'll ask afterward."

Lindsay acts like a real man-eater, but I know she's not really so predatory. I tell myself that all the time, but I still wouldn't let her date my brothers.

Back in the hall, the lights have been turned down and the music turned up. Spandau Ballet has been replaced by eighties anthems. The women are wearing a mixture of cocktail dresses and saris. Others are pretending not to care, in leather jackets and designer jeans.

There were always tribes at Oaklands. The whites were a minority. Most of the students were Banglas (Bangladeshis) with a few Pakis and Indians thrown into the mix.

I was a "curry," a "yindoo," an "elephant trainer." Brown Indian in case you're wondering. As defining details go, nothing else came close at Oaklands—not my black hair, braces or skinny legs; not having glandular fever at seven, or being able to run like the wind. Everything else paled into insignificance alongside my skin color and Sikh heritage.

It's not true that all Sikhs are called Singh. And we don't all carry curved blades strapped to our chests (although in the East End having this sort of rep isn't such a bad thing).

Even now the Banglas are sticking together. People are sitting next to the same people they sat alongside at school. Despite everything that has happened in the intervening years, the core facets of our personalities are untouched. All our flaws and strengths are the same.

On the far side of the hall I see Cate arriving. She is pale and striking, with a short expensive haircut and cheap sexy shoes. Dressed in a long light khaki skirt and a silk blouse, she looks elegant and, yes, pregnant. Her hands are smoothing her neat, compact bump. It's more than a bump. A beach ball. She hasn't long to go.

I don't want her to see me staring. I turn away.

"Alisha?"

"Sure. Who else?" I turn suddenly and put on a goofy smile.

Cate leans forward and kisses my cheek. I don't close my eyes. Neither does she. We stare at each other. Surprised. She smells of childhood.

There are fine lines at the corners of her eyes. I wasn't there to see them drawn. The small scar on her left temple, just beneath her hairline, I remember that one.

We're the same age, twenty-nine, and the same shape, except for the bump. I have darker skin and hidden depths (like all brunettes) but I can categorically state that I will never look as good as Cate. She has learned—no, that makes it sound too practiced—she was born with the ability to make men admire her. I don't know the secret. A movement of the eye, a cock of the head, a tone of voice or a touch of the arm, creates a moment, an illusion that all men gay or straight, old or young buy into.

People are watching her now. I doubt if she even realizes.

"How are you?"

"I'm fine," I answer too quickly and start again. "I'm all right."

"Just all right?"

I try to laugh. "But look at you—you're pregnant."

"Yes."

"When are you due?"

"In four weeks."

"Congratulations."

"Thank you."

The questions and answers are too abrupt and matter-of-fact. Conversation has never been this hard—not with Cate. She looks nervously over my shoulder, as if worried we might be overheard.

"Didn't you marry—?"

"Felix Beaumont. He's over there."

I follow her eyes to a tall, heavy-set figure in casual trousers and a loose white shirt. Felix didn't go to Oaklands and his real name is Buczkowski, not "Beaumont." His father was a Polish shopkeeper who ran an electronics shop on Tottenham Court Road.

Now he's deep in conversation with Annabelle Trunzo, whose dress is a scrap of material held up by her chest. If she exhales it's going to be bunched around her ankles.

"You know what I used to hate most about nights like this?" says Cate. "Having someone who looks immaculate telling me how she spent all day ferrying children to ballet or football or cricket. And then she asks the obvious question: 'Do you have any kids?' And I say, 'Nope, no children.' And she jokes, 'Hey, why don't you have one of mine?' God that pisses me off."

"Well, it won't happen anymore."

"No."

She takes a glass of wine from a passing tray. Again she glances around, looking distracted.

"Why did we fall out? It must have been my fault."

"I'm sure you remember," I say.

"It doesn't matter anymore. By the way, I want you to be a godparent."

"I'm not even a Christian."

"Oh, that doesn't matter."

Cate is avoiding whatever she really wants to talk about.

"Tell me what's wrong."

She hesitates. "I've gone too far this time, Ali. I've risked everything."

Taking her arm, I steer her toward a quiet corner. People are starting to dance. The music is too loud. Cate puts her mouth close to my ear. "You have to help me. Promise me you'll help me . . ."

"Of course."

She holds back a sob, seeming to bite down upon it. "They want to take my baby. They can't. You have to stop them—"

A hand touches her shoulder and she jumps, startled.

"Hello, gorgeous pregnant lady, who have we here?"

Cate backs away a step. "No one. It's just an old friend." Something shifts inside her. She wants to escape.

Felix Beaumont has perfect teeth. My mother has a thing about dental work. It is the first thing she notices about people.

"I remember you," he says. "You were behind me."

"At school?"

"No, at the bar."

He laughs and adopts an expression of amused curiosity.

Cate has backed farther away. My eyes find hers. The faintest shake of her head tells me to let her go. I feel a rush of tenderness toward her. She motions with her empty glass. "I'm just going to get a refill."

"Go easy on that stuff, sweetheart. You're not alone." He brushes her bump.

"Last one."

Felix watches her leave with a mixture of sadness and longing. Finally, he turns back to me.

"So is it Miss or Mrs.?"

"Pardon?"

"Are you married?"

I hear myself say "Ms." which makes me sound like a lesbian. I change it to "Miss" and then blurt, "I'm single," which appears desperate.

"That explains it."

"What?"

"Those with children have photographs. Those without have nicer clothes and fewer lines."

Is that supposed to be a compliment?

The skin around his eyes crinkles into a smile. He moves like a bear, rocking from foot to foot.

"So what do you do, Alisha?"

I hold out my hand. "My name is Alisha Barba."

He looks astonished. "Well, well, well, you *really* exist. Cate has talked about you a lot but I thought you might be one of those imaginary childhood friends."

"She's talked about me?"

"Absolutely. What do you do, Alisha?"

"I sit at home all day in my slippers watching daytime soaps and old movies on Channel 4."

He doesn't understand.

"I'm on medical leave from the Metropolitan Police."

"What happened?"

"I broke my back. Someone dropped me across a wall."

He flinches. My gaze drifts past him.

"She's coming back," he says, reading my mind. "She never leaves me talking to a pretty woman for too long."

"You must be thrilled—about the baby."

The smooth hollow beneath his Adam's apple rolls like a wave as he swallows. "It's our miracle baby. We've been trying for so long."

Someone has started a conga line on the dance floor, which snakes between the tables. Gopal Dhir grabs at my waist, pivoting my hips from side to side. Someone else pulls Felix into another part of the line and we're moving apart.

Gopal yells into my ear. "Well, well, Alisha Barba. Are you still running?"

"Only for fun."

"I always fancied you but you were far too quick for me." He yells to someone over his shoulder. "Hey, Rao! Look who it is— Alisha Barba. Didn't I always say she was cute?"

Rao has no hope of hearing him over the music, but nods vigorously and kicks out his heels.

I drag myself away.

"Why are you leaving?"

"I refuse to do the conga without a person from Trinidad being present."

Disappointed, he lets me go and rocks his head from side to side. Someone else tries to grab me but I spring away.

The crowd around the bar has thinned out. I can't see Cate. People are sitting on the steps outside and spilling into the quadrangle. Across the playground I can see the famous oak tree, almost silver in the lights. Someone has put chicken wire around the trunk to stop children climbing. One of the Banglas fell off and broke his arm during my last year—a kid called Paakhi, which is Bengali for bird. What's in a name?

The new science block squats on the far side of the quadrangle. Deserted. Crossing the playground, I push open a door and enter a long corridor with classrooms to the left. Taking a few steps, I look inside. Chrome taps and curved spouts pick up faint light from the windows.

As my eyes adjust to the darkness, I see someone moving. A woman with her dress pushed up over her waist is arched over a bench with a man between her legs.

Backing away toward the door, I sense that someone else is watching. The smallest shift of my gaze finds him.

He whispers, "Like to watch do you, yindoo?"

I catch my breath. A half breath. Paul Donavon pushes his face close to mine. The years have thinned his hair and fleshed out his cheeks but he has the same eyes. It's amazing how I can hate him with the same intensity after all this time.

Even in the half-light, I notice the tattooed cross on his neck. He sniffs at my hair. "Where's Cate?"

"You leave her alone," I say too loudly.

There are curses from the darkness. Lindsay and partner pull apart. Rocco is dancing on one leg, trying to hoist his trousers. At the far end of the corridor a door opens and light washes from outside as Donavon disappears.

"Jesus, Ali, you frightened the crap out of me," says Lindsay, tugging down her dress.

"Sorry."

"Who else was here?"

"Nobody. I'm really sorry. Just carry on."

"I think the moment's gone."

Rocco is already heading down the corridor.

"Give my best to your wife," she calls after him.

I have to find Cate now. She should be told that Donavon is here. And I want her to explain what she meant. Who wants to take her baby?

I check the hall and the quadrangle. There is no sign of her. She might have left already. How strange it is to be conscious of losing her when I've only just met her again.

I walk to the school gates. Cars are parked on either side of the road. The pavement is dotted with people. I catch a glimpse of Cate and Felix on the far side. She is talking to someone. Donavon. She has her hand on his arm.

Cate looks up and waves. I'm closing the distance between us, but she signals me to wait. Donavon turns away. Felix and Cate step between parked cars.

From somewhere behind them I hear Donavon cry out. Then comes a tortured high-pitched screech of rubber against tarmac. The wheels of a car are locked and screaming. Heads turn as if released from a catch.

Felix vanishes beneath the wheels, which rise and fall over his head with scarcely a bump. At the same moment Cate bends over the hood and springs back again. She turns her head in midair and the windscreen suddenly snaps it in reverse. She tumbles through the air in slow motion like a trapeze artist ready to be caught. But nobody waits with chalky hands.

The driver brakes and slews. Cate rolls forward, landing on her back with her arm outstretched and one leg twisted beneath her.

Like an explosion in reverse, people are sucked toward the detonation. They scramble from cars and burst from doorways. Donavon reacts quicker than most and reaches Cate first. I drop to my knees beside him.

In a moment of suspended stillness, the three of us are drawn together again. She is lying on the road. Blood seeps from her nose in a deep soft satin blackness. Spittle bubbles and froths from her slightly parted lips. She has the prettiest mouth.

I cradle her head in the crook of my arm. What happened to her shoe? She only has one of them. Suddenly, I'm fixated on a missing shoe, asking people around me. It's important that I find it. Black, with a half heel. Her skirt has ridden up. She's wearing maternity knickers to cover her bump.

A young chap steps forward politely. "I've called 999."

His girlfriend looks like she might be sick.

Donavon pulls down Cate's skirt. "Don't move her head. She has to be braced." He turns to the onlookers. "We need blankets and a doctor."

"Is she dead?" someone asks.

"Do you know her?" asks another.

"She's pregnant!" exclaims a third person.

Cate's eyes are open. I can see myself reflected in them. A burly man with a gray ponytail leans over us. He has an Irish accent.

"They just stepped out. I didn't see them. I swear."

Cate's whole body goes rigid and her eyes widen. Even with blood in her mouth she tries to cry out and her head swings from side to side.

Donavon leaps to his feet and grabs the driver's shirt. "You could have stopped, you bastard!"

"I didn't see them."

"LIAR!" His voice is hoarse with hate. "You ran them down."

The driver glances nervously around the crowd. "I don't know what he's talking about. It was an accident, I swear. He's talking crazy—"

"You saw them."

"Not until it was too late . . ."

He pushes Donavon away. Buttons rip and the driver's shirt flaps open. The tattoo on his chest is of Christ and the Crucifixion.

People have piled out of the reunion to see what the commotion is about. Some of them are yelling and trying to clear the street. I can hear the sirens.

A paramedic pushes through the crowd. My fingers are slick and warm. I feel like I'm holding Cate's head together. Two more crews arrive. The paramedics team up. I know the drill: no fire, no fuel leaks and no fallen power lines—they secure their own safety first.

I look for Felix. A dark shape is pinned beneath the rear axle of the car. Unmoving.

A paramedic crawls beneath the wheel arch. "This one's gone," he yells.

Another slides his hands beneath mine, taking hold of Cate's head. Two of them work on her.

"Airways are blocked. Using the Guedels."

He puts a plastic curved tube in her mouth and suctions out blood.

"One seventy systolic over ninety. Right pupil dilated."

"She's hypotensive."

"Put a collar on."

Someone talks into a two-way. "We got serious head trauma and internal bleeding."

"She's pregnant," I hear myself saying. I don't know if they hear me.

"BP is climbing. Low pulse."

"She's bleeding into her skull."

"Let's get her inside."

"She needs volume now."

The spine board is placed beside her and Cate is log-rolled onto her side and lifted onto a stretcher.

"She's pregnant," I say again.

The paramedic turns to me.

"Do you know her?"

"Yes."

"We got room for one. You can ride up front." He is pumping a rubber bag, forcing air into her lungs. "We need her name, DOB, address—is she allergic to any drugs?"

"I don't know."

"When is she due?"

"In four weeks."

The stretcher is in the ambulance. The paramedics climb inside. A medical technician hustles me into the passenger seat. The door shuts. We're moving. Through the window I see the crowd staring at us. Where did they all come from? Donavon is sitting in the gutter, looking dazed. I want him to look at me. I want to say thank you.

The paramedics continue working on Cate. One of them talks into a two-way using words like bradycardia and intracranial pressure. A heart monitor beeps out a broken message.

"Is she going to be all right?"

Nobody answers.

"What about the baby?"

He unbuttons her blouse. "I'm running two units."

"No, wait. I've lost her pulse."

The monitor flatlines.

"She's asystolic!"

"Starting compressions."

He rips open the final buttons, exposing her bra and torso. Both paramedics suddenly stop and raise their eyes to each other—a single look, no words, but it conveys everything. Strapped to Cate's midriff is a large piece of upholstery foam, trimmed to fit over her stomach. The prosthetic is pulled away. Cate is "pregnant" no more.

Pushing down hard on her chest, a paramedic counts the compressions, yelling the numbers. The heart monitor is competing with the siren.

"No response."

"We might have to crack her open."

"One amp of adrenaline." He bites off the cap and stabs the contents into her neck.

The next few minutes pass in a blur of flashing lights and fractured conversations. I know they're losing her. I guess I've known it all along. The dilated pupils, the bleeding inside her head—the classic signs of brain injury. Cate is broken in too many places to fix.

A thin green line on the monitor rises and falls and flattens again. They're counting each inflation with the chest compressions. One squeeze to every five compressions.

"Thommo."

"What?"

"I'm stopping the chest compressions."

"Why?"

"Because they're making her brains come out of her head."

Cate's skull is broken behind her right ear.

"Keep going."

"But—"

"Just keep going."

Half a minute passes. Hard as they try, Cate's heart won't answer.

"What are you going to do?"

"Crack her chest."

A wave of nausea washes into my mouth. I don't remember the rest of the journey or arriving at the hospital. There are no crashing doors or white coats rushing down corridors. Instead, everything appears to slow down. The building swallows Cate whole, less than whole, damaged.

Hospitals, I hate them. The smell, the pall of uncertainty, the whiteness. White walls, white sheets, white clothes. The only things not white are the bodily fluids and the Afro-Caribbean nurses.

I'm still standing near the ambulance. The paramedics return and begin mopping up the blood.

"Are you gonna be OK?" one of them asks. The pillow of upholstery foam hangs from his fist. The dangling straps look like the legs of a strange sea creature.

He hands me a damp paper towel. "You might want to use this."

I have blood on my hands; blood all over my jeans.

"You missed a bit." He motions to my cheek. I wipe the wrong one.

"Here, do you mind?"

He takes the towel and holds my chin in the palm of his hand, wiping my cheek. "There."

"Thank you."

He wants to say something. "Is she a close friend?"

"We went to school together."

He nods. "Why would she—I mean—why did she fake a pregnancy?"

I glance past him, unable to answer. It doesn't serve any purpose and makes even less sense. Cate needed to see me. She said they wanted to take her baby. What baby?

"Is she—will she be OK?"

It's his turn to not answer. The sadness in his eyes is rationed carefully because others will need it later.

A hose spits. Pink water swirls down the drain. The paramedic hands me the prosthetic and I feel something break inside me. Once I thought I had lost Cate forever. Maybe this time I have.

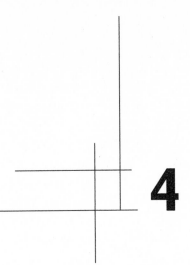

4

Hospital waiting rooms are useless, helpless places, full of whispers and prayers. Nobody wants to look at me. I have tried to clean Lindsay's top in the bathroom, scrubbing it under the tap with hand soap. I only managed to spread the stain around.

Doctors and nurses wander in and out, never able to relax. One patient on a trolley looks like a fly caught in a web of tubes and wires. The skin around his mouth is puckered and dry.

I have never really thought about death. Even when I was lying in hospital with pins holding my spine together, it didn't occur to me. I have faced off suspects, pursued cars, charged through doorways and walked into abandoned buildings but have never thought that I might die. Maybe that's one of the advantages of having little self-value.

A nurse has taken down details of Cate's family. I don't know about Felix. His mother might still be alive. Nobody can tell me anything except that Cate is in surgery. The nurses are relentlessly positive. The doctors are more circumspect. They have the truth to contend with—the reality of what they can and cannot fix.

In the midst of an ordinary evening, on a quiet street, a couple are hit by a car. One is dead. The other has horrific injuries. What happened to Cate's other shoe? What happened to her baby?

A policeman arrives to interview me. He is my age, wearing a uniform with everything polished and pressed. I feel self-conscious about my appearance.

He has a list of questions—what, where, when and why. I try to remember everything that happened. The car came out of nowhere. Donavon yelled.

"So you think it was an accident?"

"I don't know."

In my head I can hear Donavon accusing the driver of running them down. The policeman gives me a card. "If you remember anything more, give me a call."

Through the swing doors, I see Cate's family arriving. Her father, her mother in a wheelchair, her older brother, Jarrod.

Barnaby Elliot's voice is raised. "What do you mean there's no baby? My daughter is pregnant."

"What are they saying, Barnaby?" his wife asks, tugging at his sleeve.

"They're saying she wasn't pregnant."

"Then it mustn't be our Cate. They have the wrong person."

The doctor interrupts. "If you'll just wait here, I'll send someone to talk to you."

Mrs. Elliot is growing hysterical. "Does that mean she lost the baby?"

"She was never pregnant. She didn't *have* a baby."

Jarrod tries to intervene. "I'm sorry but there must be some mistake. Cate was due in four weeks."

"I want to see my daughter," demands Barnaby. "I want to see her right this minute."

Jarrod is three years older than Cate. It is strange how little I can recall of him. He kept pigeons and wore braces until he was twenty. I think he went to university in Scotland and later got a job in the city.

In contrast, nothing about Cate is remote or diffuse or gone small. I still remember when I first saw her. She was sitting on a bench outside the school gates at Oaklands wearing white socks, a short gray pleated skirt and Doc Martens. Heavy mascara bruised her eyes, which seemed impossibly large. And her teased hair had all the colors of the rainbow.

Although new to the school, within days Cate knew more kids and had more friends than I did. She was never still—always wrapping her arms around people, tapping her foot or bouncing a crossed leg upon her knee.

Her father was a property developer, she said: a two-word profession, which like a double-barreled surname gave a man gravitas. "Train driver" is also two words but my father's job didn't sound so impressive or have the same social cachet.

Barnaby Elliot wore dark suits, crisp white shirts and ties that were from one club or another. He stood twice for the Tories in Bethnal Green and each time managed to turn a safe Labour seat into an even safer one.

I suspect the only reason he sent Cate to Oaklands was to make him more electable. He liked to portray himself as a battler from "Struggle Street," with dirt under his fingernails and machine oil in his veins.

In reality, I think the Elliots would have preferred their only daughter to attend a private school, Anglican and all-girls rather than Oaklands. Mrs. Elliot, in particular, regarded it as a foreign country that she had no desire to visit.

Cate and I didn't talk to each other for almost a year. She was the coolest, most desirable girl in the whole school, yet she had a casual, almost unwanted beauty. Girls would hang around her, chatting and laughing, seeking her approval, yet she didn't seem to notice.

She talked like someone in a teen movie, smart-mouthed and sassy. I know teenagers are supposed to talk that way but I never met anyone who did except for Cate. And she was the only person I knew who could distill her emotions into drops of pure love, anger, fear or happiness.

I came from the Isle of Dogs, farther east, and went to Oaklands because my parents wanted me educated "out of the area." Sikhs were a minority, but so were whites, who were the most feared. Some regarded themselves as the true East Enders, as if there was some royal Cockney bloodline to be protected. The worst of them was

Paul Donavon, a thug and a bully, who fancied himself as a ladies' man and as a footballer. His best mate, Liam Bradley, was almost as bad. A head taller, with a forehead that blazed with pimples, Bradley looked as if he scrubbed his face with a cheese grater instead of soap.

New kids had to be initiated. Boys copped it the worst, of course, but girls weren't immune, particularly the pretty ones. Donavon and Bradley were seventeen and they were always going to find Cate. Even at fourteen she had "potential" as the older boys would say, with full lips and a J-Lo bottom that looked good in anything tight. It was the sort of bottom that men's eyes follow instinctively. Men and boys and grandfathers.

Donavon cornered her one day during fifth period. He was standing outside the headmaster's office, awaiting punishment for some new misdemeanor. Cate was on a different errand—delivering a bundle of permission notes to the school secretary.

Donavon saw her arrive in the admin corridor. She had to walk right past him. He followed her onto the stairs.

"You don't want to get lost," he said, in a mocking tone, blocking her path. She stepped to one side. He mirrored her movements.

"You got a sweet sweet arse. A peach. And beautiful skin. Let me see you walk up them stairs. Go on. I'll just stand here and you go right on ahead. Maybe you could hitch your skirt up a little. Show me that sweet sweet peach."

Cate tried to turn back but Donavon danced around her. He was always light on his feet. On the football field he played up front, ghosting past defenders, pulling them inside and out.

Big heavy fire doors with horizontal bars sealed off the stairwell. Sound echoed off the cold hard concrete but stayed inside. Cate couldn't keep focused on his face without turning.

"There's a word for girls like you," he said. "Girls that wear skirts like that. Girls that shake their arses like peaches on the trees."

Donavon put his arm around her shoulders and pressed his mouth against her ear. He pinned her arms above her head by the wrists, holding them in his fist. His other hand ran up her leg, under her skirt, pulling her knickers aside. Two fingers found their way inside her, scraping dry skin.

Cate didn't come back to class. Mrs. Pulanski sent me to look for her. I found her in the girls' toilets. Mascara stained her cheeks with black tears and it seemed like her eyes were melting. She wouldn't tell me what happened at first. She took my hand and pressed it into her lap. Her dress was so short my fingers brushed her thigh.

"Are you hurt?"

Her shoulders shook.

"Who hurt you?"

Her knees were squeezed together. Locked tight. I looked at her face. Slowly I parted her knees. A smear of blood stained the whiteness of her cotton knickers.

Something stretched inside me. It kept stretching until it was so thin it vibrated with my heart. My mother says I should never use the word "hate." You should never hate anyone. I know she's right but she lives in a sanitized Sikh-land.

The bell sounded for lunchtime. Screams and laughter filled the playground, bouncing off the bare brick walls and pitted asphalt. Donavon was on the southern edge in the quad, in the shadow of the big oak tree that had been carved with so many initials it should rightly have been dead.

"Well, what have we here," he said, as I marched toward him. "A little yindoo."

"Look at her face," said Bradley. "Looks like she's gonna explode."

"Turkey thermometer just popped out her bum—she's done."

It drew a laugh and Donavon enjoyed his moment. To his credit he must have recognized some danger because he didn't take his eyes off me. By then I had stopped a yard in front of him. My head reached halfway up his chest. I didn't think of his size. I didn't think of my size. I thought of Cate.

"That's the one who runs," said Bradley.

"Well run away little yindoo, you're smelling up the air."

I still couldn't get any words out. Disquiet grew in Donavon's eyes. "Listen, you sick Sikh, get lost."

I rediscovered my voice. "What did you do?"

"I did nothing."

A crowd had started to gather. Donavon could see them coming. He wasn't so sure anymore.

It didn't feel like me who was standing in the playground, confronting Donavon. Instead I was looking down from the branches of the tree, watching from above like a bird. A dark bird.

"Fuck off, you crazy bitch."

Donavon was fast but I was the runner. Later people said I flew.

I crossed the final yard in the beat of a butterfly's wing. My fingers found his eye sockets. He roared and tried to throw me off. I clung on in a death grip, attacking the soft tissue.

Snarling my hair in his fists, he wrenched my head backward, trying to pull me away but I wasn't letting go. He pummeled my head with his fists, screaming, "Get her off! Get her off!"

Bradley had been watching, too shocked to react. He was never sure what to do unless Donavon told him. First he tried to put me in a headlock, forcing my face into the dampness of his armpit, which smelled of wet socks and cheap deodorant.

My legs were wrapped around Donavon's waist. My fingers gouged his eyes. Bradley tried another tack. He grabbed one of my hands and uncurled my fingers, pulling my arm backward. My grip broke. I raked my fingernails across Donavon's face. Although he couldn't see anything from his streaming eyes, he lashed out, kicking me in the head. My mouth filled with blood.

Bradley had hold of my left arm, but my right was still free. In a family of boys you learn how to fight. When you're the only girl you learn how to fight dirty.

Spinning to my feet, I swung my hand at Donavon's face. My index finger and forefinger speared up his nose, hooking him like a fish. My fist closed. No matter what happened next Donavon would follow me. Bradley could break my arm, drag me backward, kick me through the goalposts and Donavon would come with me like a bull with a ring through his nose.

A moan was all I heard escape from his mouth. His arms and legs were jerking.

"Don't touch her. Don't touch her," he pleaded. "Just let her go."

Bradley loosened his grip on my left arm.

Donavon's eyes were swollen and closing. His nasal passages were turned inside out by my fingers. I held him, with his head tilted back and his lower jaw flapping open as he sucked air.

Miss Flower, the music teacher, was on playground duty that day. In truth she was having a cigarette in the staff room when someone came hurtling up the stairs to get her.

Donavon blubbered on about being sorry. I didn't say a word. It felt like none of this had happened to me. I still seemed to be watching from the branches of the tree.

Miss Flower was a fit, youthful, jolly-hockey-sticks type with a fondness for French cigarettes and the sports mistress. She took in the scene with very little fuss and realized that nobody could force me to let Donavon go. So she adopted a conciliatory approach full of comforting words and calming appeals. Donavon had gone quiet. The less he moved, the less it hurt.

I didn't know Miss Flower well but I think she got me, you know. A skinny Indian girl with braces and glasses doesn't take on the school bully without a good reason. She sat with me in the infirmary as I spat blood into a bowl. Two front teeth had been ripped out of the wire braces and were trapped in the twisted metal.

I had a towel around my neck and another across my lap. I don't know where they took Donavon. Miss Flower held an ice pack to my mouth.

"You want to tell me why?"

I shook my head.

"Well, I don't doubt he deserved it but you will have to give a reason."

I didn't answer.

She sighed. "OK, well, it can wait. First you need a clean uniform. There might be one in lost property. Let's clean up before your parents arrive."

"I want to go back to class," I lisped.

"First you need to get those teeth fixed, dear."

Finding an emergency dentist on the NHS normally meant promising your firstborn to the church but I had family connections. My uncle Sandhu has a dental practice in Ealing. (He's not really my uncle, but every older Asian who knew my family was referred to as uncle or aunt.) Uncle Sandhu had fitted my braces "at cost." Bada was so pleased that he would make me smile for visitors, showing off my teeth.

Mama rang my sister-in-law Nazeem and the two of them caught a minicab to the school. Nazeem had the twins and was pregnant again. I was whisked off to Uncle Sandhu who dismantled my braces and took photographs of my teeth. I looked six years old again and had a lisp.

The next morning was fresh and bright and possessed of an innocence so pristine it made a lie of the previous day. Cate didn't come to school. She stayed away for two weeks until we broke for the summer holidays. Miss Flower said she had pleurisy.

Sucking on my glued teeth, I went back to my classes. People treated me differently. Something had happened that day. The scales had fallen from my eyes; the earth had rotated the required number of times and I said goodbye to childhood.

Donavon was expelled from Oaklands. He joined the army, the Parachute Regiment, just in time for Bosnia. Other wars would turn up soon enough. Bradley left during the holidays and became an apprentice boilermaker. I still see him occasionally, pushing his kids on the swings on Bethnal Green.

Nobody ever mentioned what happened to Cate. Only I knew. I don't think she even told her parents—certainly not her father. Digital penetration isn't classified as rape because the law differentiates between a penis and a finger, or fist, or bottle. I don't think it should, but that's an argument for fancy defense lawyers.

People were nicer to me after my fight with Donavon. They acknowledged my existence. I was no longer just "the runner"; I had a name. One of my teeth took root again. The other turned yellow and Uncle Sandhu had to replace it with a false one.

During the holidays I had a phone call from Cate. I don't know how she found my number.

"I thought maybe you might like to catch a movie."

"You mean, you and me?"

"We could see *Pretty Woman*. Unless you've already seen it. I've been three times but I could go again." She kept talking. I had never heard her sound nervous.

"My mother won't let me see *Pretty Woman*," I explained. "She says it's about a whore."

I protested that Julia Roberts is a hooker with a heart, which only got me into trouble. Apparently, it was OK for her to use the term "whore" but I wasn't allowed to say "hooker." In the end we went to see *Ghost* with Patrick Swayze and Demi Moore.

Cate didn't say anything about Donavon. She was still beautiful, still clear-skinned, still wearing a short skirt. Sitting in the darkness, our shoulders touched and her fingers found mine. She squeezed my hand. I squeezed hers.

And that was the start of it. Like Siamese twins, we were. Salt and pepper, Miss Flower called us but I preferred "milk and cookies," which was Mr. Nelson's description. He was American and taught biology and protested when people said it was the easiest of the science electives.

Through school and then university Cate and I were best friends. I loved her. Not in a sexual way, although I don't think I understood the difference at fourteen.

Cate claimed she could predict the future. She would map out our paths, which included careers, boyfriends, weddings, husbands and children. She could even make herself miserable by imagining that our friendship would be over one day.

"I have never had a friend like you and I never shall again. Never ever."

I was embarrassed.

The other thing she said was this: "I am going to have lots of babies because they will love me and never leave me."

I don't know why she talked like this. She treated love and friendship like a small creature trapped in a blizzard, fighting for survival. Maybe she knew something then that I didn't.

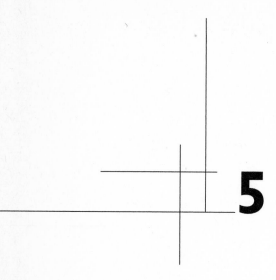

5

Another morning. The sun is shining somewhere. I can see blue sky bunched between buildings and a construction crane etched in charcoal against the light. I cannot say how many days have passed since the accident—four or fourteen. Colors are the same—the air, the trees, the buildings—nothing has changed.

I have been to the hospital every day, avoiding the waiting room and Cate's family. I sit in the cafeteria or wander the corridors, trying to draw comfort from the technology and the smiles of the staff.

Cate is in a medically induced coma. Machines are helping her to breathe. According to the hospital bulletin she suffered a perforated lung, a broken back and multiple fractures to both her legs. The back of her skull was pulverized but two operations have stopped the bleeding.

I spoke to the neurosurgeon yesterday. He said the coma was a good thing. Cate's body had shut down and was trying to repair itself.

"What about brain damage?" I asked him.

He toyed with his stethoscope and wouldn't look me in the eye. "The human brain is the most perfectly designed piece of equipment in the known universe," he explained. "Unfortunately, it is not designed to withstand a ton of metal of high speed."

"Which means?"

"We classify severe head injury as a coma score of eight or less. Mrs. Beaumont has a score of four. It is a *very* severe head injury."

At eleven o'clock the ICU posts another bulletin. Cate's condition hasn't changed. I bump into Jarrod in the cafeteria and we drink coffee and talk about everyday incidental things: jobs and families, the price of eggs, the frailty of modern paper bags. The conversation is punctuated by long pauses as though silence has become part of the language.

"The doctors say she was never pregnant," he says. "She didn't *lose* the baby. There was no miscarriage or termination. Mum and Dad are beside themselves. They don't know what to think."

"She must have had a reason."

"Yeah, well, I can't think of one." A trickle of air from the ceiling vents ruffles his hair.

"Do you think Felix knew?"

"I guess. How do you keep a secret like that from your husband?" He glances at his watch. "Have you been to see her?"

"No."

"Come on."

Jarrod leads me upstairs to the intensive care unit, along painfully white corridors that all look the same. Only two visitors per patient are allowed in the ICU. Masks must be worn and hands must be scrubbed with disinfectant.

Jarrod isn't coming with me. "There's someone already with her," he says, adding as an afterthought, "She won't bite."

My stomach drops. It's too late to back out.

The curtains are open and daylight casts a square on the floor. Mrs. Elliot in her wheelchair is trapped in the light like a hologram, her skin as pale and fine as white china.

Cate lies beside her, hostage to a tangle of tubing, plasma bags and stainless steel. Needles are driven into her veins and her head is swathed in bandages. Monitors and machines blink and buzz, reducing her existence to a digital computer game.

I want her to wake now. I want her eyes to open and for her to pluck away the breathing tube like a strand of hair caught in the corner of her mouth.

Wordlessly, Mrs. Elliot points to a chair beside the bed. "The last time I watched my daughter sleeping she was eight years old. She had come down with pneumonia. I think she caught it at one of those public swimming pools. Every time she coughed it sounded like someone drowning on dry land."

I reach across the marble sheets and take Cate's fingers in mine. I can feel her mother's eyes upon me. A cold scrutiny. She does not want me here.

I remember Mrs. Elliot when she could still walk—a tall, thin woman who always offered Cate her cheek to kiss so as not to smudge her lipstick. She used to be an actress who did mainly TV commercials and was always impeccably made-up, as though perpetually ready for her close-up. Of course, that was before she suffered a stroke that paralyzed her down her right side. Now one eyelid droops and no amount of makeup can hide the nerve damage around her mouth.

In a whisper, she asks, "Why would she lie about the baby?"

"I don't know. She was coming to see me. She said she had done something foolish and that someone wanted to take her baby."

"What baby? She was never pregnant. Never! Now they say her pelvis is so badly shattered that even if she survives she'll never be able to carry a baby."

Something shudders inside me. A déjà vu from another hospital and a different time, when *my* bones were being mended. A price is paid with every surgery.

Mrs. Elliot clutches a cushion to her chest. "Why would she do this? Why would she lie to us?"

There is no warmth in her voice, only accusation. She feels betrayed. Embarrassed. What will she tell the neighbors? I feel like lashing out and defending Cate, who deserves more than this. Instead I close my eyes and listen to the wind washing over the rooftops and the electronic beeping of the machines.

How did she do it—maintain such a lie for weeks and months? It must have haunted her. A part of me is strangely envious. I don't think I've ever wanted something *that* much, not even Olympic medals. When I missed out on the team for the Sydney Games I cried on the edge of the track but they were tears of frustration rather than disappointment. The girl who took my place *wanted* it more.

I know that I shouldn't compare Olympic selection with motherhood. Perhaps my opinions are clouded by the medical reality of a patched pelvis and a reinforced spine that can never withstand the trials of pregnancy and labor. Wanting children is a dangerous ambition for me.

Squeezing Cate's hand, I hope she knows I'm here. For years I wanted her to call, to be friends again, to need me. And just when it finally happened, she's been snatched away like a half-finished question. I have to find out what she wanted. I have to understand why.

—————

Euston Traffic Garage is in Drummond Crescent, tucked between Euston Station and the British Library. The spire of Saint Aloysius Church rises above it like a rocket on a launchpad.

The Collision Investigation Unit is an odd place, a mixture of high-tech gadgetry and old-fashioned garage, with hoists, grease traps and machine tools. This is where they do the vehicular equivalents of autopsies and the process is much the same. Bodies are opened, dismantled, weighed and measured.

The duty officer, a roly-poly sergeant in overalls, peers up from the twisted front end of a car. "Can I help you?"

I introduce myself, showing him my badge. "There was a traffic accident on Friday night on Old Bethnal Green Road. A couple were knocked down."

"Yeah, I looked at that one." He wipes his hands on a rag and tucks it back into his pocket.

"One of them is a friend of mine."

"She still alive?"

"Yes."

"Lucky."

"How far are you with the investigation?"

"Finished. Just got to write it up."

"What do you think happened?"

"Thought it was pretty obvious. Your friend and her husband tried to tackle a minicab." He doesn't mean to sound callous. It's just his way. "Maybe the driver could've put the brakes on a bit sooner. Sometimes you can be unlucky. Choose the wrong moment to check your mirrors and that fraction of a second comes off your reaction time. Might've made a difference. Might not. We'll never know."

"So you're not going to charge him?"

"What with?"

"Dangerous driving, negligence, there must be something."

"He was licensed, insured, registered and roadworthy—I got nothing on this guy."

"He was traveling too fast."

"He says they stepped out in front of him. He couldn't stop."

"Did you examine the car?"

"At the scene."

"Where is it now?"

He sighs. "Let me explain the facts of life to you, Detective Constable. You see that yard out there?" He motions to an open roller door leading to a walled yard. "There are sixty-eight vehicles—every one of them involved in a serious accident. We have thirteen reports due for the coroner, two dozen submissions for criminal trials and I spend half my time in the witness box and the other half up to me elbows in motor oil and blood. There are no *good* traffic accidents but from my point of view the one on Friday night was better than most because it was simple—sad, but simple. They stepped out from between parked cars. The driver couldn't stop in time. End of story."

The genial curiosity on his face has vanished. "We checked the brakes. We checked his license. We checked his driving record. We checked his blood alcohol. We took a statement at the scene and let the poor guy go home. Sometimes an accident is just an accident. If you have evidence to the contrary, hand it over. Otherwise, I'd appreciate if you let me get on with my job."

There is a moment when we eyeball each other. He's not so much angry as disappointed.

"I'm sorry. I didn't mean to question your expertise."

"Yes you did." His face softens. "But that's OK. I'm sorry about your friend."

"Would you mind if I took a look at the driver's statement?"

He doesn't see a problem with that. He leads me to an office and motions to a chair. A computer hums on the desk and box files line the shelves like cardboard bricks. The sergeant hands me a file and a video. For a moment he hovers near the door, unwilling to leave me alone.

The driver's name was Earl Blake and his occupation is listed as stevedore. He was moonlighting as a minicab driver to make extra money, he said.

The video is time coded down to the second and begins with wide-angle shots of the street, taken in the shaky camera style of a holiday video. Partygoers are milling outside the gates of Oaklands, some still holding drinks or draped with streamers.

Earl Blake is in the distance, talking to a policeman. He notices the camera and seems to turn away. It might mean nothing.

There are statements from a dozen witnesses. Most heard the screech of brakes and saw the impact. Farther along the road, two cabbies were parked near the corner of Mansford Street. The mini-cab came past them slowly, as though searching for an address.

I look for any mention of Donavon. His name and address were taken down by investigators but there isn't a statement.

"Yeah, I remember him," says the sergeant. "He had a tattoo." He points to his neck, tracing a cross below his Adam's apple. "He said he didn't see a thing."

"He *saw* it happen."

The sergeant raises an eyebrow. "That ain't what he told me."

I make a note of Donavon's address on a scrap of paper.

"You're not trying to run a private investigation here are you, Detective Constable?"

"No, sir."

"If you have any important information regarding this accident, you are obliged to make it known to me."

"Yes, sir. I have no information. Mr. Donavon tried to save my friend's life. I just want to thank him. Good manners, you see. My mother bred them into me."

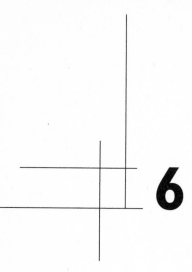

6

Earl Blake's address is a small terrace off Pentonville Road in the neglected end of King's Cross. There is nobody home. My legs have gone to sleep I've been sitting here for so long, staring out the windscreen, tapping a rhythm on the wheel.

A drug pusher leans against a low wall outside a pub on the corner, his face half hidden under the brim of a baseball cap. Two teenage girls walk by and he says something, smiling. They toss back their hair and sashay a little faster.

A red hatchback pulls into a parking space ahead of me. A woman in her fifties emerges, dressed in a nurse's uniform. She collects a bag of groceries from the boot and walks to the terrace, cursing as she drops her keys.

"Are you Mrs. Blake?" I ask.

"Who wants to know?" Her blue-gray hair is lacquered into place.

"I'm looking for your husband."

"You trying to be funny?"

She has opened the door and stepped inside.

"Your husband was involved in a car accident last Friday night."

"Not bloody likely."

She is disappearing down the hallway.

"I'm talking about *Earl* Blake."

"That's his name."

"I need to speak to him."

Shouting over her shoulder: "Well, missy, you're six years too late. That's when I buried him."

"He's dead!"

"I sure hope so." She laughs wryly.

The house smells of damp dog and toilet freshener.

"I'm a police officer," I call after her. "I'm sorry if there's been a mistake. Do you have a son called Earl?"

"Nope."

Dumping her shopping on a table in the kitchen, she turns. "Listen, love, either come in or stay out. This place costs a fortune to bloody heat."

I follow her into the house and shut the door. She has taken a seat at the table and kicked off her shoes, rubbing her feet through her support hose.

I look around. There are medications lined up on the windowsill and food coupons stuck under fridge magnets. A picture of a baby in a hollowed-out pumpkin is on the calendar.

"Put the kettle on will you, love."

The tap spits and belches.

"I'm sorry about your husband."

"Nowt for you to be sorry about. He dropped dead right there—face-first into his egg and chips. He was moaning about how I over-cooked the eggs and then whump!" Her hand topples onto the table. "I told him not to wear his underwear to breakfast but he never listened. All the neighbors watched him wheeled out of here in his old Y-fronts."

She tosses her shoes in the corner beside the back door. "I know all men leave eventually but not when you've just made 'em egg 'n' chips. Earl was always bloody inconsiderate."

Mrs. Blake pushes herself upward and warms the teapot. "You're not the first, you know."

"What do you mean?"

"Some bloke came here yesterday. He didn't believe me either when I said Earl was dead. He said Earl owed him money. As if! Can't see him gambling from beyond."

"What did this man look like?"

"Had this tattoo on his neck. A cross."

Donavon is searching for Blake.

"I hate tattoos," she continues. "Earl had 'em on his forearms. He was in the merchant navy before I met him. Traveled all over the place and came back with these *souvenirs*. I call 'em skin complaints."

"Did he have one just here?" I point to my chest. "A Crucifixion scene."

"Earl weren't religious. He said religion was for people who believed in hell."

"Do you have a photograph of him?"

"Yeah, a few. He was handsome once."

She leads me to the sitting room, which is full of seventies furniture and faded rugs. Rummaging in a cupboard next to the gas fire, she pulls out a photo album.

"Course it's easier keeping the place clean now. He was a real slob. Dropped clothes like they was crumbs."

She hands me a snapshot. Earl is wearing a jacket with a fur collar and fluorescent strips. He looks nothing like the driver of the minicab, although both are roughly the same age.

"Mrs. Blake, do you ever get mail for your late husband?"

"Yeah, sure, junk stuff. Banks are always sending him applications for credit cards. What's he going to do with a credit card, eh?"

"Did you cancel his driver's license?"

"Didn't bother. I sold his old van. Bought meself the hatchback. Reckon the dealer ripped me off, the Paki bastard. No way that thing had done only four thousand miles."

She realizes her mistake. "No offense, love."

"I'm not Pakistani."

"Right. I don't know much about the difference."

She finds me another photograph.

"Do you ever take in lodgers or have visitors staying?"

"Nah."

"Ever had a break-in?"

"Yeah, a few years back." She looks at me suspiciously.

I try to explain that someone has stolen her husband's identity, which is not as difficult as it sounds. A bank statement and a gas bill is all it takes to get a credit report, which will yield a National Insurance number and a list of previous addresses. The rest falls into place—birth certificates, credit cards, a passport.

"Earl never did anything wrong," says Mrs. Blake. "Never did much right either." She overbalances a little as she stands and her forearms wobble beneath the short sleeves of her uniform.

I don't stay for a cup of tea, which disappoints her. Letting myself out, I stand for a moment on the front steps, raising my face to the misty rain. Three kids are practicing their literacy skills on a wall across the road.

Farther down the street is a triangular garden with benches and a playground surrounded by a semicircle of plane trees and a copper beech. Something catches my eye beneath the lower branches.

When soldiers are trained to hide in the jungle, they are told four main things that will give them away: movement, shape, shine and silhouette. Movement is the most important. That's what I notice. A figure stands from a bench and begins walking away. I recognize his gait.

It is strange how I react. For years, whenever I have conjured up Donavon's face, panic has swelled in the space between my heart and lungs. I'm not frightened of him now. I want answers. Why is he so interested in Cate Beaumont?

He knows I've clocked him. His hands are out of his pockets, swinging freely as he runs. If I let him reach the far side of the park I'll lose him in the side streets.

Rounding the corner, I accelerate along the path which is flanked by a railing fence and tall shrubs. An old Royal Mail sorting office is on the opposite corner, with tall windows edged in painted stone. Turning left, I follow the perimeter fence. The exit is ahead. Nobody emerges. He should be here by now.

I pause at the gate, listening for hard heels on the pavement. Nothing. A motorcycle rumbles to life on the far side of the park. He doubled back. Clever.

Run, rabbit, run. I know where you live.

———————

My hallway smells of bleach and the stale backdraft of a vacuum cleaner. My mother has been cleaning. That's one of the signs that my life isn't all that it should be. No matter how many times I complain that I don't need a cleaner, she insists on catching a bus from the Isle of Dogs just to "straighten a few things up."

"I am defrosting the freezer," she announces from the kitchen.

"It doesn't need defrosting. It's automatic."

She makes a *pfffhh* sound. Her blue-and-green sari is tucked up into her support stockings, making her backside appear enormous. It is an optical illusion just like her eyes behind her glasses, which are as wet and brown as fresh cow dung.

She is waiting for a kiss on the cheek. I have to bend. She is scarcely five feet tall and shaped like a pear, with sticky-out ears that help her hear like a bat and X-ray vision that only mothers possess. She also has an oddly selective sense of smell, which can pick up the scent of perfume from fifty feet, yet allows her to sniff the crotches of my four brothers' underpants to establish if they need washing. I feel like retching at the thought of it.

"Why is there a padlock on my Hari's door?"

"Privacy, perhaps."

"I found it open."

That's strange. Hari is always very careful about locking the door.

Mama holds my face in her hands. "Have you eaten today?"

"Yes."

"You're lying. I can tell. I have brought some dahl and rice."

She uses perfect schoolbook English, the kind they used to teach in the dark ages when she went to school.

I notice a suitcase in the corner. For a moment I fear she might be planning to stay but one suitcase would never be enough.

"Your father was cleaning out the attic," she explains.

"Why?"

"Because he has nothing else to do." She sounds exasperated.

My father has retired after thirty-five years driving mainline trains and is still making the adjustment. Last week he went through my pantry checking use-by dates and putting them in order.

Mama opens the suitcase. Lying neatly across the top is my old Oaklands school uniform. I feel a stab of recognition and remember Cate. I should phone the hospital for an update on her condition.

"I didn't want to throw things away without asking you," she explains. There are scarves, scrapbooks, photo albums, diaries and running trophies. "I had no idea you had a crush on Mr. Elliot."

"You *read* my diary!"

"It fell open."

Matricide is a possibility.

She changes the subject. "Now you're coming early on Sunday to help us cook. Make sure Hari wears something nice. His ivory shirt."

My father is having his sixty-fifth birthday and the party has been planned for months. It will include at least, one eligible Sikh bachelor, no doubt. My parents want me to marry a good Sikh boy, bearded of course; not one of those clean-shaven Indians who thinks he's a Bollywood film star. This ignores the fact that all my brothers cut their hair, apart from Prabakar, the eldest, who is the family's moral guardian.

I know that all parents are considered eccentric by their children, but mine are particularly embarrassing. My father, for example, is a stickler for conserving energy. He studies the electricity bill every quarter and compares it to previous quarters and previous years.

Mama crosses entire weeks off the calendar in advance so that she "doesn't forget."

"But how will you know what day it is?" I once asked her.

"Everyone knows what day it is," she replied.

You cannot argue with logic like that.

"By the way, your phone is fixed," she announces. "A nice man came this afternoon."

"I didn't report a problem."

"Well, he came to fix it."

A chill travels across my skin as if someone has left a door open. I fire off questions: What did he look like? What was he wearing? Did he have identification? Mama looks concerned and then frightened.

"He had a clipboard and a box of tools."

"But no ID."

"I didn't ask."

"He should have shown it to you. Did you leave him alone?"

"I was cleaning."

My eyes dart from one object to the next, taking an inventory. Moving upstairs, I search my wardrobes and drawers. None of my jewelry is missing. My bank statements, passport and spare set of keys are still in the drawer. Carefully, I count the pages of my checkbook.

"Perhaps Hari reported the fault," she says.

I call him on his mobile. The pub is so noisy he can barely hear me.

"Did you report a problem with the phone?"

"What?"

"Did you call British Telecom?"

"No. Was I supposed to?"

"It doesn't matter."

My mother rocks her head from side to side and makes concerned noises. "Should we call the police?"

The question had already occurred to me. What would I report? There was no break-in. Nothing has been taken as far as I can tell. It is either the perfect crime or no crime at all.

"Don't worry about it, Mama."

"But the man—"

"He was just fixing the telephone."

I don't want her worrying. She spends enough time here already.

Mama looks at her watch. If she doesn't leave now she won't be home for dinner. I offer to drive her and she smiles. It is the widest, most radiant smile ever created. No wonder people do as she says—they want to see her smile.

On the bedside table is a book that I started reading last night. The bookmark is in the wrong place—twenty pages forward. Perhaps I moved it inadvertently. Paranoia is not reality on a finer scale; it is a foolish reaction to unanswered questions.

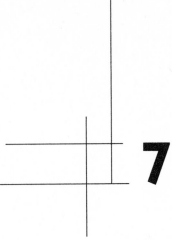

7

On her very last day of being sixteen Cate found her mother lying unconscious in the kitchen. She had suffered something called a hemorrhagic stroke, which Cate explained as being like a "brain explosion."

Ruth Elliot had two subsequent strokes in hospital, which paralyzed her down her right side. Cate blamed herself. She should have been at home. Instead we'd sneaked out to watch the Beastie Boys at the Brixton Academy. Cate let a guy kiss her that night. He must have been at least twenty-five. Ancient.

"Maybe I'm being punished for lying," she said.

"But your mum is the one *really* being punished," I pointed out.

Cate started going to church after that—for a while at least. I went with her one Sunday, kneeling down and closing my eyes.

"What are you doing?" she whispered.

"Praying for your mum."

"But you're not an Anglican. Won't your god think you're changing teams?"

"I don't think it matters which god fixes her up."

Mrs. Elliot came home in a wheelchair, unable to talk properly. In the beginning she could only say one word: "When," uttered more as a statement than a question.

No matter what you said to her, she answered the same way.

"How are you today, Mrs. Elliot?"

"When, when, when."

"Have you had your tea?"

"When, when, when."

"I'm just going to study with Cate."

"When, when."

I know it sounds horrible but we used to play tricks on her.

"We have a biology test, Mrs. E."

"When, when."

"On Friday."

"When, when, when."

"In the morning."

"When, when."

"About half past nine."

"When, when."

"Nine thirty-four to be precise. Greenwich mean time."

They had a nurse to look after her. A big Jamaican called Yvonne, with pillow breasts and fleshy arms and mottled pink hands. She used to wear electric colors and men's shoes and she blamed her bad complexion on the English weather. Yvonne was strong enough to scoop Mrs. Elliot up in her arms and lift her into the shower and back into her wheelchair. And she talked to her all the time, having long conversations that sounded completely plausible unless you listened closely.

Yvonne's greatest gift, however, was to fill the house with laughter and songs, lifting the gloom. She had children of her own— Caspar and Bethany—who had steel-wool hair and neon smiles. I don't know about her husband—he was never mentioned—but I know Yvonne went to church every Sunday and had Tuesdays off and baked the best lime cheesecake in creation.

On weekends I sometimes slept over at Cate's place. We rented a video and stayed up late. Her dad didn't come home until after nine. Tanned and tireless, he had a deep voice and an endless supply of corny jokes. I thought him unbelievably handsome.

The tragedy of his wife's condition gained a lot of sympathy for Barnaby. Women, in particular, seemed to admire his devotion to his crippled wife and how he went out of his way to make her feel special.

Ruth Elliot, however, didn't seem to share this admiration. She recovered her speech after months of therapy and attacked Barnaby at every opportunity, belittling him in front of Yvonne and his children and his children's friends.

"Did you hear that?" she'd say as the front door opened. "He's *home*. He *always* comes home. Who does he smell like tonight?"

"Now, now, Ruth, please," Barnaby would say, but she wouldn't stop.

"He smells of soap and shampoo. He always smells of soap and shampoo. Why does a man shower *before* he comes home?"

"You know the reason. I've been playing tennis at the club."

"He washes before he comes home. Washes the smell away."

"Ruth, darling," Barnaby tried to say. "Let's talk about this upstairs."

She would fight at his hands and then surrender as he lifted her easily from her chair and carried her up the sixteen stairs. We would hear her screaming and finally crying. He would put her to bed, settle her like a child, and then rejoin us in the kitchen for hot chocolate.

When I first met Cate, Barnaby was already forty, but looked good for his age. And he could get away with things because he was so supremely confident. I saw him do it countless times at restaurants, on school open days and in the middle of the street. He could say the most outrageous things, using double entendres and playful squeezes and women would simply giggle and go weak at the knees.

He called me his "Indian princess" and his "Bollywood beauty" and, one time, when he took us horse riding, I actually felt dizzy when he put his hands around my waist and lifted me down from the saddle.

I would never have confessed it to anyone, but Cate guessed the truth. It wasn't hard. I was always inviting myself back to her place and making excuses to talk to her father. She didn't even know about the times I rode my bicycle past his office, hoping he might see me and wave. Twice I ran into open car doors.

Cate, of course, found my infatuation hilarious beyond measure, thus ensuring I have never admitted to loving any man.

See the sort of stuff I remember! It's all coming back, the good, the bad and the ugly. My mind aches.

I've been dreading this moment—seeing Barnaby again. Ever since the accident he has slept at Cate's house, according to Jarrod. He hasn't been to work or answered calls.

The front door has stained-glass panels and a tarnished knocker in the shape of a naked torso. I grab her hips. Nobody answers. I try again.

A lock turns. The door opens a crack. Unshaven and unwashed, Barnaby doesn't want to see me. Self-pity needs his full attention.

"Please, let me in."

He hesitates but the door opens. I move inside, stepping around him as though he's surrounded by a force field. The place is musty and closed up. Windows need opening. Plants need watering.

I follow him to the kitchen and dining area, open plan, looking out into the garden. Cate's touches are everywhere from the French provincial dining table to the art deco posters on the walls. There are photographs on the mantel. One of them, a wedding picture, shows Cate in a twenties flapper dress trimmed with mother-of-pearl.

Folding himself onto a sofa, Barnaby crosses his legs. A trouser cuff slides up to reveal a bald shin. People used to say he was ageless and joke about him having a portrait in his attic. It's not true. His features are too feminine to age well. Instead of growing character lines he has wrinkled and one day, ten years from now, he'll wake up an old man.

I never imagined speaking to him again. It doesn't seem so hard, although grief makes everything more intimate.

"They always say that a father is the last person to know anything," he says. "Cate used to laugh at me. 'Dear old Dad,' she said. 'Always in the dark.' "

Confusion clouds his eyes. Doubt.

"Did Felix know?"

"They weren't sleeping together."

"He told you that."

"Cate wouldn't let him touch her. She said it might harm the baby. They slept in different beds—in different rooms."

"Surely a husband would—"

"Marriage and sex aren't mutually inclusive," he says, perhaps too knowingly. I feel myself growing uncomfortable. "Cate even told Felix he could see a prostitute if he wanted. Said she wouldn't mind.

What sort of wife says that? He should have seen something was wrong."

"Why couldn't she conceive?"

"Her womb destroyed his sperm. I don't know the medical name for it. They tried for seven years. IVF, drugs, injections, herbal remedies; they exorcised the house of evil spirits and sprinkled Chinese lemongrass oil on the garden. Cate was a walking bloody textbook on infertility. That's why it came as such a surprise. Cate was over the moon—I've never seen her happier. I remember looking at Felix and he was trying hard to be excited—I guess he was—but it's like he had a question inside him that wouldn't go away."

"He had doubts?"

"For years his wife rejects his sperm and then suddenly she's pregnant? Any man would have doubts."

"But if that's the case—"

"He *wanted* to believe, don't you see? She convinced everyone."

Standing, he motions me to follow. His slippers flap gently against his heels as he climbs the stairs. The nursery door is open. The room is freshly painted and papered. The furniture new. A cot, a changing table, a comfortable chair with a Winnie the Pooh pillow.

Opening a drawer, he takes out a folder. There are receipts for the furniture and instructions for assembling the cot. He up-ends an envelope, shaking it gently. Two sheets of photographs, monochrome images, drop into his hand. Ultrasound pictures.

Each photograph is only a few inches square. The background is black, the images white. For a moment it's like looking at one of those Magic Eye pictures where a 3-D image emerges from within. In this case I see tiny arms and legs. A face, eyes, a nose . . .

"They were taken at twenty-three weeks."

"How?"

"Felix was supposed to be there but Cate messed up the days. She came home with the photographs."

The rest of the file contains testimony of an unborn baby's existence. There are application forms to the hospital, appointment slips, medical reports, correspondence and receipts for the nursery furniture. An NHS pamphlet gives details of how to register the birth. Another lists the benefits of folic acid in early pregnancy.

There are other documents in the drawer, including a bundle of private letters tucked in a corner, bank statements, a passport and health insurance certificates. A separate file contains details of Cate's IVF treatments. There appear to have been five of them. Sohan Banerjee, a fertility specialist in Wimbledon, is mentioned several times.

"Where was she planning to have the baby?"

"Chelsea and Westminster Hospital."

I look at a brochure for prenatal classes. "What I can't understand is how it was supposed to end. What was Cate going to do in four weeks?"

Barnaby shrugs. "She was going to be exposed as a liar."

"No, think about it. That prosthetic was almost a work of art. She must have altered it two or three times over the months. She also had to forge medical letters and appointment slips. Where did she get the ultrasound pictures? She went to all that effort. Surely she had a plan."

"Like what?"

"Maybe she organized a surrogacy or a private adoption."

"Why keep it a secret?"

"Perhaps she couldn't let anyone know. Commercial surrogacy is illegal. Women can't accept money to have a baby. I know it sounds far-fetched but isn't it worth considering?"

He scoffs and smites at the air between us. "So a month from now my daughter was going to nip off somewhere, dump the padding and come back with a baby, custom-made, ready to order from the baby factory. Maybe Ikea does them nowadays."

"I'm just looking for reasons."

"I *know* the reason. She was obsessed. Desperate."

"Enough to explain these?" I point to the ultrasound pictures.

Reaching down, he opens the second drawer and retrieves a different file. This one contains court transcripts, charge sheets and a judgment.

"Eighteen months ago Cate was caught stealing baby clothes from *Mothercare*. She said it was a misunderstanding, but we knew it was a cry for help. The magistrates were very kind. They gave her a suspended sentence.

"She had counseling for about six months, which seemed to help. She was her old self again. There were obvious places she had to avoid like parks and playgrounds, schools. But she couldn't stop torturing herself. She peered into prams and struck up conversations with mothers. She got angry when she saw women with big families, who were pregnant again. It was unfair, she said. They were being greedy.

"She and Felix looked into adopting a baby. They went for the interviews and were screened by social workers. Unfortunately, the shoplifting conviction came back to haunt Cate. The adoption committee deemed her mentally unstable. It was the final straw. She lost it completely. Felix found her sitting on the floor of the nursery, clutching a teddy bear, saying, 'Look! It's a beautiful baby boy.' She was taken to hospital and spent a fortnight in a psych ward. They put her on antidepressants."

"I had no idea."

He shrugs. "So you see, Alisha, you shouldn't make the mistake of putting rational thoughts in my daughter's head. Cate didn't have a plan. Desperation is the mother of bad ideas."

Everything he says makes perfect sense but I can't forget the image of Cate at the reunion, begging me to help her. She said they wanted to take her baby. Who did she mean?

There is nothing as disarming as a heartfelt plea. Barnaby's natural caution wavers.

"What do you want?"

"I need to see telephone records, credit card receipts, check stubs and diaries. Have any large sums of money been withdrawn from Cate or Felix's bank accounts? Did they travel anywhere or meet anyone new? Was she secretive about money or appointments? I also need to see her computer. Perhaps her e-mails can tell me something."

Unable to push his tongue around the word no, he hedges. "What if you find something that embarrasses this family?"

His wretchedness infuriates me. Whatever Cate might have done, she needs him now.

The doorbell rings. He turns toward the sound, surprised. I follow him down the stairs and wait in the hallway as he opens the front door.

Yvonne gives a deep-throated sob and throws her arms around his shoulders, crushing his head to her chest.

"I'm sorry. I'm so sorry," she wails. Her eyes open. "Alisha?"

"Hello, Yvonne."

Manhandling Barnaby out of the way, she smothers me in her cleavage. I remember the feeling. It's like being wrapped in a fluffy towel, fresh from the dryer. Gripping my forearms, she holds me away. "Look at you! You're all grown up."

"Yes."

"You cut your lovely hair."

"Ages ago."

Yvonne hasn't changed. If anything she is a little fatter and her pitted face has fleshed out. Overworked veins stand out on her calves and she's still wearing men's shoes.

Even after Ruth Elliot recovered her speech, Yvonne stayed with the family, cooking meals, washing clothes and ironing Barnaby's shirts. She was like an old-fashioned retainer, growing old with them.

Now she wants me to stay, but I make excuses to leave. As I reach the car, I can still feel Barnaby's stubble on my cheeks where he kissed me goodbye. Glancing back at the house I remember a different tragedy, another goodbye. Voices from the past jostle and merge. The sadness is suffocating.

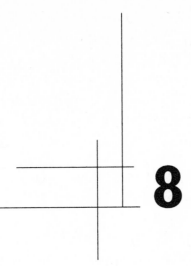

8

Donavon gave the police an address in Hackney, not far from London Fields. Set back from the road, the crumbling terrace house has a small square front yard of packed dirt and broken concrete. A sun-faded red Escort van is parked in the space, alongside a motorcycle.

A young woman answers the door. She's about twenty-five with a short skirt, a swelling pregnancy and acne scars on her cheeks. Cotton wool is wedged between her toes and she stands with her heels planted and toes raised.

"I'm looking for Donavon."

"Nobody here by that name."

"That's too bad. I owe him some money."

"I can give it to him."

"You said he didn't live here."

"I meant he wasn't here right now," she says curtly. "He might be around later."

"I'd prefer to give it to him personally."

She considers this for a moment, still balancing on her heels. "You from the council?"

"No."

"A welfare officer?"

"No."

She disappears and is replaced by Donavon.

"Well, well, if it isn't yindoo."

"Give it a rest, Donavon."

He runs his tongue along a nick in his front tooth while his eyes roam up and down over me. My skin is crawling.

"Didn't your mother ever tell you it's not polite to stare?"

"My mother told me to beware of strangers who tell lies about owing me money."

"Can I come in?"

"That depends."

"On what?"

"I'm fucking certain I ordered a Thai girl but I guess you'll do."

He hasn't changed. The pregnant girl is standing behind him. "This is my sister, Carla," he says.

She nods, sullenly.

"It's nice to meet you, Carla. I went to school with your brother. Did you go to Oaklands?"

Donavon answers for her. "I sort of shat in that particular nest."

"Why did you run yesterday?"

He shrugs. "You got the wrong guy."

"I know it was you."

He holds up his hands in mock surrender. "Are you gonna arrest me, Officer? I hope you brought your handcuffs. That's always fun."

I follow him along the hallway, past a coatrack and assorted shoes. Carla continues painting her nails at the kitchen table. She is flexible and shortsighted, pulling her foot almost up to her nose as she dabs on the varnish with a thin brush, unconcerned about exposing her knickers.

A dog beneath the table thumps its tail several times but doesn't bother rising.

"You want a drink?"

"No. Thank you."

"I do. Hey, Carla, nip up the road and get us a few cans."

Her top lip curls as she snatches the twenty-quid note from his fist.

"And this time I want the change back."

Donavon gives a chair a gentle shake. "You want to sit down?"

I wait for him to be seated first. I don't feel comfortable with him standing over me. "Is this your place?" I ask.

"My parents'. My dad's dead. Mum lives in Spain."

"You joined the army."

"Yeah, the Paras." His fingers vibrate against the tabletop.

"Why did you leave?"

He motions to his leg. "A medical discharge. I broke my leg in twelve places. We were on a training jump above Andover. One of the newbies wrapped his chute around mine and we came down under the one canopy. Too fast. They wouldn't let me jump after that. They said I'd get a pension but the government changed the rules. I got to work."

I glance around the kitchen, which looks like a craft workshop with boxes of leather strips, crystals, feathers and painted clay beads. On the table I notice a reel of wire and pliers.

"What are you making?"

"I sell stuff at the markets. Trinkets and shit. Don't make much, you know . . ."

The statement trails off. He talks a little more about the Paras, clearly missing army life, until Carla returns with a six-pack of draft and a packet of chocolate biscuits. She retreats to the stairs with the biscuits, eating them while listening to us. I can see her painted toes through a gap in the stair rails.

Donavon opens a can and drinks noisily. He wipes his mouth.

"How is she?"

"She might be brain damaged."

His face tightens. "What about the baby?"

"She wasn't pregnant."

"What?"

"She was faking it."

"What do you mean—faking it? Why would she . . . ? Makes no fucking sense."

The phantom pregnancy seems harder for him to accept than Cate's medical condition.

"Why are you interested in Earl Blake?"

"Same reason as you."

"Yeah, sure. What difference does it make to you?"

"You wouldn't understand."

"Try me."

"Fuck you!"

"You wish!"

"The bastard could have stopped," he says suddenly, his anger bordering on violence.

"Did you see the car speed up? Did it veer toward them?"

A shake of the head.

"Then why are you so sure?"

"He was lying."

"Is that it?"

He raises one shoulder as if trying to scratch his ear. "Just forget it, OK?"

"No, I want to know. You said the driver was lying. Why?"

He goes quiet. "I just know. He lied. He ran them down."

"How can you be sure?"

He turns away, muttering, "Sometimes I just am."

My mother always told me that people with green eyes are related to fairies, like the Irish, and that if I ever met someone with one green eye and one brown one, it meant that person had been taken over by a fairy, but not in a scary way. Donavon is seriously scary. The bones of his shoulders shift beneath his shirt.

"I found out some stuff about Blake," he says, growing calmer. "He signed on with the minicab firm a week ago and only ever worked days. At the end of every shift he handed over eighty quid for the lease of the car but the mileage didn't match the fares. He can't have done more than a few miles. He told another driver that he had regular customers who liked to have him on call. One of them was a film producer but there's no way some hotshot film producer is going around London in a beat-up Vauxhall Cavalier."

He straightens up, into the story now. "So I ask myself, 'Why does a guy need a car all day if it's not going anywhere?' Maybe he's watching someone—or waiting for them."

"That's a big leap."

"Yeah, well, I saw the look Cate gave him. She recognized him."

He noticed it too.

Kicking back his chair, he stands and opens a kitchen drawer.

"I found this. Cate must have dropped it."

He hands me a crumpled envelope. My name is on the front of it. The swirls and dips of the handwriting belong to Cate. Lifting the flap, I pull out a photograph. A teenage girl gazes absently at the camera. She has fine limbs and ragged dark hair, trimmed by the wind. Her wide lips curl down at the edges making her look melancholy rather than gloomy. She is wearing jeans, sandals and a cotton shirt. Her hands are by her sides, palms open, with a white band on her wrist.

I turn the photograph over. There is a name written on the back. Samira.

"Who is she?" asks Donavon.

"I don't know."

"What about the number?"

In the bottom right-hand corner there are ten digits. A phone number, perhaps.

I study the image again as a dozen different questions chase one another. Cate faked her pregnancy. Does this girl have anything to do with it? She looks too young to be a mother.

I take out my mobile and punch in the number. A recorded voice announces it is unavailable. The area code doesn't belong in the U.K. It could be international.

The fight seems to have gone out of Donavon. Maybe alcohol mellows him.

"What are you gonna do?" he asks.

"I don't know yet."

On my feet, I turn to leave. He calls after me, "I want to help."

"Why?"

He's still not going to tell me.

Carla intercepts me before I reach the front door.

"He's losing it," she whispers. "He used to have it together but something happened in Afghanistan or wherever the hell they sent him. He's not the same. He doesn't sleep. He gets obsessed about stuff. I hear him at night, walking about."

"You think he needs help?"

"He needs something."

9

Chief Superintendent Lachlan North has an office on the eleventh floor of New Scotland Yard overlooking Victoria Street and Westminster Abbey. He is standing by the window, beside a telescope, peering into the eyepiece at the traffic below.

"If that moron thinks he can turn there . . ."

He picks up a two-way radio and communicates a call-sign to traffic operations.

A tired voice answers. "Yes, sir."

"Some idiot just did a U-turn in Victoria Street. Did you see it?"

"Yes, sir, we're onto him."

The Chief Superintendent is talking while still peering through the telescope. "I can get his number plate."

"It's under control, sir."

"Good work. Over and out."

Reluctantly, he turns away from the telescope and sits down. "There are some dangerous bloody morons loose on our roads, Detective Constable Barba."

"Yes, sir."

"In my experience, the morons are more dangerous than the criminals."

"There are more of them, sir."

"Yes. Absolutely."

He dips his head into a drawer and retrieves a dark green folder. Shuffling through the contents, he clears his throat and smiles, attempting to appear warmer and fuzzier. A nagging doubt hooks me in the chest.

"The results of your medical have been reviewed, DC Barba, along with your psychological evaluation. I must say you have made a remarkable recovery from your injuries. Your request to return to active duty with the Diplomatic Protection Group has also been noted. Courageous is the word that comes to mind." He tugs at his cuffs. Here it comes. "But under the circumstances, having reviewed the matter thoroughly, it has been decided to transfer you out of the DPG. You might be a little gun-shy, you see, which is hardly a good thing when protecting diplomats and foreign heads of state. Could be embarrassing."

"I'm not gun-shy, sir. Nobody fired a gun at me."

He raises his hand to stop me. "Be that as it may, we have a responsibility to look after our foreign guests and while I have every confidence in you, there is no way of testing your fitness when push comes to shove and Abdul the terrorist takes a potshot at the Israeli ambassador." He taps the folder several times with his finger to stress the point.

"The most important part of my job is shuffling people and priorities. It is a thankless task but I don't ask for medals or commendations. I am simply a humble servant of the public." His chest swells. "We don't want to lose you, DC Barba. We need more women like you in the Met, which is why I am pleased to offer you a position as a recruitment officer. We need to encourage more young women into the Met, particularly from minority communities. You can be a role model."

A mist seems to cloud my vision. He stands now, moving back to the window where he bends to peer through his telescope again.

"Unbelievable! Moron!" he screams, shaking his head.

He turns back to me, settling his haunch on the corner of the desk. A print behind his head is a famous depiction of the Bow Street Runners, London's renowned early police force.

"Great things are expected of you, DC Barba."

"With all due respect, sir, I am not gun-shy. I am fitter than ever. I can run a mile in four and a half minutes. I'm a better shot than anyone at the DPG. My high-speed defensive driving skills are excellent. I am the same officer as before—"

"Yes, yes, you're very capable I'm sure, but the decision has been made. It's out of my hands. You'll report to the Police Recruitment Center at Hendon on Monday morning."

He opens his office door and waits for me to leave. "You're still a very important member of the team, Alisha. We're glad to have you back."

Words have dried up. I know I should argue with him or slam my fist on his desk and demand a review. Instead, I meekly walk out the door. It closes behind me.

Outside, I wander along Victoria Street. I wonder if the Chief Superintendent is watching me. I'm tempted to look up toward his window and flip him the bird. Isn't that what the Americans call it?

Of course, I don't. I'm too polite, you see. That's my problem. I don't intimidate. I don't bully. I don't talk in sporting clichés or slap backs or have a wobbly bit between my legs. Unfortunately, it's not as though I have outstanding feminine wiles to fall back on such as a killer cleavage or a backside like J-Lo. The only qualities I bring to the table are my gender and ethnic credibility. The Metropolitan Police want nothing else from me.

I am twenty-nine years old and I still think I'm capable of something remarkable in my life. I am different, unique, beyond compare. I don't have Cate's luminous beauty or infinite sadness, or her musical laugh or the ability to make all men feel like warriors. I have wisdom, determination and steel.

At sixteen I wanted to win Olympic gold. Now I want to make a difference. Maybe falling in love will be my remarkable deed. I will explore the heart of another human being. Surely that is challenge enough. Cate always thought so.

When I need to think I run. When I need to forget I run. It can clear my thoughts completely or focus them like a magnifying glass that dwarfs the world outside the lens. When I run the way I know I can, it all happens in the air, the pure air, floating above the ground, levitating the way great runners imagine themselves in their dreams.

The doctors said I might never walk again. I confounded predictions. I like that idea. I don't like doing things that are predictable. I don't want to do what people expect.

I began with baby steps. Crawl before you can walk, Simon my physiotherapist said. Walk before you can run. He and I conducted an ongoing skirmish. He cajoled me and I cursed him. He twisted my body and I threatened to break his arm. He said I was a crybaby and I called him a bully.

"Rise up on your toes."

"I'm trying."

"Hold on to my arm. Close your eyes. Can you feel the stretch in your calf?"

"I can feel it in my eyeballs."

After months in traction and more time in a wheelchair, I had trouble telling where my legs stopped and the ground began. I bumped into walls and stumbled on pavements. Every set of stairs was another Everest. My living room was an obstacle course.

I gave myself little challenges, forcing myself out on the street every morning. Five minutes became ten minutes, became twenty minutes. After every operation it was the same. I pushed myself through winter and spring and a long hot summer when the air was clogged with exhaust fumes and heat rose from every brick and slab.

I have explored every corner of the East End, which is like a huge, deafening factory with a million moving parts. I have lived in other places in London and never even made eye contact with neighbors. Now I have Mr. Mordecai next door, who mows my postage-stamp-size lawn, and Mrs. Goldie across the road picks up my dry cleaning.

There is a jangling, squabbling urgency to life in the East End. Everyone is on the make—haggling, complaining, gesticulating and slapping their foreheads. These are the "people of the abyss" according to Jack London. That was a century ago. Much has changed. The rest remains the same.

For nearly an hour I keep running, following the Thames past Westminster, Vauxhall and the old Battersea Power Station. I recognize where I am—the back streets of Fulham. My old boss lives near here, in Rainville Road: Detective Inspector Vincent Ruiz, retired.

We talk on the phone every day or so. He asks me the same two questions: are you okay, and do you need anything. My answers are always: yes, I'm okay; and no, I don't need anything.

Even from a distance I recognize him. He is sitting in a folding chair by the river, with a fishing rod in one hand and a book on his lap.

"What are you doing, sir?"

"I'm fishing."

"You can't really expect to catch anything."

"No."

"So why bother?"

He sighs and puts on his ah-grasshopper-you-have-much-to-learn voice.

"Fishing isn't always about catching fish, Alisha. It isn't even about the expectation of catching fish. It is about endurance, patience and most importantly"—he raises a can of draft—"it is about drinking beer."

Sir has put on weight since he retired—too many pastries over coffee and the *Times* crossword—and his hair has grown longer. It's strange to think he's no longer a detective, just an ordinary citizen.

Reeling in his line, he folds up his chair.

"You look like you've just run a marathon."

"Not quite that far."

I help him carry his gear across the road and into a large terrace house, with lead-light windows above empty flower boxes. He fills the kettle and moves a bundle of typed pages from the kitchen table.

"So what have you been doing with yourself, sir?"

"I wish you wouldn't call me sir."

"What should I call you?"

"Vincent."

"How about DI?"

"I'm not a detective inspector anymore."

"It could be like a nickname."

He shrugs. "You're getting cold. I'll get you a sweater."

I hear him rummaging upstairs and he comes down with a cardigan that smells of lavender and mothballs. "My mother's," he says apologetically.

I have met Mrs. Ruiz just the once. She was like something out of a European fairy tale—an old woman with missing teeth, wearing a shawl, rings and chunky jewelry.

"How is she?"

"Mad as a meat ax. She keeps accusing the staff at the hostel of giving her enemas. Now *there's* one of life's lousy jobs. You got to feel sorry for that poor bastard."

Ruiz laughs out loud, which is a nice sound. He's normally one of the most taciturn of men, with a permanent scowl and a generally low opinion of the human race, but that has never put me off. Beneath his gruff exterior I know there *isn't* a heart of gold. It's more precious than that.

I spy an old-fashioned typewriter in the corner.

"Are you writing, DI?"

"No." He answers too abruptly.

"You're writing a book."

"Don't be daft."

I try not to smile but I know my lips are turning up. He's going to get cross now. He hates people laughing at him. He takes the manuscript and tries to stuff it into an old briefcase. Then he sits back at the table, nursing his cup of tea.

I let a decent interval go by. "So what's it about?"

"What?"

"Your book."

"It's not a book. It's just some notes."

"Like a journal."

"No. Like *notes*." That settles the issue.

I haven't eaten since breakfast. Ruiz offers to make me something. Pasta puttanesca. It is perfect—far too subtle for me to describe and far better than anything I could have cooked. He puts shavings of Parmesan on slices of sourdough and toasts them under the griller.

"This is very good, DI."

"You sound surprised."

"I *am* surprised."

"Not all men are useless in the kitchen."

"And not all women are domestic goddesses." I talk to my local Indian takeout more often than I do my mother. It's called the tandoori diet.

Ruiz was there the day my spine was crushed. We have never really spoken about what happened. It's like an undeclared pact. I know he feels responsible but it wasn't his fault. He didn't force me to be there and he can't make the Met give me my old job back.

The dishes are washed and packed away.

"I am going to tell you a story," I tell him. "It's the sort of story you like because it has a puzzle at the center. I don't want you to interrupt and I won't tell you if it's real or invented. Just sit quietly. I need to put all the details in order to see how it sounds. When I'm finished I will ask you a question and you can tell me if I'm totally mistaken. Then I will let you ask me one question."

"Just one?"

"Yes. I don't want you to tear apart my logic or pick holes in my story. Not now. Tomorrow maybe. Is it a deal?"

He nods.

Carefully, I set out the details, telling him about Cate, Donavon and Earl Blake. Like a tangle in a fishing line, if I pull too tightly the story knots together and it becomes harder to separate fact from supposition.

"What if Cate arranged a surrogacy and something went wrong? Could there be a baby out there somewhere—Cate's baby?"

"Commercial surrogacy is illegal," he says.

"It still happens. Women volunteer. They get their expenses paid, which is allowed, but they cannot profit from the birth."

"Usually they're related in some way—a sister or a cousin."

I show him the photograph of Samira. He searches her face for a long time as though she might tell him something. Turning it over he notices the numbers.

"The first four digits could be a mobile phone prefix but not in the U.K.," he says. "You need the exact country code or you won't be able to call it."

It's my turn to be surprised again.

"I'm not a complete technophobe," he protests.

"You're typing your *notes* on an ink ribbon."

He glances at the old typewriter. "Yeah, well, it has sentimental value."

The clouds have parted just long enough to give us a sunset. The last golden rays settle on the river. In a few minutes they'll be gone, leaving behind a raw, damp cold.

"You promised me a question," he says.

"One."

"Do you want a lift home?"

"Is that it?"

"I thought maybe we could swing by Oaklands and you could show me where it happened."

The DI drives an old Mercedes with white leather seats and soft suspension. It must guzzle petrol and makes him look like a lawn bowler, but Ruiz has never been one to worry about the environment or what people think of him.

I feel strange sitting in the passenger seat instead of behind the wheel. For years it was the other way around. I don't know why he chose me to be his driver, but I heard the gossip about the DI liking pretty faces. He's really not like that.

When I first moved out of uniform into the Serious Crime Group, the DI showed me respect and gave me a chance to prove myself. He didn't treat me any differently because of my color or my age or my being a woman.

I told him I wanted to become a detective. He said I had to be better, faster and cleverer than any man who wanted the same position. Yes, it was unfair. He wasn't defending the system—he was teaching me the facts of life.

Ruiz was already a legend when I did my training. The instructors at Hendon used to tell stories about him. In 1963, as a probationary constable, he arrested one of the Great Train Robbers, Roger Cordrey, and recovered £141,000 of the stolen money. Later, as a detective, he helped capture the Kilburn rapist, who had terrorized North London for eight months.

I know he's not the sort to reminisce or talk about the good old days but I sense he misses a time when it was easier to tell the villains from the constabulary and the general public respected those who tried to keep them safe.

He parks the car in Mansford Street and we walk toward the school. The Victorian buildings are tall and dark against the ambient light. Fairy lights still drip from the windows of the hall. In my imagination I can see the dark stain on the tarmac where Cate fell. Someone has pinned a posy to the nearest lamppost.

"It's a straight line of sight," he says. "They can't have looked."

"Cate turned her head."

"Well she can't have seen the minicab. Either that or he pulled out suddenly."

"Two cabdrivers say they saw the minicab farther along the street, barely moving. They thought he was looking for an address."

I think back, mentally replaying events. "There's something else. I think Cate recognized the driver."

"She knew him?"

"He might have picked her up earlier as a fare."

"Or followed her."

"She was frightened of him. I could see it in her eyes."

I mention the driver's tattoo. The Crucifixion. It covered his entire chest.

"A tattoo like that might be traceable," says the DI. "We need a friend on the inside."

I know where he's going with this.

"How is 'New Boy' Dave?" he asks. "You two still bumping uglies?"

"That would be none of your business."

Sikh girls blush on the inside.

———————

Dave King is a detective with the Serious Crime Group (Western Division), Ruiz's old squad. He's in his early thirties with a tangle of gingery hair that he cuts short so it doesn't escape. He earned the nickname "New Boy" when he was the newest member of the SCG, but that was five years ago. He's now a detective sergeant.

Dave lives in a flat in West Acton, just off the Uxbridge Road, where gas towers dominate the skyline and trains on the Paddington line rattle him awake every morning.

It is a typical bachelor pad in progress, with a king-size bed, a wide-screen TV, a sofa, and precious little else. The walls are half stripped and the carpet has been ripped up but not replaced.

"Like what you've done to the place," observes Ruiz sardonically.

"Yeah, well, I been sort of busy," says Dave. He looks at me as if to say, *What's going on?*

Pecking him on the cheek, I slip my hand under his T-shirt and run my fingers down his spine. He's been playing rugby and his hair smells of mown grass.

Dave and I have been sleeping together, on and off, for nearly two years. Ruiz would smirk over the "on and off" part. It's the longest relationship of my life—even discounting the time I spent convalescing in hospital.

Dave thinks he wants to marry me but he hasn't met my family. You don't marry a Sikh girl. You marry her mother, her grandmother, her aunties, her brothers . . . I know all families have baggage but mine belongs in one of those battered suitcases, held together with string, that you see circling endlessly on a luggage carousel.

Dave tries to outdo me by telling stories about his family, particularly his mother who collects roadkill and keeps it in her freezer. She is on a mission to save badgers, which includes lobbying local councils to build tunnels beneath busy roads.

"I don't have anything to drink," he says apologetically.

"Shame on you," says Ruiz, who is pulling faces at the photographs on the fridge. "Who's this?"

"My mother," says Dave.

"You take after your father then."

Dave clears the table and pulls up chairs. I go through the story again. Ruiz then adds his thoughts, giving the presentation added gravitas. Meanwhile, Dave folds and unfolds a blank piece of paper. He wants to find a reason not to help us.

"Maybe you should wait for the official investigation," he suggests.

"You know things get missed."

"I don't want to tread on any toes."

"You're too good a dancer for that, 'New Boy,' " says Ruiz, cajoling him.

I can be shameless. I can bat my big brown eyelashes with the best of them. Forgive me, sisters. Taking the piece of paper from Dave's hand, I let my fingers linger on his. He chases them, not wanting to lose touch.

"He had an Irish accent but the most interesting thing is the tattoo." I describe it to him.

Dave has a laptop in the bedroom on a makeshift desk made from a missing bathroom door and saw horses. Shielding the screen from me, he types in a username and a password.

The Police National Computer is a vast database that contains the names, nicknames, aliases, scars, tattoos, accents, shoe size, height, age, hair color, eye color, offense history, associates and modus operandi of every known offender and person of interest in the U.K. Even partial details can sometimes be enough to link cases or throw up names of possible suspects.

In the good old days almost every police officer could access the PNC via the Internet. Unfortunately, one or two officers decided to make money selling the information. Now every request—even a license check—has to be justified.

Dave types in the age range, accent and details of the tattoo. It takes less than fifteen seconds for eight possible matches. He highlights the first name and the screen refreshes. Two photographs appear—a front view and a profile of the same face. The date of birth, antecedents and last known address are printed across the bottom. He is too young; too smooth-skinned.

"That's not him."

Candidate number two is older with horn-rimmed glasses and bushy eyebrows. He looks like a librarian caught in a pedophile sweep. Why do all mug shots look so unflattering? It isn't just the harsh lighting or plain white background with its black vertical ruler measuring the height. Everybody looks gaunt, depressed, worst of all, guilty.

A new photograph appears. A man in his late forties with a shaved head. Something about his eyes makes me pause. He looks arrogant; as if he knows he is cleverer than the vast majority of his fellow human beings and this inclines him to be cruel.

I reach toward the computer screen and cup my hand over the top of the image, trying to imagine him with a long gray ponytail.

"That's him."

"Are you sure?"

"Absolutely."

His name is Brendan Dominic Pearl—born in 1958 in Rathcoole, a Loyalist district of north Belfast.

"IRA," whispers Dave.

"How do you know?"

"It's the classic background." He scrolls down the screen to the biography. Pearl's father was a boilermaker on the Belfast docks. His elder brother, Tony, died in an explosion in 1972 when a bomb accidentally detonated in a warehouse being used as a bomb-making factory by the IRA.

A year later, aged fifteen, Brendan Pearl was convicted of assault and firearms offenses. He was sentenced to eighteen months of juvenile detention. In 1977 he launched a mortar attack on a Belfast police station that wounded four people. He was sentenced to twelve years.

At the Maze Prison in 1981 he joined a hunger strike with two dozen Republican prisoners. They were protesting about being treated as common criminals instead of prisoners of war. The most celebrated of them, Bobby Sands, died after sixty-six days. Pearl slipped into a coma in the hospital wing but survived.

Two years later, in July 1983, he and fellow inmate Frank Farmer climbed out of their compound onto the prison roof and gained access to the Loyalist compound. They murdered a paramilitary leader, Patrick McNeill, and maimed two others. Pearl's sentence was increased to life.

Ruiz joins us. I point to the computer screen. "That's him—the driver."

His shoulders suddenly shift and his eyes search mine.

"Are you sure?"

"Yes. Why? What's wrong?"

"I know him."

It's my turn to be surprised.

Ruiz studies the picture again as if the knowledge has to be summoned up or traded for information he doesn't need.

"There are gangs in every prison. Pearl was one of the IRA's enforcers. His favorite weapon was a metal pole with a curved hook something like a marlin spike. That's why they called him the Shankhill Fisherman. You don't find many fish in the Maze but he found another use for the weapon. He used to thread it through the bars while prisoners were sleeping and open their throats with a flick of the wrist, taking out their vocal chords in the process so they couldn't scream for help."

Cotton wool fills my esophagus. Ruiz pauses, his head bent, motionless.

"When the Good Friday peace agreement was signed more than four hundred prisoners were released from both sides—Republicans and Loyalists. The British government drew up a list of exemptions—people they wanted kept inside. Pearl was among them. Oddly enough, the IRA agreed. They didn't want Pearl any more than we did."

"So why isn't he still in prison?" asks Dave.

Ruiz smiles wryly. "That's a very good question, 'New Boy.' For forty years the British government told people it wasn't fighting a war in Northern Ireland—it was a 'police operation.' Then they signed the Good Friday Agreement and declared, 'The war is over.'

"Pearl got himself a good lawyer and that's exactly what he argued. He said he was a prisoner of war. There should be *no* exemptions. Bombers, snipers and murderers had been set free. Why was *he* being treated differently? A judge agreed. He and Frank Farmer were released on the same day."

A palm glides over his chin, rasping like sandpaper. "Some soldiers can't survive the peace. They need chaos. Pearl is like that."

"How do you know so much about him?" I ask.

There is sadness in his eyes. "I helped draw up the list."

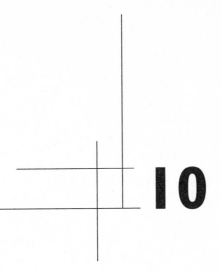

10

"New Boy" Dave shifts beside me, draping his arm over my breasts. I lift it away and tuck it under his pillow. He sleeps so soundly I can rearrange his body like a stop-motion puppet.

A digital clock glows on the bedside table. I lift my head. It's after ten on Sunday morning. Where are the trains? They didn't wake me. I have less than an hour and a half to shower, dress and get ready for my father's birthday.

Rolling out of bed, I look for my clothes. Dave's clothes. My running gear is still damp from yesterday.

He reaches for me, running his thumbs beneath the underside of my breast, tracing a pattern that only men can find.

"You trying to sneak away?"

"I'm late. I have to go."

"I wanted to make you breakfast."

"You can drive me home. Then you have to find Brendan Pearl."

"But it's Sunday. You never said—"

"That's the thing about women. We don't *say* exactly what we want but we reserve the right to be mighty pissed off when we don't get it. Scary isn't it?"

Dave makes coffee while I use the shower. I keep pondering how Brendan Pearl and Cate Beaumont could possibly know each other. They come from different worlds, yet Cate recognized him. It doesn't *feel* like an accident. It never did.

On the drive to the East End, Dave chats about work and his new boss. He says something about being unhappy but I'm not really listening.

"You could come over later," he says, trying not to sound needy. "We could get a pizza and watch a movie."

"That would be great. I'll let you know."

Poor Dave. I know he wants something more. One of these days he's going to take my advice and find another girlfriend. Then I'll have lost something I never tried to hold.

Things I like about him: He's sweet. He changes the sheets. He tolerates me. I feel safe with him. He makes me feel beautiful. And he lets me win at darts.

Things I don't like about him: His laugh is too loud. He eats junk food. He listens to Mariah Carey CDs. And he has hair growing on his shoulders. (*Gorillas* have hair on their shoulders.) Christ I can be pedantic!

His rugby mates have nicknames like Bronco and Sluggo and they talk in this strange jargon that nobody else can understand unless they follow rugby and appreciate the finer points of mauling, rucking and lifting. Dave took me to watch a game one day. Afterward we all went to the pub—wives and girlfriends. It was OK. They were all really nice and I felt comfortable. Dave didn't leave my side and kept sneaking glances at me and smiling.

I was only drinking mineral water but I shouted a round. As I waited at the bar I could see the corner tables reflected in the mirror.

"So what are we doing after?" asked Bronco. "I fancy a curry."

Sluggo grinned. "Dave's already had one."

They laughed and a couple of the guys winked at each other. "I bet she's a tikka masala."

"No, definitely a vindaloo."

I didn't mind. It was funny. I didn't even care that Dave laughed too. But I knew then, if not before, that my initial instincts were right. We could share a bath, a bed, a weekend, but we could never share a life.

We pull up in Hanbury Street and straightaway I realize that something is missing.

"I'll kill him!"

"What's wrong?"

"My car. My brother has taken it."

I'm already calling Hari's mobile. Wind snatches at his words. He's driving with the window open.

"Hello?"

"Bring back my car."

"Sis?"

"Where are you?"

"Brighton."

"You're joking! It's Dad's birthday."

"Is that *today*?" He starts fumbling for excuses. "Tell him I'm on a field trip for university."

"I'm not going to lie for you."

"Oh, come on."

"No."

"All right, I'll be there."

I look at my watch. I'm already late. "I hate you, Hari."

He laughs. "Well, it's a good thing I love you."

Upstairs I throw open wardrobes and scatter my shoes. I have to wear a sari to keep my father happy. Saris and salvation are mixed up in his mind—as though one is going to bring me the other, or at least get me a husband.

"New Boy" Dave is downstairs.

"Can you call me a cab, please?"

"I'll take you."

"No, really."

"It won't take more than a few minutes—then I'll go to work."

Back in my room, I wrap the sari fabric around my body, right to left, tucking the first wrap into my petticoat, making sure the bottom edge is brushing my ankles. Then I create seven pleats down the center, making sure they fall with the grain of the fabric. Holding the pleats in place, I take the remaining length of sari behind my back, across my body and drape it over my left shoulder.

This one is made of Varanasi silk, elaborately brocaded in red and green, with delicate figures of animals sewn with metallic silver thread along the border.

Pinning up my hair with a golden comb, I put on makeup and jewelry. Indian women are expected to wear lots of jewelry. It is a sign of wealth and social standing.

Sitting on the stairs, I buckle my sandals. Dave is staring at me.

"Is something wrong?"

"No."

"Well, what are you gawping at?"

"You look beautiful."

"Yeah, right." *I look like a Ratner's display window.*

I bat his hands away as he reaches out for me. "No touching the merchandise! And for God's sake, don't have an accident. I don't want to die in these clothes."

My parents live in the same house where I grew up. My mother doesn't like change. In her perfect world, children would never leave home or discover how to cook or clean for themselves. Since this is impossible, she has preserved our childhoods in bric-a-brac and become the full-time curator at the Barba family museum.

As soon as I turn into the cul-de-sac I feel a familiar heat in my cheeks. "Just drop me off here."

"Where's the house?"

"Don't worry. This will be fine."

We pull up outside a small parade of shops. Fifty yards away my niece and nephew play in the front garden. They go tearing inside to announce my arrival.

"Quick, quick, turn round!"

"I can't turn round."

It's too late! My mother appears, waddling down the road. My worst nightmare is coming true.

She kisses me three times, squeezing me so hard that my breasts hurt.

"Where is Hari?"

"I reminded him. I even ironed his shirt."

"That boy will be the death of me." She points to her temple. "See my gray hairs."

Her gaze falls on "New Boy" Dave. She waits for an introduction.

"This is a friend from work. He has to go."

Mama makes a *pffffhh* sound. "Does he have a name?"

"Yes, of course. Detective Sergeant Dave King. This is my mother."

"It's nice to meet you, Mrs. Barba. Ali has told me so much about you."

My mother laughs. "Will you stay for lunch, Detective Sergeant?"

"No, he has to go."

"Nonsense. It's Sunday."

"Police have to work weekends."

"Detectives are allowed to have lunch breaks. Isn't that right?"

Then my mother smiles and I know I've lost. Nobody can ever say no to that smile.

Small feet patter down the hallway ahead of us. Harveen and Daj are fighting over who's going to break the news that Auntie Ali has brought someone with her. Harveen comes back and takes my hand, dragging me into the kitchen. There are frown lines on her forehead at the age of seven. Daj is two years older and, like every male member of my family, is improbably handsome (and spoiled).

"Have you brought anything for us?" he asks.

"Only a kiss."

"What about a present?"

"Only for Bada."

Benches are covered with food and the air is heavy with steam and spices. My two aunts and my sisters-in-law are talking over one another amid the clatter and bang of energetic cooking. There are hugs and kisses. Glasses graze my cheekbones and fingers tug at my sari or straighten my hair, without my relatives ever taking their eyes from "New Boy" Dave.

My aunties, Meena and Kala, couldn't be less alike as sisters. Meena is quite masculine and striking, with a strong jaw and thick eyebrows. Kala, by contrast, is unexceptional in almost every way, which might explain why she wears such decorative spectacles, to give her face more character.

Meena is still fussing with my hair. "Such a pretty thing to be unmarried; such lovely bones."

A baby is thrust into my arms—the newest addition to the family. Ravi is six weeks old, with coffee-bean-colored eyes and rolls of fat on his arms that you could lose a sixpence inside.

Cows might be sacred to Hindus, but babies are sacred to Sikhs, boys more so than girls. Ravi latches on to my finger and squeezes it until his eyes fold shut.

"She's so good with children," says Mama, beaming. Dave should be squirming but he's actually enjoying this. Sadist!

The men are outside in the garden. I can see my father's blue turban above them all. His beard is swept back from his cheeks and crawls down his neck like a silver trickle of water.

I count heads. There are extras. My heart sinks. They've invited someone for me to meet.

My mother ushers Dave outside. He glances over his shoulder at me, hesitating before obeying her instructions. Down the side steps, along the mildewed path, past the door to the laundry, he reaches the rear garden. Every face turns toward him and the conversation stops.

It's like the parting of the Red Sea, as people step back and "New Boy" Dave faces my father. It's eyeball to eyeball but Dave doesn't flinch, which is to his credit.

I can't hear what they're saying. My father glances up toward the kitchen window. He sees me. Then he smiles and thrusts out his hand. Dave takes it and suddenly conversation begins again.

My mother is at the sink, peeling and slicing mangoes. She slides the knife blade easily beneath the pale yellow flesh. "We didn't know you were going to bring a friend."

"I didn't bring him."

"Well, your father has invited someone. You must meet his guest. It's only polite. He is a doctor."

"A very fine one," echoes Auntie Kala. "Very successful."

I scan the gathering and pick him out. He is standing with his back to me, dressed in a Punjabi suit that has been laundered and starched to attention.

"He's fat."

"A sign of success," says Kala.

"It takes a big hammer to hammer a big nail," adds Meena, cackling like a schoolgirl. Kala disapproves.

"Oh, don't give me that look, sister. A wife has to learn how to keep her husband happy in the boudoir." The two of them continue arguing while I go back to the window.

The stranger in the garden turns and glances up at me. He holds up his glass, as if offering me a toast. Then he shakes it from side to side, indicating its emptiness.

"Quickly, girl, take him another drink," says Meena, handing me a jug.

Taking a deep breath, I walk down the side steps into the garden. My brothers whistle. They know how much I hate wearing a sari. All the men turn toward me. I keep my eyes focused on my sandals.

My father is still talking to Dave and my uncle Rashid, a notorious butt-squeezer. My mother claims it is an obsessive-compulsive disorder but I think he's just a lech. They are talking about cricket. The men in my family are obsessed with the game even when the summer is over.

Most Indian men are small and elegant with delicate hands but my brothers are strapping, rugged types, except for Hari, who would make a beautiful woman.

Bada kisses my cheek. I bow to him slightly. He ushers his guest closer and makes the formal introductions.

"Alisha, this is Dr. Sohan Banerjee."

I nod, still not raising my eyes.

The name is familiar. Where have I heard it before?

Poor Dave doesn't understand what's going on. He's not a Sikh, which is probably a good thing. If I'd brought a Sikh home my parents would have killed a goat.

Dr. Banerjee stands very straight and bows his head. My father is still talking. "Sohan contacted me personally and asked if he could meet you, Alisha. Family to family—that is how it should be done."

I'm not meant to comment.

"He has more than one medical degree," he adds.

He has more than one chin.

I don't know how much worse this day could get. People are watching me. Dave is on the far side of the garden talking to my eldest brother, Prabakar, the most religious member of the family, who won't approve.

The doctor is talking to me. I have to concentrate on his words. "I believe you are a police officer."

"Yes."

"And you live separately from your parents. Very few single Indian girls have property. So why aren't you married?"

The bluntness of the question surprises me. He doesn't wait for an answer. "Are you a virgin?"

"Excuse me?"

"I'm assuming your mother explained the facts of life to you."

"It's none of your business."

"No comment means yes."

"No, it doesn't."

"In my experience it does. Do you drink?"

"No."

"See? You don't have to be so defensive. My parents think I should marry a girl from India because village girls are hard workers and good mothers. This may be so but I don't want a peasant girl who can't eat with a knife and fork."

Anger rises in my throat and I have to swallow hard to keep it down. I give him my politest smile. "So tell me Dr. Banerjee—"

"Call me Sohan."

"Sohan, do you ever masturbate?"

His mouth opens and closes like a ventriloquist's dummy. "I hardly think—"

"No comment means yes."

The flash of anger in his eyes is like a bloodred veil. He grinds his teeth into a smile. "Touché."

"What kind of doctor are you?"

"An obstetrician."

Suddenly I remember where I've read his name. It was in the file that Barnaby Elliot showed me. Sohan Banerjee is a fertility specialist. He performed Cate's IVF procedures.

There are 100,000 Sikhs in London and what—maybe 400 obstetricians? What are the chances of Cate's doctor showing up here?

"We have a mutual acquaintance," I announce. "Cate Beaumont. Did you hear about the accident?"

He shifts his gaze to the mottled green roof of my father's shed. "Her mother telephoned me. A terrible thing."

"Did she tell you that Cate faked her pregnancy?"

"Yes."

"What else did she say?"

"It would be highly unethical to reveal the details of our conversation." He pauses and adds, "Even to a police officer."

My eyes search his or perhaps it's the other way round. "Are you deliberately trying to withhold information from a police investigation?"

He smiles warily. "Forgive me. I thought this was a birthday party."

"When did you last see Cate?"

"A year ago."

"Why couldn't she conceive?"

"No reason at all," he says blithely. "She had a laparoscopy, blood tests, ultrasounds and a hysteroscopy. There were no abnormalities, adhesions or fibroids. She *should* have been able to conceive. Unfortunately, she and her husband were incompatible. Felix had a low sperm count, but married to someone else he may well have fathered a child without too much difficulty. However, in this case, his sperm were treated like cancerous cells and were destroyed by his wife's immune system. Pregnancy was theoretically possible but realistically unlikely."

"Did you ever suggest surrogacy as an option?"

"Yes, but there aren't many women willing to have a child for another couple. There was also another issue . . ."

"What issue?"

"Have you heard of achondrogenesis?"

"No."

"It is a very rare genetic disorder, a form of lethal dwarfism."

"What does that have to do with Cate?"

"Her only known pregnancy resulted in a miscarriage at six months. An autopsy revealed severe deformities in the fetus. By some twisted chance of fate, a reverse lottery, she and Felix each carried a recessive gene. Even, if by some miracle, she could conceive, there was a 25 percent chance it would happen again."

"But they kept trying."

He raises his hand to stop me. "Excuse me, Alisha, but am I to understand from your questions that you are investigating this matter in some official capacity?"

"I'm just looking for answers."

"I see." He ponders this. "If I were you, I would be very careful. People can sometimes misconstrue good intentions."

I'm unsure if this is advice or a warning but he holds my gaze until I feel uncomfortable. There is an arrogance about Banerjee that is typical of his generation of educated Sikhs, who are more pukka than any Englishman you will ever meet.

Finally, he relaxes. "I will tell you this much, Alisha. Mrs. Beaumont underwent five IVF implants over a period of two years. This is very complex science. It is not something you do at home with a glass jar and a syringe. It is the last resort, when all else fails."

"What happened in Cate's case?"

"She miscarried each time. Less than a third of IVF procedures result in a birth. My success rate is at the high end of the scale, but I am a doctor not a miracle worker."

For once the statement doesn't sound conceited. He seems genuinely disappointed.

Aunt Meena calls everyone inside for lunch. The tables have been set up with my father at the head. I am seated among the women. The men sit opposite. "New Boy" Dave and Dr. Banerjee are side by side.

Hari arrives in time for pudding and is treated like a prodigal son by my aunts, who run their fingers through his long hair. Leaning down, he whispers into my ear, "Two at once, sis. And I had you down as an old maid."

My family are noisy when we eat. Plates are passed around. People talk over one another. Laughter is like a spice. There is no ceremony but there are rituals (which are not the same thing). Speeches are made, the cooks must be thanked, nobody talks over my father and all disagreements are saved for afterward.

I don't let Dave stay that long. He has work to do. Sohan Banerjee also prepares to leave. I still don't understand why he's here. It can't be just a coincidence.

"Would you accede to seeing me again, Alisha?" he asks.

"No, I'm sorry."

"It would make your parents very happy."

"They will survive."

He rocks his head from side to side and up and down. "Very well. I don't know what to say."

"Goodbye is traditional."

He flinches. "Yes. Goodbye. I wish your friend Mrs. Beaumont a speedy recovery."

Closing the front door, I feel a mixture of anxiety and relief. My life has enough riddles without this one.

Hari meets me in the hallway. His dark eyes catch the light and he puts his arms around me. My mobile is open in his fingers.

"Your friend Cate died at one o'clock this afternoon."

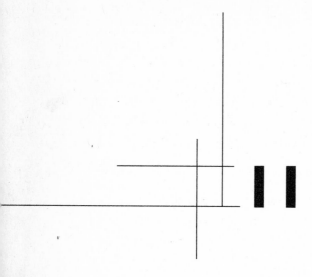

There are cars parked in the driveway and in the street outside the Elliots' house. Family. A wake. I should leave them alone. Even as I debate what to do I find myself standing at the front door ringing the bell.

It opens. Barnaby is there. He has showered, shaved and tidied himself up but his eyes are watery and unfocused.

"Who is it, dear?" asks a voice from inside.

He stiffens and steps back. Wheels squeak on the parquetry floor and Cate's mother rolls into view. She is dressed in black making her face appear even more spectral.

"You must come in," she says, her lips peeled back into a pained smile.

"I'm so sorry about Cate. If there's anything I can do."

She doesn't answer. Wheels roll her away. I follow them inside to the sitting room, which is full of sad-eyed friends and family. A few of them I recognize. Judy and Richard Sutton, a brother and sister. Richard was Barnaby's campaign manager in two elections and Judy works for Chase Manhattan. Cate's aunt Paula is talking to Jarrod and in the corner I spy Reverend Lunn, an Anglican minister.

Yvonne is crumpled on a chair, talking and sobbing at the same time. Her clothes, normally so bright and vibrant, now mirror her mood, black. Her two children are with her, both grown up, more English than Jamaican. The girl is beautiful. The boy could name a thousand places he'd prefer to be.

Yvonne cries a little harder when she sees me, groaning as she raises her arms to embrace me.

Before I can speak, Barnaby grips my forearm, pulling me away.

"How did you know about the money?" he hisses. I can smell the alcohol on his breath.

"What are you talking about?"

The words catch in his throat. "Somebody withdrew £80,000 from Cate's account."

"Where did she get that sort of money?"

He lowers his voice even further. "From her late grandmother. I checked her bank account. Half the money was withdrawn last December and the other half in February."

"A bank check?"

"Cash. The bank won't tell me any more."

"And you have no idea why?"

He shakes his head and stumbles forward a pace. I steer him toward the kitchen where "get well soon" cards lie open on the table amid torn envelopes. They seem pointless now; forlorn gestures swamped by a greater grief.

Filling a glass from the tap, I hand it to him. "The other day you mentioned a doctor, a fertility specialist."

"What about him?"

"Did you ever meet him?"

"No."

"Do you know if he ever suggested alternatives to IVF like adoption or surrogacy?"

"Not that I heard. He didn't overstate Cate's chances, I know that much. And he wouldn't implant more than two embryos each time. He had another policy—three strikes and you're out. Cate begged him to let her try again so he gave her five chances."

"Five?"

"They harvested eighteen eggs but only twelve were viable. Two embryos were implanted each time."

"But that only accounts for ten—what about the remaining two eggs?"

He shrugs. "Dr. Banerjee wouldn't go again. He saw how fragile Cate had become, emotionally. She was falling apart."

"She could have gone to another clinic."

"Felix wouldn't let her. The hormones, the tests, the tears—he wouldn't put her through it again."

None of this explains the money. Eighty thousand pounds isn't just given away. Cate was trying to buy a baby but something went wrong. That's why she contacted me.

I go over the story again, laying out the evidence. Some of the details and half-truths have taken on the solidity of facts. I can see what Barnaby's thinking. He's worried about his political ambitions. This sort of scandal would kill his chances stone dead.

"That's why I need to see Cate's computer," I say.

"She doesn't have one."

"Have you looked?"

"Yes."

The glass clinks against his teeth. He's lying to me.

"The files you showed me—and Cate's letters—can I borrow them?"

"No."

My frustration is turning to anger. "Why are you doing this? How can I make you understand?"

His hand touches my knee. "You could be nicer to me."

Ruth Elliot materializes in the kitchen, her wheels silent this time. She looks at me as though she's spat out a frog.

"People are beginning to leave, Barnaby. You should come and say goodbye."

He follows her to the front door. I grab my coat and slip past them.

"Thank you for coming, dear," she says mechanically, reaching up from her wheelchair. Her lips are as dry as paper on my forehead.

Barnaby puts his arms around me and I move my weight so our thighs lose contact. His lips brush my left earlobe.

"Why do women always do this to *me*?"

Driving away, I can still feel the warmth of his breath. Why do men always think it is about *them*?

I'm sure I could find an excuse or make an argument for what I'm about to do, but whatever way you dress it up, it's still breaking the law. A half brick. An overcoat. The pane of glass shatters and falls inward. So far it's vandalism or criminal damage. I reach inside and unlock the door. Now it's illegal entry. If I find the laptop it's going be theft. Is this what they mean by the slippery slope of crime?

It's after midnight. I'm wearing black jeans, leather gloves and a royal blue turtleneck sweater Auntie Meena knitted me. I have brought with me a large roll of black plastic, some duct tape, a torch and a USB drive for downloading computer files.

I close my eyes. The layout of the ground floor rises up in front of me. I remember it from three days ago. Glass crunches under my sneakers. A red light blinks on the answering machine.

It shouldn't have come to this. Barnaby lied to me. It's not that I suspect him of anything serious. Good people protect those they love. But sometimes they don't recognize how good intentions and blind loyalty can twist their reasoning.

He's frightened of what I might find. *I'm* frightened. He's worried that he didn't really know his daughter. *I'm* worried too.

I climb the stairs. In the nursery I take the roll of black plastic and cover the window, sealing the edges with duct tape. Now it's safe to turn on the torch.

Precautions like this might be unnecessary but I can't afford to have the neighbors investigating or someone calling the police. My career (what career?) already hangs on a thread. I open the dresser drawer. The files have gone, along with the bundle of letters.

Moving from room to room I repeat the process, searching wardrobes and drawers beneath beds.

Next to the main bedroom there is a study with a desk and filing cabinet. The lone window is partially open. I glance outside to a moonlit garden, blanketed by shadows and fallen leaves.

Unfurling another sheet of black plastic, I seal the window before turning on my torch. Beneath the desk, just above the skirting board, I notice a phone outlet. The top drawer contains software and instructions for an ADSL connection. I was right about the computer. Right about Barnaby.

Opening the remaining drawers, I find the usual office supplies—

marker pens, a stapler, paper clips, a ball of rubber bands, Post-it notes, a cigarette lighter . . .

Next I search the filing cabinet, leafing through the hanging files. There are no labels or dates. I have to search each one. Plastic sheaths contain the domestic bills. Each telephone account has a list of outgoing calls to mobiles and long-distance numbers. I can possibly trace them but it will take days.

Among the invoices there is one from an Internet company. People sometimes leave copies of their e-mails on their server but I need Cate's password and username.

Having finished in the study I move on to the main bedroom, which is paper-free except for the bookshelves. Barnaby said Felix was sleeping in the guest room. His side of the wardrobe is empty. Cate slept on the right side of the bed. Her bedside drawer has night cream, moisturizer, emery boards and a picture frame lying face-down. I turn it over.

Two teenage girls are laughing at the camera; arms draped over each other's shoulders; seawater dripping from their hair. I can almost taste the salt on their skin and hear the waves shushing the shingles.

Every August the Elliot family used to rent a cottage in Cornwall and spend their time sailing and swimming. Cate invited me one year. I was fifteen and it was my first proper beach holiday.

We swam, rode bikes, collected shells and watched the boys surfing at Widemouth Bay. A couple of them offered to teach Cate and me how to surf but Barnaby said that surfers were deadbeats and potheads. Instead he taught us how to sail in a solo dinghy on Padstow Harbour and the Camel Estuary. He could only take one of us out at a time.

I was embarrassed by my lime-green gingham seersucker one-piece, which my mother had chosen. Cate let me borrow one of her bikinis. As we sat side by side, Barnaby's leg would sometimes touch mine. And to balance the boat we had to lean out over the water and he put his arm around my waist. I liked the way he smelled of salt and suntan lotion.

Of an evening we played games like charades and Trivial Pursuit. I tried to sit next to him because he would nudge me in the ribs when he told one of his jokes or lean against me until we toppled over.

"You were flirting with him," said Cate after we'd gone to bed. We were sharing the loft. Mr. and Mrs. Elliot had the largest bedroom on the floor below and Jarrod had a room to himself at the back of the house.

"No, I wasn't."

"You *were*."

"Don't be ridiculous."

"It's disgusting. He's old enough to be—"

"Your father?"

We laughed. She was right, of course. I did flirt with Barnaby and he flirted back because he knew no other way to behave with women or girls.

Cate and I were lying on top of the bedclothes, unable to sleep because it was so hot. The loft had no insulation and seemed to trap the heat from the day.

"Do you know your problem?" she said. "You've never actually kissed a boy."

"Yes, I have."

"I'm not talking about your brothers. I mean a proper French kiss—with tongues."

I grew embarrassed.

"You should practice."

"Pardon?"

"Here, do this." She pressed her thumb and forefinger together. "Pretend this is a boy's lips and kiss them."

She held my hand and kissed it, snaking her tongue between my thumb and forefinger until they were wet with saliva.

"Now you try it." She held out her hand. It tasted of toothpaste and soap. "No, too much tongue. Yeuch!"

"*You* used a lot of tongue."

"Not that much." She wiped her hand on the sheets and looked at me with impatient affection. "Now you have to remember positioning."

"What do you mean?"

"You have to tilt your head to the right or left so you don't bang noses. We're not Eskimos."

She tossed her ponytail over her shoulder and pulled me close. Cupping my face, she pressed her lips against mine. I could feel her heart beating and the blood pulsing beneath her skin. Her tongue brushed along my lips and danced over my teeth. We were breathing the same air. My eyes stayed closed. It was the most amazing feeling.

"Wow, you're a fast learner," she said.

"You're a good teacher."

My heart was racing.

"Maybe we shouldn't do that again."

"It did feel a bit weird."

"Yeah. Weird."

I rubbed my palms down the front of my nightdress.

"Yeah, well, now you know how to do it," said Cate, picking up a magazine.

She had kissed a lot of boys, even at fifteen, but she didn't brag about it. Many more followed—pearls and pebbles strung around her neck—and as each one came and went there was scarcely a shrug of resignation or sadness.

I brush my fingers over the photograph and contemplate whether to take it with me. Who would know? At the same moment an answer occurs to me. Retracing my steps to the study, I open the desk drawer and spy the cigarette lighter. When we were kids and I stayed the night with Cate, she would sneak cigarettes upstairs and lean out the window so her parents didn't smell the smoke.

Tearing the plastic sheet from the sash window, I slide the lower pane upward and brace my hands on the sill as I lean outside, sixteen feet above the garden.

In the darkness I follow the line of a rainwater pipe that is fixed to the bricks with metal brackets. I need more light. Risking the torch, I direct the beam onto the pipe. I can just make out the knotted end of a thin cord, looped over the nearest bracket, beyond reach.

What did she use?

I look around the study. At the back of the desk, hard against the wall, is a wire coat hanger stretched to create a diamond shape with a hook on one end. Back at the window, I lean out and snag the loop of cord on the hook, pulling it toward me. The cord runs across the wall and over a small nail before dropping vertically. As I pull it a paint can emerges from the foliage of the garden. It rises toward me until I can lean out and grab it.

Pulling it inside, I use a coin to lever open the lid. Inside is half a packet of cigarettes and a larger package wrapped in plastic and held together with rubber bands. Retrieving it, I close the lid of the paint can and let the nylon cord slip through my fingers as I lower it back into the shrubs.

Returning to the main bedroom, I slip off the rubber bands from the package and unfold what turns out to be a plastic bag with documents pressed into the bottom corner. I spread the contents on the duvet: two airline boarding passes, a tourist map of Amsterdam and a brochure.

The boarding passes are for a British Midlands flight from Heathrow to Schiphol Airport in the Netherlands on the ninth of February, returning on the eleventh.

The tourist map has a picture of the Rijksmuseum on the front cover and is worn along the folds. It seems to cover the heart of Amsterdam where the canals and streets follow a concentric horseshoe pattern. The back of the map has bus, tram and train routes, flanked by a list of hotels. One of them is circled: the Red Tulip Hotel.

I pick up the brochure. It appears to promote a charity—the New Life Adoption Center, which has a phone number and a post box address in Hayward's Heath, West Sussex. There are pictures of babies and happy couples, along with a quote: "Isn't it nice to know when you're not ready to be a mother, somebody else is?"

Unfolding the brochure there are more photographs and testimonials.

"HOPING TO ADOPT? If you are looking for a safe, successful adoption we can help! Since 1995 we have helped hundreds of couples adopt babies. Our select group of caring professionals can make your dream of a family come true."

On the opposite page is a headline: ARE YOU PREGNANT AND CONSIDERING WHAT TO DO?

"We can help you! We offer assistance and encouragement during and after your pregnancy and can provide birthparent scholarships. Open adoption means YOU make the choices."

Underneath is a photograph of a child's hand clinging to the finger of an adult.

Someone called Julie writes: "Thank you for turning my unexpected pregnancy into a gift from God to all involved."

On the opposite page are further testimonials, this time from couples.

"Choosing adoption brought us a beautiful daughter and made our lives complete."

A loose page slips from the center of the brochure.

"This child could be yours," it reads. "Born this month: a boy, white, with an unknown father. The mother, 18, is a prostitute and former drug user, now clean. This baby could be yours for a facilitation fee and medical expenses."

Returning the documents to the plastic bag, I snap the rubber bands in place.

The phone number on the back of Samira's photograph needed a foreign prefix. Cate visited the Netherlands in February. She announced she was twelve weeks pregnant in May.

I pick up the telephone next to the bed and call international inquiries. It feels wrong to call from the scene of the crime, as though I'm confessing. An operator gives me the country code for the Netherlands. Adding "31" this time, I call the number.

It connects. The ring tone is long and dull.

Someone picks up. Silence.

"Hello?"

Nothing.

"Hello, can you hear me?"

Someone is breathing.

"I'm trying to reach Samira. Is she there?"

A guttural voice, bubbling with phlegm, answers me. "Who is calling?"

The accent might be Dutch. It sounds more East European.

"A friend."

"Your name?"

"Actually, I'm a friend of a friend."

"Your name and your friend's name?"

Distrust sweeps over me like a cold shadow. I don't like this voice. I can feel it searching for me, reaching inside my chest, feeling blindly for my soft center, my soul.

"Is Samira there?"

"There is nobody here."

I try to sound calm. "I am calling on behalf of Cate Beaumont. I have the rest of the money."

I am extrapolating on the known facts, which is just a fancy way of saying that I'm winging it. *How much further can I go?*

The phone goes dead.

Not far enough.

Putting the receiver back on its cradle, I smooth the bed and pick up my things. As I turn toward the door I hear a tinkling sound. I know what it is. I made just such a sound when I smashed a pane of glass in the French doors.

Someone is in the house. What are the chances of two intruders on the same night? Slim. None. Tucking the package into the waistband of my jeans, I peer over the banister. There are muffled voices in the hall. At least two. A torch beam passes the bottom of the stairs. I pull back.

What to do? I shouldn't be here. Neither should they. Ahead of me are the stairs to the loft. Climbing them quickly, I reach a door that opens on stiff hinges.

From downstairs: "Did you hear something?"

"What?"

"I thought I heard something."

"Nah."

"I'll check upstairs."

One of them sounds Irish. It could be Brendan Pearl.

"Hey!"

"What?"

"You notice that?"

"What?"

"The windows are covered in plastic. Why would they do that?"

"Fucked if I know. Just get on with it."

The loft seems to be full of odd angles and narrow corners. My eyes are getting used to the dark. I can make out a single bed, a cabinet, a fan on a stand and cardboard boxes of clutter and bric-a-brac.

Squeezing into a space formed by the cabinet and the sloping roof, I pull boxes in front of me. I need a weapon. The iron bed has heavy brass balls on the bedposts. I unscrew one of them quietly and peel off a sock, slipping the ball inside. It slips down to the toe and I weigh it in my hands. It could break bones.

Returning to my hiding place, I listen for footsteps on the stairs and watch the door. I have to call the police. If I flip open my phone the screen will light up like a neon sign saying, "Here I am! Come and get me!"

Shielding it in both hands, I dial 999. An operator answers.

"Officer in trouble. Intruders on premises."

I whisper the address and my badge number. I can't stay on the line. The phone closes and the screen goes dark. Only my breathing now and the footsteps . . .

The door opens. A torch beam flashes and swings across the room. I can't see the figure behind it. He can't see me. He stumbles over a box and sends Christmas baubles spilling across the floor. The light finds one of them close to my feet.

He puts the torch on the bed, facing toward him. It reflects off his forehead. Brendan Pearl. All my weight is on the balls of my feet, ready to fight. What's he doing?

There is something in his fist. A box-like can. He presses it and a stream of liquid arcs from the nozzle, shining silver in the torch beam. He presses again, soaking the boxes and drawing patterns on the walls. Fluid splashes across my forehead, leaking into my eyes.

Red hot wires stab into my brain and the smell catches in the back of my throat. Lighter fluid. Fire!

The pain is unimaginable, but I mustn't move. He's going to set fire to the house. I have to get out. I can't see. Vibrations on the stairs. He's gone. Crawling from my hiding place, I reach the door and press my ear against it.

My eyes are useless. I need water to flush them out. There's a bathroom on the first floor as well as an en suite in the main bedroom. I can find them but only if Pearl has gone. I can't afford to wait.

Something breaks with a crack and topples over downstairs. My vision is blurred but I see a light. Not light. Fire!

The ground floor is ablaze and the smoke is rising. Clinging to the handrail, I make it down to the landing. Feeling my way along the wall, I reach the en suite and splash water into my eyes. I can see only blurred outlines, shadows instead of sharp detail.

The smoke is getting thicker. On my hands and knees, I feel my way across the bedroom, smelling the lighter fluid on the carpet. When the fire reaches this floor it will accelerate. The study window is still open. I crawl across the landing, bumping my head against a wall. My fingers find the skirting board. I can feel the heat.

Finding the window, I lean outside and take deep breaths between spluttering coughs. There is a whooshing sound behind me. Flames sweep past the open door. Hungry. Feeding on the accelerant.

Climbing onto the window ledge I look down. I can just make out the garden, sixteen feet below. A jump like that will break both my legs. I turn my head toward the downpipe bolted to the wall. My eyes are useless. How far was it? Four feet. Maybe a little more.

I can feel the heat of the fire on the backs of my legs. A window blows out beneath me. I hear glass scattering through the shrubbery.

I have to back myself to do this. I have to trust my memory and my instincts. Toppling sideways, I reach out, falling.

My left hand brushes past the pipe. My right hand hooks around it. Momentum will either pull me loose or rip my shoulder out. Two hands have it now. My hip crashes against the bricks and I hang on.

Hand below hand, I shimmy toward the ground. Sirens are coming. My feet touch soft earth and I wheel about, stumbling a dozen paces before tripping over a flower bed and sprawling on my face.

Every window at the rear of the house is lit up. Through my watery eyes it sounds and looks like a university party. The ultimate housewarming.

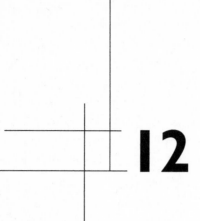

12

Two detectives have turned up. One of them I remember from training college, Eric Softell. The name sounds like a brand of toilet paper, which is why they nicknamed him "Arsewipe" at training college. Not me, of course. Sikh girls don't risk calling people names.

"I heard you were off the force," he says.

"No."

"Still running?"

"Yes."

"Not fast enough from what I hear." He grins at his partner, Billy Marsh, a detective constable.

Stories about the camaraderie of police officers are often sadly overstated. I don't find many of my colleagues particularly lovable or supportive, but at least most of them are honest and some of them are keepers like DI Ruiz.

A paramedic has flushed out my eyes with distilled water. I'm sitting on the back ramp of the ambulance, head tilted, while he tapes cotton wool over my left eye.

"You should see an eye specialist," he says. "It can sometimes take a week before the full damage is clear."

"Permanent damage?"

"See the specialist."

Behind him fire hoses snake across the gleaming road and firemen in reflective vests are mopping up. Structurally, there is still a house on the block, but the insides are gutted and smoking. The loft collapsed under the weight of water.

I called Hari to come and get me. Now he's watching the firemen with a mixture of awe and envy. What boy doesn't want to play with a hose?

Sensing the animosity between Softell and me, he tries to step in and play the protective brother, which doesn't really suit him.

"Listen, punka-wallah, why don't you run along and fetch us a cup of tea?" says Softell.

Hari doesn't understand the insult but he recognizes the tone.

I should be angry but I'm used to remarks like this from people like Softell. During probationer training a group of us were given riot shields and sent to the parade ground. Another band of recruits were told to attack us verbally and physically. There were no rules, but we weren't able to retaliate. Softell spat in my face and called me a "Paki whore." I practically thanked him.

My left thigh is slightly corked; my knuckles are scraped and raw. There are questions. Answers. The name Brendan Pearl means nothing to them.

"Explain to me again what you were doing in the house."

"I was driving by. I saw a burglary in process. I called it in."

"From inside the house?"

"Yes, sir."

"So you followed them inside?"

"Yes."

Softell shakes his head. "You just happened to be driving past a friend's house and you saw the same man who was driving the car that ran her down. What do you think, Billy?"

"Sounds like bullshit to me." Marsh is the one taking notes.

"How did you get lighter fluid in your eyes?"

"He was spraying it around."

"Yeah, yeah, while you were *hiding* in the corner."

Arsehole!

Casually, he props his foot on the tray of the ambulance. "If you were just gonna hide in there, why bother going in at all?"

"I thought there was only one of them."

I'm digging myself into a hole.

"Why didn't you phone for backup *before* you went in?"

Deeper and deeper.

"I don't know, sir."

Drops of water have beaded on the polished toe of his shoe.

"You see how it looks, don't you?" Softell says.

"How does it look?"

"A house burns down. A witness comes forward who is covered in lighter fluid. Rule number one when dealing with arson—nine times out of ten, the person who yells 'fire' is the person who starts the fire."

"You can't be serious. Why would I do that?"

His shoulders lift and drop. "Who knows? Maybe you just like burning shit."

The whole street has been woken. Neighbors are standing on the pavement in dressing gowns and overcoats. Children are jumping on a hose and dancing away from a leak that sprays silver under the streetlight.

A black cab pulls up outside the ring of fire engines. Ruiz emerges. He steps through the ring of rubberneckers, ignoring the constable who is trying to keep them back.

After pausing to appraise the house, he continues along the road until he reaches me. The white eye patch makes me look like a reverse pirate.

"Do you ever have a *normal* day?" he asks.

"Once. It was a Wednesday."

He looks me up and down. I'm putting most of my weight on one leg because of my thigh. Surprisingly, he leans forward and kisses my cheek, an absolute first.

"I thought you retired," says Billy Marsh.

"That's right, son."

"Well, what are you doing here?"

"I asked him to come," I explain.

Ruiz is sizing up the detectives. "Mind if I listen in?"

It sounds like a question only it isn't. The DI manages to do that sometimes—turn questions into statements.

"Just don't get in the bloody way," mumbles Softell.

Marsh is on the phone calling for a Scene of Crime team to sweep the house and garden for clues. The fire brigade will launch its own investigation. I hobble away from the ambulance, which has another call. Ruiz takes my arm.

Hari is still here. "You can go home now," I tell him.

"What about you?"

"I could be a while."

"You want me to stay?"

"That's OK."

He glances at Softell and whispers, "Do you know that prick?"

"He's OK."

"No wonder people dislike coppers."

"Hey!"

He grins. "Not you, sis."

There are more questions to answer. Softell becomes less interested in what I was doing in the house and more interested in Brendan Pearl.

"So you think this arson attack is linked to the deaths of the Beaumonts?"

"Yes."

"Why would Pearl burn down their house?"

"Perhaps he wanted to destroy evidence—letters, e-mails, phone records—anything that might point to him."

I explain about Cate's fake pregnancy and the money missing from Cate's account. "I think she arranged to buy a baby, but something went wrong."

Marsh speaks: "People adopt foreign kids all the time—Chinese orphans, Romanians, Koreans. Why would you buy a child?"

"She tried to adopt and couldn't."

"How do you buy one?"

I don't have the answers. Softell glances at Billy Marsh. There is a beat of silence and something invisible passes between them.

"Why didn't you report any of this earlier?"

"I couldn't be sure."

"So you went looking for evidence. You broke into the house."

"No."

"Then you tried to cover your tracks with a can of lighter fluid and a cock-'n'-bull story."

"Not true."

Ruiz is nearby, clenching and unclenching his fists. For the first time I notice how old he looks in a shapeless overcoat, worn smooth at the elbows.

"Hey, Detective Sergeant, I know what you're thinking," he says. "You want some kitchen-sink, bog-standard example of foul play you can solve by nine o'clock and still make your ballet lesson. This is one of your colleagues, one of your own. Your job is to believe her."

Softell puffs up, too stupid to keep his mouth shut. "And who do you think you are?"

"Godzilla."

"Who?"

Ruiz rolls his eyes. "I'm the monster that's going to stomp all over your fucking career if you don't pay this lady some respect."

Softell looks like he's been bitch-slapped. He takes out his mobile and punches in a number. I overhear him talking to his superintendent. I don't know what he's told. Ruiz still has a lot of friends in the Met, people who respect what he's done.

When the call finishes Softell is a chastened man. A task force investigation has been authorized and a warrant issued for the arrest of Brendan Pearl.

"I want you at the station by midday to make a statement," he says.

"I can go?"

"Yeah."

Ruiz won't let me drive. He takes me home in my car. Squeezed behind the wheel of my hatchback, he looks like a geriatric Noddy.

"Was it Pearl?"

"Yes."

"Did you see him?"

"Yes."

Taking one hand off the wheel, he scratches his chin. His ring finger is severed below the first knuckle, courtesy of a high-velocity bullet. He likes to tell people his third wife attacked him with a meat cleaver.

I tell Ruiz about the boarding passes and the brochure for the New Life Adoption Center. We both know stories about stolen and trafficked babies. Most stray into the realm of urban myth—baby farms in Guatemala and runaways snatched from the streets of São Paulo for organ harvesting.

"Let's just say you're right and Cate Beaumont organized some sort of private adoption or to buy a baby. Why go through the pretense of pregnancy?"

"Perhaps she wanted to convince Felix the baby was his."

"That's a pretty ambitious goal. What if the kid looks nothing like him?"

"A lot of husbands are happy to *believe* they've fathered a child. History is littered with mistakes."

Ruiz raises an eyebrow. "You mean lies."

I rise to the bait. "Yes, women can be devious. Sometimes we have to be. We're the ones who get left changing nappies when some bloke decides he's not ready to commit or to get rid of his Harley or his porn collection."

Silence.

"Did that sound like a rant?" I ask.

"A little."

"Sorry."

Ruiz begins thinking out loud, trawling through his memory. That's the thing about the DI—nothing is ever forgotten. Other people grimace and curse, trying to summon up the simplest details but Ruiz does it effortlessly, recalling facts, figures, quotes and names.

"Three years ago the Italian police smashed a ring of Ukrainian human traffickers who were trying to sell an unborn baby. They ran a kind of auction looking for the highest bidder. Someone offered to pay £250,000."

"Cate traveled to Amsterdam in February. She could have arranged a deal."

"Alone?"

"I don't know."

"How did they communicate with her?"

I think back to the fire. "We might never know."

He drops me home and arranges to meet me in the morning.

"You should see an eye specialist."

"First I have to make a statement."

Upstairs, I pull the phone jack from the wall and turn off my mobile. I have talked to enough people today. I want a shower and a warm bed. I want to cry into a pillow and fall asleep. A girl should be allowed.

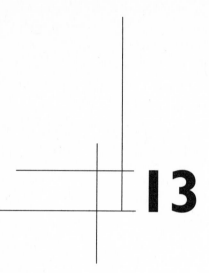

13

Wembley Police Station is a brand-new building decked in blue and white on the Harrow Road. The new national stadium is almost a mile away with soaring light towers visible above the rooftops.

Softell keeps me waiting before taking my statement. His attitude has changed since last night. He has looked up Pearl on the computer and the interest sparks in his eyes like a gas ring igniting. Softell is the sort of detective who goes through an entire career with his head under his armpit, not understanding people's motives or making any headline arrests. Now he can sense an opportunity.

The deaths of Cate and Felix Beaumont are a side issue. A distraction. I can see what he's going to do: he'll dismiss Cate as a desperate woman with a history of psychiatric problems and a criminal record. Pearl is the man he wants.

"You have no evidence a baby ever existed," he says.

"What about the missing money?"

"Someone probably ripped her off."

"And then killed her."

"Not according to the vehicle accident report."

Softell hands me a typed statement. I have to sign each page and initial any changes. I look at my words. I have lied about why I was at the house and what happened before the fire. Does my signature make it worse?

Taking back the statement, he straightens the pages and punches the stapler. "Very fucking professional," he sneers. "You know it never stops—the lying. Once you start it just keeps getting worse."

"Yeah, well, you'd know," I say, wishing I could think of a put-down that wasn't so lame. Mostly, I wish I could tear up the statement and start again.

Ruiz is waiting for me in the foyer.

"How's the eye?"

"The specialist said I should wear an eye patch for a week."

"So where is it?"

"In my pocket."

Stepping on a black rubber square, the doors open automatically.

"Your boyfriend has called six times in the last hour. Ever thought of getting a dog instead?"

"What did you tell him?"

"Nothing. That's why he's here."

I look up and see Dave leaning on Ruiz's car. He wraps me in a bear hug with his face in my hair. Ruiz turns away as though embarrassed.

"Are you smelling me, Dave?"

"Yup."

"That's a bit creepy."

"Not to me. I'm just glad you're in one piece."

"Only bruises."

"I could kiss them better."

"Perhaps later."

Dressed in a dark blue suit, white shirt and maroon tie, Dave has tidied up since his promotion, but I notice a brown sauce stain on the tie that he hasn't managed to sponge away. My mother would recognize a detail like that. Scary.

My stomach is empty. I haven't eaten since yesterday.

We find a café near Wembley Central with a smudged black-board menu and enough grease in the air to flatten Dave's hair. It's an old-fashioned "caff" with Formica tables, paper napkins, and a nervy waitress with a nose stud.

I order tea and toast. Ruiz and Dave choose the all-day breakfast—otherwise known as the 999 because it's a heart attack on a plate. Nobody says anything until the food is consumed and tea poured. The DI has milk and sugar.

"There is a guy I used to play rugby with," he says. "He never talked about his job, but I know he works for MI5. I called him this morning. He told me an interesting thing about Brendan Pearl."

"What's that?"

Ruiz takes out a tattered notebook held together with a rubber band. Loose pages tumble through his fingers. A lot of detectives don't believe in keeping notes. They want their memories to be "flexible" should they ever get in the witness box. Ruiz has a memory like the proverbial steel trap, yet he still backs it up on paper.

"According to my friend, Pearl was last known to be working as a security consultant for a construction company in Afghanistan. Three foreign contractors were killed in mid-September 2004 in a convoy traveling on the highway leading from the main airport to central Kabul when a suicide bomber drove into them. Pearl was among the wounded. He spent three weeks in a German hospital and then signed himself out. Nobody has heard from him since then."

"So what's he doing here?" asks Dave.

"And how did Cate meet him?" I add.

Ruiz gathers the pages and slips the rubber band around them. "Maybe we should check out this New Life Adoption Center."

Dave disagrees. "It's not *our* investigation."

"Not *officially*," concedes the DI.

"Not even unofficially."

"It's an *independent* investigation."

"Unauthorized."

"*Unconstrained.*"

Interrupting them, I suggest, "You could come with us, Dave."

He hesitates.

Ruiz spies an opening. "That's what I like about you, Dave. You're a freethinker. Some people think the modern British detective has become timid and punctilious, but not you. You're a credit to the Met. You're not frightened to have an opinion or act on a hunch."

It's like watching a fisherman casting a fly. It curls through the air, settles on the water and drifts downstream, drifting, drifting . . .

"I suppose it wouldn't hurt to check it out," says Dave.

There are no signs pointing out the New Life Adoption Center, either in the nearest village or at the gates, which are flanked by sandstone pillars. A loose gravel driveway curves through fields and crosses a single-lane stone bridge. Friesians dot the pasture and scarcely stir as we pass.

Eventually, we pull up in front of a large Adam's-style house, in the noise shadow of Gatwick Airport. I take Dave's arm.

"OK, we've been married for six years. It was a big Sikh wedding. I looked beautiful of course. We've been trying for a baby for five years but your sperm count is too low."

"Does it have to be *my* sperm count?"

"Oh, don't be so soft! Give me your ring."

He slides a white gold band from his pinkie and I place it on my ring finger.

Ruiz has stayed behind in the village pub, chatting with the locals. So far we've established that the adoption center is a privately run charity operating out of a former stately home, Followdale House. The founder, Julian Shawcroft, is a former executive director of the Infertility and Planned Parenthood Clinic in Manchester.

A young woman, barely out of her teens, answers the doorbell. She's wearing woolly socks and a powder-blue dressing gown that struggles to hide her pregnancy.

"I can't really help you," she confides immediately. "I'm just minding the front desk while Stella has a tinkle."

"Stella?"

"She's in charge. Well, not really in charge. Mr. Shawcroft is *really* in charge but he's often away. He's here today, which is unusual. He's the chairman or the managing director. I can never work out the difference. I mean, what does an MD do and what does a chairman do? I'm talking too much, aren't I? I do that sometimes. My name is Meredith. Do you think Hugh is a nice boy's name? Hugh Jackman is very cute. I can't think of any other Hughs."

"Hugh Grant," I suggest.

"Cool."

"Hugh Hefner," says Dave.

"Who's he?" she asks.

"It doesn't matter," I tell her, glaring at Dave.

Meredith's hair is just long enough to pull into a ponytail and her nail polish is chipped where she has picked it off.

The lobby of the house has two faded Chesterfields on either side of a fireplace. The staircase, with its ornate banister, is sealed off by a blue tasseled rope hung from brass posts.

She leads us to an office in a side room. Several desks have computers and a photocopier spits out pages as a light slides back and forth beneath the glass.

There are posters on the wall. One of them shows a couple swinging an infant between their outstretched hands, except the child is cut out like a missing piece of a jigsaw puzzle. Underneath the caption reads: IS THERE A CHILD-SIZE HOLE IN YOUR LIFE?

Through French doors I can see a rose garden and what might once have been a croquet lawn.

"When are you due?" I ask.

"Two weeks."

"Why are you here?"

She giggles. "This is an adoption center, silly."

"Yes, but people come to adopt a baby, not to have one."

"I haven't decided yet," she says in a matter-of-fact way.

A woman appears—Stella—apologizing for the delay. She looks very businesslike in a dark polo-neck, black trousers and imitation snakeskin shoes with pointed toes and kitten heels.

Her eyes survey me up and down, as though taking an inventory. "Nope, the womb is vacant," I feel like saying. She glances at her diary.

"We don't have an appointment," I explain. "It was rather a spur-of-the-moment decision to come."

"Adoption should never be spur-of-the-moment."

"Oh, I don't mean *that* decision. We've been talking about it for months. We were in the neighborhood."

Dave chips in. "I have an aunt who lives close."

"I see."

"We want to adopt a baby," I add. "It's all we think about."

Stella takes down our names. I call myself Mrs. King, which doesn't sound as weird as it probably should.

"We've been married six years and trying to have a baby for five."

"So you're looking to adopt because you can't have your own baby?"

It's a loaded question. "I come from a big family. I wanted the same. But even though we want our own children, we always talked about adopting."

"Are you prepared to take an older child?"

"We'd like a baby."

"Yes, well, that may be so, but there are very few newborn babies put up for adoption in this country. The waiting list is very long."

"How long?"

"Upward of five years."

Dave blows air through his cheeks. He's better at this than I expected. "Surely it can be fast-tracked in some way," he says. "I mean, even the slowest of wheels can be *oiled*."

Stella seems to resent the suggestion. "Mr. King, we are a non-profit charity governed by the same rules and regulations as local authority adoption services. The interests of the child come *first* and *last*. Oil doesn't enter into it."

"Of course not. I didn't mean to suggest—"

"My husband works in management," I explain contritely. "He believes that almost any problem can be solved by throwing more people or money at it."

Stella nods sympathetically and for the first time seems to consider my skin color. "We do facilitate intercountry adoptions, but there are no children made available from the subcontinent. Most people are choosing to adopt from Eastern Europe."

"We're not fussy," adds Dave. I kick him under the desk. "We're not fazed, I mean. It's not a race thing."

Stella is eyeing him cautiously. "There are many *bad* reasons to adopt. Some people try to save their marriage, or replace a child who has died, or they want a fashion accessory because all their friends have one."

"That's not us," I say.

"Good. Well even with intercountry adoptions, the assessment and approval process is exactly the same as for adopting a child in this country. This includes full medicals, home visits, criminal record checks and interviews with social workers and psychologists."

She stands and opens a filing cabinet. The form is thirty pages long.

"I was wondering if Mr. Shawcroft was here today."

"Do you know him?"

"Only by reputation. That's how I heard about the center—through a friend."

"And what's your friend's name?"

"Cate Beaumont."

I get no sense of whether she's heard the name before.

"Mr. Shawcroft is normally very busy fund-raising but fortunately he's here today. He might be able to spare you a few minutes."

She excuses herself and I can hear her walking upstairs.

"What do you think?" whispers Dave.

"Watch the door." Skirting the desk, I open the drawer of the filing cabinet.

"That's an illegal search."

"Just *watch* the door."

My fingers are moving over the files. Each adoptive family appears to have one but there is no "Beaumont" or "Elliot." Some folders are marked by colored stickers. There are names typed on the labels. At first glance I think they might be children, but the ages are all wrong. These are young women.

One name jumps out at me. Carla Donavon. Donavon's younger sister. His *pregnant* sister. A coincidence? Hardly.

"Those files are confidential." The disembodied voice startles me.

I look to Dave. He shakes his head. There is an intercom on the desk. I scan the ceiling and spy a small security camera in the corner. I should have seen it earlier.

"If you want to know something, Mrs. King, you should ask," says the voice. "I assume that's your real name or perhaps you have lied about that as well."

"Do you always eavesdrop on people?" I say.

"Do you always illegally search someone's office and look at highly confidential files? Who exactly are you?"

Dave answers, "Police officers. I'm Detective Sergeant Dave King. This is Detective Constable Alisha Barba. We are making inquiries about a woman we believe may have been one of your clients."

The faint buzzing of the intercom goes silent. A side door opens. A man enters, in his mid-fifties, with a sturdy frame and a broad face that creases momentarily as he smiles disarmingly. His hair, once blond, now gray, has tight curls like wood shavings from a lathe.

"I'm sure there must be a law against police officers misrepresenting who they are and conducting unauthorized searches."

"The drawer was open. I was simply closing it."

This triggers a smile. He has every right to be angry and suspicious. Instead he finds it amusing. He makes a point of locking the filing cabinet before addressing us again.

"Now that we know exactly who we are, perhaps I could give you a guided tour and you could tell me what you're doing here."

He leads us into the lobby and through the French doors onto the terrace. The young woman we saw earlier is sitting on a swing in the garden. Her dressing gown billows as she rocks back and forth, getting higher and higher.

"Be careful, Meredith," he calls. And then to us. "She's a clumsy young thing."

"Why is she here?"

"Meredith hasn't decided what she wants to do. Giving up a baby is a difficult and courageous decision. We help young women like her to decide."

"You try to convince her."

"On the contrary. We offer love and support. We teach parenting skills so she'll be ready. And if she decides to give up her baby, we have scholarships that can help her find a flat and get a job. We operate open adoptions."

"Open?"

"The birth mothers and adoptive parents get to know one another and often stay in touch afterward."

Shawcroft chooses an unraked gravel path around the southern end of the house. Large bay windows reveal a lounge. Several young women are playing cards in front of a fire.

"We offer prenatal classes, massage therapy and have quite a good gymnasium," he explains.

"Why?"

"Why not?"

"I don't understand why it's necessary."

Shawcroft has an eye for an opening. It gives him the opportunity to explain his philosophy and he does so passionately, haranguing the historical attitudes that saw young unmarried mothers demonized or treated like outcasts.

"Single motherhood has become more acceptable but it is still a challenging choice," he explains. "That's why I established this center. There are far too many orphans and unwanted children in our society and overseas, with too few options available to improve their lives.

"Have you any idea how slow, bureaucratic and unfair our adoption system is? We leave it in the hands of people who are underfunded, understaffed and inexperienced—people who play God with the lives of children."

Dave has dropped back.

"I began out of a small office in Mayfair. There was just me. I charged £50 for a two-hour consultancy session. Two years later I had a full-time staff of eight and had completed more than a hundred adoptions. Now we're here." He gestures to Followdale House.

"How can you afford this place?"

"People have been very generous—new parents and grandparents. Some leave us money as bequests or make donations. We have a staff of fourteen, including social workers, counselors, career advisers, health visitors and a psychologist."

In one corner of the garden I notice a golf bag propped beneath an umbrella and a bucket of balls waiting to be hit. There are calluses on his fingers.

"My one indulgence," he explains, gazing over the fence into the pasture. "The cows are rather ball-shy. I have developed an incurable slice since my operation."

"Operation?"

"My hip. Old age catching up on me."

He picks up a club and swings it gently at a rosebush. A flower dissolves in a flurry of petals. Examining his fingers, he opens and closes his fist.

"It's always harder to hold a club in the winter. Some people wear gloves. I like being able to *feel* the grip."

He pauses and turns to face me. "Now, Detective Constable, let's dispense with the pretense. Why are you here?"

"Do you know someone called Cate Beaumont?"

"No." The answer is abrupt.

"You don't need to check your client files?"

"I remember all of them."

"Even those who don't succeed?"

"*Especially* those who don't succeed."

Dave has joined us. He picks a metal-headed driver and eyes a Friesian in the distance before thinking better of it.

"My friend faked her pregnancy and emptied her bank account. I think she arranged to buy a baby."

"Which is illegal."

"She had one of your brochures."

"Which is *not* illegal." Shawcroft doesn't take offense or become defensive. "Where is your friend now?"

"She's dead. Murdered."

He repeats the word with renewed respect. His hands are unfailingly steady.

"The brochure contained an advertisement for a baby boy whose mother was a prostitute and a former drug addict. It mentioned a facilitation fee and medical expenses."

Shawcroft lets his palm glide over his cheek, giving himself time. For a moment something struggles inside him. I want a denial. There isn't one.

"The facilitation fee is to cover paperwork such as visas and birth certificates."

"Selling children is illegal."

"The baby was not for sale. Every applicant is properly vetted. We require referees and assessment reports. There are group workshops and familiarization. Finally, there is an adoption panel that must approve the adopter before a child can be matched to them."

"If these adoptions are aboveboard, why are they advertised using post box numbers?"

He gazes straight ahead as if plotting the distance of his next shot.

"Do you know how many children die in the world every year, Alisha? Five million. War, poverty, disease, famine, neglect, land mines and predators. I have seen children so malnourished they don't have the energy to swat flies away and starving women holding babies to their withered breasts, desperate to feed them. I have seen them throw their babies over the fences of rich people's houses or, worse still, into the River Ganges because they can't afford to look after them. I have seen AIDS orphans, crack babies and children sold into slavery for as little as £15. And what do we do in this country? We make it *harder* for people to adopt. We tell them they're too old, or the wrong color, or the wrong religion."

Shawcroft makes no attempt to hide the bitterness in his voice. "It takes courage for a country to admit it can't take care of its smallest and weakest. Many countries who are not so brave would prefer to see abandoned children starve than to leave for a better life.

"The system is unfair. So, yes, I sometimes cut corners. In some countries contracts can be signed with birth mothers. Hollywood movie stars do it. Government ministers do it. Children can be rescued. Infertile couples can have families."

"By *buying* babies."

"By *saving* them."

For all his avuncular charm and geniality, there is steel in this man's nature and something vaguely dangerous. A mixture of sentimentality and spiritual zeal that fortifies the hearts of tyrants.

"You think that what I'm doing is immoral. Let me tell you what's more immoral. Doing *nothing*. Sitting back in your comfortable chair in your comfortable home thinking that just because you sponsor a child in Zambia you're doing enough."

"It shouldn't mean breaking the law."

"Every family that adopts here is vetted and approved by a panel of experts."

"You're profiting from their desperation."

"All payments go back into the charity."

He begins listing the number of foreign adoptions the center has overseen and the diplomatic hurdles he has had to overcome. His arguments are marshalled so skillfully that I have no line of reasoning to counter them. My objections sound mean-spirited and hostile. I should apologize.

"Your friend's death is very unfortunate, DC Barba, but I would strongly counsel you against making any rash or unfounded claims about what we do here. Police knocking on doors, asking questions, upsetting families, that would be very unfortunate."

He has made his first mistake. I can accept his passionate beliefs and his rationale for them, but I don't appreciate emotional black-mail.

Stella appears on the terrace and calls to Shawcroft, miming a phone call with her hand.

"I have to go," he says, smiling tiredly. "The baby you referred to was born in Washington four weeks ago. A boy. A young couple from Oxford are adopting him."

I watch him return along the path, gravel rasping beneath his soft-soled shoes. Meredith is still in the garden. He motions for her to come inside. It is getting cold.

"New Boy" Dave falls into step beside me and we follow the path in the opposite direction toward the car park, passing a statue of a young girl holding an urn and another of a Cupid with a missing penis.

"So what do you think?" he asks.

"What sort of adoption center has surveillance cameras?"

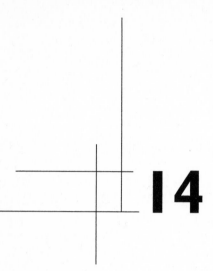

14

"Finding Donavon" sounds like the title of an Irish art-house movie directed by Neil Jordan. "Deconstructing Donavon" is another good title and that's exactly what I plan to do when I find him.

Maybe it's a coincidence, maybe it's not a coincidence, but I don't like the way that his name keeps popping up whenever I trace Cate's movements. Donavon claims to know when someone is lying. That's because he's an expert on the subject—a born deceiver.

On the drive back to London we go over the details of our meeting with Shawcroft. Ruiz doesn't see a problem with adoption having a financial element if couples are vetted properly. Too much control allows black markets to flourish. Perhaps he's right, but a zealot like Shawcroft can turn compassion into a dangerous crusade.

"New Boy" Dave has work to do. We drop him at the Harrow Road police station and I make him promise to run a check on Shawcroft. He kisses my cheek and whispers, "Leave this alone."

I can't. I won't. He adds something else. "I *did* like being married to you."

Timewise it was even shorter than Britney Spears's first wedding, but I don't tell him that.

Nobody answers the door at Donavon's house. The curtains are drawn and his motorbike isn't parked outside. A neighbor suggests we try the markets in Whitechapel Road. Donavon has a weekend stall there.

Parking behind the Royal London Hospital, we follow the insurrection of noise, color and movement. Dozens of stalls spill out from the pavement. Everything is for sale—Belgian chocolates from Poland, Greek feta from Yorkshire, Gucci handbags from China and Rolex watches draped inside trench coats.

Traders yell over one another.

"Fresh carnations. Two-fifty a bunch!"

"Live mussels!"

"Garden tomatoes as red as your cheeks!"

I can't see Donavon but I recognize his stall. Draped from the metal framework there are dozens of intricate necklaces or perhaps they're wind chimes. They twirl in the light breeze, fragmenting the remains of the sunlight. Beneath them, haphazardly displayed, are novelty radios, digital clocks and curling tongs from Korea.

Carla looks cold and bored. She's wearing red woolen tights and a short denim skirt stretched over her growing bump.

I close the gap between us and slide my hand under her sweater, across her abdomen until I feel the warmth of her skin.

"Hey!"

I pull my hand away as if scalded. "I just wanted to be sure."

"Sure about what?"

"It doesn't matter."

Carla looks at me suspiciously and then at Ruiz. A faint, fast vibration is coming off her, as though something terrible and soundless is spinning inside.

"Have you seen him?" she asks anxiously.

"Who?"

"Paul. He hasn't been home in two days."

"When did you last see him?"

"On Saturday. He had a phone call and went out."

"Did he say where?"

"No. He never leaves it this long. He always calls me."

Female intuition is often a myth. Some women just *think* they're more intuitive. I know I'm letting the sisters down by saying that, but gender isn't a factor. It's blood. Families can tell when something is wrong. Carla's eyes dart across the crowd as though assembling a human jigsaw puzzle.

"When are you due?" I ask.

"Christmas."

"What can you tell me about the New Life Adoption Center?"

Her mouth seems to frame something she's too embarrassed to admit. I wait for her.

"I don't know what sort of mother I'm gonna make. Paul says I'll be fine. He says I learned from one of the *worst* so I won't make the same mistakes our mum did." Her hands are trembling. "I didn't want an abortion. It's not because of any religious thing. It's just how I feel, you know. That's why I thought about adoption."

"You went to see Julian Shawcroft."

"He offered to help me. He said there were scholarships, you know. I always wanted to be a makeup artist or a beautician. He said he could arrange it."

"If you gave up the baby?"

"Yeah, well, you can't do both, eh? Not look after a baby and work full-time—not without help."

"So what did you decide?" asks the DI.

Her shoulders grow rounder. "I keep changing me mind. Paul wants me to keep it. He says he'll look after us all." She gnaws at a reddened fingernail.

A crew-cutted teenager stops and picks up a transistor radio shaped like a Pepsi can.

"Don't waste your money—this stuff is shite," says Carla. The youth looks hard done by rather than grateful.

"How did you hear about the New Life Adoption Center?"

"A friend told Paul about it."

"Who?"

Carla shrugs.

Her mauve-tinted eyelids tremble. She doesn't have the where-withal to lie to me. She can't see a reason. Glancing above her head, I notice the feathers and beads.

I have seen one of these ornaments before—at Cate's house, in the nursery. It was hanging above the new cot.

"What are they?" I ask.

Carla unhooks one from the metal frame above her and hangs it from her finger, watching me through a wooden circle crisscrossed with colored thread and hung with feathers and beads.

"This is a dream catcher," she explains. "American Indians believe the night air is filled with dreams, some good and some bad. They hang a dream catcher over a child's bed so it can catch dreams as they flow by. The good dreams know how to slip through the holes and slide down the soft feathers where they land gently on the child's head. But the bad dreams get tangled in the web and perish when the sun comes up."

Blowing gently, she makes the feathers bob and swirl.

Donavon didn't go to the reunion to "make his peace" with Cate. He had seen her before. He gave her a dream catcher or she bought one from him.

"How well did your brother know Cate Beaumont?"

Carla shrugs. "They were friends, I guess."

"That's not possible."

She bridles. "I'm not lying. When Paul was in the Paras, she wrote to him. I seen the letters."

"Letters?"

"He brought them home from Afghanistan. He kept her letters."

I hear myself quizzing her, wanting to know the where, when and why, but she can't answer for her brother. Trying to pin her down to specific dates and times makes her even more confused.

Ruiz intervenes and I feel a twinge of guilt at having browbeaten a pregnant woman who's worried about her brother.

The afternoon sun is sliding below rooftops, leaving behind shadows. Stallholders are shutting up, loading wares into boxes, bags and metal trunks. Buckets of ice are tipped into the gutter. Plastic awnings are rolled and tied.

After helping Carla load up the red Escort van, we follow her home. The house is still empty. There are no messages waiting for her on the answer phone. I should be angry with Donavon, yet I feel a nagging emptiness. This doesn't make any sense. Why would Cate write letters to someone who sexually assaulted her? She was talking to him the night of the reunion. What were they saying?

Ruiz drops me home. Turning off the engine, we stare at the streetscape as if expecting it to suddenly change after more than a century of looking almost the same.

"You want to come in?"

"I should go."

"I could cook."

He looks at me.

"Or we could get takeaway."

"Got any alcohol?"

"There's an off-licence on the corner."

I can hear him whistling his way up the street as I open the front door and check my answering machine. All the messages are for Hari. His girlfriends. I should double his rent to pay the phone bill.

The doorbell rings. It should be Ruiz—only it's not. A younger man has come to the door, dressed in a pepper-gray suit. Clean-shaven with broad shoulders and Nordic features, his rectangular glasses seem too small for his face. Behind him are two more men, who are standing beside cars that are double-parked and blocking the street. They look official, but not like police officers.

"DC Barba, we need you to accompany us." He makes a clicking sound with his tongue that might be a signal or a sign of nerves.

"Why? Who are you?"

He produces a badge. SOCA. The Serious Organized Crime Agency. The organization is less than a year old and the media have labeled it Britain's answer to the FBI, with its own Act of Parliament, budget and extraordinary powers. What do they want with me?

"I'm a police officer," I stammer.

"I know who you are."

"Am I under arrest?"

"Important people wish to speak to you."

I look for Ruiz. He's hurrying down the pavement with a half bottle of Scotch tucked in his coat pocket. One of the men beside the cars tries to step in front of him. The DI feints left and drops his shoulder, propelling him over a low brick wall into a muddy puddle. This could get ugly.

"It's all right, sir."

"Who are they?"

"SOCA."

The look on his face says it all. Fear and loathing.

"You might want to pack a few things for the journey," says the senior officer. He and Ruiz are sizing each other up like roosters in a henhouse.

I pack a sports bag with a pair of jeans, knickers and a light-weight sweater. My gun is wrapped in a cloth on top of a kitchen cabinet. I contemplate whether I should take it with me, but dismiss the idea as being too hostile. I have no idea what these people want, but I can't risk antagonizing them.

Ruiz follows me to the car. A hand is placed on the back of my head as I slide into the rear seat. The brake is released suddenly and I'm thrown back against the new-smelling leather.

"I hope we haven't spoiled your plans for the evening, DC Barba," says the gray-suited man.

"You know my name, can I have yours?"

"Robert Forbes."

"You work for SOCA?"

"I work for the government."

"Which *part* of the government?"

"The part people don't often talk about." He makes the clicking sound again.

The car has reached the end of Hanbury Street. Beneath a streetlight, a solitary spectator, clad in black leather, leans against a motorcycle. A helmet dangles from his right hand. A fag end burns in his fist. It's Donavon.

Traffic meanders at an agonizingly slow pace, shuffling and pausing. I can only see the back of the driver's head. He has a soldier's hair-cut and wraparound sunglasses like Bono, who also looks ridiculous wearing sunglasses at night.

I'm trying to remember what I've read about SOCA. It's an amalgam of the old National Crime Squad and National Criminal Intelligence Service, along with elements of Customs and Excise and the Immigration Service. Five thousand officers were specially cho-sen with the aim of targeting criminal gangs, drug smugglers and people traffickers. The boss of the new agency is a former head of MI5.

"Where are you taking me?"

"To a crime scene," says Forbes.

"What crime? There must be some mistake."

"You are Alisha Kaur Barba. You are twenty-nine years of age. You work for the London Metropolitan Police, most recently for the Diplomatic Protection Group. You have four brothers. Your father is a retired train driver. Your mother takes in sewing. You went to Falcon Street Primary School and to Oaklands Secondary. You graduated from London University with a degree in sociology and topped your class at Hendon Police Training College. You are an expert markswoman and former champion athlete. A year ago you were injured trying to apprehend a suspect who almost snapped your spine. You accepted a bravery medal but refused a disability pension. You seem to have recovered quite well."

"I set off metal detectors at airports."

I don't know if his knowledge is supposed to impress or intimidate me. Nothing else is said. Forbes is not going to answer my questions until he's ready. Silence is part of the softening-up process. Ruiz taught me that.

We take the A12 through Brentwood and out of London. I don't like the countryside at night. Even in moonlight it looks bruised and sullen like a week-old fall down the stairs.

Forbes takes several phone calls, answering yes or no but offering nothing more apart from the clicking sound in his throat. He is married. The gold band on his wedding finger is thick and heavy. Someone at home irons his shirts and polishes his shoes. He is right-handed. He's not carrying a gun. He knows so much about me that I want to even the scales.

We continue through Chelmsford in Essex before bypassing Colchester and turning east toward Harwich along the A120. Convoys of prime movers and semitrailers begin to build up ahead of us. I can smell the salt in the air.

A large sign above the road welcomes us to Harwich International Port. Following the New Port Entrance Road through two roundabouts we come to the freight entrance. Dozens of trucks are queuing at the gates. A customs officer with a light wand and a fluorescent vest waves us through.

In the distance I see the Port of Felixstowe. Massive gantry cranes tower above the ships, lifting and lowering containers. It looks like a scene from *War of the Worlds* where alien machines have landed and are creating hatchlings for the next generation. Row after row of containers are stacked on top of one another, stretching for hundreds of yards in every direction.

Now Forbes decides to speak to me again.

"Have you ever been here before, DC Barba?"

"No."

"Harwich is a freight and passenger port. It handles cruise ships, ferries, bulk carriers and roll-on, roll-off vessels. Thousands of vehicles pass through here every day from Denmark, Sweden, Belgium, Germany and the Hook of Holland."

"Why am I here?"

He motions ahead of us. The car slows. In the middle of the customs area a Scene of Crime tent has been erected. Police cars are circled like wagons around it.

Arc lights inside the tent throw shadows against the fabric walls, revealing the outline of a truck and people moving inside, silhouetted like puppets in a Kabuki theater.

Forbes is out of the car, walking across the tarmac. The ticking of the cooling engine sounds like a clock. At that moment a side flap of the tent is pushed open. A SOCO emerges wearing overalls and white rubber gloves that peel off his hands like a second skin.

I recognize him. George Noonan, a forensic pathologist. They call him "the Albino" because of his pale skin and snow-white hair. Dressed in white overalls, white gloves and a white hat, he looks like a fancy-dress spermatozoon.

He spends a few minutes talking to Forbes. I'm too far away to hear what they say.

Forbes turns toward me, summoning me forward. His face is set hard like the wedge of an ax.

The tent flap opens. Plastic sheets cover the ground, weighed down with silver boxes of forensic equipment and cameras. A truck is parked at the center, with its twin rear doors open. Inside there are wooden pallets holding boxes of oranges. Some of these have been shifted to one side to form a narrow aisle just wide enough for a person to squeeze through to the far end of the lorry.

A camera flash illuminates a cavity within the pallets. At first I think there might be mannequins inside it, broken models or clay figurines. Then the truth reaches me. Bodies, I count five of them, are piled beneath a closed air vent. There are three men, a woman and a child. Their mouths are open. Breathless. Lifeless.

They appear to be Eastern European dressed in cheap mismatched clothes. An arm reaches up as if suspended by a wire. The lone woman has her hair pulled back. A tortoiseshell hair clip has come loose and dangles on her cheek from a strand of hair. The child in her arms is wearing a Mickey Mouse sweatshirt and clutching a doll.

The flashgun pops again. I see the faces frozen in place, trapped in that moment when their oxygen ran out and their dreams turned to dust on dry tongues. It is a scene to haunt me, a scene that changes everything. And although I can't picture the world they came from, which seems impossibly strange and remote, their deaths are somehow unbearably close.

"They died in the past twelve hours," says Noonan.

Automatically, I transfer this into personal time. What was I doing? Traveling to West Sussex. Talking to Julian Shawcroft at the adoption center.

Noonan is holding several bloody fingernails collected in a plastic bag. I feel my stomach lurch.

"If you're going to puke, Detective Constable, you can get the hell away from *my* crime scene," he says.

"Yes, sir."

Forbes looks at Noonan. "Tell her how they died."

"They suffocated," he replies wearily.

"Explain it to us."

The request is for my benefit. Forbes wants me to hear this and to smell the sweet stench of oranges and feces. Noonan obliges.

"It begins with a rising panic as one fights for each breath, sucking it in, wanting more. The next stage is quiescence. Resignation. And then unconsciousness. The convulsions and incontinence are involuntary, the death throes. Nobody knows what comes first— oxygen deprivation or carbon dioxide poisoning."

Taking hold of my elbow, Forbes leads me out of the truck. A makeshift morgue has been set up to take the bodies. One of them is already on a gurney, lying faceup, covered in a white sheet. Forbes runs his fingers over the cloth.

"Someone inside the truck had a mobile," he explains. "When

they began to suffocate they tried to call someone and reached an emergency number. The operator thought it was a hoax because the caller couldn't give a location."

I look toward the massive roll-on, roll-off ferry with its open stern doors.

"Why am I here?"

He flicks his wrist and the sheet curls back. A teenage boy with fleshy limbs and dark hair lies on the slab. His head is almost perfectly round and pink except for the blueness around his lips and the overlapping folds of flesh beneath his chin.

Forbes hasn't moved. He's watching me from behind his rectangular glasses.

I drag my eyes away. With a birdlike quickness he grips my arm. "This is all he was wearing—a pair of trousers and a shirt. No labels. Normally, clothes like this tell us nothing. They're cheap and mass produced." His fingers are digging into me. "These clothes are different. There was something sewn into the lining. A name and address. Do you know whose name? Whose address?"

I shake my head.

"Yours."

I try not to react but that in itself is a reaction.

"Can you explain that?" he asks.

"No."

"Not even a vague notion."

My mind is racing through the possibilities. My mother used to put labels on my clothes because she didn't want me losing things. My name, not my address.

"You see how it looks," he says, clicking his tongue again. "You have been implicated in a people-trafficking investigation and potentially a murder investigation. We think his name is Hassan Khan. Does that mean anything to you?"

"No."

"The lorry is Dutch registered. The driver is listed on the passenger manifest as Arjan Molenaar."

Again I shake my head.

Numbness rather than shock seeps through me. It feels like someone has walked up and hit me in the back of the head with a metal tray and the noise is still ringing in my ears.

"Why weren't they found sooner?"

"Do you know how many lorries pass through Harwich every day? More than ten thousand. If Customs searched every one of them there'd be ships queued back to Rotterdam."

Noonan joins us, leaning over the body and talking as though the teenager were a patient and not a corpse.

"All right young fellow, *please* try to be candid. If you open up to the process in good faith we'll find out more about you. Now let's take a look."

He peers closer, almost putting his lips on the boy's cheek. "There is evidence of petechial hemorrhages, pinpoint, less than one millimeter on the eyelids, lips, ears, face and neck, consistent with lack of oxygen to the tissue . . ."

He holds up an arm, examining the skin.

"The scarring indicates an old thermal injury to the left forearm and hand. Something very intense, perhaps a blast."

I notice dozens of smaller scars on his chest. Noonan takes an interest, using a ruler to measure them.

"Very unusual."

"What are they?"

"Knife wounds."

"He was stabbed?"

"Someone sliced him up." He flicks an imaginary knife through the air. "None of the wounds is particularly deep. The blade threatened no organs or major blood vessels. Excellent control."

The pathologist sounds impressed—like one surgeon admiring the work of another.

He sees something else. Lifting the boy's right arm, he turns it outward, displaying the wrist. A small tattooed butterfly hovers halfway between the palm and elbow. Noonan takes a measurement and speaks into a digital recorder.

Forbes has shown me enough.

"I wish to go home now," I say.

"I still have questions."

"Do I need a lawyer?"

The question disappoints him. "I can provide you with someone if you wish."

I know I should be more concerned but the desire for knowledge overrides my natural caution. It's not about being invincible or believing my innocence will protect me. I've seen too many miscarriages of justice to be so optimistic.

The terminal has a café for freight drivers. Forbes takes a table and orders coffee and a bottle of water.

For the next hour he dissects my personal life, my friends and associates. Over and over I make the same point. I have no idea how my name and address were sewn into the clothes of Hassan Khan.

"Is it my color?" I ask him eventually.

His countenance falls. "Why do people *always* do that? Play the race card. Whenever someone from a minority background is questioned I can guarantee it's coming. This has nothing to do with your color or your religion or where you were born. *Your* name and address were sewn into a dead kid's clothes. An illegal. That's what makes you a person of interest."

I wish I could take the question back.

He takes out a half packet of cigarettes and counts them, rationing himself. "Have you any idea how big it is—people trafficking?" He puts the packet away, clicking his tongue as though admonishing himself.

"More than 400,000 people were trafficked into Western Europe last year. The Italian Mafia, the Russians, the Albanians, the Japanese Yakuza, the Chinese Snakeheads—they're all involved. And beneath the big syndicates are thousands of smaller freelance gangs that operate with nothing more than a couple of mobile phones, a speed boat and a transit van. They corrupt border guards, politicians, police and customs officers. They are bottom-feeding scum who prey on human misery. I hate them. I really do."

His eyes are locked on mine. His tongue is making that sound again. I suddenly realize what he reminds me of: the roadrunner. Wile E. Coyote was always trying to catch that arrogant, beeping bird, coming up with ridiculous booby traps and snares. Just *once* I wanted the coyote to win. I wanted the hundred-pound barbell or the bundle of dynamite or the slingshot to work, so he could ring that scrawny bird's neck.

As if on cue there is a *beep beep* from Forbes's pager. He makes a phone call on the far side of the cafeteria. Something must have been said during the call because his demeanor changes.

"I'm sorry for keeping you so long, DC Barba."

"So I can leave?"

"Yes, of course, but it's very late. Accommodation has been arranged in town. The pub looks quite nice. I can have you driven back to London in the morning."

He tugs nervously at the cuffs of his jacket, as though worried the sleeves might be shrinking. I wonder who called. Sikh girls don't have friends in high places.

The pub is quaint and rustic, although I've never been exactly sure what "rustic" means. The restaurant annex has low ceilings with fishing nets strung from the beams and a harpoon bolted above the bar.

Forbes invites me to dinner. "I'm a detective inspector but you don't have to consider it an order," he says, trying to be charming.

I can smell the kitchen. My stomach rumbles. Perhaps I can find out more about Hassan Khan.

Shrugging off his gray jacket, Forbes stretches his legs beneath the table and makes a fuss over ordering and tasting the wine.

"This is very good," he comments, holding his glass up to the light. "Are you sure you won't have some?" Without waiting for me to answer he pours himself another glass.

I have been calling him Mr. Forbes or sir. He says I should call him Robert. I don't give him permission but he calls me Alisha anyway. He asks if I'm married.

"You know that already."

"Yes, of course."

He has pale Nordic eyes and his bottom teeth are crooked but he has a pleasant smile and an easy laugh. The clicking sound seems to go away when he relaxes. Perhaps it's a nervous thing, like a stutter.

"So what about your family?" he asks. "When did they come to Britain?"

I tell him about my grandfather who was born in a small village in Gujarat and joined the British Army at fourteen where he became a kitchen hand and then a chef. After the war a major in the Royal Artillery brought him back to England to cook for his family. My grandfather traveled on a steamer that took three weeks to get from Bombay to England. He came alone. That was in 1947.

He earned three pounds a week, but still managed to save enough for my grandmother to join him. They were the first Indians in Hertfordshire but they later moved to London.

My only memory of my grandparents is a story they told me about their first winter in England. They had never seen snow and said it looked like a scene from a Russian fairy tale.

I don't always understand irony, but my grandfather spent his entire life trying to become white only to be crushed by an overturned coal truck on Richmond Hill that painted him as black as soot.

Forbes has finished a second bottle of wine and grown melancholy.

"I have to use the bathroom," he says.

I watch him weave between tables, leading with his left shoulder and then his right. On his way back he orders a brandy. He talks about growing up in Milton Keynes, a planned town that didn't exist before the 1960s. Now he lives in London. He doesn't mention a wife but I know there's one at home.

I want to talk to him about the illegals before he gets too drunk. "Have you managed to trace the truck?" I ask.

"Shipping containers have codes. They can be tracked anywhere in the world."

"Where did it come from?"

"The truck left a factory on the outskirts of Amsterdam early yesterday. The locks are supposed to be tamperproof."

"How did you know Hassan Khan's name?"

"He had papers. We found a cloth bag tied around his waist. According to the Dutch police, he arrived in Holland nineteen months ago from Afghanistan. He and a group of asylum seekers were living above a Chinese restaurant in Amsterdam."

"What else was in the bag?"

Forbes lowers his eyes. "Drawings and photographs. I could show them to you . . ." He pauses. "We could go to my room."

"Alternatively, you could bring the bag downstairs," I suggest.

He runs his socked foot up my calf and gives me his bad little boy smile.

I want to say something disagreeable but can't find the words.

I'm never good at put-downs. Instead I smile politely and tell him to quit while he's ahead.

He frowns. He doesn't understand.

For the love of God, you're not even attractive. Call your wife and wish her good night.

Forbes stumbles as he climbs the stairs. "I guess we hit the old vino pretty hard, eh?"

"One of us did."

He fumbles in his pocket for his key and makes several unsuccessful attempts to find the keyhole. I take it from him. He collapses on the bed and rolls over, spread-eagled like a sacrifice to the demon god of drink.

I take off his shoes and hang his jacket over the chair. The calico bag is on the bedside table. As I leave I slide the security bar across the door frame so that the door doesn't close completely.

Back in my room I call Ruiz and "New Boy" Dave. Dave wants to come and get me. I tell him to stay put. I'll call him in the morning.

Fifteen minutes later I go back to Forbes's room. The door is still ajar and he's snoring. I cross the floor, listening for a change in his breathing. My fingers close around the calico bag. He doesn't stir.

Suddenly, there's another sound. A singsong ring tone.

I drop to the floor and crouch between the radiator and the curtain.

If Forbes turns on the lamp he'll see me or he'll notice that the bag is missing.

Rolling half out of bed, he reaches for his jacket, fumbling with his mobile.

"Yeah. I'm sorry, babe, I should have called. I got in late and I didn't want to wake you or the kids . . . No, I'm fine, not drunk. Just a few glasses . . . No, I didn't see the news tonight . . . That's really great . . . Yeah . . . OK . . . I'll call you in the morning . . . Go to sleep now . . . Love you too."

He tosses the phone aside and stares at the ceiling. For a moment I think he's falling back to sleep until he groans and rolls out of bed. The bathroom light blinks on. Behind him, my hiding place is neatly framed by the radiance. He drops his boxers and urinates.

Sliding out of the light, I cross the floor and ease the door shut behind me. Dizzy and trembling, I have broken one of Ruiz's fundamental rules: when under stress always remember to breathe.

Back in my room, I tip the contents of the calico bag onto the bed. There is a pocketknife with one broken blade and the other intact, a small mirror, a medicine bottle full of sand, a charcoal drawing of two children and a battered circular biscuit tin.

Every object is significant. Why else would he carry them? These are the wordly possessions of a sixteen-year-old boy. They can't possibly breathe life into his lungs or tell me his fears and desires. They aren't enough. He deserves more.

The biscuit tin contains a tarnished military medal and a black-and-white photograph folded in half. It appears to show a group of workers standing in front of a factory with a corrugated-iron roof and wooden shutters on the windows. Packing crates are stacked against the wall, along with drums and pallets.

There are two lines of workers. Those in the front row are sitting on stools. At the center is a patriarch or the factory owner in a high-backed chair. Ramrod straight, he has a stern countenance and a far-off stare. One hand is on his knee. The other is missing and the sleeve of his coat is tied off at the elbow.

Beside him is another man, physically similar, perhaps his brother. He is wearing a small fez and has a neatly trimmed beard. He also is missing a hand and his left eye appears to be an empty socket. I glance along the two rows of workers, many of who are maimed or crippled or incomplete. There are people on crutches, others with skin like melted plastic. A boy in the front row is kneeling on a skateboard. No, not kneeling. What I first imagine are his knees, poking out from beneath short trousers, are the amputated stumps of his thighs.

None of the workers is smiling. They are olive-skinned men with blurred features and no amount of magnifying will make the image any clearer or the men appear any less stiff and glowering.

I put the photograph back in the tin and examine the rest of the curios and ornaments. The charcoal drawing is creased at the corners. The two children, a boy and a girl, are about six and eight. Her arm is around his shoulders. She has a high forehead and a straight part in her hair. He looks bored or restless, with a spark of light in his eyes from an open window. He wants to be outside.

The paper is soft in my fingers. A fixative has been sprayed on the charcoal to stop it smudging. In the bottom left-hand corner there is a signature. No, it's a name. Two names. The drawing is of Hassan as a young boy and his sister, Samira.

Lying back, I stare at the ceiling and listen to the deep night. It is so quiet I can hear myself breathing. What a beautiful sound.

This is a story of parts. A chronicle of fictions. Cate faked her pregnancy. Brendan Pearl ran her and Felix down. Her doctor lied. Donavon lied. An adoption agency lied. People are being trafficked. Babies are being bought and sold.

I once read that people caught in avalanches can't always tell which way is up or down and don't know which direction to dig. Experienced skiers and climbers have a trick. They dribble. Gravity shows them the way.

I need a trick like that. I am submerged in something dark and dangerous and I don't know if I'm escaping or burying myself deeper. I'm an accidental casualty. Collateral damage.

My dreams are real. As real as dreams can be. I hear babies crying and mothers singing to them. I am being chased by people. It is the same dream as always but I never know who they are. And I wake at the same moment, as I'm falling.

I call Ruiz again. He picks up on the second ring. The man never sleeps.

"Can you come and fetch me?"

He doesn't ask why. He puts down the phone and I imagine him getting dressed and getting in his car and driving through the countryside.

He is thirty years older than me. He has been married three times and has a private life with more ordnance than a live firing range but I know and trust him more than anyone else.

I know what I'm going to do. Up until now I have been trying to imagine Cate's situation—the places she went to, what she tried to hide—but there is no point in calling the same phone numbers or mentally piecing together her movements. I have to follow her footsteps, to catch up.

I am going to Amsterdam to find Samira. I look at the clock. Not tomorrow. Today.

Two hours later I open the door to Ruiz. Sometimes I wonder if he knows my thoughts or if he's the one who puts them in my mind in the first place and then reads them like counting cards in a poker game.

"We should go to Amsterdam," he says.

"Yes."

BOOK TWO

The bitterest tears shed over graves
are for words left unsaid and deeds
left undone.

—HARRIET BEECHER STOWE

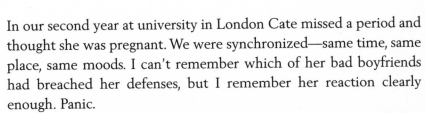

In our second year at university in London Cate missed a period and thought she was pregnant. We were synchronized—same time, same place, same moods. I can't remember which of her bad boyfriends had breached her defenses, but I remember her reaction clearly enough. Panic.

We did a home pregnancy test and then another. I went with her to the family planning clinic, a horrible green building in Greenwich not far from the observatory. Where time began, life ended.

The nurse asked Cate some questions and told her to go home and wait another seven days. Apparently, the most common reason for a false negative is testing too early.

Her period arrived.

"I might have been pregnant and miscarried," she said afterward. "Perhaps if I had wanted it more."

Later, apropos of nothing, she asked, "What do they do with them?"

"With what?"

"With the aborted babies."

"They don't call them babies. And I guess they get rid of them."

"Get rid of them?"

"I don't know, OK?"

I wonder if a scare such as this, a near miss, came back to haunt her during the years of trying to fall pregnant. Did she tell Felix? Did she wonder if God was punishing her for not loving the first one enough?

I *remember* the name of the bad boyfriend. We called him Handsome Barry. He was a Canadian ski instructor with a year-round suntan and incredibly white teeth. What is it about male ski instructors? They take on this God-like aura in the mountains as if the rarefied air makes them look more handsome or (more likely) women less discerning.

We were working during the Christmas break at a ski lodge in the French Alps in the shadow of Mont Blanc (which didn't ever throw a shadow since the clouds never lifted).

"Have you ever seen a Sikh ski?" I asked Cate.

"You can be the first," she insisted.

We shared a room in Cell Block H, the nickname for the staff quarters. I worked as a chambermaid five days a week, from six in the morning until mid-afternoon. I rarely saw Cate who worked nights at a bar. She practiced her Russian accent by pretending to be Natalia Radzinsky, the daughter of a countess.

"Where on earth did you sleep with Barry?" I asked.

"I borrowed your house key. We used one of the guest suites."

"You did what?"

"Oh, don't worry. I put down a towel."

She seemed more interested in my love life. "When are you going to lose your virginity?"

"When I'm ready."

"Who are you waiting for?"

I told her "Mr. Right," when really I meant "Mr. Considerate" or "Mr. Worthy" or any "mister" who *wanted* me enough.

Maybe I was my mother's daughter after all. She was already trying to find me a husband—my cousin Anwar, who was reading philosophy at Bristol University. Tall and thin with large brown eyes and little wire spectacles, Anwar had great taste in clothes and liked Judy Garland records. He ran off with a boy from the university bookshop, although my mother still won't accept that he's gay.

———

Ruiz has scarcely said a word since our flight left Heathrow. His silences can be so eloquent.

I told him that he didn't have to come. "You're retired."

"True, but I'm not dead," he replied. The faintest of smiles wrinkled the corners of his eyes.

It's amazing how little I know about him after six years. He has children—twins—but doesn't talk about them. His mother is in a retirement home. His stepfather is dead. I don't know about his real father, who's never come up in conversation.

I have never met anyone as self-sufficient as Ruiz. He doesn't appear to hunger for human contact or *need* anyone. You take those survivor shows on TV where people are separated into competing tribes and try to win "immunity." Ruiz would be a tribe of one—all on his own. And the grumpy old bugger would come out on top every time.

Amsterdam. It makes me think of soft drugs, sanctioned prostitution and wooden shoes. This will be my first visit. Ruiz is also a "Dutch virgin" (his term, not mine). He has already given me his thumbnail appraisal of the Dutch. "Excellent lager, a few half-decent footballers and the cheese with the red wax."

"The Dutch are very polite," I offered.

"They're probably the nicest people in the world," he agreed. "They're so amenable that they legalized prostitution and marijuana rather than say no to anyone."

For all his Gypsy blood Ruiz has never been a wanderer. His only foreign holiday was to Italy. He is a creature of habit—warm beer, stodgy food and rugby—and his xenophobia is always worse the farther he gets from home.

We managed to get bulkhead seats which means I can take off my shoes and prop my feet against the wall, showing off my pink-and-white-striped socks. The seat between us is empty. I've claimed it with my book, my bottle of water and my headphones. Possession is nine-tenths of the law.

Outside the window the Dutch landscape is like an old snooker table, patched with different squares of felt. There are cute farmhouses, cute windmills and occasional villages. This whole below-sea-level thing is quite strange. Even the bridges would be underwater if the dikes ever failed. But the Dutch are so good at reclaiming land that they'll probably fill in the North Sea one day and the M11 will stretch all the way to Moscow.

On the journey from the airport our taxi driver seems to get lost and drives us in circles, crossing the same canals and the same bridges. The only clue we have to Cate's movements is the tourist map of central Amsterdam and a circle drawn around the Red Tulip Hotel.

The desk clerk greets us with a wide smile. She is in her mid-twenties, big boned and a pound or two away from being overweight. Behind her is a notice board with brochures advertising canal boat cruises, bicycle tours, and day trips to a tulip farm.

I slide a photograph of Cate across the check-in counter. "Have you seen her?"

She looks hard. Cate is worth a long look. The woman doesn't recognize her.

"You could ask some of the other staff," she says.

A porter is loading our cases onto a trolley. In his fifties, he's wearing a red waistcoat stretched tight over a white shirt and a paunch, putting the buttons under pressure.

I show him the photograph. His eyes narrow as he concentrates. I wonder what he remembers about guests—their faces, their cases, the tips they leave?

"Room 12," he announces, nodding vigorously. His English is poor.

Ruiz turns back to the desk clerk. "You must have a record. She might have stayed here during the second week of February."

She glances over her shoulder, worried about the manager, and then taps at the keyboard. The screen refreshes and I glance down the list. Cate isn't there. Wait! There's another name I recognize: "Natalia Radzinsky."

The porter claps his hands together. "Yes, the countess. She had one blue bag." He measures the dimensions in the air. "And a smaller one. Very heavy. Made of metal."

"Was she with anyone?"

He shakes his head.

"You have a very good memory."

He beams.

I look at the computer screen again. I feel as though Cate has left me a clue that nobody else could recognize. It's a silly notion, of course, to imagine the dead leaving messages for the living. The arrogance of archaeologists.

The Red Tulip Hotel has sixteen rooms, half of them overlooking the canal. Mine is on the first floor and Ruiz's room is above me. Sunlight bounces off the curved windows of a canal boat as it passes, taking tourists around the city. Bells jangle and bike riders weave between pedestrians.

Ruiz knocks on my door and we make a plan. He will talk to the Immigration and Naturalization Service (IND), which deals with asylum seekers in the Netherlands. I will visit Hassan Khan's last known address.

I take a taxi to Gerard Doustraat in a quarter known as de Pijp, or "the Pipe" as my driver explains. He calls it the "real Amsterdam." Ten years ago it had a seedy reputation but is now full of restaurants, cafés and bakeries.

The Flaming Wok is a Chinese restaurant with bamboo blinds and fake bonsai trees. The place is empty. Two waiters are hovering near the kitchen door. Asian. Neat, wearing black trousers and white shirts.

From the front door I can see right through to the kitchen where pots and steamers hang from the ceiling. An older man, dressed in white, is preparing food. A knife stutters in his hand.

The waiters speak menu English. They keep directing me to a table. I ask to see the owner.

Mr. Weng leaves his kitchen, wiping his hands on a towel. He bows to me.

"I want to know about the people who were living upstairs."

"They gone now."

"Yes."

"You want to rent frat? One bedroom. Very crean."

"No."

He shrugs ambivalently and points to a table, motioning me to sit, before he orders tea. The waiters, his sons, compete to carry out the instructions.

"About the tenants," I say.

"They come, they go," he replies. "Sometimes full. Sometimes empty." His hands flutter as he talks and he clasps them occasionally, as if fearful they might fly away.

"Your last tenants, where were they from?"

"Everywhere. Estonia, Russia, Uzbekistan . . ."

"What about this boy?" I show him the charcoal drawing of Hassan. "He's older now. Sixteen."

He nods energetically. "This one okay. He wash the dishes for food. Others take food from bins."

The green tea has arrived. Mr. Weng pours. Tea leaves circle in the small white cups.

"Who paid the rent?"

"Pay money up front. Six months."

"But you must have had a lease."

Mr. Weng doesn't understand.

"A contract?"

"No contract."

"What about the electricity, the telephone?"

He nods and smiles. He's too polite to tell me that he doesn't have an answer.

I point to the girl in the drawing and take out the photograph of Samira. "What about this girl?"

"Many girls in and out." He makes a circle with his left forefinger and thumb and thrusts a finger through the hole. "Prostitutes," he says apologetically, as though sorry for the state of the world.

I ask to see the flat. One of his sons will show me. He takes me through a fire door that opens into an alley and leads me up a rear staircase to where he unlocks a door.

I have been in depressing flats before, but few have disheartened me as quickly as this one. It has one bedroom, a lounge, a kitchen and a bathroom. The only furniture is a low chest of drawers with a mirror on top and a sofa with cigarette burns.

"The mattresses were thrown away," Mr. Weng's son explains.

"How many lived here?"

"Ten."

I get the impression he knew the occupants better than his father.

"Do you remember this girl?" I show him the photograph.

"Maybe."

"Did she stay here?"

"She visited."

"Do you know where she lives?"

"No."

The tenants left nothing behind except a few cans of food, some old pillows and a couple of used international phone cards. There are no clues here.

Afterward, I catch a taxi and meet Ruiz at a bar in Nieumarkt, a paved open square not far from the Oude Kerk. Most of the outside tables are empty. It is getting too late in the year for backpackers and American tourists.

"I didn't think you were going to buy one of those, sir," I say, pointing to his guidebook.

"Yeah, well, I hate asking directions," he grumbles. "I'm sure someone is going to say, "You want to go *where?*" That's when I'll discover I'm in the wrong bloody country."

A couple at the next table are locals. They could be having an argument or agreeing completely. I can't tell.

"The Dutch can squeeze more vowels into a sentence than anyone else in the world," says Ruiz, too loudly. "And that Dutch 'j' is a deliberate bloody provocation."

He goes back to his guidebook. We're sitting on the western flank of the red light district, in an area known as de Walletjes (the Little Walls).

"That building with all the turrets is the Waag," he explains. "It used to be a gatehouse to the old city."

A young waitress has come to take our order. Ruiz wants another beer, "with less froth and more Heineken." She smiles at me sympathetically.

Opening his marbled notebook, Ruiz relates how Hassan and Samira Khan were smuggled across the German border into the Netherlands in the luggage compartment of a tourist coach in April 2005. They were taken to an application center at Ter Apel and were interviewed by the Immigration and Naturalization Service. Hassan claimed to be fifteen and Samira seventeen. They told the authorities they were born in Kabul and had spent three years living in a refugee camp in Pakistan. After their mother died of dysentery, their father, Hamid Khan, took the children back to Kabul where he was shot dead in 1999. Hassan and Samira were sent to an orphanage.

"That's the story they told in every interview, together and independently. Never wavered."

"How did they get here?"

"Traffickers, but they both refused to name names." Ruiz consults his notebook again. "After they were screened, they were housed at a center for underage asylum seekers operated by the Valentine Foundation. Three months later they were moved to the campus at Deelen where 180 children are housed. In December last year both their visas were revoked."

"Why?"

"I don't know. They were given twenty-eight days to leave the Netherlands. An appeal was lodged but they disappeared."

"Disappeared?"

"Not many of these people hang around to get deported."

"What do you mean 'these people'?"

Ruiz looks at me awkwardly. "Slip of the tongue." He pauses to sip his beer. "I have the name of a lawyer who represented them. Lena Caspar. She has an office here in Amsterdam."

White froth clings to his top lip. "There's something else. The boy made an earlier North Sea crossing. He was picked up and sent back to the Netherlands within twenty-four hours."

"Guess he tried again."

"Second time unlucky."

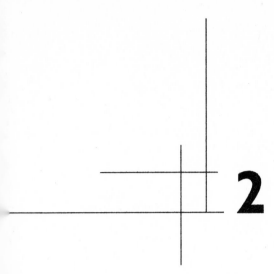

2

The lawyer's office is on Prinsengracht in a four-story building that deviates from the vertical by a degree or two, leaning out over the brick-paved street. A high arched doorway leads to a narrow court-yard where an old woman is swabbing flagstones with a mop and bucket. She points to the stairs.

On the first floor we enter a waiting room full of North Africans, many with children. A young man looks up from a desk, pushing his Harry Potter glasses higher up his nose. We don't have an appointment. He flicks through the pages of a daily schedule.

At that moment a door opens behind him and a Nigerian woman appears, dressed in a voluminous floral dress. A young girl clings to her hand and a baby is asleep on her shoulder.

For a moment I don't see anyone else. Then a small woman emerges, as if appearing from the folds of the Nigerian's dress.

"I'll send you a copy of the papers once I've lodged the appeal," she says. "You must let me know if you change your address."

Dressed in a long-sleeved cotton blouse, black cardigan and gray trousers, she looks very lawyerly and businesslike, despite her dimin-utive stature. Smiling absently at me as though we might have met, she glances at Ruiz and shudders.

"Mrs. Caspar, excuse this interruption. Could we have a word?"

She laughs. "How very English that sounds. Just the one word? I'm almost tempted to say yes just to hear which one you might choose." The skin around her eyes wrinkles like peach stones. "I'm very busy today. You'll have to wait until—"

She stops in mid-sentence. I am holding up a photograph of Samira. "Her brother is dead. We have to find her."

Mrs. Caspar holds her office door open until we follow her inside. The room is almost square, with highly polished wood floors. The house has belonged to her family for generations, she explains. The law practice was her grandfather's and then her father's.

Despite volunteering this information, Mrs. Caspar has a lawyer's natural caution.

"You don't look like a police officer," she says to me. "I thought you might require my services." She turns her attention to Ruiz. "*You*, however, look exactly like a policeman."

"Not anymore."

"Tell me about Hassan," she says, turning back to me. "What happened to him?"

"When did you last see him?"

"Eleven months ago."

I describe the discovery of his body in the truck and how my name and address were sewn into his clothes. Turning her face to the window, Mrs. Caspar might be close to tears, but I doubt if such a woman would let strangers see her emotions.

"Why would he have your name?"

"I don't know. I was hoping you could tell me."

She shakes her head.

"I am trying to find Samira."

"Why?"

How do I answer this? I plunge straight in. "I think a friend of mine who couldn't have children tried to buy a baby in Amsterdam. I think she met Samira."

"Samira doesn't have a baby."

"No, but she has a womb."

Mrs. Caspar looks at me incredulously. "A Muslim girl doesn't rent her womb. You must be mistaken."

The statement has the bluntness and certainty of fact or dogma. She crosses the office and opens a filing cabinet, taking out a folder. Sitting at her desk, she scans the contents.

"My government does not welcome asylum seekers. They have made it more and more difficult for them. We even have a minister of immigration who claims that only 20 percent of applicants are 'real refugees'—the rest are liars and frauds.

"Unfortunately, legitimate asylum seekers are being demonized. They are treated like economic refugees, roaming between countries looking for someone to take them in."

The bitterness in her voice vibrates her tiny frame.

"Samira and Hassan had no papers when they arrived. The IND claimed they destroyed them on purpose. They didn't believe Samira was a minor. She looked closer to twelve than twenty, but they sent her for tests."

"Tests?"

"An age evaluation test. They x-rayed her collarbone, which is supposed to establish if someone is older or younger than twenty. Hassan had his wrist x-rayed. A report was prepared by Harry van der Pas, a physical anthropologist at Tilburg University.

"It backfired on them. Samira appeared even younger. Poor diet and malnutrition had stunted her growth. They gave them both temporary visas. They could stay, but only until further checks were done."

Mrs. Caspar turns a page in the folder.

"Nowadays the policy is to return underage asylum seekers to their own country. Hassan and Samira *had* no family. Afghanistan can scarcely feed its own people. Kabul is a city of widows and orphans."

She slides a page of notes toward me—a family history. "They were orphans. Both spoke English. Their mother was educated at Delhi University. She worked as a translator for a publishing company until the Taliban took over."

I look at the notes. Samira was born in 1987 during the Soviet occupation of Afghanistan. She was two years old when the Soviets left and ten when the Taliban arrived.

"And their father?"

"A factory owner."

I remember Hassan's photograph.

"They made fireworks," explains Mrs. Caspar. "The Taliban closed the factory down. Fireworks were forbidden. The family fled to Pakistan and lived in a refugee camp. Their mother died of dysentery. Hamid Khan struggled to raise his children. When he grew tired of living like a beggar in a foreign country, he took his family back to Kabul. He was dead within six months."

"What happened?"

"Samira and Hassan witnessed his execution. A teenager with a Kalashnikov made him kneel on the floor of their apartment and shot him in the back of the head. They threw his body from a window into the street and wouldn't let his children collect it for eight days, by which time the dogs had picked it over."

Her voice is thick with sadness. "There is an Afghan proverb. I heard Samira say it: To an ant colony dew is a flood."

It doesn't need any further explanation.

"When did you last see her?"

"Mid-January. She surprised me on my birthday. She made me fireworks. I don't know how she managed to buy the chemicals and powder. I had never seen anything so beautiful."

"What about their application for asylum?"

The lawyer produces another letter. "Eighteen is a very important age for an asylum seeker in this country. Once you reach this age you are treated as an adult. Samira's temporary residency was revoked. She was deemed to be old enough to look after Hassan, so his visa was also canceled. Both were denied asylum and told they had to leave.

"I lodged an appeal, of course, but I couldn't prevent them being forced onto the street. They had to leave the campus at Deelen. Like a lot of young people denied asylum, they chose to run rather than wait to be deported."

"Where?"

She opens her arms, palms upward.

"How can we find Samira?"

"You can't."

"I have to try. Did she have any friends at the campus?"

"She mentioned a Serbian girl. I don't know her name."

"Is she still there?"

"No. She was either deported or she ran away."

Mrs. Caspar looks at Ruiz and back to me. The future is mapped out in the lines on her face. It is a difficult journey.

"I have a friend—a retired policeman like you, Mr. Ruiz. He has spent half his life working in the red light district. He knows everyone—the prostitutes, pimps, dealers and drug addicts. Walls have mice and mice have ears. He can hear what the mice are saying."

She takes down the name of our hotel and promises to leave a message.

"If you find Samira, be careful with her. When she finds out about her brother she will hurt in places where it matters most."

"You think we'll find her?"

She kisses my cheeks. "There is always a way from heart to heart."

Back at the Red Tulip I call DI Forbes. Straightaway he demands to know where I am. A quiet inner voice tells me to lie. It's a voice I've been hearing a lot lately.

"Have you interviewed the truck driver?" I ask.

"Are you in Amsterdam?" he counters.

"What did he tell you?"

"You can't just *leave* the fucking country. You're a suspect."

"I wasn't made aware of any restrictions."

"Don't give me that crap! If you're running a parallel investigation I'll have you up on disciplinary charges. You can forget about your career. You can forget about coming home."

I can hear the annoying click in his voice. It must drive his wife mad—like living with a human metronome.

Eventually he calms down when I tell him about Hassan. We swap information. The truck driver has been charged with manslaughter, but there is a complication. U.K. immigration officers received a tip-off about a suspect vehicle before the roll-on, roll-off ferry docked in Harwich. They had the license number and were told to look for a group of illegal immigrants.

"Who provided the tip-off?"

"The Port Authority in Rotterdam received an anonymous phone call two hours after the ferry sailed. We think it came from the traffickers."

"Why?"

"They were setting up a decoy."

"I don't understand."

"They were sacrificing a small number of illegals who would tie up resources. Customs and immigration would be so busy that they wouldn't notice a much larger shipment."

"On the same boat?"

"Two articulated lorries haven't been accounted for. The companies listed on the freight manifest are nonexistent. They could have smuggled a hundred people in the back of those trucks."

"Could the air vents have been closed deliberately—to create a more effective decoy?"

"We may never know."

"I don't want a health club, I want a gym," I tell the desk clerk who doesn't appreciate the difference. I shadow box and she backs away. Now she understands.

I know a little about gyms. In our last year at Oaklands, I convinced Cate to take karate classes with me. They were held in a grungy old gym in Penwick Street, mostly used by boxers and old guys in sleeveless vests whose veins would pop out of their heads when they were on the bench press.

The karate instructor was Chinese with a Cockney accent and everyone called him "Peking," which got shortened to "P.K.," which he didn't seem to mind.

There was a boxing ring and a weight-training room with mirrors and a separate annex with mats on the floor for karate. P.K. spent the first few lessons explaining the principles behind karate, which didn't particularly interest Cate. "The mental discipline, physical training and study help build respect toward our fellow man," he said.

"I just want to be able to kick them in the balls," said Cate.

"The two Japanese characters that make up the word 'karate' have the literal meaning of 'empty hands,' " explained P.K. "It is a system of self-defense that has evolved over hundreds of years. Every move is based on a knowledge of the muscles and joints and the relationship between movement and balance."

Cate raised her hand. "When do I learn to hit people?"

"You will be taught the techniques of counterattack."

He then described how the word "karate" came from Mandarin and Cantonese phrases like "chan fa" and "ken fat," which sent Cate into a fit of giggles. The literal meaning is "The Law of the Fist." Attacks to the groin of an opponent are frowned upon by most martial arts. Karate also doesn't approve of targeting the hip joints, knee joints, insteps, shins, upper limbs and face.

"What's the bloody point?" muttered Cate.

"I think he means in competition."

"Forget competition. I want to hurt their balls."

She persevered with learning the theory but every week she pestered him with the same question: "When do we learn the groin kick?"

P.K. finally relented. He gave Cate a private lesson after the gym had closed. The blinds were drawn and he turned off all the lights except for the one over the ring.

She came out looking flushed and smiling, with a mark on her neck that looked suspiciously like a love bite. She didn't go back to self-defense classes again.

I kept going, working my way through the belts. P.K. wanted me to go for black but I was already at the police training college.

Ruiz is on his second beer when I get to the restaurant. He's watching the pizza chef spin a disk of dough in the air, draping it over his knuckles before launching it again.

The waiters are young. Two of them are watching me, commenting to each other. They're trying to fathom my relationship with Ruiz. What is a young Asian woman doing with a man twice her age? I'm either a mail-order bride or his mistress, they think.

The café is nearly empty. Nobody eats this early in Amsterdam. An old man with a dog sits near the front door. He slips his hand beneath the table with morsels of food.

"She could be anywhere," says Ruiz.

"She wouldn't have left Amsterdam."

"What makes you so sure?"

"Hassan was only sixteen. She wouldn't leave him."

"He made *two* North Sea crossings without her."

I have no answer.

So far we have been trying to make inquiries without drawing attention to ourselves. Why not change our tactics? We could print up posters or place an advertisement.

Ruiz doesn't agree. "Cate Beaumont tried to take this public and look what happened. This isn't some seat-of-the-pants operation where someone panicked and killed the Beaumonts. We're dealing with an organized gang—guys like Brendan Pearl."

"They won't expect it."

"They'll know we're looking."

"We'll flush them out."

Ruiz continues to argue, but he understands my point. Chance or fate will not decide what takes place next. We can *make* things happen.

Hotel rooms in strange cities are lonely places where the human spirit touches rock bottom. I lie on the bed but cannot sleep. My head refuses to abandon the image of a child in a Mickey Mouse T-shirt, lying next to his mother, beneath a closed air vent.

I want to rewind the clock back to the night of the reunion and further. I want to sit down with Cate and take turns at talking and crying and saying we're sorry. I want to make up for the last eight years. Most of all, I want to be forgiven.

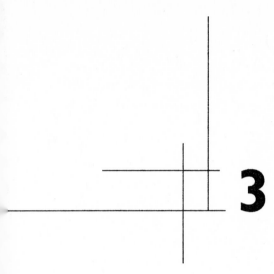

3

A mobile vibrates gently beneath my pillow.

I hear Ruiz's voice. "Rise and shine."

"What time is it?"

"Just gone seven. There's someone downstairs. Lena Caspar sent him."

Pulling on my jeans, I splash water on my face and brush my hair back in a band.

Nicolaas Hokke is in his mid-sixties with short springy gray hair and a beard. His six-foot frame helps hide the beginnings of a paunch beneath a scuffed leather jacket.

"I understand you need a guide," he says, taking my hand in both of his. He smells of tobacco and talcum powder.

"I'm looking for a girl."

"A girl?"

"An asylum seeker."

"Hmmm. Let's talk over breakfast."

He knows a place. We can walk. The intersections are a flurry of trams, cars and bicycles. Hokke negotiates them with the confidence of a deity crossing a lake.

Already I am falling for Amsterdam. It is prettier and cleaner than London with its cobbled squares, canals and wedding-cake façades. I feel safer here: the anonymous foreigner.

"Often people want tours of the red light district," Hokke explains. "Writers, sociologists, foreign politicians. I take them twice— once during daylight and again at night. It is like looking at different sides of the same coin, light and dark."

Hokke has an ambling gait with his hands clasped behind his back. Occasionally, he stops to point out a landmark or explain a sign. "Straat" means street and "steeg" means lane.

"This was your beat?" asks Ruiz.

"Of course."

"When did you retire?"

"Two years ago. And you?"

"A year."

They nod to each other as if they share an understanding.

Turning a corner, I get my first glimpse of Amsterdam's famous "windows." Initially, they appear to be simple glass doors with wooden frames and brass numbers. The curtains are drawn across some of them. Others are open for business.

Only when I draw closer do I see what this means. A skinny dark woman in a sequined bra and G-string is sitting on a stool with her legs crossed and boots zipped up to her knees. Under the black lights the bruises on her thighs appear as pale blotches.

The blatancy of her pose and her purpose diminishes a small part of me. She watches me aggressively. She doesn't want me with these men. I will stop them coming to her door.

Negotiating more of the narrow lanes, we pass windows that are so close on either side that it is like being at a tennis match and following the ball back and forth across the net. In contrast, Ruiz looks straight ahead.

A large Dominican woman calls out to Hokke and waves. Dressed in a red tasseled push-up bra that underpins a massive bust, she is perched on a stool with her legs crossed and stomach bulging over her crotch.

Hokke stops and talks to her in Dutch.

"She has four children," he explains. "One of them is at university. Twenty years a prostitute but she's still a woman."

"What do you mean a woman?"

"Some of them turn into whores."

He waves to several more prostitutes, who blow him kisses or tease him by slapping their wrists. Farther down the street an older woman comes out of a shop and throws her arms around him like a long lost son. She presses a bag of cherries into his hand.

"This is Gusta," he explains, introducing us. "She still works the windows."

"Part-time," she reminds him.

"But you must be—"

"Sixty-five," she says proudly. "I have five grandchildren."

Hokke laughs at our surprise. "You're wondering how many customers would sleep with a grandmother."

Gusta puts her hands on her hips and rolls them seductively. Hokke looks for a polite way to answer our question.

"Some of the younger, prettier girls have men queuing up outside their windows. They are not concerned if a man comes back to them. There will be plenty more waiting. But a woman like Gusta cannot rely on a sweet smile and a firm body. So she has to offer quality of service and a certain expertise that comes with experience."

Gusta nods in agreement.

Hokke doesn't seem to resent or disapprove of the prostitutes. The drug addicts and dealers are a different story. A North African man is leaning on the railing of a bridge. He recognizes Hokke and dances toward him. Hokke doesn't stop moving. The African has betel-stained teeth and dilated pupils. Hokke's face is empty, neutral. The African jabbers in Dutch, grinning wildly. Hokke carries on walking.

"An old friend?" I ask.

"I've known him thirty years. He's been a heroin addict for this much time."

"It's remarkable he's still alive."

"Addicts do not die from the drugs, they die from the lifestyle," he says adamantly. "If drugs were less expensive he wouldn't have to steal to afford them."

On the far side of the bridge, we meet another junkie, younger and even less appealing. He points the glowing end of a cigarette at me and talks to Hokke in a wheedling voice. An argument ensues. I don't know what they're saying.

"I asked him if he was clean," Hokke explains.

"What did he say?"

"He said: 'I am always clean.' "

"You argued."

"He wanted to know if you were for sale."

"Is he a pimp?"

"When it suits him."

We reach the café and take a table outside under the bare branches of a large tree that is threaded with fairy lights. Hokke drinks his coffee black and orders a slice of sourdough toast with jam. Afterward, he fills a pipe, so small that it seems almost designed for an apprentice smoker.

"My one vice," he explains.

Ruiz laughs. "So in all those years you were never tempted."

"Tempted?"

"To sleep with some of the women in the windows. There must have been opportunities."

"Yes, opportunities. I have been married forty years, Vincent. I hope I can call you Vincent. I have slept with only my wife. She is enough for me. These women are in business. They should not be expected to give away their bodies for free. What sort of businesswoman would do that?"

His face almost disappears behind a cloud of pipe smoke.

"This girl you want to find, you think she might be a prostitute?"

"She was trafficked out of Afghanistan."

"Afghani prostitutes are rare. The Muslim girls are normally Turkish or Tunisian. If she is illegal she won't be working the windows unless she has false papers."

"Are they difficult to get?"

"The Nigerians and Somalis swap papers because they all look alike but the windows are normally the easiest to police. The streets and private clubs are more difficult. It is like an iceberg—we see only the tip. Beneath the waves there are hundreds of prostitutes, some underage, working from parking lots, toilets and private houses. Customers find them through word of mouth and mobile telephones."

I tell him about Samira disappearing from the care center.

"Who brought her to the Netherlands?" he asks.

"Traffickers."

"How did she pay them?"

"What do you mean?"

"They will want something in return for smuggling her."

"She and her brother are orphans."

He empties his pipe, tapping it against the edge of an ashtray.

"Perhaps they haven't yet paid." Refilling it again he explains how gangs operate within the asylum centers. They pick up girls and turn them into prostitutes, while the boys are used as drug runners or beggars.

"Sometimes they don't even bother kidnapping children from the centers. They collect them for the weekend and bring them back. This is safer for the pimps because the girls don't disappear completely and trigger an investigation. Meanwhile, they are fed, housed and learn a bit of Dutch—paid for by the Dutch government."

"You think that's what happened to Samira?"

"I don't know. If she is young she will be moved between cities or sold to traffickers in other countries. It is like a carousel. Young and new girls are prized as fresh meat. They generate more money. By moving them from place to place, it is harder for the police or their families to find them."

Hokke gets to his feet and stretches. He beckons us to follow him. We turn left and right down the cobbled lanes, moving deeper into the red light district. More windows are open. Women tap on the glass to get Hokke's attention. A Moroccan shakes her breasts at him. Another slaps her rump and sways to a song that only she can hear.

"Do you know them all?" I ask.

He laughs. "Once perhaps, yes. I heard all their stories. Now there is a kind of wall between the police and the prostitutes. In the old days most of them were Dutch. Then the Dominicans and Columbians moved in. Then the Surinamese. Now we have Nigerians and girls from Eastern Europe."

Each of the streets is different, he explains. The Oudekerksteeg is the African quarter. The South Americans are on Boomsteeg; the Asians on Oudekennissteeg and Barndesteeg, while Bloedstraat has the transsexuals. The Eastern European girls are on Molensteeg and along the Achterburgwal.

"It is getting harder to make money. A prostitute needs at least two clients before her rent for the window is paid. Another four clients are needed for the pimp's share. Six men have used her and she still hasn't earned anything for herself.

"In the old days prostitutes would save up to buy a window and then become the landlady, renting to other girls. Now companies own the windows and sometimes use them to launder money by claiming the girls earn more than they do."

Hokke doesn't want to sound melancholy but can't help himself. He yearns for the old days.

"The place is cleaner now. Less dangerous. The problems have gone out farther, but they never disappear."

We are walking alongside a canal, past strip clubs and cinemas. From a distance the sex shops look like souvenir sellers. Only up close do the bright novelty items become dildos and fake vaginas. I am fascinated and disturbed in equal parts; torn between looking away and peering into the window to work out what the various things are for.

Hokke has turned into a lane and knocks on a door. It is opened by a large man with a bulging stomach and sideburns. Behind him is a small room barely big enough for him to turn around. The walls are lined with porn videos and film reels.

"This is Nico, the hardest working projectionist in Amsterdam."

Nico grins at us, wiping his hands on his shirtfront.

"This place has been here longer than I have," explains Hokke. "Look! It still shows Super-8 films."

"Some of the actresses are grandmothers now," says Nico.

"Like Gusta," adds Hokke. "She was very beautiful once."

Nico nods in agreement.

Hokke asks him if he knows of any Afghani girls working the windows or clubs.

"Afghani? No. I remember an Iraqi. You remember her, Hokke? Basinah. You had a beating heart for her."

"Not me," laughs the former policeman. "She had problems with her landlord and wanted me to help."

"Did you arrest him?"

"No."

"Did you shoot him?"

"No."

"You weren't a very successful policeman, were you, Hokke? Always whistling. The drug dealers heard you coming from two streets away."

Hokke shakes his head. "When I wanted to catch them I didn't whistle."

I show Nico the photograph of Samira. He doesn't recognize her.

"Most of the traffickers deal with their own. Girls from China are smuggled by the Chinese; Russians smuggle Russians." He opens his hands. "The Afghanis stay at home and grow poppies."

Nico says something to Hokke in Dutch.

"This girl. Why do you want to find her?"

"I think she knows about a baby."

"A baby?"

"I have a friend." I correct myself. "I *had* a friend who faked her pregnancy. I think she arranged to get a baby from someone in Amsterdam. My friend was murdered. She left behind this photograph."

Hokke is filling his pipe again. "You think this baby was being smuggled?"

"Yes."

He stops in mid-movement, the match burning in his fingers. I have surprised him—a man who thought he had seen and heard it all after thirty years in this place.

Ruiz is waiting outside, watching the carnival of need and greed. There are more people now. Most have come to see but not touch the famous red light district. One group of Japanese tourists is shepherded by a woman holding a bright yellow umbrella above her head.

"Samira had a brother," I explain to Hokke and Nico. "He went missing from the care center at the same time. Where would he go?"

"Boys can also become prostitutes," says Hokke, in a matter-of-fact way. "They also carry drugs or pick pockets or become beggars. Look at Central Station. You'll see dozens of them."

I show them the charcoal drawing of Hassan. "He had a tattoo on the inside of his wrist."

"What sort of tattoo?"

"A butterfly."

Hokke and the projectionist exchange glances.

"It is a property tattoo," says Nico, scratching his armpit. "Somebody owns him."

Hokke stares into the blackened bowl of his pipe. Clearly, it is not good news.

I wait for him to explain. Choosing his words carefully, he reveals that certain criminal gangs control areas of the city and often claim ownership over asylum seekers and illegals.

"She should stay away from de Souza," says Nico.

Hokke holds a finger to his lips. Something passes between them.

"Who is de Souza?" I ask.

"Nobody. Forget his name."

Nico nods. "It is for the best."

There are more windows open. More customers. The men don't raise their eyes as they pass one another.

Prostitution has always confused me. When I was growing up, movies like *Pretty Woman* and *American Gigolo* glamorized and sanitized the subject. My first glimpse of real prostitutes was with Cate. We were in Leeds for an athletics meeting. Near the railway station, where most of the cheap hotels could be found, we saw women on street corners. Some of them appeared washed out and unclean—nothing like Julia Roberts. Others looked so carnivorous that they were more like angler fish than objects of desire.

Maybe I have a naïve view of sex as being beautiful or magical or otherworldly. It *can* be. I have never liked dirty jokes or overtly sexual acts. Cate called me a prude. I can live with that.

"What are you thinking, sir?"

"I'm wondering why they do it," Ruiz replies.

"The women?"

"The men. I don't mind someone warming my toilet seat for me but there's some places I don't want to come second, or third . . ."

"You think prostitution should be illegal?"

"I'm just making an observation."

I tell him about an essay I read at university by Camille Paglia, who claimed that prostitutes weren't the victims of men but their conquerors.

"That must have set the feminists afighting."

"Rape alarms at ten paces."

We walk in silence for a while and then sit down. A swathe of sunshine cuts across the square. Someone has put up a soapbox beneath a tree and is preaching or reciting something in Dutch. It could be *Hamlet*. It could be the telephone directory.

Back at the hotel we start making calls—working through a list of charities, refugee advocates and support groups. Hokke has promised us more names by tomorrow. We spend all afternoon on the phones but nobody has any knowledge of Samira. Perhaps we are going to have to do this the old-fashioned way—knocking on doors.

On Damrak I find a print shop. A technician enlarges the photograph of Samira and uses a color copier to produce a bundle of images. The smell of paper and ink fills my head.

Ruiz will take the photograph to Central Station and show it around. I'll try the women in the windows, who are more likely to talk to me. Ruiz is completely happy with the arrangement.

Before I leave I call Barnaby Elliot to ask about the funerals. The moment he hears my voice he starts accusing me of having burned down Cate and Felix's house.

"The police say you were there. They say you reported the fire."

"I reported a break-in. I didn't start a fire."

"What were you doing there? You wanted her computer and her letters. You were going to steal them."

I don't respond, which infuriates him even more.

"Detectives have been here asking questions. I told them you were making wild allegations about Cate. Because of you they won't release the bodies. We can't arrange the funerals—the church, the readings, the death notices. We can't say goodbye to our daughter."

"I'm sorry about that, Barnaby, but it's not my fault. Cate and Felix were murdered."

"SHUT UP! JUST SHUT UP!"

"Listen to me—"

"No! I don't want to hear any more of your stories. I want you to leave my family alone. Stay away from us."

As soon as he hangs up my mobile chirrups like a fledgling.

"Hello? Alisha? Hello."

"I can hear you, Mama."

"Is everything OK?"

"Yes, fine."

"Did Hari call you?"

"No."

"A Chief Superintendent North has been trying to reach you. He said you didn't turn up for work."

Hendon! My new job as a recruitment officer. I totally forgot.

"He wants you to call him."

"OK."

"Are you sure everything is all right?"

"Yes, Mama."

She starts telling me about my nieces and nephews—which ones are teething, smiling, walking or talking. Then I hear about the dance recitals, soccer games and school concerts. Grandchildren are at the center of her life. I should feel usurped but the emotion is closer to emptiness.

"Come round for lunch on Sunday. Everyone will be here. Except for Hari. He has a study date."

That's a new name for it.

"Bring that nice sergeant." She means "New Boy" Dave.

"I didn't *bring* him last time."

"He was very nice."

"He's not a Sikh, Mama."

"Oh, don't worry about your father. He's all bark and no bite. I thought your friend was very polite."

"Polite."

"Yes. You can't expect to marry a prince. But with a little patience and hard work, you can *make* one. Look how well I did with your father."

I can't help but love her. She kisses the receiver. Not many people still do that. I kiss her back.

As if on cue I get a call from "New Boy" Dave. Maybe they're working in cahoots.

"Hello, sweet girl."

"Hello, sweet boy." I can hear him breathing as distinctly as if he were standing next to me.

"I miss you."

"A *part* of you misses me."

"No. All of me."

The odd thing is that I miss him too. It's a new feeling.

"Have you found her?"

"No."

"I want you to come home. We need to talk."

"So let's talk."

He has something he wants to say. I can almost hear him rehearsing it in his mind. "I'm quitting the force."

"Good God!"

"There's a little sailing school on the south coast. It's up for sale."

"A sailing school."

"It's a good business. It makes money in the summer and in the winter I'll work on the fishing boats or get a security job."

"Where will you get the money?"

"I'm going to buy it with Simon."

"I thought he was working in San Diego?"

"He is, but he and Jacquie are coming home."

Simon is Dave's brother. He is a sailmaker or a boat designer—I can never remember which one.

"But I thought you *liked* being a detective."

"It's not a good job if I ever have a family."

Fair point. "You'll be closer to your mum and dad." (They live in Poole.)

"Yeah."

"Sailing can be fun." I don't know what else to say.

"Here's the thing, Ali. I want you to come with me. We can be business partners."

"Partners?"

"You know I'm in love with you. I want to get married. I want us to be together." He's talking quickly now. "You don't have to say anything yet. Just think about it. I'll take you down there. I've found a cottage in Milford-on-Sea. It's beautiful. Don't say no. Just say maybe. Let me show you."

I feel something shift inside me and I want to take his large hand in my two small hands and kiss his eyelids. Despite what he says, I know he wants an answer. I can't give him one. Not today, nor tomorrow. The future is an hour-by-hour panorama.

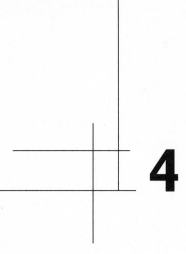

4

Once more I walk past the Oude Kerk and Trompettersteeg. Hokke
was right—the red light district is different at night. I can almost
smell the testosterone and used condoms.

As I pass each window, I press a photograph against the glass.
Some of the prostitutes shout at me or shake their fingers angrily.
Others offer seductive smiles. I don't want to meet their eyes, but I
must make sure they look at Samira.

I walk through Goldbergersteeg and Bethlemsteeg, making a
mental note of those windows where the curtains are closed so I can
return later. Only one woman tries to encourage me indoors. She
puts two fingers to her lips and pokes her tongue between them. She
says something in Dutch. I shake my head.

In English this time. "You want a woman." She shakes her claret
covered breasts.

"I don't sleep with women."

"But you've thought about it."

"No."

"I can be a man. I have the tools." She is laughing at me now.

I move on, around the corner, along the canal through Boomsteeg to Molensteeg. There are three windows side by side, almost
below ground. The curtain is open on the center one. A young woman

raises her eyes. Black lights make her blond hair and white panties glow like neon. A tiny triangle barely covers her crotch and two higher on her chest are pulled together to create a cleavage. The only other shadows darken the depression on either side of her pubic bone where the bikini is stretched tightly across her hips.

A balloon hangs from the window. Streamers. Birthday decorations? I hold the photograph against the glass. A flash of recognition. Something in her eyes.

"You know her?"

She shakes her head. She's lying.

"Help me."

There are traces of beauty in her cheekbones and the curve of her jaw. Her hair is parted. The thin scalp line is dark instead of white. She lowers her eyes. She's curious.

The door opens. I step inside. The room is scarcely wide enough for a double bed, a chair and a small sink attached to the wall. Everything is pink, the pillows, sheets and the fresh towel lying on top. One entire wall is a mirror, reflecting the same scene so it looks like we're sharing the room with another window.

The prostitute sips from a can of soft drink. "My name is Eve—just like the first woman." She laughs sarcastically. "Welcome to my Garden of Eden."

Leaning down she picks up a packet of cigarettes beneath her stool. Her breasts sway. She hasn't bothered closing the curtain. Instead she stays by the window. I look at the bed and the chair, wondering where to sit.

Eve points to the bed. "Twenty euros, five minutes."

Her accent is a mixture of Dutch and American. It's another testament to the power of Hollywood which has taught generations of people in distant corners of the world to speak English.

I hand over the money. She palms it like a magician making a playing card disappear.

I hold up the photograph again. "Her name is Samira."

"She's one of the pregnant ones."

I feel myself straighten. Invisible armor. Knowledge.

Eve shrugs. "Then again, I could be wrong."

The thumbprint on her forearm is a bruise. Another on her neck is even darker.

"Where did you see her? When?"

"Sometimes I get asked to help with the new ones. To show them."

"To show them what?"

She laughs and lights a cigarette. "What do *you* think? Sometimes they watch me from the chair or from the bed, depending on what the customer has paid for. Some of them like being watched. Makes it quicker."

I'm about to ask about why she needs a chair, when I notice the strip of carpet on the floor to protect her knees.

"But you said she was pregnant. Why would you need to show her this?"

She rolls her eyes. "I'm giving you the *five*-minute version. That's what you paid for."

I nod.

"I saw her the first time in January. I remember because it was so cold that day." She motions to the sink. "Cold water only. Like ice. They brought her to watch. Her eyes were bigger than this." The prostitute makes fists with her hands. "I thought she was going to throw up. I told her to use the sink. I knew she was never going to make it as one of us. It's only sex. A physical act. Men come and go. They cannot touch me here or here," she says pointing to her heart and her head. "This girl acted as though she was saving herself. Another fucking virgin!" She flicks the ash from her cigarette.

"What happened?"

"Time's up." She holds out her hand for more money.

"That wasn't five minutes."

She points to the wall behind me. "You see that clock? I lie on my back and watch it for a living. Nobody judges five minutes like I do."

I hand her another twenty euros. "You said she was pregnant."

"That was the next time I saw her." Eve mimes the bump. "She was at a doctor's clinic in Amersfoort. She was in the waiting room with a Serbian girl. Both of them were pregnant. I figured it was a welfare scam or they were trying to stay in the country by having a baby."

"Did you talk to her?"

"No. I remember being surprised because I thought she was going to be the world's last virgin." The cigarette is burning near her knuckles.

"I need the name and address of the clinic."

"Dr. Beyer. You'll find him in the book."

She crushes the cigarette beneath a sling-back shoe. A knock on the glass catches her attention. A man outside points first to me and then to Eve.

"What's your name?" she whispers conspiratorially.

"Alisha."

She reaches for the door. "He wants both of us, Alisha."

"Don't open it!"

"Don't be so shy. He looks clean. I have condoms."

"I'm not a—"

"Not a whore. Not a virgin either. You can make some money. Buy some decent clothes."

There is a small commotion outside. More men are peering through the window. I'm on my feet. I want to leave. She is still trying to convince me. "What have you got to lose?"

I want to say my self-respect.

She opens the door. I have to squeeze past her. Her fingernail runs down my cheek and the tip of her tongue moistens her bottom lip. Men crowd the passageway, where the cobbles are slick and hard. I have to shoulder my way past them, smelling their bodies, brushing against them. My foot strikes a step and I stumble. A hand reaches out to help me but I slap it away irrationally, wanting to scream abuse at him. I was right about Samira. Right about the baby. That's why Cate faked her pregnancy and carried Samira's photograph.

A small patch of gray sky appears above the crush. Suddenly I'm out, in a wider street, drawing deep breaths. The dark water of the canal is slashed with red and lilac. I lean over a railing and vomit, adding to the color.

My mobile vibrates. Ruiz is on the move.

"I might have found someone," he says, puffing slightly. "I was showing Samira's photograph around Central Station. Most people didn't want to know but this one kid acted real strange when he saw the picture."

"You think he knew her?"

"Maybe. He wouldn't tell the truth if God Almighty asked him for it."

"Where is he now?"

"He took off. I'm fifty yards behind him."

The DI rattles off a description of a teenage boy in a khaki camouflage jacket, jeans and sneakers.

"Damn!"

"What's up?"

"My mobile is running low. Should have charged it last night. Nobody ever bloody calls me."

"I do."

"Yeah, well, that just goes to show you should get a life. I'll try to give you a cross street. There's a canal up ahead."

"Which one?"

"They all look the same."

I hear music in the background and a girl shouting from the windows.

"Hold on. Barndesteeg," he says.

Standing in the ocher glow of a streetlight, I open a tourist map and run my finger down the names until I find the street grid reference. They're not far away.

Movies and TV shows make it look easy to follow someone and not be seen, but the reality is very different. If this were a proper police tail, we'd have two cars, a motorcyclist and two, maybe three officers on foot. Every time the target turned, someone new would be behind him. We don't have that luxury.

Crossing over Sint Jansbrug, I walk quickly along the canal. Ruiz is a block farther east, heading toward me along Stoofsteeg. The teenager is going to walk straight past me.

The pavement is crowded. I have to step left and right, brushing shoulders with passersby. The air is thick with hashish and fried-food smells.

I don't see him until the last moment. He's almost past me. Gaunt-cheeked, hair teased with fingers and gel, he skips from the pavement to the gutter and back again, dodging people. He's carrying a canvas bag over his shoulder. A bottle of soft drink protrudes from the top. He looks over his shoulder. He knows he's being followed but he's not scared.

Ruiz has dropped back. I take over. We reach the canal and cross the bridge, almost retracing my steps. The boy walks nearer the water than the buildings. If he wants to lose a tail, why take the open side of the street?

Then it dawns on me—he's *leading* Ruiz away. Someone at the station must have known Samira. He didn't want Ruiz finding them.

The teenager stops moving and waits. I walk past him. The DI doesn't appear. The kid thinks he's safe but doubles back to make sure.

When he moves again he doesn't look back. I follow him through the narrow lanes until he reaches Warmoesstraat and then Dam Square. He waits near a sculpture until a slender girl appears, dressed in jeans and a pink corduroy jacket. Her hair is short and straight, the color of tea.

He argues and gesticulates, miming with his hands. I call Ruiz on the mobile. "Where are you?"

"Behind you."

"Was there a girl at the station in jeans and a pink jacket? Dark haired. Late teens. Pretty for now."

"Samira?"

"No. Another girl. I think he was trying to lead you away. He didn't want you finding her."

They're still arguing. The girl shakes her head. He tugs at her coat sleeve. She pulls away. He shouts something. She doesn't turn.

"They're splitting up," I whisper into my mobile. "I'll follow the girl."

She has a curious body, a long torso and short legs, with slightly splayed feet when she walks. She takes a blue scarf from her pocket and wraps it over her head, tying it beneath her chin. It is a hijab— a head covering. She could be Muslim.

I stay close behind her, aware of the crowds and the traffic. Trams joust on tracks that divide the wider roads. Cars and bicycles weave around them. She is so small. I keep losing sight of her.

One moment she's in front of me and the next— Where has she gone? I sprint forward, looking vainly in doorways and shop windows. I search the side streets, hoping for a glimpse of her pink jacket or the blue of her hijab.

Standing on a traffic island, I turn full circle and step forward. A bell sounds urgently. My head turns. An unseen hand wrenches me backward as a tram washes past in a blur of noise and rushing air.

The girl in the pink jacket is staring at me, her heart beating faster than mine. The smudges beneath her eyes are signs of the premature or the beaten down. She knew I was following her. She saved me.

"What's your name?"

Her lips don't move. She turns to leave. I have to sprint several yards to get in front of her.

"Wait! Don't leave. Can we talk?"

She doesn't answer. Perhaps she doesn't understand.

"Do you speak English?" I point to myself. "My name is Alisha."

She steps around me.

"Wait, please."

She steps around me again. I have to dodge people as I try to walk backward and talk to her at the same time. I hold my hands together as if praying. "I'm looking for Samira."

She doesn't stop. I can't *make* her talk to me.

Suddenly, she enters a building, pushing through a heavy door. I don't see her use a key or press a buzzer. Inside smells of soup and electric warmth. A second door reveals a large stark room full of tables and scraping chairs. People are sitting and eating. A nun in a black tunic fills bowls of soup from a trolley. A bikie type with a long beard hands out plates and spoons. Someone else distributes bread rolls.

An old man at the nearest table leans low over his food, dipping chunks of bread into the steaming mixture. He crooks his right arm around the bowl as though protecting it. Beside him a tall figure in a woolen cap is trying to sleep with his head on the table. There must be thirty people in the dining room, most with ragtag clothes, body tics and empty stomachs.

"Wou je iets om te eten?"

I turn to the voice.

In English this time: "Would you like something to eat?"

The question belongs to an elderly nun with a narrow face and playful eyes. Her black tunic is trimmed with green and her white hair sweeps back from her brow until it disappears beneath a wimple.

"No, thank you."

"There is plenty. It is good soup. I made it myself."

A work apron, the width of her shoulders, reaches down to her ankles. She is collecting plates from the tables, stacking them along her arm. Meanwhile, the girl has lined up metal tins in front of the soup pot.

"What is this place?"

"We are Augustinians. I am Sister Vogel."

She must be in her eighties. The other nuns are of similar vintage although not quite so shrunken. She is tiny, scarcely five feet tall, with a voice like gravel spinning in a drum.

"Are you sure you won't eat?"

"No. Thank you." I don't take my eyes off the girl.

The nun steps in front of me. "What do you want with her?"

"Just to talk."

"That's not possible."

"Why?"

"She will not hear you."

"No, you don't understand. If I can just speak—"

"She *cannot* hear you." Her voice softens. "She is one of God's special children."

I finally understand. It's not about language or desire. The girl is deaf.

The soup tins have been filled. The girl screws a lid on each tin and places them in a shoulder bag. She raises the strap over her head, adjusting it across her chest. She unfolds a paper napkin and wraps two pieces of bread. A third piece she takes with her, nibbling at the edges.

"Do you know her name?" I ask.

"No. She comes three times a week and collects food."

"Where does she live?"

Sister Vogel isn't going to volunteer the information. There is only one voice she obeys—a higher authority.

"She's done nothing wrong," I reassure her.

"Why do you wish to speak with her?"

"I'm looking for someone. It's very important."

Sister Vogel puts down the soup dishes and wipes her hands on her apron. Rather than walking across the room she appears to float a fraction above the wooden floorboards in her long tunic. I feel leaden-footed alongside her.

She steps in front of the girl and taps the palm of her hand before making shapes with her fingers.

"You can sign!" I say.

"I know some of the letters. What do you wish to ask?"

"Her name."

They sign to each other.

"Zala."

"Where is she from?"

"Afghanistan."

I take the photograph from my pocket. Sister Vogel takes it from me. The reaction is immediate. Zala shakes her head adamantly. Fearfully. She won't look at the image again.

Sister Vogel tries to calm her down. Her voice is soft. Her hands softer. Zala continues to shake her head, without ever lifting her gaze from the floor.

"Ask her if she knows Samira."

Sister Vogel tries to sign but Zala is backing away.

"I need to know where Samira is."

The nun shakes her head, scolding me. "We don't frighten people away from here."

Zala is already at the door. She can't run with the soup weighing her down. As I move to follow her, Sister Vogel grabs my arm. "Please, leave her alone."

I look at her imploringly. "I can't."

Zala is on the street. She looks back over her shoulder. Her cheeks are shining under the streetlamps. She's crying. Hair has escaped from beneath her hijab. She cannot spare a hand to brush it away from her face.

The DI isn't answering his mobile. His battery must be dead. Dropping back, I stay behind Zala as she leads me away from the convent. The streets and canals are no longer familiar. They are lined with aging, psoriatic houses, subdivided into bedsits, flats and maisonettes. Doorbell pushers form neat lines.

We pass a small row of shops that are shuttered and locked. At the next corner Zala crosses the road and enters a gate. It belongs to a large, rundown apartment block at the heart of a T junction. The shrubs outside are like puffs of green against the darkness of the bricks. There are bars on the downstairs windows and shutters on the upper floors. Lights burn behind them.

I walk past the gate and check there are no other entrances. I wish Ruiz were here. What would he do? Knock on the door? Introduce himself? No, he'd wait and watch. He'd see who was coming and going. Study the rhythm of the place.

I look at my watch. It has just gone eight. Where is he? With luck, he'll get my text message with the address.

The wind has picked up. Leaves dance with scraps of paper at my feet. Hidden in a doorway, I'm protected by the shadows.

I don't have the patience for stakeouts. Ruiz is good at them. He can block everything out and stay focused, without ever daydreaming or getting distracted. When I stare at the same scene for too long it becomes burned into my subconscious, playing over and over on a loop until I don't register the changes. That's why police surveillance teams are rotated every few hours. Fresh eyes.

A car pulls up. Double-parks. A man enters the building. Five minutes later he emerges with three women. Neatly groomed. Dressed to kill. Ruiz would say it smells like sex.

Two different men stop outside to smoke. They sit on the steps with their legs splayed, comfortable. A young boy creeps up behind one of them and covers his eyes playfully. Father and son wrestle happily until the youngster is sent back inside. They look like immigrants. It's the sort of place Samira would go, seeking safety in numbers.

I can't stay here all night. And I can't afford to leave and risk losing my link to her. It's almost nine. Where the hell is Ruiz?

The men on the steps look up as I approach.

"Samira Khan?"

One of them tosses his head, indicating upstairs. I step around them. The door is open. The foyer smells of cooking spices and a thousand extinguished cigarettes.

Three children are playing at the base of the stairs. One of them grabs hold of my leg and tries to hide behind me before dashing off again. I climb to the first landing. Empty gas bottles have collected against the walls beside bags of rubbish. A baby cries. Children argue. Canned laughter escapes through thin walls.

Two teenage girls are sitting outside a flat, heads together, swapping secrets.

"I'm looking for Samira."

One of them points upstairs.

I climb higher, moving from landing to landing, aware of the crumbling plaster and buckling linoleum. Laundry hangs over banisters and somewhere a toilet has overflowed.

I reach the top landing. A bathroom door is open at the far end of the corridor. Zala appears in the space. A bucket of water tilts her shoulders. In the dimness of the corridor I notice another open door. She wants to reach it before I do. The bucket falls. Water spills at her feet.

Against all my training I rush into a strange room. A dark-haired girl sits on a high-backed sofa. She is young. Familiar. Even dressed in a baggy jumper and peasant skirt she is obviously pregnant. Her shoulders pull forward as if embarrassed by her breasts.

Zala pushes past me, putting her body between us. Samira is standing now, resting a hand on the deaf girl's shoulder. Her eyes travel over me, as though putting me in context.

"I don't want to hurt you."

In textbook English: "You must leave here. It is not safe."

"My name is Alisha Barba."

Her eyes bloom. She knows my name.

"Please leave. Go now."

"Tell me how you know me?"

She doesn't answer. Her right hand moves to her distended abdomen. She caresses it gently and sways slightly from side to side as if rocking her passenger to sleep. The motion seems to take the fight out of her.

She signs for Zala to lock the door and pushes her toward the kitchen where speckled linoleum is worn smooth on the floor and a shelf holds jars of spices and a sack of rice. The soup canisters are washed and drying beside the sink.

I glance around the rest of the apartment. The room is large and square. Cracks edge across the high ceiling and leaking water has blistered the plaster. Mattresses are propped against the wall, with blankets neatly folded along the top. A wardrobe has a metal hanger holding the doors shut.

There is a suitcase, a wooden trunk, and on the top a photograph in a frame. It shows a family in a formal pose. The mother is seated holding a baby. The father is standing behind them, a hand on his wife's shoulder. At her feet is a small girl—Samira—holding the hem of her mother's dress.

I turn back to her. "I've been looking for you."

"Please go."

I glance at the swell of her pregnancy. "When are you due?"

"Soon."

"What are you going to do with the baby?"

She holds up two fingers. For a moment I think she's signing something to Zala but this has nothing to do with deafness. The message is for me. Two babies! Twins.

"A boy and a girl," she says, clasping her hands together, beseeching me. "Please go. You cannot be here."

Hair prickles on the nape of my neck. Why is she so terrified?

"Tell me about the babies, Samira. Are you going to keep them?"

She shakes her head.

"Who is the father?"

"Allah the Redeemer."

"I don't understand."

"I am a virgin."

"You're pregnant, Samira. You understand how that happens."

She confronts my skepticism defiantly. "I have never lain down with a man. I *am* a virgin."

What fantasies are these? It's ridiculous. Yet her certainty has the conviction of a convert.

"Who put the babies inside you, Samira?"

"Allah."

"Did you see him?"

"No."

"How did he do it?"

"The doctors helped him. They put the eggs inside me."

She's talking about IVF. The embryos were implanted. That's why she's having twins.

"Whose eggs were put inside you?"

Samira raises her eyes to the question. I know the answer already. Cate had twelve viable embryos. According to Dr. Banerjee there were five IVF procedures using two eggs per treatment. That leaves two eggs unaccounted for. Cate must have carried them to Amsterdam. She arranged a surrogacy.

That's why she had to fake her pregnancy. She was going to give Felix his *own* child—a perfect genetic match that nobody could prove wasn't theirs.

"Please leave," says Samira. Tears are close.

"Why are you so frightened?"

"You don't understand."

"Just tell me why you're doing this."

She pushes back her hair with her thumb and forefinger. Her wide eyes hold mine until the precise moment that it becomes uncomfortable. She is strong-willed. Defiant.

"Did someone pay you money? How much? Did Cate pay you?"

She doesn't answer. Instead she turns her face away, gazing at the window, a dark square against a dark wall.

"Is that how you know my name? Cate gave it to you. She said that if anything happened, if anything went wrong, you had to contact me. Is that right?"

She nods.

"I need to know why you're doing this. What did they offer you?"

"Freedom."

"From what?"

She looks at me as though I'll never understand. "Slavery."

I kneel down, taking her hand, which is surprisingly cool. There is a speck of sleep in the corner of her eye. "I need you to tell me exactly what happened. What were you told? What were you promised?"

There is a noise from the corridor. Zala reappears. Terror paints her face and her head swings from side to side, looking for somewhere to hide.

Samira motions for her to stay in the kitchen and turns to face the door. Waiting. A brittle scratching. A key in the lock. My nerve ends are twitching.

The door opens. A thin man with pink-rimmed eyes and bad teeth seems to spasm at the sight of me. His right hand reaches into a zipped nylon jacket.

"Wie bent u?" he barks.

I think he's asking who I am.

"I'm a nurse," I say.

He looks at Samira. She nods.

"Dr. Beyer asked me to drop by and check on Samira on my way home. I live not far from here."

The thin man makes a sucking sound with his tongue and his

eyes dart about the room as though accusing the walls of being part of the deceit. He doesn't believe me, but he's not sure.

Samira turns toward me. "I have been having cramps. They keep me awake at night."

"You are *not* a nurse," he says accusingly. "You don't speak Dutch!"

"I'm afraid you're mistaken. English is the official language of the European Union." I use my best Mary Poppins voice. Officious. Matter-of-fact. I don't know how far I can push him.

"Where do you live?"

"Like I said, it's just around the corner."

"The address?"

I remember a cross street. "If you don't mind I have an examination to conduct."

He screws his mouth into a sneer. Something about his defiance hints at hidden depths of brutality. Whatever his relationship to Samira or Zala, he terrifies them. Samira mentioned slavery. Hassan had a property tattoo on his wrist. I don't have all the answers but I have to get them away from here.

The thin man barks a question in Dutch.

Samira nods her head, lowering her eyes.

"Lieg niet tegen me, kutwijf. Ik vermoord je."

His right hand is still in his jacket. Lithe and sinewy like a marathon runner, he weighs perhaps 180 pounds. With the element of surprise I could possibly take him.

"Please leave the room," I tell him.

"No. I stay here."

Zala is watching from the kitchen. I motion her toward me and then unfold a blanket, making her hold it like a curtain to give Samira some privacy.

Samira lies back on the couch and lifts her jumper, bunching it beneath her breasts. My hands are damp. Her thighs are smooth and a taut triangle of white cotton lies at the top of them. The skin of her swollen belly is like tracing paper, stretched so tightly I can see the faint blue veins beneath the surface.

The babies move. Her entire torso seems to ripple. An elbow or a knee creates a peak and then slips away. I can feel the outline of tiny bodies beneath her skin, hard little skulls and joints.

She lifts her knees and raises her hips, indicating I should remove her underwear. She has more of an idea of what to do than I have. Her minder is still at the door. Samira fixes him with a defiant glare as if to say: You want to see this?

He can't hold her gaze. Instead he turns away and walks into the kitchen, lighting a cigarette.

"You lie so easily," Samira whispers.

"So do you."

"Who is he?"

"Yanus. He looks after us."

I look around the room. "He's not doing such a good job."

"He brings food."

Yanus is back at the doorway.

"Well the babies are in good position," I say loudly. "They're moving down. The cramps could be Braxton Hicks, which are like phantom contractions. Your blood pressure is a little higher than it has been."

I don't know where this information is coming from; some of it must be via verbal osmosis, having heard my mother's graphic descriptions of my nieces and nephews arriving in the world. I know far more than I want to about mucus plugs, fundal measurements and crowning. In addition to this, I am a world authority on pain relief—epidurals, pethidine, Entonox, TENS machines and every homeopathic, mind-controlling family remedy in existence.

Yanus turns away again. I hear him punch keys on his mobile phone. He's calling someone. Taking advice. Time is running out.

"You met a friend of mine. Cate Beaumont. Do you remember her?"

Samira nods.

"Do your babies belong to her?"

The same nod.

"Cate died last Sunday. She was run down and killed. Her husband is also dead."

Samira doubles over as though her unborn have understood the news and are grieving already. Her eyes flood with a mixture of disbelief and knowing.

"I can help you," I plead.

"Nobody can help me."

Yanus is in the doorway. He reaches into his jacket again. I can see his shadow lengthening on the floor. I turn to face him. He has a can of beans in his fist. He swings it, a short arc from the hip. I sense it coming but have no time to react. The blow sends me spinning across the room. One side of my head is on fire.

Samira screams. Not so much a scream as a strangled cry.

Yanus is coming for me again. I can taste blood. One side of my face is already beginning to swell. He hits me, using the can like a hammer. A knife flashes in his right hand.

His eyes are fixed on mine with ecstatic intensity. This is his calling—inflicting pain. The blade twirls in front of me doing figure eights. I was supposed to take him by surprise. The opposite happened. I underestimated him.

Another blow connects. Metal on bone. The room begins to blur.

Some things, real things, seem to happen half in the mind and half in the world; trapped in between. The mind sees them first, like now—a boot swings toward me. I glimpse Zala hanging back. She wants to look away but can't drag her gaze from me. The boot connects and I see a blaze of color.

Fishing roughly in my pockets, Yanus takes out my mobile, my passport, a bundle of Euros . . .

"Who are you?"

"I'm a nurse."

"Leugenaar!"

He holds the knife against my neck. The point pricks my skin. A ruby teardrop is caught on the tip of the blade.

Zala moves toward him. I yell at her to stop. She can't hear me. Yanus swats her away, with the can of beans. Zala drops and holds her face. He curses. I hope he broke his fingers.

My left eye is closing and blood drips from my ear, warming my neck. He forces me upright, pulling my arms back and looping plastic cuffs around my wrists. The ratchets pull them tighter, pinching my skin.

He opens my passport. Reads the name.

"Politieagent! How did you find this place?" He spits toward Zala. "*She* led you here."

"If you leave us alone I won't say anything. You can walk out of here."

Yanus finds this amusing. The point of his knife traces across my eyebrow.

"My partner knows I'm here. He's coming. He'll bring others. If you leave now you can get away."

"What are you doing here?"

"Looking for Samira."

He speaks to Samira in Dutch. She begins gathering her things. A few clothes, the photograph of her family . . .

"Wait for me outside," he tells her.

"Zala."

"Outside."

"Zala," she says again, more determined.

He waves the knife in her face. She doesn't flinch. She is like a statue. Immovable. She's not leaving without her friend.

The door suddenly blasts inward as if blown from its hinges. Ruiz fills the frame. Sometimes I forget how big he can make himself.

Yanus barely flinches. He turns, knife first. Here is a fresh challenge. The night holds such promise for him. Ruiz takes in the scene and settles on Yanus, matching his intensity.

But I can see the future. Yanus is going to take Ruiz apart. Kill him slowly. The knife is like an extension of him, a conductor's baton directing an invisible orchestra. Listening to voices.

The DI has something in his hand. A half brick. It's not enough. Yanus braces his legs apart and raises a hand, curling a finger to motion him onward.

Ruiz swings his fist, creating a disturbance in the air. Yanus feints to the left. The half brick comes down and misses. Yanus grins. "You're too slow, old man."

The blade is alive. I scarcely see it move. A dark stain blossoms on Ruiz's shirtsleeve, but he continues stepping forward, forcing Yanus to retreat.

"Can you walk, Alisha?"

"Yes, sir."

"Get up and get out."

"Not without you, sir."

"Please, for once in your life—"

"I'll kill you both," says Yanus.

My hands are bound behind me. I can't do anything. The acid sting of nausea rises in my throat. Samira goes ahead of me, stepping into the corridor. Zala follows, still holding her cheek. Yanus yells to her in Dutch, threateningly. He lunges at Ruiz who dodges the blade. I turn outside the door and run toward the stairs, waiting for the sound of a body falling.

On every landing I shoulder the locked doors, banging my head against them and yelling for help. I want someone to untie my hands, to call the police, to give me a weapon. Nobody answers. Nobody wants to know.

We reach the ground floor and the street, turning right and heading for the canal. Samira and Zala are ahead of me. What a strange trio we make hustling through the darkness. We reach the corner. I turn to Samira. "I have to help him." She understands. "I want you to go straight to the police."

She shakes her head. "They'll send me back."

I haven't time to argue. "Then go to the nuns. Quickly. Zala knows the way."

I can feel the adrenaline still pumping through my body. Running now, aware of the void in my stomach, I sprint toward the house. There are people milling outside. They're surrounding a figure slumped on the steps. Ruiz. Someone has given him a cigarette. He sucks it greedily, drawing in his cheeks and then exhaling slowly.

Relief flows through me like liquid beneath my skin. I don't know whether to weep or laugh or do both. Blood soaks his shirt. A fist is pressed against his chest.

"I think maybe you should take me to a hospital," he says, struggling to breathe.

Like a crazy woman, I begin yelling at people to call an ambulance. A teenager summons the courage to tell me there's one coming.

"I had to get close," Ruiz explains in a hoarse whisper. His brow and upper lip are dotted with beads of sweat. "I had to let him stab me. If he could reach me I could *reach him*."

"Don't talk. Just be still."

"I hope I killed the bastard."

More people emerge from the flats. They want to come and see the bleeding man. Someone cuts away my cuffs and the plastic curls like orange peel at my feet.

Ruiz gazes at the night sky above the rooftops.

"My ex-wives have been wishing this on me for a long while," he says.

"That's not true. Miranda is still in love with you."

"How do you know?"

"I can see it. She flirts with you all the time."

"She can't help herself. She flirts with everyone. She does it to be nice."

His breathing is labored. Blood gurgles in his lungs.

"Wanna hear a joke?" he says.

"Don't talk. Sit quietly."

"It's an old one. I like the old ones. It's about a bear. I like bears. Bears can be funny."

He's not going to stop.

"There's this family of polar bears living in the Arctic in the middle of winter. The baby polar bear goes to his mother one day and says, 'Mum? Am I really a *polar bear?*'

" 'Of course you are, son,' she says.

"And the cub replies, 'Are you sure I'm not a panda bear or a black bear?'

" 'No, you're definitely not. Now run outside and play in the snow.'

"But he's still confused so the baby polar bear goes looking for his father and finds him fishing at the ice hole. 'Hey, Dad, am I a polar bear?'

" 'Well, of course, son,' he replies gruffly.

" 'Are you sure I don't have any grizzly in me or maybe koala?'

" 'No, son, I can tell you now that you're a hundred percent purebred polar bear, just like me and your mother. Why in the world do you ask?'

" 'Because I'm freezing my butt off out here!' "

The DI laughs and groans at the same time. I put my arms around his chest, trying to keep him warm. A mantra, unspoken, grows louder in my head: "Please don't die. Please don't die. Please don't die."

This is my fault. He shouldn't be here. There's so much blood.

5

Regret is such an odd emotion because it invariably comes a moment too late, when only our imagination can rewrite what has happened. My regrets are like pressed flowers in the pages of a diary. Brittle reminders of summers past; like the last summer before graduation, the one that wasn't big enough to hold its own history.

It was supposed to be the last hurrah before I entered the "real world." The London Metropolitan Police had sent me an acceptance letter. I was part of the next intake for the training college at Hendon. The class of 1998.

When I went to primary school I never imagined getting to secondary school. And at Oaklands I never imagined the freedom of university. Yet there I was, about to graduate, to grow up, to become a full-fledged, paid-up adult with a tax file number and a student loan to repay. "Thank God we'll never be forty," Cate joked.

I was working two jobs—answering phones at my brothers' garage and working weekends on a market stall. The Elliots invited me to Cornwall again. Cate's mother had suffered her stroke by then and was confined to a wheelchair.

Barnaby still had political ambitions but no safe seat had become available. He wasn't made of the right stuff—not old school enough to please the die-hard Conservatives and not female, famous or ethnic enough to satisfy modernizers in the party.

I still thought he was handsome. And he continued to flirt with me, finding reasons to lean against me or punch my arm or call me his "Bollywood beauty" or his "Indian princess."

On Sunday mornings the Elliots went to church in the village, about a ten-minute walk away. I stayed in bed until after they'd gone.

I don't know why Barnaby came back, what excuse he made to the others. I was in the shower. Music videos were turned up loud on the TV. The kettle had boiled. The clock ticked as if nothing had happened.

I didn't hear him on the stairs. He just appeared. I held the towel against me but didn't cry out. He ran his fingers slowly over my shoulder and along my arms. Perfect fingernails. I looked down. I could see his gray trousers and the tips of his polished shoes growing out from under his cuffs.

He kissed my throat. I had to throw my head back to make room for him. I looked up at the ceiling and he moved his lips lower to the space between my breasts. I held his head and pushed against him.

My hair was long back then, plaited in a French braid that reached down to the small of my back. He held it in his fists, wrapping it around his knuckles like a rope. Whispering in my ear, sweet nothings that meant more, he pushed down on my shoulders, wanting me to kneel. Meanwhile, the TV blared and the clock ticked and the water in the kettle cooled.

I didn't hear the door open downstairs or footsteps on the stairs. I don't know why Cate came back. Some details don't matter. She must have heard our voices and the other noises. She must have known but she kept coming closer until she reached the door, drawn by the sounds.

In real estate location is everything. Barnaby was standing naked behind me. I was on all fours with my knees apart. Cate didn't say a word. Having seen enough she stayed there watching more. She didn't see me fighting or struggling. I *didn't* fight or struggle.

This is the way I remember it. The way it happened. All that was left was for Cate to tell me to leave and that she never wanted to see me again. And time enough for her to lie sobbing on her bed. A single bed away, I packed my bag, breathing in her grief and trying to swallow something that I couldn't spit out.

Barnaby drove me to the station in silence. The seagulls were crying, accusing me of betrayal. The rain had arrived, drowning summer.

It was a long journey back to London. I found Mama at her sewing machine, making a dress for my cousin's wedding. For the first time in years I wanted to crawl onto her lap. Instead I sat next to her and put my head on her shoulder. Then I cried.

Later that night I stood in front of the bathroom mirror with Mama's big dressmaking scissors and cut my hair for the first time. The blades carved through my tresses and sent them rocking to the tiles. I trimmed it as short as the scissors allowed, nicking my skin so that blood stained the blades and tufts of hair stood out from my skull like sprouts of wheat germ.

I can't explain why. Somehow the act was palliative. Mama was horrified. (She would have been less shocked if I'd sliced open my wrists.)

I left messages for Cate and wrote her notes. I couldn't visit her house without risking meeting her father—or worse, her mother. What if Ruth Elliot knew? I caught the same buses and trains as Cate. I orchestrated chance meetings and sometimes I simply stalked her, but it made no difference. Being sorry wasn't enough. She didn't want to see me or talk to me.

Eventually I stopped trying. I locked myself away for hours, coming out only to run and to eat. I ran a personal best a month later. I no longer wanted to catch up with the future—I was running away from the past. I threw myself into my police training, studying furiously. Filling notebooks. Blitzing exams.

My hair grew back. Mama calmed down. I used to daydream, in the years that followed, that Cate and I would find each other and somehow redeem the lost years. But a single image haunted me— Cate standing silently in the doorway, watching her father fuck her best friend to the rhythm of a ticking clock and a cooling kettle.

In all the years since, not a day has passed when I haven't wanted to change what happened. Cate did not forgive me. She hated me with a hatred more fatal than indifference because it was the opposite of love.

After enough time had passed, I didn't think about her every hour or every day. I sent her cards on her birthday and at Christmas. I heard about her engagement and saw the wedding photographs in a photographer's window in Bethnal Green Road. She looked happy. Barnaby looked proud. Her bridesmaids (I knew all their names) wore the dresses she always said she wanted. I didn't know Felix. I didn't know where they'd met or how he'd proposed. What did she see in him? Was it love? I could never ask her.

They say time is a great healer and a lousy beautician, but it didn't heal my wounds. It covered them over with layers of regret and awkwardness like pancake makeup. Wounds like mine don't heal. The scars simply grow thicker and more permanent.

The curtains sway back and forth, breathing in and then out like lungs drawing restless air. Light spills from around the edges. Another day.

I must have dozed off. I rarely sleep soundly anymore. Not like I did as a child when the world was still a mystery. Now I snatch awake at the slightest noise or movement. The scars on my back are throbbing, telling me to stand and stretch.

Ruiz is lying on a bed in the dimness. Wires, fluids and machines have captured him. A mask delivers oxygen. Three hours ago surgeons inserted a tube in his chest and reinflated his right lung. They stitched his arm, commenting on his many scars.

My ear is wrapped in bandages and an ice pack has melted on my cheek. The swelling has gone down but the bruising will be ugly. At least I can let down my hair to hide the worst of it.

The doctors and nurses have been very kind. They wanted me to leave the DI's room last night. I argued. I begged. Then I seem to remember lying down on the linoleum floor, challenging them to carry me out. They let me stay.

I feel numb. Shell-shocked. This is my fault. I close my eyes to the darkness and listen to him breathing. Someone has delivered a tray with a glass of orange juice under a frilled paper lid. There are biscuits. I'm not hungry.

So this is all about a baby. Two babies. Cate Beaumont tried unsuccessfully to get pregnant through IVF. She then met someone who convinced her that for £80,000 another woman would have a baby for her. Not just any baby. Her own genetic offspring.

She traveled to Amsterdam where two of her fertilized embryos were implanted into the womb of an Afghani teenager who owed money to people smugglers. Both embryos began growing.

Meanwhile, in London Cate announced she was "pregnant." Friends and family celebrated the news. She began an elaborate deception that she had to maintain for nine months. What went wrong? Cate's ultrasound pictures—the fake ones—showed only one baby. She didn't expect twins.

Someone must have arranged the IVF procedure. Doctors were needed. Fertility specialists. Midwives. Minders.

A nurse appears at the door, an angel in off-white. She walks around the bed and whispers in my ear. A detective has come to interview me.

"He won't wake yet," she whispers, glancing at Ruiz. "I'll keep watch."

A local politieagent has been sitting outside the room all night. He looks very smart in dark blue trousers, light blue shirt, tie and jacket. Now he's talking to a more senior colleague. I wait for them to finish.

The senior detective introduces himself as Spijker, making it sound like a punishment. He doesn't give me a first name. Maybe he only has the one. Tall and thin with a narrow face and thinning hair, he looks at me with watery eyes as though he's already having an allergic reaction to what I might say.

A small mole on his top lip dances up and down as he speaks. "Your friend will be all right, I think."

"Yes, sir."

"I shall need to talk to him when he wakes up."

I nod.

We walk to the patient lounge, which is far smarter than anything I've seen in a British hospital. There are eggs and cold meats and slices of cheese on a platter, along with a basket of bread rolls. The detective waits for me to be seated and takes out a fountain pen, resting it on a large white pad. His smallest actions have a function.

Spijker explains that he works for the Youth and Vice Squad. Under normal circumstances, this might sound like an odd combination but not when I look at Samira's age and what she's been through.

As I tell him the story, explaining events, it strikes me how implausible it all sounds. An Englishwoman transports fertilized embryos to Amsterdam inside a small cooler box. The eggs are placed in the womb of an unwilling surrogate. A virgin.

Spijker leans forward, with his hands braced on either side of his chair. For a moment I think he might suffer from piles and want to relieve some of the pressure.

"What makes you think this girl was forced to become pregnant?"

"She told me."

"And you believe her?"

"Yes, sir."

"Perhaps she agreed."

"No. She owed money to traffickers. Either she became a prostitute or she agreed to have a baby."

"Trafficking is a very serious crime indeed. Commercial surrogacy is also illegal."

I tell him about the prostitute on Molensteeg who mentioned seeing a second pregnant girl. A Serb. Samira had a Serbian friend on the campus, according to Lena Caspar.

There could be others. Babies born at a price, ushered into the world with threats and blackmail. I have no idea how big this is, how many people it touches.

Spijker's face gives nothing away. He speaks slowly, as if practicing his English. "And this has been the purpose of your visit to Amsterdam?"

The question has a barbed tip. I have been waiting for this—the issue of jurisdiction. What is a British police officer doing investigating possible crimes in the Netherlands? There are protocols to be followed. Rules to be obeyed.

"I was making private inquiries. It is not an official investigation."

Spijker seems satisfied. His point has been made. I have no authority in the Netherlands.

"Where is this woman—the pregnant one?"

"Safe."

He waits, expecting an address. I explain about Samira's asylum appeal and the deportation order. She's frightened of being sent back to Afghanistan.

"If this girl is telling the truth and becomes a witness there are laws to protect her."

"She could stay?"

"Until the trial."

I want to trust him—I want Samira to trust him—yet there is something in his demeanor that hints at skepticism. The notepad and fountain pen have not been touched. They are merely props.

"You tell a very interesting story, Detective Constable. A very interesting story, indeed." The mole on his top lip is quivering. "However, I have heard a different version. The man we found unconscious at the scene says he returned home and found you in his apartment. You claimed to be a nurse and that you were trying to examine his fiancée."

"His fiancée!"

"Yes indeed his fiancée. He says that he asked you for some proof of your identity. You refused. Did you conduct a physical examination of Miss Khan?"

"She *knew* I wasn't a nurse. I was trying to help her."

"Mr. Yanus further claims that he was attacked by your colleague as he endeavored to protect his fiancée."

"Yanus had a knife. Look at what he did!"

"In self-defense."

"He's lying."

Spijker nods, but not in agreement. "You see my dilemma, DC Barba. I have two different versions of the same event. Mr. Yanus wants you both charged with assault and abducting his fiancée. He has a good lawyer. A very good lawyer indeed."

"This is ridiculous! Surely you can't believe him."

The detective raises a hand to silence me. "We Dutch are famous for our open minds but do not mistake this openness for ignorance or naïveté. I need evidence. Where is the pregnant girl?"

"I will take you there, but I must talk to her first."

"To get your stories straight, perhaps?"

"No!" I sound too strident. "Her brother died three days ago. She doesn't know."

We drive in silence to my hotel. I am given time to shower and change. Spijker waits in the lobby.

Peeling off my clothes, I slip on a hotel robe and sit cross-legged on the bed, leafing through the messages that were waiting at reception. "New Boy" Dave has phoned four times, my mother twice and Chief Superintendent North has left a terse six-word "please explain." I screw it into a ball and flush it away. Maybe this is what he meant by shuffling people and priorities.

I should call Ruiz's family. Who, exactly? I don't have numbers for his children or any of his ex-wives—not even the most recent, Miranda.

I pick up the phone and punch the numbers. Dave is at the station. I hear other voices in the background.

"Hello, sweet girl, where have you been?"

"My mobile was stolen."

"How?"

"There was an accident."

His mood alters. "An accident!"

"Not really an accident." *I'm not doing this very well.*

"Hang on." I hear him apologizing to someone. He takes me somewhere private.

"What's wrong? Are you all right?"

"The DI is in hospital. Someone stabbed him."

"Shit!"

"I need a favor. Find a number for his ex-wife."

"Which one?"

"Miranda. Tell her that he's in the Academisch Medisch Centrum. It's a hospital in Amsterdam."

"Is he going to be all right?"

"I think so. He's out of surgery."

Dave wants the details. I try to fudge them, making it sound like a wrong-place-at-the-wrong-time scenario. Bad luck. He isn't convinced. I know what's coming now. He's going to get clingy and pathetic and ask me to come home and I'll be reminded of all the reasons I don't want to be married to someone.

Only he doesn't. He is matter-of-fact and direct, taking down the number of the hospital, along with Spijker's name. He's going to find out what the Dutch police are doing.

"I found Samira. She's pregnant."

I can hear Dave's mind juddering through the consequences. He is careful and methodical, like a carpenter who measures twice and cuts once.

"Cate paid for a baby. A surrogate."

"Jesus, Ali."

"It gets worse. She donated the embryos. There are twins."

"Who owns the babies?"

"I don't know."

Dave wants the whole story but I don't have time. I'm about to hang up when he remembers something.

"I know it's probably not the time," he says, "but I had a phone call from your mother."

"When?"

"Yesterday. She invited me to lunch on Sunday."

She threatened to do it and she went and did it!

He's waiting for a response.

"I don't know if I'll be home by then," I say.

"But you *knew* about the invite?"

"Yes, of course," I lie. "I told her to invite you."

He relaxes. "For a moment I thought she might have gone behind your back. How embarrassing would that be—my girlfriend's mother arranging dates for me? Story of my life—mothers liking me and their daughters running a mile."

Now he's blathering.

"It's all right, Dave."

"Brilliant."

He doesn't want to hang up. I do it for him. The shower is running. I step beneath the spray and flinch as the hot water hits my cheek and the cut on my ear. Washed and dried, I open my bag and take out my Dolce & Gabbana pants and a dark blouse. I see less of me in the mirror than I remember. When I ran competitively my best weight was 123 pounds. I got heavier when I joined the Met. Night shifts and canteen food will do that to you.

I have always been rather un-girlie. I don't have manicures or pedicures and I only paint my nails on special occasions (so I can chip it off when I get bored).

The day I cut my hair was almost a rite of passage. When it grew back I got a sensible layered shag cut. My mother cried. She's never been one to ration tears.

Ever since my teens I have lived in fear of saris and skirts. I didn't wear a bra until I was fourteen and my periods started after everyone else's. I imagined them banked up behind a dam wall and when the gates opened it was going to be like a scene from a Tarantino film, without Harvey Keitel to clean up afterward.

In those days I didn't imagine ever feeling like a woman, but slowly it happened. Now I'm almost thirty and self-conscious enough to wear makeup—a little lip gloss and mascara. I pluck my eyebrows and wax my legs. I still don't own a skirt and every item in my wardrobe, apart from my jeans and my saris, is a variant on the color black. That's okay. Small steps.

I make one more phone call. It diverts between numbers and Lena Caspar answers. A public address system echoes in the background. She is on a railway platform. There is a court hearing in Rotterdam, she explains. An asylum seeker has been charged with stealing groceries.

"I found Samira."

"How is she?"

"She needs your help."

The details can wait. I give her Spijker's name and phone number. Samira will need protection and guarantees about her status if they want her to give evidence.

"She doesn't know about Hassan."

"You have to tell her."

"I know."

The lawyer begins thinking out loud. She will find someone to take over the court case in Rotterdam. It might take a few hours.

"I have a question."

My words are drowned out by a platform announcement. She waits. "I'm sorry. What did you say?"

"I have a hypothetical question for you."

"Yes?"

"If a married couple provided a fertilized embryo to a surrogate mother who later gave birth, who would the baby belong to?"

"The birth mother."

"Even if genetically it had the DNA of the couple?"

"It doesn't matter. The law in the Netherlands is the same as the law in the U.K. The birth mother is the legal mother. Nobody else has a claim."

"What about the father?"

"He can apply for access, but the court will favor the mother. Why do you want to know?"

"Spijker will explain."

I hang up and take another look in the mirror. My hair is still wet. If I wear it down it will hide the swelling on my cheek. I'll have to stop my natural inclination to push it behind my ears.

Downstairs I find the detective and desk clerk in conversation. A notebook is open. They stop talking when they see me. Spijker is checking my details. I would do the same.

It is a short drive to the Augustinian Convent. We turn along Warmoesstraat and pull into a multistory car park. The African parking attendant comes running over. Spijker shows him a badge and tears up the parking stub.

Against his better judgment he has agreed to let me see Samira first. I have twenty minutes. Descending the concrete steps, I push open a heavy fire door. Across the street is the convent. A familiar figure emerges from the large front door. Dressed in her pink jacket and a long ankle-length skirt, Zala puts her head down and hustles along the pavement. Her blue hijab hides the bruising on her face. She shouldn't be outside. I fight the urge to follow her.

A large ruddy-faced nun answers the door. Like the others she is creased and crumbling, trying to outlive the building. I am led down a corridor to Sister Vogel's office, which contains a curious mixture of the old and the new. A cabinet with a glass-front full of books is stained the same dark color as the mahogany desk. In the corner there is a fax machine and a photocopier. A heart-shaped box of candies sits on the mantel, alongside photographs that could be of her nieces and nephews. I wonder if Sister Vogel ever regrets her calling. God can be a barren husband.

She appears beside me. "You didn't tell me you were a police officer."

"Would it have made a difference?"

She doesn't answer. "You sent more people for me to feed."

"They don't eat very much."

She folds her arms. "Is this girl in trouble?"

"Yes."

"Has she been abandoned?"

"Abused."

Sorrow fills every crease and wrinkle of her face. She notices the bruising on my cheek and reaches toward it sympathetically. "Who did this to you?"

"It doesn't matter. I must talk to Samira."

She takes me to a room on the second floor which is stained with the same dark panels. Samira is at the window when the door opens. She's wearing a long dress, buttoned down the middle, with a Peter Pan collar. The light from the window paints an outline of her body inside it. Watching me carefully, she takes a seat on the sofa. Her pregnancy rests on her thighs.

Sister Vogel doesn't stay. As the door closes, I glance around the room. On the wall there is a painting of the Virgin Mary and the baby Jesus. Both are pictured beside a stream, where fruit hangs from trees and fat naked cherubs dance above the water.

Samira notices me looking at it. "Are you a Christian?"

"A Sikh."

She nods, satisfied.

"Do you dislike Christians?"

"No. My father told me that Christians believe less than we believe. I don't know if that is true. I am not a very good Muslim. I sometimes forget to pray."

"How often are you supposed to pray?"

"Five times a day, but my father always said that three was enough."

"Do you miss him, your father?"

"With every breath."

Her copper-colored eyes are flecked with gold and uncertainty. I can't imagine what they've seen in her short life. When I picture Afghanistan I see women draped in black like covered statues, mountains capped with snow, old caravan trails, unexploded mines, scorching deserts, terra-cotta houses, ancient monuments and one-eyed madmen.

I introduce myself properly this time and tell Samira how I found her. She looks away self-consciously when I mention the prostitute on Molensteeg. At the same time she holds her hand to her chest, pressing down. I see pain on her forehead.

"Are you OK?"

"Heartburn. Zala has gone to get medicine." She glances at the door, already missing her friend.

"Where did you meet her?"

"At the orphanage."

"You didn't leave Afghanistan together."

"No. We had to leave her behind."

"How did she get here?"

"In the back of a truck and then by train."

"By herself?"

Samira's face softens. "Zala can always find a way to make herself understood."

"Has she always been deaf?"

"No."

"What happened?"

"Her father fought with the mujahideen against the Taliban. When the Talibs took over they punished their enemies. Zala and her mother were imprisoned and tortured with acid and melted plastic. Her mother took eight days to die. By then Zala could not hear her screaming."

The statement sucks the oxygen from the room and I feel myself struggling for breath. Samira looks toward the door again, waiting for Zala. Her fingers are splayed on her belly as if reading the bumps and kicks. What must it feel like—to have something growing inside you? A life, an organism that takes what it needs without asking or sharing, stealing sleep, changing hormones, bending bones and squeezing organs. I have heard my friends and sisters-in-law complain of weak nails, molting hair, sore breasts and stretch marks. It is a sacrifice men could not make.

Samira is watching me. She has something she wants to ask.

"You said Mrs. Beaumont is dead."

"Yes."

"What will happen now to her babies?"

"It is your decision."

"Why?"

"They belong to you."

"No!"

"They're your babies."

Her head pivots from side to side. She is adamant.

Standing suddenly, she rocks slightly and reaches out her hand, bracing it on the back of the sofa. Crossing the room, she stares out the window, hoping to see Zala.

I'm still contemplating her denial. Does she love her unborn twins? Does she imagine a future for them? Or is she simply carrying them, counting down the days until the birth, when her job is done?

"When did you meet Mrs. Beaumont?"

"She came to Amsterdam. She bought me clothes. Yanus was there. I had to pretend I didn't speak English but Mrs. Beaumont talked to me anyway. She gave me a piece of paper with your name. She said if I was ever in trouble I had to find you."

"When was this?"

"In February I saw her the first time. She came to see me again in September."

"Did she know you were having twins?"

She shrugs.

"Did she know why?"

"What do you mean?"

"Did she know about the debt? Did she know you were *forced* to get pregnant?"

Her voice softens. "She thanked me. She said I was doing a good thing."

"It is a crime to force someone to have a baby. She did a very *foolish* thing."

Samira shrugs, unwilling to be so harsh. "Sometimes friends do foolish things," she says. "My father told me that true friends are like gold coins. Ships are wrecked by storms and lie for hundreds of years on the ocean floor. Worms destroy the wood. Iron corrodes. Silver turns black but gold doesn't change in seawater. It loses none of its brilliance or color. It comes up the same as it went down. Friendship is the same. It survives shipwrecks and time."

The swelling in my chest suddenly hurts. How can someone so young be so wise?

"You must tell the police what happened."

"They will send me back."

"These people have done very bad things. You owe them nothing."

"Yanus will find me. He will never let me go."

"The police can protect you."

"I do not trust them."

"Trust me."

She shakes her head. She has no reason to believe me. Promises don't fill stomachs or bring back dead brothers. She still doesn't know about Hassan. I can't bring myself to tell her.

"Why did you leave Kabul?"

"Brother."

"Your brother?"

"No. An Englishman. We called him Brother."

"Who is he?"

"A saint."

Using her forefinger she traces the outline of a cross on her neck. I think of Donavon's tattoo. Is it possible?

"This Englishman, was he a soldier?"

"He said he was on a mission from God."

She describes how he visited the orphanage, bringing food and blankets. There were sixty children aged between two and sixteen, who slept in dormitories, huddling together in winter, surviving on scraps and charity.

When the Taliban were in control they took boys from the orphanage to fill their guns with bullets and the girls were taken as wives. The orphans cheered when the Northern Alliance and the Americans liberated Kabul, but the new order proved to be little different. Soldiers came to the orphanage looking for girls. The first time Samira hid under blankets. The second time she crawled into the latrine. Another girl threw herself off the roof rather than be taken.

I'm amazed at how ambivalent she sounds. Fateful decisions, issues of life and death, are related with the matter-of-factness of a shopping list. I can't tell if she's inured to shock or overcome by it.

"Brother" paid off the soldiers with medicine and money. He told Samira that she should leave Afghanistan because it wasn't safe. He said he would find her a job in London.

"What about Hassan?"

"Brother said he had to stay behind. I said I would not go without him."

They were introduced to a trafficker called Mahmoud, who arranged their passage. Zala had to stay behind because no country would accept a deaf girl, Mahmoud told them.

Hassan and Samira were taken overland to Pakistan by bus and smuggled south through Quetta and west into Iran until they reached Tabriz near the Turkish border. In the first week of spring they walked across the Ararat mountain range and almost succumbed to the freezing nights and the wolves.

On the Turkish side of the mountains, sheep farmers smuggled them between villages and arranged their passage to Istanbul in the back of a truck. For two months brother and sister worked in a sweatshop in the garment districts of Zeytinburnu, sewing sheepskin waistcoats.

The trafficking syndicate demanded more money to get them to England. The price had risen to ten thousand American dollars. Samira wrote a letter to "Brother" but didn't know where to send it. Finally they were moved. A fishing boat took them across the Aegean Sea to Italy where they caught a train to Rome with four other illegals. They were met at the station and taken to a house.

Two days later, they met Yanus. He took them to a bus depot and put them inside the luggage compartment of a tourist coach that traveled through Germany to the Netherlands. "Don't move, don't talk—otherwise you will be found," he told them. When the coach arrived at the Dutch border they were to claim asylum. He would find them.

"We are supposed to be going to England," Samira said.

"England is for another day," he replied.

The rest of the story matches what I've already learned from Lena Caspar.

Sister Vogel knocks softly on the door. She is carrying a tray of tea and biscuits. The delicate cups have chipped handles. I pour the tea through a broken strainer. Samira takes a biscuit and wraps it in a paper napkin, saving it for Zala.

"Have you ever heard the name Paul Donavon?"

She shakes her head.

"Who told you about the IVF clinic?"

"Yanus. He said we had to pay him for our passage from Kabul. He threatened to rape me. Hassan tried to stop him but Yanus cut him over and over. A hundred cuts." She points to her chest. Noonan found evidence of these wounds on Hassan's torso.

"What did Yanus want you to do?"

"To become a whore. He showed me what I would have to do—sleep with many men. Then he gave me a choice. He said a baby would pay off my debt. I could remain a virgin."

She says it almost defiantly. This is a truth that sustains Samira. I wonder if that's why they chose a Muslim girl. She would have done almost anything to protect her virginity.

I still don't know how Cate became involved. Was it her idea or Donavon's?

Spijker is waiting outside. I can't delay this. Opening my satchel I take out the charcoal drawing, smoothing the corners.

Excitement lights Samira's eyes from within. "Hassan! You've seen him!"

She waits. I shake my head. "Hassan is dead."

Her head jerks up as though tied to a cord. The light in her eyes is replaced by anger. Disbelief. I tell her quickly, hoping it might spare her, but there is no painless way to do this. His journey. His crossing. His fight to stay alive.

She puts her hands over her ears.

"I'm sorry, Samira. He didn't make it."

"You're lying! Hassan is in London."

"I'm telling the truth."

She rocks from side to side, her eyes closed and her mouth opening and closing soundlessly. The word she wants to say is no.

"Surely you must be wondering why you haven't heard from him," I say. "He should have called by now or written to you. You sewed my name into his clothes. That's how I found you." I close the gap between us. "I have no reason to lie to you."

She stiffens and pulls away, fixing me with a gaze of frightening intensity.

Spijker's voice echoes from downstairs. He has grown tired of waiting.

"You must tell the police everything you have told me."

She doesn't answer. I don't know if she understands.

Turning toward the window, she utters Zala's name.

"Sister Vogel will look after her."

She shakes her head stubbornly, her eyes full of imbecile hope. "I will find her. I'll look after her."

For a moment something struggles inside her. Then her mind

empties and she surrenders. Fighting fate is too difficult. She must save herself to fight whatever fate throws up.

———

There is a pharmacy in the heart of de Walletjes, explains Sister Vogel. The pharmacist is a friend of hers. This is where she sent Zala. She was carrying a note.

Turning each corner I expect to see a flash of pink or her blue hijab coming toward me. I pass a greengrocer and catch the scent of oranges, which makes me think of Hassan. What will happen to Samira now? Who will look after her?

I turn into Oudekerksteeg. There is still no sign of Zala. A touch on my arm makes me turn. For a second I don't recognize Hokke, who is wearing a woolen cap. With his light beard it makes him look like a North Sea fisherman.

"Hello, my friend." He looks at me closely. "What have you done to yourself?" His finger traces the bruising on my cheek.

"I had a fight."

"Did you win?"

"No."

I look over his shoulder, scanning the square for Zala. My sense of urgency makes him turn his own head.

"Are you still looking for your Afghani girl?"

"No, a different one this time."

It makes me sound careless—as though I lose people all the time. Hokke has been sitting in a café. Zala must have passed by him but he doesn't remember her.

"Perhaps I can help you look."

I follow him, scanning the pedestrians, until we reach the pharmacy. The small shop has narrow aisles and neatly stacked shelves. A man in a striped shirt and white coat is serving customers at a counter. When he recognizes Hokke he opens his arms and they embrace. Old friends.

"A deaf girl—I'd remember her," he announces, breaking into English.

"She had a note from Sister Vogel."

The pharmacist yells to his assistant. A head pops out from behind a stand of postcards. More Dutch. A shrug. Nobody has seen her.

Hokke follows me back onto the street. I walk a few paces and stop, leaning against a wall. A faint vibration is coming off me; a menacing internal thought spinning out of control. Zala has not run away. She would not leave Samira willingly. Ever.

Police headquarters is on one of the outer canals, west of the city. Fashioned by the imagination of an architect, it looks scrubbed clean and casts a long shadow across the canal. The glass doors open automatically. CCTV cameras scan the foyer.

A message is sent upstairs to Spijker. His reply comes back: I'm to wait in the reception area. None of my urgency has any effect on the receptionist, who has a face like the farmer's daughter in *American Gothic*. This is not my jurisdiction. I have no authority to make demands or throw my weight around.

Hokke offers to keep me company. At no point has he asked how I found Samira or what happened to Ruiz. He is content to accept whatever information is offered rather than seeking it out.

So much has happened in the past week yet I feel as though I haven't moved. It's like the clock on the wall above the reception desk, with its white face and thick black hands that refuse to move any faster.

Samira is somewhere above me. I don't imagine there are many basements in Amsterdam—a city that seems to float on fixed pontoons held together by bridges. Perhaps it is slowly sinking into the ooze like a Venice of the north.

I can't sit still. I should be at the hospital with Ruiz. I should be starting my new job in London or resigning from it.

Across the foyer the double doors of a lift slide open. There are voices, deep, sonorous, laughing. One of them belongs to Yanus. His left eye is swollen and partially closed. Head injuries are becoming a fashion statement. He isn't handcuffed, nor is he being escorted by police.

The man beside him must be his lawyer. Large and careworn, with a broad forehead and broader arse, his rumpled suit has triple vents and permanent creases.

Yanus looks up at me and smiles with his thin lips.

"I am very sorry for this misunderstanding," he says. "No hard feelings."

He offers me his hand. I stare at it blankly. Spijker appears at his left shoulder, standing fractionally behind him.

Yanus is still talking. "I hope Mr. Ruiz is being looked after. I am very sorry I stabbed him."

My eyes haven't left Spijker. "What are you doing?"

"Mr. Yanus is being released. We may need to question him again later."

The fat lawyer is tapping his foot on the floor impatiently. It has the effect of making his face wobble. "Samira Khan has confirmed that Mr. Yanus is her fiancé. She is pregnant by him." His tone is extravagantly pompous, with just a hint of condescension. "She has also given a statement corroborating his account of what happened last night."

"No!"

"Fortunately, for you, Mr. Yanus has agreed not to make a formal complaint against you or your colleague for assault, malicious wounding and abducting his fiancée. In return, the police have decided not to lay charges against him."

"Our investigations are continuing," counters Spijker.

"Mr. Yanus has cooperated fully," retorts the fat lawyer, dismissively.

Lena Caspar is so small that I almost don't see her behind him. I can sense my gaze flicking from face to face like a child waiting for a grown-up to explain. Yanus has withdrawn his hand. Almost instinctively he slides it inside his jacket, where his knife would normally be.

I imagine that I must look dazed and dumbstruck, but the opposite is true. I can see myself reflected in the dozens of glass panels around the walls and the news hasn't altered my demeanor at all. Internally, the story is different. Of all the possible outcomes, this one couldn't be anticipated.

"Let me talk to Samira."

"That's not possible."

Lena Caspar puts her hand on my arm. "She doesn't want to talk to anyone."

"Where is she?"

"In the care of the Immigration and Naturalization Service."

"Is she going to be deported?"

The fat lawyer answers for her. "My client is applying for a visa that will allow his fiancée to remain in the Netherlands."

"She's *not* his fiancée!" I snap.

The lawyer inflates even further (it barely seems possible). "You are very fortunate, Miss Barba, that my client is so willing to forgive. You would otherwise be facing very serious charges. Mr. Yanus now demands that you leave him alone, along with his fiancée. Any attempt by you to approach either of them will be taken very seriously."

Yanus looks almost embarrassed by his own generosity. His entire persona has softened. The cold, naked, unflinching hatred of last night has gone. It's like watching a smooth ocean after a storm front has passed. He extends his hand again. There is something in it this time—my mobile phone and passport. He hands them to me and turns away. He and the fat lawyer are leaving.

I look at Spijker. "You know he's lying."

"It makes no difference," he replies.

Mrs. Caspar wants me to sit down.

"There must be something," I say, pleading with her.

"You have to understand. Without Samira's testimony there *is* no case to answer, no evidence of forced pregnancies or a black market in embryos and unborn babies. The proof might lie in DNA or paternity tests, but these can't be done without Samira's permission and invasive surgery that could endanger the twins."

"Zala will confirm my story."

"Where is she?"

The entrance doors slide open. The fat lawyer goes first. Yanus pulls a light blue handkerchief from his pocket and wipes his forehead. I recognize the fabric. He rolls it over and over in his fingers. It's not a handkerchief. It's a headscarf. Zala's hijab!

Spijker sees me moving and holds me back. I fight against his arms, yelling accusations out the door. Yanus turns and smiles, showing a few teeth at the sides of his mouth. A shark's smile.

"See in his hand—the scarf," I cry. "That's why she lied."

Mrs. Caspar steps in front of me. "It's too late, Alisha."

Spijker releases my arms slowly and I shake his fingers loose. He's embarrassed at having touched me. There's something else in his demeanor. Understanding. He *believes* me! He had no choice but to release Yanus.

Frustration, disappointment and anger fill me until I feel like screaming. They have Zala. Samira is sure to follow. For all the bruises and bloodshed, I haven't even slowed them down. I'm like Wile E. Coyote, flattened beneath a rock, listening to the Road Runner's infernal, triumphant, infuriating "beep, beep!"

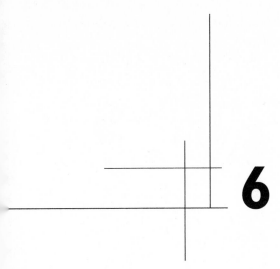

6

Ruiz's skin is a pallid gray and his eyes are bloodshot from the morphine. The years have mugged him in his sleep and he looks every one of his sixty birthdays.

"I knew you were gonna be okay," I say. "Your hide is thicker than a rhino's."

"Are you saying my arse looks big in these pajamas?"

"Not in *those* pajamas."

The curtains are open and the remains of the day are collecting on the far horizon.

It might be the morphine or his ridiculous male pride, but the DI keeps bragging about the number of stitches he needed in his chest and arm. Next we'll be comparing scars. I don't need a comparison—mine are bigger than his.

Why is it always a competition with men? Their egos are so fragile or their hormones so strong that they have to prove themselves. What tossers!

I give him a big wet kiss on his cheek. He's lost for words.

"I brought you something, sir."

He gives me a quick look, unsure whether to trust me. I pull a bottle of Scotch from a paper bag. It's a private joke. When I was lying in hospital with a busted spine Ruiz brought me a bottle. It's still the only time I've ever had alcohol. A one-off drink, sucked through a crazy straw, that made my eyes water and my throat burn. What do people see in alcohol?

I crack the seal and pour him a drink, adding a little water.

"You're not having one?"

"Not this time. You can have mine."

"That's very generous of you."

A nurse walks in. The DI hides the glass. I hide the bottle. She hands him a little plastic cup with two pills inside. The fact that we've stopped talking and look guilty encourages her to pause at the door. She says something in Dutch. It might be "bottom's up," but I doubt it.

"I think I'm going to stay here," says Ruiz. "The food is much better than the NHS muck and the nurses have a certain charm. They remind me of my house mistresses at boarding school."

"That sounds disturbingly like a sexual fantasy."

He half grins. "Not completely."

He takes another sip. "Have you ever thought about what you'd like to happen when you die? The arrangements."

"I've made a will."

"Yeah, but did you stipulate anything for the funeral? Cremation or burial or having your ashes sprinkled off the end of Margate Pier?"

"Not specifically." This is getting rather morbid.

"I want my ashes put into a rocket."

"Sure, I'll put in a call to NASA."

"In a *firework* rocket. I want to be blasted into a thousand falling stars. They can do that now—put ashes in fireworks. I read about it somewhere."

"Go out with a bang."

"A blaze of glory."

He smiles and holds out his glass for more. "Not yet, of course."

"Of course."

The truth is, *I have* thought about it. Dying. During the autumn and winter of my discontent—the months of surgery and physiotherapy, when I couldn't wash, feed or care for myself—a small, secret, childlike part of me feared that I would never walk again. And an unspoken, guilt-ridden, adult part of me decided I would rather die if that happened.

Everyone thinks I'm so strong. They expect me to face autumns and winters like that and bitch-slap them down, make them heel. I'm not so strong. I only pretend.

"I had a phone call from Miranda today," the DI announces. "I still don't know how she got the number or knew I was in hospital. As far as I can tell I was unconscious for most of yesterday." His eyes narrow. "Try not to look so sheepish, my little lambkin."

"I told you she still cares about you."

"But can't *live* with me."

"That's because you're grumpy."

"And you're an expert in these things, I suppose."

"Well 'New Boy' Dave has asked me to marry him." The statement blurts from me, unplanned, spontaneous.

Ruiz ponders it. "I didn't think he had the courage."

"You think he's afraid of me?"

"Any man with any sense should be a little bit afraid of you."

"Why?"

"I mean that in the nicest possible way." His eyes are dancing.

"You said I was too sharp for him."

"And you said that any man who could *fit* into your pants couldn't *get* into your pants."

"He loves me."

"That's a good start. How about you?"

I can't answer. I don't know.

It's strange talking about love. I used to hate the word. Hate is too strong. I was sick of reading about it in books, hearing it in songs, watching it in films. It seemed such a huge burden to place on another person—to love them; to give them something so unbelievably fragile and expect them not to break it or lose it or leave it behind on the No. 96 bus.

I thought I had a choice. Fall in love. Don't fall in love. He loves me. He loves me not. See, I'm not so smart!

My mind drifts back to Samira. I don't know what to do. I'm out of ideas. Up until now I've been convinced that I would find Cate's babies and then—what then? What did I imagine would happen? Cate broke the law. She rented a womb. Perhaps she didn't realize that Samira would be forced to cooperate. I can give her the benefit of *that* doubt.

Cate always walked close to the edge. Closer to death, closer to life. She had a crazy streak. Not all the time, just occasionally. It's like when the wind changes suddenly before a storm and kids go wild, running around in circles like swirling scraps of paper caught in the updraft. Cate would get that same gleam in her eye and drift onto the wrong side of crazy.

She is more memory than reality. She belongs to a time of teenage crushes, first kisses, crowded lecture halls and smoky pubs. Even if she had lived, we might have had nothing in common except the past.

I should let it go. When Ruiz is well enough, I'll take him home. I'll swallow my pride and take whatever job I'm offered or I'll marry Dave and we'll live in Milford-on-Sea. I shouldn't have come to Amsterdam. Why did I ever imagine I could make a difference? I can't bring Cate back. Yet for all this, I still can't shake one fundamental question: What will happen to the babies?

Yanus and his cronies will sell them to the highest bidder. Either that or they'll be born in the Netherlands and put up for adoption. Worse still, they'll be sent back to Kabul along with Samira, who will be ostracized and treated as an outcast. In some parts of Afghanistan they still stone women for having children out of wedlock.

Cate lied and deceived. She broke the law. I still don't know why Brendan Pearl killed her, although I suspect it was to stop her from talking. She came to me. I guess that makes me partially responsible.

Am I guilty of anything else? Is there something else I should have done? Perhaps I should tell Felix's family that their son would have become a father in a few weeks. Barnaby and Ruth Elliot are pseudo-grandparents to surrogate twins.

I didn't imagine ever feeling sorry for Barnaby—not after what happened. I thought I saw his true nature on the day he dropped me at the railway station in Cornwall. He couldn't even look at me or say the word goodbye.

I still don't know if he told his wife. I doubt it. Barnaby is the type to deny, deny and deny, until faced with incontrovertible proof. Then he will shrug, apologize and play the tragic hero, brought down by loving too much rather than too little.

When I first saw him at the hospital, when Cate was in a coma, it struck me how he was still campaigning, still trying to win votes. He caught glimpses of his reflection in the glass doors, making sure he was doing it right, the grieving. Maybe that's unfair—kicking a man when he's down.

Ruiz is asleep. I take the glass from his hand and rinse it in the sink. Than I tuck the bottle into my bag.

I'm still no closer to knowing what to do. It's like running a race where I cannot tell how many laps there are to go or who's winning or who's been lapped. How do I know when to kick on the final bend and start sprinting for home?

A taxi drops me at the hotel. The driver is listening to a football game being broadcast on the radio. The commentator has a tenor voice that surges with the ebb and flow of the action. I have no idea who is playing but I like the thunderous sound of the crowd. It makes me feel less melancholy.

There is a white envelope poking out of my pigeonhole at the reception desk. I open it immediately.

Three words: "Hello, sweet girl."

The desk clerk moves her eyes. I turn. "New Boy" Dave is standing behind me.

His arms wrap around me and I bury my face in his shirt. I stay there. Holding him tightly. I don't want him to see my tears.

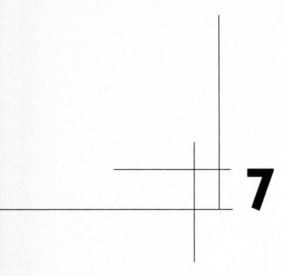

7

One second I'm sleeping and the next I'm awake. I look at the clock. Four a.m. Dave is lying next to me on his side with his cheek pressed flat against the sheet and his mouth vibrating gently.

Last night we didn't talk. Exhaustion and a hot shower and the touch of his hands put me to sleep. I'll make it up to him when he wakes. I'm sure it doesn't do much for the male ego, having a woman fall asleep on them.

Propped on one elbow, I study him. His hair is soft and rumpled like a tabby cat with tiny flecks of blond amid the ginger. He has a big head. Does that mean he would have big babies, with big heads? Involuntarily I squeeze my thighs together.

Dave scratches his ear. He has nice ears. The one I can see has the faintest hint that at one time it might have been pierced. His hand is stretched toward me on the sheet. The nails are wide and flat, trimmed straight across. I touch his fingers with mine, awkward at being so happy.

Yesterday was perhaps the worst day of my life, and I held him last night like a shipwrecked sailor clinging to the debris. He made me feel safe. He wrapped his arms around me and the pain leaked away.

Maybe that's why I feel this way, lying so still—not wanting this moment to end.

I have no experience of love. Ever since adolescence I have avoided it, renounced it, longed for it. (Such a dichotomy is one of the symptoms.) I have been an agony aunt for all my girlfriends, listening to their sob stories about arranged marriages, unfaithful husbands, men who won't call or commit, missed periods, sexual neuroses, wedding plans, postnatal depression and failed diets. I know all about other people's love affairs but I am a complete novice when it comes to my own. That's why I'm scared. I'm sure to mess it up.

Dave touches my bruised cheek. I flinch. "Who did that?" he asks.

"His name is Yanus."

I can almost see him storing this information away for future reference. He and Ruiz are similar in that way. There is nothing half-cocked or hotheaded about them. They can wait for their shot at revenge.

"You were lucky he didn't break your cheekbone."

"He could have done a lot worse."

I step closer and kiss him on the lips, quickly, impulsively. Then I turn and go to shower. Spinning back to say something, I catch him punching the air in victory.

He blushes.

"It wasn't *that* good a kiss."

"It was to me."

Later, he sits on the bed and watches me dress, which makes me feel self-conscious. I keep my back to him. He reaches across and cups my breasts before my bra embraces them.

"I volunteer for this job," he says.

"That's very noble, but you're not holding my breasts all day."

I gently push his hands away and continue dressing.

"You really like me, don't you?" he says. His big goofy grin is reflected in the wardrobe mirror.

"Don't push it," I warn him.

"But you do. You *really* like me."

"That *could* change."

His laugh isn't entirely convincing.

We breakfast at a café on Paleisstraat near Dam Square. Blue-and-white trams clatter and fizz past the window beneath humming wires. A weak sun is barely breaking through the clouds and a wind tugs at the clothes of pedestrians and cyclists.

The café has a zinc-topped counter running the length of one side. Arranged above it is a blackboard menu and barrels of wine or port. The place smells of coffee and grilled cheese. My appetite is coming back. We order sliced meats, bread and cheese; coffee with frothed milk.

I take Dave through everything that's happened. Occasionally he interrupts with a question, but mostly he eats and listens. This whole affair is laced with half-truths and concocted fictions. The uncertainties and ambiguities seem to outweigh the facts and they nag at me, making me fretful and uncomfortable.

I borrow his notebook and write down names.

> Brendan Pearl
> Yanus
> Paul Donavon
> Julian Shawcroft

On the opposite side of the page I write another list: the victims.

> Cate and Felix Beaumont
> Hassan Khan
> Samira Khan

There are likely to be others. Where do I list those who fall in between, people like Barnaby Elliot? I still think he lied to me about Cate's computer. And Dr. Banerjee, her fertility specialist. It was more than a coincidence that he turned up at my father's birthday party.

I'm not sure what I hope to achieve by writing things down. Perhaps it will give me a fresh slant on events or throw up a new link.

I have been searching for a central figure behind events but maybe that's too simplistic a notion. People could all be linked like spokes of a wheel that only touch in the center.

There is another issue. Where was the baby—or the babies—going to be handed over? Perhaps Cate planned to take a holiday or a weekend break to the Netherlands. She would go into "labor"; tell everyone she had given birth and then bring her newborn home to live happily ever after.

Even a baby needs travel documents. A passport. Which means a birth certificate, statutory declarations and signed photographs. I should call the British consulate in The Hague and ask how British nationals register a foreign birth.

In a case like this it would be much easier if the baby were born in the same country as the prospective parents. It could be a home birth or in a private house, without involving a hospital or even a midwife.

Once the genetic parents took possession of the baby nobody could ever prove it didn't belong to them. Blood samples, DNA and paternity tests would all confirm their ownership.

Samira said Hassan was going to the U.K. ahead of her. She expected to follow him. What if that's where they plan to take her? It would also explain why Cate gave Samira my name in case something went wrong.

"Last night you said you were giving up and going home," says Dave.

"I know. I just thought—"

"You said yourself that these babies belong to Samira. They always have."

"Someone killed my friend."

"You can't bring her back."

"They torched her house."

"It's not your case."

I feel a surge of anger. Does he really expect me to leave this to Softell and his imbecile mates? And Spijker doesn't fill me with confidence after letting Yanus go.

"Last night you were crying your eyes out. You said it was over."

"That was last night." I can't hide the anger in my voice.

"What's changed?"

"My mind. It's a woman's prerogative."

I want to say, *Don't be a fucking jerk, Dave, and stop quoting me back to myself.*

What is it about men? Just when you think they're rational members of the human race they go all Neanderthal and protective. Next he'll be asking me how many partners I've had and if the sex was any good.

We're drawing stares from other patrons. "I don't think we should talk about it here," he whispers.

"We're not going to talk about it at all." I get up to leave.

"Where are you going?"

I want to tell him it's none of his damn business. Instead I say that I have an appointment with Samira's lawyer, which isn't entirely true.

"I'll come with you."

"No. You go and see Ruiz. He'll appreciate that." My voice softens. "We'll meet up later."

Dave looks miserable but doesn't argue. Give him his due—he's a quick learner.

———

Lena Caspar's waiting room is being vacuumed and tidied. Magazines sit neatly stacked on a table and the toys have been collected in a polished wooden crate. Her desk is similarly neat and empty except for a box of tissues and a jug of water on a tray. Even the wastepaper basket is clean.

The lawyer is dressed in a knee-length skirt and a matching jacket. Like many women of a certain age, her makeup is applied perfectly.

"I cannot tell you where Samira is," she announces.

"I know. But you can tell me what happened yesterday."

She points to a chair. "What do you want to know?"

"Everything."

The lawyer places her palms flat on the desk. "I knew something was wrong when I saw the interpreter. Samira's English is perfect, yet she pretended not to understand what I said to her. Everything had to be translated back and forth. Samira volunteered no information without being prompted."

"Did Yanus spend any time alone with her?"

"Of course not."

"Did she see him?"

"Yanus took part in a lineup. She picked him out through a two-way mirror."

"He couldn't see Samira?"

"No."

"Did Yanus have anything in his hands?"

She sighs, irritated at my pedantry.

I press her. "Did he have something in his hands?"

She is about to say no but remembers something. "He had a blue handkerchief. He was pushing it into his fist like a magician preparing a conjuring trick."

How did he find Zala? Nobody knew she was at the convent except the nuns. Sister Vogel wouldn't have given her up. De Walletjes is a small place. What did the lawyer once say to me? The walls have mice and the mice have ears.

Mrs. Caspar listens patiently while I explain what I think happened. Zala is not her concern. She has four hundred asylum seekers on her books.

"What will happen to Samira now?" I ask.

"She will be sent back to Afghanistan, which is I think a better option than marrying Yanus."

"He is not going to marry her."

"No."

"He is going to find her and take her babies."

She shrugs. How can she blithely accept such an outcome? Leaning on the windowsill, she looks down at the courtyard where pigeons peck at the base of a lone tree.

"Some people are born to suffer," she says pensively. "It never stops for them, not for a second. Look at the Palestinians. The same is true of Afghanis and Sudanese, Ethiopians and Bangladeshis. War, famine, droughts, flood, the suffering never stops. They are made for it—sustained by it.

"We in the West like to think it can be different; that we can change these countries and these people because it makes us feel better when we tuck our own children into their warm beds with full stomachs and then pour ourselves a glass of wine and watch someone else's tragedy unfold on CNN." She stares down at her hands as if she despises them. "Unless we truly understand what it's like to walk in their shoes, we should not judge people like Samira. She is only trying to save what she has left."

Something else trembles in her voice. Resignation. Acceptance. Why is she so ready to give up? In that split second I realize there is something that she's not telling me. Either she can't bring herself to do it or Spijker has warned her off. With her innate sense of honesty and justice, she will not lie to me directly.

"What happened to Samira?"

"She went missing last night from the migrant center at Schiphol Airport."

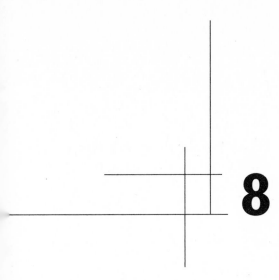

8

There is a scientific theory called the uncertainty principle that
states it is impossible to truly observe something without altering it.
I have done more than observe. By finding Samira I have changed
the course of events.

During the taxi journey to police headquarters my fists are
clenched and my fingernails dig into the soft flesh. I want to scream.
I warned Spijker this would happen. I said Samira would run or
Yanus would find her.

I don't expect him to see me. He will hide behind his workload
or make excuses that I've wasted enough of his time already. Again
I wait in the foyer. This time the summons comes. Perhaps he has a
conscience after all.

The corridors are lined in light gray carpet and dotted with
palms. It feels more like a merchant bank than a police station.

Spijker is jacketless. His sleeves are rolled up. The hair on his
forearms is the color of his freckles. The door closes. His jacket swings
from a hanger behind it.

"How long are you intending to remain in Amsterdam?" he asks.

"Why, sir?"

"You have already stayed longer than is usual. Most visitors are
here for a day or two."

"Are you advising me to leave?"

"I have no authority to do that." He spins on his chair, gazing out the window. His office looks east across the theater district to the neo-Gothic spires of the Rijksmuseum. Lined on the windowsill are tiny cacti in painted clay pots. This is his garden—fleshy, bulbous and spiky.

I had a speech prepared during my taxi ride, when I vented my spleen and caused the taxi driver a few anxious moments, peering into the rear mirror. Now all my best lines seem pointless and wasted. I wait for the detective to speak.

"I know what you think, DC Barba. You think I have dropped the ball on this. That is a rugby term, yes? A British game not a Dutch one. In the Netherlands we do not *pick up* the ball. Only a goalkeeper can do this."

"You should have protected her."

"She *chose* to escape."

"She's eight months pregnant and eighteen years old. You couldn't hold her for twenty-four hours."

"Did you want me to handcuff her?"

"You could have stopped her."

"I am trying to keep this investigation low key. I don't want it reaching the media. Black market babies make dramatic headlines."

"So it was a political decision?"

"There is no politics in the Dutch police."

"No?"

"No one has talked politics to me."

Despite his down-turned mouth and sad eyes, Spijker comes across as an optimist, a man who has faith in the human condition.

"I have twenty years' service. I know how to make a case. I am like the little pig that builds his house out of bricks. You are like the little pig who builds her house from straw. Do you remember what happens to such a house?" He puffs out his cheeks and blows. A flake of cigarette ash swirls from his desk into my lap.

Sporting metaphors and fairy-tale metaphors, what next? He opens the top drawer of his desk, withdrawing a file.

"There is a fertility clinic in Amersfoort. It has a very good reputation and has helped thousands of couples to begin a family. Occasionally, when IVF has been unsuccessful, the clinic has agreed to implant embryos into the uterus of a surrogate mother. This is called gestational surrogacy. In 2002 there were only four such procedures out of 1,500 normal IVF implantations. In 2003 and 2004 there were two in total." He glances at the file. "In the past year there have been twenty-two."

"Twenty-two! That's an increase of more than tenfold."

"Gestational surrogacy is legal in the Netherlands. Commercial surrogacy is not. Nor is blackmail or bonded slavery."

"Directors of the clinic and staff insist they are unaware of any wrongdoing. They also insist the surrogate mothers were properly screened. They were examined physically, financially and psychologically.

"On January 26 this year Samira Khan underwent this examination. She was asked questions about her menstrual cycle and was given pills and injections—estrogen and progesterone—to prepare her uterus for the implantation.

"On February 10 she returned to the clinic. The embryo transfer took less than fifteen minutes. A soft tube was inserted through her vagina to a predetermined position. A small inner catheter was then loaded with two embryos and these were injected into the uterus. Samira Khan was told to lie still for thirty minutes and then discharged. She was taken to the car park in a wheelchair and driven away by Yanus. Her pregnancy was confirmed two weeks later. Twins."

Spijker finally looks up at me. "But you know this already."

There are other papers in his file.

"Do you have the names of the intended parents?"

"Legal contracts are required between couples and the surrogate mothers. The clinic does not draw up these contracts, but requires a written statement from a lawyer confirming they exist."

"Have you seen the contracts?"

"Yes."

For a moment I think he's going to wait for me to ask, but he is not a cruel man.

"Each copy of the contract was signed by Samira Khan and countersigned by Cate Beaumont. Is this what you wish to know?"

"Yes."

He returns the folder to the drawer and rises from his seat, surveying the view from his window with a mixture of pride and protectiveness.

"Of the twenty-two procedures I mentioned, eighteen resulted in pregnancies. One of the failures involved a woman named Zala Haseeb. Doctors discovered she was unable to fall pregnant because of earlier damage to her reproductive organs caused by blunt force trauma."

"She was tortured by the Taliban."

He doesn't turn from the window but I know he hears me.

"Twelve of the surrogate mothers are past term but we have no confirmation of the births. Normally the clinic monitors every stage of the pregnancy and keeps a record of each outcome for statistical purposes. In this case, however, it lost track of the women."

"Lost track of them!"

"We are in the process of finding them. The clinic has provided us with their names but the addresses appear to be fictitious."

"I don't think you'll find any trace of the births in the Netherlands," I say. "I think the mothers were smuggled across borders or overseas to where the intended parents live. This meant the babies could be handed over immediately after they were born and registered without any questions."

Spijker sees the logic of this. "We are tracking the intended parents through financial transactions. There are receipts and statutory declarations."

"Who drew up the contracts?"

"A legal firm here in Amsterdam."

"Are they being investigated?"

Spijker pauses for a brief moment. "You met the senior partner yesterday. He represents Mr. Yanus."

His gaze builds into a stare. For the first time I realize what a burden he carries. I have been chasing the truth about a single woman. He now has a case that touches dozens, perhaps hundreds of people's lives.

Spijker turns away from the window. After a long silence he speaks. "Do you have children?"

"No, sir."

"I have four of them."

"Four!"

"Too many, not enough—I can't decide." A smile flirts with his lips. "I understand what it means to people; how they can want a child so badly that they will do almost anything." He leans slightly forward, inclining his head to one side. "Do you know the legend of Pandora's box, DC Barba?"

"I've heard the term."

"The box didn't belong to Pandora; it was built by the Greek god Zeus and it was crammed full of all the diseases, sufferings, vices and crimes that could possibly afflict humanity. I cannot imagine such a malignant brew. The god Zeus also created Pandora—a beautiful woman, inquisitive by nature. He knew that she wouldn't be able to resist peeking inside the mysterious box. She heard pitiful whispers coming from inside. So she raised the lid just a little. And all the ills of the world flew out, fastening upon the carefree and innocent, turning their cries of joy into wails of despair."

His fingers open showing me his palms. Empty. This is what he fears. An investigation like this risks tearing apart entire families. How many of these babies are in loving homes? Consider how lucky they are when so many children are abused and unwanted. The argument triggers a feeling of déjà vu. Julian Shawcroft had made a similar case when I visited him at the adoption center.

I understand the concerns, but my best friend was murdered. Nothing anyone says to me will justify her death and their ominous warnings sound hollow when I picture Cate lying broken on the road.

The briefing is over. Spijker stands rather formally and escorts me downstairs.

"I spoke to a Chief Superintendent North of Scotland Yard last evening. He informed me that you are absent without leave from the London Metropolitan Police. You are facing disciplinary proceedings for neglect of duty."

There is nothing I can say.

"I also spoke to a Detective Inspector Forbes who is investigating the deaths of illegals on a ferry at Harwich. You are helping him with this investigation. There was also, I think, a Detective Sergeant Softell, who wishes to speak to you about a suspicious fire."

Spijker could have used the term "suspect" but is far too polite.

"These men have asked me to put you on the first available flight back to London, but as I explained to them, I have no authority for this." He pinches the bridge of his nose between his thumb and forefinger. "I also assume you do not wish to leave Amsterdam without your friend Mr. Ruiz. I spoke to him this morning. He is recovering well."

"Yes, sir."

"He has great affection for you."

"We have known each other a long time."

"He believes that you will make a very fine investigator. He used a term I am not familiar with. He said you were 'sharper than a pointy stick.' "

That sounds like the DI.

"I understand why you are here and why you will stay a little longer, but now it is time for you to leave this investigation to me."

"What about Samira?"

"I will find her."

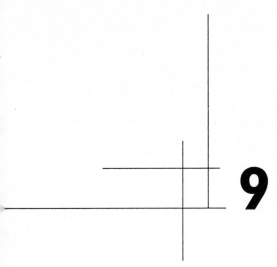

9

I don't normally notice people when I run. I shut out the world, floating over the ground like a vague impression. Today is different. I can hear people talking, arguing and laughing. There are muffled footsteps and car doors closing, the hum of traffic and machines.

"New Boy" Dave is at the hospital with Ruiz. That's where I'm heading, although the strangeness of the city makes it difficult to get my bearings. There are twin church steeples ahead of me. I turn again, running past flat-fronted shops with barred windows or metal shutters. Some of the alleys and lanes are only wide enough for bicycles or pedestrians.

By the time I find the hospital it is almost dark. The corridors are quiet and rain streaks the windows. "New Boy" Dave puts his jacket around my shoulders to stop me from getting cold. Ruiz is asleep.

"How is he?"

"Bored shitless. Today he tried to organize a mass escape from the hospital to the nearest pub. He convinced two guys to join him—both amputees. He said they were legless already so it shouldn't matter."

"How far did they get?"

"As far as the hospital gift shop. One of the nurses uncovered the escape plot and called security."

"What did the DI say?"

"He said the Resistance would spring him tomorrow."

Dave has been talking to the doctors. Ruiz should be able to leave hospital in a few days but he won't be able to fly for a month.

"We can take the ferry," I suggest.

Dave is toying with my fingers, running his thumb across the palm. "I was sort of hoping you might fly home with me tomorrow. I have an Old Bailey trial on Monday."

"I can't leave the DI. We started this together."

He understands. "What are you going to do about the job?"

"I haven't decided."

"You're supposed to have started."

"I know."

There's something else he wants to ask. His forehead creases, wrestling with the question.

"Have you thought about the other thing?" he asks. He's referring to the sailing school and the cottage by the sea. Marriage. The future. I'm still amazed that he plucked up the courage to ask me. The sense of expectation and dread must be killing him. Sometimes life is like the movies, with the audience barracking, "Just ask her. Just ask her."

"I thought you always wanted to be a detective," I say.

"I wanted to be a fireman when I was six. I got over it."

"I fell in love with Mr. Sayer, my piano teacher, and wanted to be a concert pianist."

"I didn't know you played."

"It's still open to debate."

He's waiting for my answer.

"So what happened, Dave? What made you decide to quit?"

He shrugs.

"Something must have triggered it."

"You remember Jack Lonsdale?"

"I heard he got wounded."

Dave silences his hands by putting them in his pockets. "We were following up a tip-off about a bail jumper on the White City Estate. A drug dealer. It's a god-awful place at the best of times but this was Saturday night in mid-July. Hot. We found the place okay and knocked on the door. It was supposed to be a simple pickup. I was putting handcuffs on the dealer when his fifteen-year-old kid came out of the kitchen and stuck a knife in Jack's chest. Right there." He points to the spot. "The kid was hanging off the blade trying to scramble his guts, but I managed to pry him loose. His eyes were like saucers. He was higher than a 747. I tried to get Jack out to the car but there were two hundred people outside the flat, most of them West Indian, screaming abuse and throwing shit. I thought we were gonna die."

"Why didn't you tell me?"

"You had your own shit to deal with."

"How's Jack now?"

"They had to take out part of his bowel and he's taken early retirement. The dealer finished up in Brixton. His kid went to a foster home. His mother was dead, I think."

Dave lowers his eyes, unwilling to look at me. "I know it makes me sound like a coward but I keep thinking how it could have been me spilling blood on that filthy floor—or worse, it could have been you."

"It doesn't make you a coward. It makes you human."

"Yeah, well, that's when I got to thinking about doing something else."

"Maybe you just need a sea change."

"Maybe."

"Maybe you don't really want to marry me."

"Yes I do."

"Would you still want to marry me if we didn't have children?"

"What do you mean?"

"I'm asking."

"But you *want* children, right?"

"What if I couldn't have children?"

Dave straightens up. He doesn't understand.

I try to explain. "Sometimes children just don't arrive. Look at Cate. She couldn't get pregnant and it twisted her up inside until she did something foolish. Don't you think if two people love each other that should be enough?"

"Yeah, I guess."

He still doesn't get my point. There is nowhere else for me to go except the truth. Words tumble out and I'm surprised at how organized they sound. Almost perfect sentences.

A woman's pelvis is meant to expand and tilt forward as a baby grows inside her. Mine can't do this. I have metal plates and rods holding my spine together. My pelvis cannot bend or twist. Pregnancy would put enormous strain on the disks and joints of my lower back. I risk being paralyzed and nursing a baby from a wheelchair.

He looks stunned. Desolate. It doesn't matter what he says now because I have glimpsed his soul. He wants to raise a child. And for the first time in my life, I realize that I want one too. I *want* to be a mother.

In the hours that follow all possibilities are considered. On the taxi ride to the hotel, over dinner, afterward in bed, Dave talks of second opinions, alternatives and operations. We use up so much air in the room that I can scarcely breathe. He hasn't answered my original question. The most important one. He hasn't said if it matters.

While on the subject of true confessions, I tell him about sleeping with Barnaby Elliot and falling out with Cate. There are moments when I see him flinch but he needs to hear this. I am not the person he imagines.

My mother says the truth is unimportant when it comes to love. An arranged marriage is all about the fictions that one family tells another. Perhaps she's right. Perhaps falling in love is about inventing a story and accepting the truth of it.

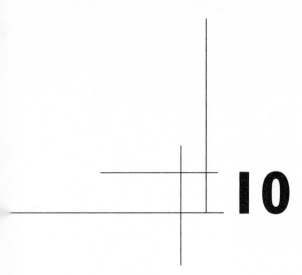

10

I wake in the early hours, with his heart against my back and his arm around me. A part of me wants to stay like this, not moving, scarcely breathing. Another part wants to run down the hotel corridor, the stairs, along the street, out of the city, away!

Slipping out of bed and into the bathroom, I dress in jeans and a blouse and fill the pockets of my jacket with cash and my mobile. I bend to lace my boots, accepting the dull ache in my spine for what it is, a part of me now.

Daylight is leaking over the rooftops and the streets are beginning to stir. A machine with spinning brushes seems to be polishing the cobblestones with overnight rain. Most of the windows are closed in de Walletjes, with curtains drawn. Only the desperate and the lonely are on the streets at this hour.

I wonder if this is what it feels like to be a refugee—to be a stranger in a place, despairing and hopeful all at once. Waiting for what will come next. I have never lived like this.

Hokke is waiting for me at the café. He knows about Samira. "A bird told me," he says, raising his eyes. As if signaled, a pigeon flutters onto a branch above us.

The air inside the café is noisy with whistling steam and banging pots. Counter staff and waitresses acknowledge Hokke with waves, shouts and handshakes. He leaves me for a moment, threading his way between tables. The kitchen door is open. Bending low over sinks, scrubbing pans, are three young men who greet Hokke with respect. He ruffles their hair and shares a joke.

I glance around the café, which is almost empty except for a table of hippies who seem to be communicating in a code of clicks and clacks from their beaded hair. On her own, a young teenage girl nurses a hot drink. Waiflike and hollow-eyed, she is just the sort pimps prey upon with warm meals and promises.

Hokke has returned. He, too, notices the girl. Summoning a waitress, he quietly orders breakfast for the girl, thick toast, jam, cheese and ham. She accepts it warily, expecting there to be strings attached, and eats greedily.

His attention turns to me.

"I have to find Samira," I tell him.

"Again."

"Refugees have networks. You said so. You mentioned a name: de Souza. Could he help me?"

Hokke puts a finger to his lips. He leans closer, speaking out of the corner of his mouth like a prisoner under the eye of a warder. "Please be very careful when you speak such a name."

"Who is he?"

Hokke doesn't answer immediately. He pours coffee from a pot, tapping metal against glass. "Despite what you have read, the Netherlands is defined more by what it forbids than by what it permits. We do not have slums. Graffiti is cleaned away quickly. Broken windows are repaired. Abandoned vehicles are towed. We expect our trains and trams to run on time. We queue. It doesn't change the people, of course, just the aesthetics."

He gestures with a slight nod toward the kitchen. "There are half a million illegal workers in the Netherlands—Iranians, Sudanese, Afghanis, Bosnians, Kosovars, Iraqis. They work in restaurants, hotels, laundries and factories. Newspapers wouldn't be delivered without them, hotel sheets wouldn't be laundered, houses wouldn't be cleaned. People complain, but we cannot do without them."

A pipe appears in his hand. He packs it slowly, pressing tobacco into the bowl with his thumb. A match flares and flickers as he sucks in a breath.

"Imagine a person who could control a workforce such as this. He would be more powerful than any trade union leader or politician."

"Is there such a person?"

His voice drops to a whisper. "His name is Eduardo de Souza. Nobody has more real power in this city than he does. He has an army of couriers, cleaners, drivers and spies. He can get you anything: a pistol, a fake passport, a kilo of the finest Afghani heroin. Drugs and prostitution are only a small part of it. He knows which politicians are sleeping with which girls and which illegals are looking after their children or cleaning their houses or tending their gardens. That is *real* power. Destiny making."

He sits back, his soft blue eyes blinking through the smoke.

"You admire him."

"He is a very interesting man."

His answer strikes me as peculiar. It carries a hint that there are things he hasn't told me.

"How long have you known him?"

"Many years."

"Is he a friend?"

"Friendship is something I find harder to understand as I get older."

"Will he help me find Samira?"

"He could be behind it all."

"Why do you say that?"

"Yanus once worked for him."

He places his hands on the table and wearily pushes himself to his feet.

"I will get a message to him."

His pipe slips into his jacket pocket. He won't let me pay for breakfast. The bill has been covered, he says, nodding toward the owner.

Outside it is raining again. The puddles are shiny and black as oil. Hokke offers me an umbrella. "I will call you in a few hours. Give my regards to DI Ruiz. Tell him that old policemen never die. They just miss a beat."

Barnaby answers his cell phone quickly as if he's been expecting a call. It must also be raining in London. I hear car tires swishing on a wet road and raindrops on his umbrella. I ask about the funerals. There is a long pause. I swap the phone between hands.

"Saturday at the West London Crematorium. They won't release the bodies until Wednesday."

There is another silence. The knowledge of Samira and the twins expands in my chest. Lawyers and medical ethicists can debate all they want about who "owns" the twins, but it doesn't change the fact that Cate provided the embryos. Barnaby should know.

"There's something I have to tell you."

He grunts a response.

"I know why Cate faked her pregnancy. She arranged a surrogate. Her embryos were implanted in someone else's womb."

Something shifts deep in his chest. A groan. "I told you to leave my daughter's affairs alone."

I don't expect this reaction. Surely he must be curious. Doesn't he want to know the outcome? Then it dawns on me that none of this is new. He knows already.

He lied about finding Cate's computer, which means he must have read her e-mails. If he knows, why hasn't he gone to the police?

"What are you doing Barnaby?"

"I'm getting my grandchildren."

He has no idea what he's dealing with. "Listen to me, Barnaby. This isn't what you think. Cate broke the law."

"What's done is done."

"These men are killers. You can't negotiate with them. Look what happened to Cate."

He isn't listening. Instead he charges ahead, trying to attach logic and fairness to what should happen next.

"Stop, Barnaby. This is crazy."

"It's what Cate would have wanted."

"No. You'll get yourself killed. Just tell me where you are. Let's sit down and talk."

"Stay out of this. Don't interfere."

The line goes dead. He won't answer again.

Before I can dial Spijker there is another call. DI Forbes's voice is hoarse with a cold and the clicking sound in his throat is muffled by phlegm. I can imagine one of his children bringing the infection home from school and spreading it through the house like a domestic plague.

"Having a nice holiday?"

"It's not a holiday."

"You know the difference between you and me? I don't run away when things get tough. I'm a professional. I stick with the job. I got a wife and kids, responsibilities . . ."

And wandering hands.

He sneezes and blows his nose. "I'm still waiting for your fucking statement."

"I'm coming home."

"When?"

"By Friday."

"Well you can expect a warm welcome. A Chief Superintendent North has been on the phone. Says you didn't show up for work. He's not happy."

"It's not important," I say, trying to change the subject. I ask him about the two trucks that couldn't be accounted for on the ferry that carried Hassan and the other illegals. One was stolen from a German freight yard three months ago, he says. It was resprayed and registered in Holland. According to the manifest it was carrying plumbing supplies from a warehouse in Amsterdam, but the pickup address doesn't exist. The second truck was leased from an owner-driver five weeks ago. He thought it was doing a run from Spain to the Netherlands. The leasing documents and bank accounts are in false names.

This case is populated with people who seem to be ghosts, floating across borders with false papers. People like Brendan Pearl.

"I need a favor."

He finds this amusing. "I shouldn't even be talking to you."

"We're on the same side."

"Cellar-dwellers."

"Running into form."

"What do you want?"

"I need you to check the Customs and Immigration files for the past two years. Among the stowaways and illegals were any of them pregnant?"

"Off the top of my head I can think of two in the past three months. They were hidden in the back of a container."

"What happened to them?"

"I don't know."

"Can you find out?"

"Yeah, sure. Along with a thousand other fucking things on my plate."

I feel the heat in my cheeks.

"There's something else. Hassan Khan has a sister, Samira. She's pregnant. I think traffickers are going to try to move her into the U.K."

"When?"

"I don't know. You might want to give Customs a heads-up."

"I'm not a free agent here."

"It's only a phone call. If you don't want to do it, just say so."

"How are they going to move her?"

"They'll probably stick to what they know."

"We can't search every truck and container."

I can hear him scratching a note on a pad. He asks me about Spijker and I give him the nuts and bolts of the surrogacy scam.

"I've never known anyone who attracts trouble like you do," he says.

"You sound like my mother."

"Do you take any notice of *her*?"

"Not much."

The call ends and I close my eyes for a moment. When I open them again, I see a class of schoolchildren with their teacher. The girls are dressed like Madeline in navy blue raincoats with yellow hats, and they are all holding hands as they wait for the traffic lights to change. Inexplicably, I feel a lump forming in my throat. I'll never have one of those.

A police car is parked outside the hotel. A uniformed officer waits in reception, standing almost to attention.

"New Boy" Dave hovers like a jealous suitor. "Where have you been?"

"I had to see someone."

He grips my hand tightly.

The officer introduces himself and holds out a police radio. I place it against my ear. Spijker's voice comes from far away. I can hear water. Seagulls. "We've found someone."

"Who is it?"

"I'm hoping you can tell me."

Something soft and wet flips over in my stomach.

The officer takes back the radio to receive further instructions.

"I'll come with you," says Dave.

"What about your flight?"

"There's still time."

We sit in silence on the journey. Frustration is etched into his forehead. He wants to say something planned, thought-out, about last night but it's not the right time.

I feel oddly ambivalent. Maybe that means I'm not ready to marry and I'm not really in love. The whole idea was one of those "what if" moments that doesn't survive the hangover or the harsh light of day.

The Dutch officer has a vocabulary of four English words and is unwilling or unable to explain where we're going. Meanwhile, he navigates the narrow streets and bridges, taking us through an industrial area with docks and warehouses. We seem to pass the same gray squares of water several times before pulling up beside a weathered wooden pier. Police cars nose together as though drinking from the same trough.

Spijker is a head taller than the other detectives. He is wearing a dark suit and polished shoes but still seems miscast in life; as though he's playing dress-up in his father's clothes.

There is a wooden ramp that slopes into the water from the dock. Halfway down it is a Zodiac made of heavy rubberized canvas with a wooden bottom. Another is already waiting on the water with four men on board.

Spijker hands me a pair of rubber boots and a waterproof jacket to wear over my sweater. He finds similar clothes for Dave and then pulls on his own rubber boots.

The Zodiac launches in a fluid movement. Spijker holds out his hand and helps me step on board. The throttle engages and we pull away. The sky is like a solid gray sheet with no depth at all. A quarter mile off I see the flat of a paddle, lifting and dipping, as a canoeist follows the shore. Farther out is a ferry, snub-nosed and puffing smudges of black smoke.

I try to orientate myself. Some six miles to the west is the North Sea. We seem to be following a western dock. The air smells sweet—of chocolate. Perhaps there is a factory nearby. Dave is beside me. I feel him when I rock sideways, brushing his left arm with my breast.

Spijker is comfortable steering a boat. Perhaps it rubs off, living below sea level, protected by dikes and flood barriers.

"How much do you know about the sea, DC Barba?"

What is there to know? It's cold, it's wet, it's salty . . .

"My father was a merchant seaman," he explains without waiting for me to answer. "He divorced my mother when I was seven but I used to spend holidays with him. He didn't go to sea anymore and he wasn't the same man on shore. He seemed smaller."

Dave hasn't said much since I introduced them to each other, but now he mentions the sailing school he wants to buy. Soon they're discussing skiffs and sail area. I can actually picture Dave in an Aran sweater, ducking beneath a boom. He seems suited to outdoors, big spaces full of wind and sky and water.

Five hundred yards ahead of us is a container ship. The Port of Amsterdam spent millions thinking they could match Rotterdam as a hub for international trade, explains Spijker. "It is never going to be so."

Passing the ship, we come to a wooden pier rising twenty feet above the waterline supported by pylons and beams. A floating platform is moored on the nearside.

Spijker disengages the throttle and the engine idles. He steadies the Zodiac and throws a rope around a rusting cleat on the platform, drawing us closer. At the same moment a spotlight is switched on and swings into the darker shadows beneath the pier, searching amid the weathered gray wood. A flash of white appears. A figure suspended above the water, gazing down at me. A noose is looped around her neck. Another rope around her waist disappears into the water, obviously weighted down.

The body swings slightly as if moved by an unseen hand and her outstretched toes seem to pirouette on the surface of the water.

"Is it the deaf girl?" asks Spijker.

Zala's eyes are open. Two crimson orbs. Blood vessels have burst in the whites and her pupils seem to have disappeared. She's dressed in the same skirt and pink jacket that I last saw her wearing. Salt in the air has stiffened the fabric.

The Zodiac is rising and sinking on the slight swell. Spijker steadies it and I step onto the platform. A metal ladder, bolted to a pylon, leads up to the pier. Seagulls watch from the navigation buoys and a nearby barge. The other Zodiac has arrived, carrying ropes and a stretcher cage.

Spijker climbs the ladder and I follow him. Dave is behind me. The planks of the pier are old and deeply furrowed, with gaps in between that are wide enough for me to see the top of Zala's head and her shoulders.

The rope around her neck is tied to a metal bollard normally used for mooring ships.

A police officer in climbing gear abseils over the side. He swings in a harness beside her body and we watch in silence as Zala is lashed into a stretcher cage. The rope around her waist is tied to a cinder block. I can see the cement dust on her hands and the front of her jacket.

They made her jump. The certainty is like a vision. She held the cinder block in her arms and they pushed her the final step. She dropped fifteen feet before the rope stopped her. The cement brick tore from her fingers and kept falling until the second rope, tied around her waist, pulled taut. My stomach shares the drop.

"A fisherman found her just before nine thirty," says Spijker. "He reported it to the coast guard." He swivels to a junior officer, seeking confirmation.

"What made you think . . . ?" I can't finish the question.

"She fitted the description."

"How did she get out here?"

Spijker motions along the pier. "It's fenced off. Warning signs. Of course, that only encourages people."

"You're not thinking suicide?"

"Your deaf girl didn't carry that lump of concrete out here by herself."

In the distance there are whitecaps where the water is less sheltered from the wind. A fishing boat is coming in, its windows flashing in a rare shaft of sunlight.

Despite his veteran's cynicism, Spijker needs to show compassion and offer condolences. Somehow I have become his only link to this girl.

"She came from Kabul. She was an orphan," I explain.

"Another one."

"What do you mean?"

"The list of surrogates from the IVF clinic. At least ten of them were orphans. It's making them difficult to find."

Orphans. Illegal immigrants. What a perfect combination of the unwanted and the desperate.

"Samira mentioned a visitor to the orphanage. A westerner who said he could organize a job for her. He had a cross on his neck. I might know who it is." I give him Donavon's name and he promises to check the files.

The dock gates have been unlocked at the far end of the pier. A forensic team arrives in a van. A second car is summoned to take us back to our hotel.

As I walk along the pier I feel that Amsterdam has changed and become darker and more dangerous. I long for the familiar. Home.

Dave falls into step beside me.

"Are you all right?"

"Fine."

"It's not your fault."

"What do you know about it?" I snap. Straightaway, I feel angry with myself. He's done nothing wrong. After a few minutes I try to assuage my guilt. "Thanks for being here. I'm sorry about last night. Forget everything I said."

"I think we should talk about it some more."

"There's nothing to talk about."

"I love you."

"But it's different now, isn't it?"

Dave puts his hand on my forearm to stop me. "I don't care. I want to be with you."

"You say that now, but think about in five years or ten years. I couldn't do that to you."

An abandoned crane is rusting on the shoreline. It looks like wreckage from an ancient war. Zala's body is still spinning in my mind, pirouetting on her toes in the waves.

I have been a fool. My good intentions have set off a chain of events that have led to this. And I don't know where it ends or who else will be hurt. I am certain of only one thing: I want to spend every waking moment hunting down the people who took Cate from me and who did this to Zala. This is not about an eye for an eye. It's bigger than that. I want to make their misery more poignant and horrific than anything they have inflicted upon others. Never in my life have I felt so capable of killing someone.

———

Dave's hair is combed. His bag is packed. A taxi is booked for the airport. The clock hasn't moved. Not even a second. I swear it. I hate the last hour before someone leaves. Everything has been said and done. Minutes drag out. Statements are repeated. Tickets are checked.

"It's time to leave this alone," says Dave, rinsing his toothbrush. "It's over."

"How did we get to over?"

"Maybe you think," he says, choosing his words with care, "that this is about you and me. It's not. I'd tell you the same thing if I didn't love you."

"But that's why you *should* understand."

He picks up his bag and puts it down again.

"You could come with me."

"I'm not leaving Ruiz."

He puts on his jacket.

"You could stay," I suggest.

"I have to give evidence in court."

"I need you."

"You don't *need* anyone."

It's not meant to wound but I flinch as though struck.

He opens the door slowly. All the while I'm hoping he'll turn back, take me in his arms, force me to look in his eyes, tell me he doesn't care about anything except me, that he understands.

The door closes behind him. My chest is suddenly empty. He's taken my heart.

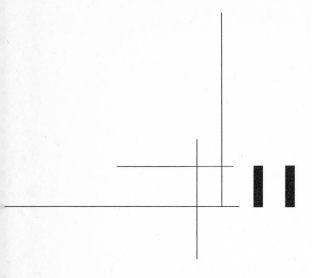

For twenty minutes I stare at the door, wishing it would open, hoping that he'll come back.

When I was lying in hospital with my damaged spine, fearing I would never walk again, I started to say cruel things to people. I criticized nurses and complained about the food. I called one male orderly Fat Albert after the Bill Cosby character.

"New Boy" Dave came to visit me every day. I remember screaming at him and calling him a moron. He didn't deserve it. I felt sorry for myself because everybody else felt sorry for me. And being cruel to people took my mind off myself for a while.

Dave didn't come to see me after that. I wanted to call him. I wanted to say I was sorry for being mad and could he please come back. I didn't. Instead I wrote him a letter. What a gutless wonder! I don't deserve him.

My mobile rattles on the table.

"You didn't come to lunch today."

"I'm still overseas, Mama."

"Your auntie Meena made kulfi. It's your favorite."

It was my favorite at age six.

"All the boys came. Even Hari."

Typical. He doesn't show up unless he can show me up.

"Your friend Detective King phoned to say he couldn't make it."

"I know, Mama."

"But another very eligible gentleman was here. He was disappointed not to see you."

"Whose arm did you twist this time?"

"Dr. Banerjee seems to be very fond of you."

It cannot be a coincidence. "What did he want?"

"He brought you flowers—such a thoughtful man. And his table manners are impeccable."

If we get married I'll have clean tablecloths.

"Where did you tell him I was?"

"I said you were in Amsterdam. You're being very secretive about this. You know I don't like secrets."

She carries on describing the good doctor and a funny story he told her about his baby nephew. I don't hear the punch line. I'm too busy trying to connect him to Samira.

Banerjee collected twelve viable embryos from Cate. Instead of six cycles of IVF, there were only five, which meant two embryos remained, frozen and stored in liquid nitrogen. He gave them to Cate, which means he knew about her surrogacy plan. That's why he arranged an invitation to my father's birthday party. He tried to warn me off.

"I have to go, Mama."

"When will you be home?"

"Soon."

I hang up and call "New Boy" Dave, who is just boarding his flight.

"Does this mean you miss me?"

"It's a given. I need a favor."

He sighs. "Just the one?"

"When you get back to London, run a ruler over Dr. Sohan Banerjee."

"He was at your father's party."

"That's him."

"What do you want to know?"

"Does he have any links with fertility clinics outside of the U.K.? Also check if he has any links with adoption agencies or children's charities."

"I'll see what I can do."

A stewardess is telling him to turn off his phone.

"Safe journey."

"You too."

Forbes's cold is getting worse and he's developed a seal-like cough punctuated by the clicking in his throat. He sounds like a boom box.

"You should have stayed home," I suggest.

"My house is full of sick people."

"So you decided to infect the rest of the population."

"That's me. Patient Zero."

"Did you find them—the pregnant asylum seekers?"

"I should have locked you up when I had the chance." He blows his nose. "They arrived in early July hidden in a shipping container. A Russian, aged eighteen, and an Albanian, twenty-one. Both looked ready to drop any time. They were fingerprinted, issued with identification papers and taken to a reception center in Oxfordshire. Three days later they were taken to a bed-and-breakfast accommodation in Liverpool. They had two weeks to fill out a statement of evidence form and meet with a lawyer but neither of them showed up. They haven't been seen since."

"What about the babies?"

"There's no record of the births at any NHS hospital but that doesn't prove anything. A lot of people have them at home these days—even in the bath. Thank Christ our tub wasn't big enough."

I have a sudden mental image of his wife, whalelike in the family bathtub.

"It still doesn't make much sense," he says. "One of the attractions of the U.K. for asylum seekers is free health care. These women could have had their babies in an NHS hospital. The government also provides a one-off grant of £300 for a newborn baby, as well as extra cash for milk and nappies. This is on top of the normal food vouchers and income support. These women claimed to have no family or friends in the U.K. who could support them, yet they didn't take advantage of the welfare benefits on offer. Makes you wonder how they survived."

"Or if they did."

He doesn't want to go there.

Ruiz is waiting for me downstairs at the Academisch Medisch Centrum. He looks like a kid being picked up from summer camp, without the peeling nose or poison ivy stings.

"The staff wished me a long and healthy life," he says. "They also told me never to get sick in the Netherlands again."

"Touching."

"I thought so. I'm a medical bloody miracle." He holds up the stump of his missing finger and begins counting. "I've been shot, almost drowned and now stabbed. What's left?"

"They could blow you up, sir."

"Been tried. Brendan Pearl and his IRA chummies fired a mortar into a Belfast police station. Missed me by that much." He does his Maxwell Smart impersonation.

He pauses at the revolving door. "Have you been crying, grasshopper?"

"No, sir."

"I thought you might have been pining."

"Not pining, sir."

"Women are allowed to be warm and fuzzy."

"You make me sound like a stuffed animal."

"With very sharp teeth."

He's in a good mood. Maybe it's the morphine. It doesn't last long. I tell him about Zala and can see the tension rise to his shoulders and move to his neck. His eyes close. He takes a ragged breath as though the pain has suddenly returned.

"They're going to smuggle Samira into Britain," I say.

"You can't be certain of that."

"It happened to the others. The babies are delivered in the same country as the parents lived."

"The Beaumonts are dead."

"They'll find other buyers."

"Who are *they*?"

"Yanus. Pearl. Others."

"What does Spijker say?"

"He says I should go home."

"A wise man."

"Hokke says there is someone who might help us find Samira."

"Who is he?"

"Eduardo de Souza. Yanus used to work for him."

"This gets better and better."

My mobile is ringing. Hokke is somewhere noisy. The red light district. He spends more time there now than when he was walking the beat.

"I will pick you up at seven from the hotel."

"Where are we going?"

"Answers at seven."

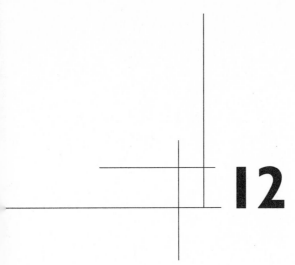

12

An enormous dishwater moon has risen in the east and seems to move across the sky, following our taxi. Even in darkness I recognize some of the roads. Schiphol Airport is not far from here.

This is a different area of Amsterdam. The chocolate-box façades and historic bridges have been replaced by the functional and harsh—cement-gray apartment blocks and shops protected by metal shutters. Only one store is open. A dozen black youths are standing outside.

De Souza doesn't have a fixed address, Hokke explains. He moves from place to place, never staying more than a night in any one bed. He lives with the people he employs. They protect him.

"Be very careful what you say to him. And don't interrupt when he speaks. Keep your eyes down and your hands by your sides."

We have pulled up outside an apartment block. Hokke opens the door for me.

"Aren't you coming with me?"

"You must go alone. We will wait here."

"No," declares Ruiz. "I am going with her."

Hokke responds with equal passion. "She goes alone or there will be nobody waiting to meet her."

Ruiz continues to protest but I push him back into the car where he grimaces as he folds his arms across his bandaged chest.

"Remember what I told you," says the Dutchman, pointing toward a building that is identical to the one next to it and the one next to that. A teenage boy leans against a wall. A second one watches us from an upstairs window. Lookouts. "You must go now. Phone me if there's a problem."

I walk away from the taxi. The boy leaning against the wall has gone. The second teenager is still at the window. I walk through a concrete archway into a quadrangle. Lights shine on water. Chinese lanterns are strung from the branches of a leafless tree growing amid the weeds.

Pushing through a fire door, I climb the stairs, counting off the floors. Turning left at the landing, I find the second door. A bell sounds when I push a small white button.

Another teenager appears at the door. His polished black eyes examine me but turn away when I meet his gaze. Shoes and sandals are lined up in the narrow hallway. The teenager points to my boots. I take them off.

The floor creaks idly as I follow him to a living area. A group of five men in their forties and fifties are seated on cushions arranged at the edges of a woven rug.

Eduardo de Souza is immediately recognizable because of his place at the center. Dressed in white pantaloons and a dark shirt, he looks Turkish or possibly Kurdish, with a high forehead and carved cheekbones. Unfurling his legs, he rises and touches my hand briefly.

"Welcome, Miss Barba, I am Eduardo de Souza."

His neatly trimmed beard is black and gray—the gray like slivers of ice hanging on dark fur. Nobody speaks or moves, yet there is a perceptible energy in the air, a sharpening of focus. I keep my gaze down as eyes roam over me.

Through the doorway to the kitchen I spy a young Nigerian woman in a flowing dress of bright colors. Three children, two boys and a girl, jostle at the doorway, regarding me with fascination.

De Souza speaks again. "These are friends of mine. This is Sunday. He is our host this evening."

Sunday smiles. He is Nigerian and his teeth are a brilliant white. Each of the men introduces himself in turn. The first is Iranian with a Swiss German accent. His name is Farhad and his eyes are set so deep in his skull that I can scarcely see them. Beside him is Oscar, who looks Moroccan and speaks with a French accent.

Finally, there is Dayel, a smooth-shaven Indian, with an oil burn on his neck.

"One of your countrymen, although not a Sikh," says de Souza. Dayel smiles at the introduction.

How does he know I'm a Sikh?

There is a spare brocade cushion beside him. I am expected to sit. Sunday's wife enters the room carrying a tray of mismatched glasses and begins pouring sweet tea. Her hair is braided into a curtain of long beaded plaits. She smiles shyly at me. Her teeth are perfect and her wide nose flares gently as she breathes.

Dishes arrive. A meal. Holding his hands together, de Souza studies me above his steepled fingers, weighing up whether or not to help me. His English is perfect, overlaid with an educated British accent that is especially noticeable on the long vowels.

"This area of Amsterdam is called Bijlmermeer," he says, glancing at the window. "In October 1992 a cargo jet took off from Schiphol and lost two engines. It buried itself into an apartment block like this one, full of immigrant families who were sitting down to an evening meal. Fifty apartments were destroyed by the initial impact. Another hundred burned afterward as jet fuel ran through the streets like a river of fire. People threw themselves off balconies and rooftops to escape the flames.

"At first they said the death toll was 250. Later they dropped the estimate to 75 and officially only 43 people died. The truth is, nobody knows the true number. Illegal immigrants have no papers and they hide from the police. They are ghosts."

De Souza hasn't touched the food, but seems particularly satisfied to see the others eating.

"Forgive me, Miss Barba, I talk too much. My friends here are too polite to tell me to be quiet. It is customary for a guest to bring something to the feast or provide some form of entertainment. Do you sing or dance?"

"No."

"Perhaps you are a storyteller."

"I don't really understand."

"You will tell us a story. The best of them seem to me to be about life and death, love and hate, loyalty and betrayal." He waves his hand as if stirring the air. His amber eyes are fixed on mine.

"I am not a very good storyteller."

"Let us be the judge of that."

I tell him the story of two teenage girls who met at school and became best friends. Soul mates. Later, at university, one of them slept with the other's father. He seduced her. She allowed herself to be seduced. The friendship was over.

I don't mention names, but why would I tell them such a personal story?

Seamlessly, I begin talking about a second pair of teenage girls, who met in a city of widows and orphans. People traffickers smuggled them out of Afghanistan as far as Amsterdam. They were told that they owed a debt for their escape. Either they became prostitutes or carried a baby for a childless couple. Virgins were implanted with embryos in a ritualized form of medical rape. They were the perfect incubators. Factories. Couriers.

Even as I tell this story, a sense of alarm dries my throat. Why have I told de Souza such personal stories? For all I know he is involved. He could be the ringleader. I don't have time to consider the implications. I don't know if I care. I have come too far to back out.

There is a moment of silence when I finish. De Souza leans forward and takes a chocolate from a platter, rolling it over his tongue before chewing it slowly.

"It is a good story. Friendship is a difficult thing to define. Oscar here is my oldest friend. How would you define friendship, Oscar?"

Oscar grunts slightly, as though the answer is obvious. "Friendship is about choice and chemistry. It cannot be defined."

"But surely there is something more to it than that."

"It is a willingness to overlook faults and to accept them. I would let a friend hurt me without striking back," he says, smiling, "but only once."

De Souza laughs. "Bravo, Oscar, I can always rely on you to distill an argument down to its purest form. What do you think, Dayel?"

The Indian rocks his head from side to side, proud that he has been asked to speak next.

"Friendship is different for each person and it changes throughout our lives. At age six it is about holding hands with your best friend. At sixteen it is about the adventure ahead. At sixty it is about reminiscing." He holds up a finger. "You cannot define it with any one word, although honesty is perhaps the closest word—"

"No, not honesty," Farhad interrupts. "On the contrary, we often have to protect our friends from what we truly think. It is like an unspoken agreement. We ignore each other's faults and keep our confidences. Friendship isn't about being honest. The truth is too sharp a weapon to wield around someone we trust and respect. Friendship is about self-awareness. We see ourselves through the eyes of our friends. They are like a mirror that allows us to judge how we are traveling."

De Souza clears his throat now. I wonder if he is aware of the awe he inspires in others. I suspect he is too intelligent and too human to do otherwise.

"Friendship cannot be defined," he says sternly. "The moment we begin to give reasons for being friends with someone we begin to undermine the magic of the relationship. Nobody wants to know that they are loved for their money or their generosity or their beauty or their wit. Choose one motive and it allows a person to say, 'Is that the *only* reason?' "

The others laugh. De Souza joins in with them. This is a performance.

He continues: "Trying to explain why we form particular friendships is like trying to tell someone why we like a certain kind of music or a particular food. We just do."

He focuses on me now. "Your friend's name is Cate Beaumont."

How does he know that?

"Were you ever jealous of her?"

"I don't know what you mean."

"Friends can be jealous of each other. Oscar, here, is envious of my position and my wealth."

"Not at all, my friend," he beseeches.

De Souza smiles knowingly. "Did you envy Cate Beaumont's beauty or her success?"

"Sometimes."

"You wished she had less and you had more."

"Yes."

"That is natural. Friendships can be ambiguous and contradictory."

"She is dead now," I add, although I sense he knows this already.

"She paid money for a baby. A criminal act," he states piously.

"Yes."

"Are you trying to protect her?"

"I'm trying to rescue the surrogate mother and the babies."

"Perhaps you want a baby for yourself?"

My denial is too strident. I make it worse. "I have never . . . I don't . . ."

He reaches into a small pouch tied to the belt of his tunic. "Do you think I am a criminal, Miss Barba?"

"I don't know enough—"

"Give me your opinion."

I pause. The faces in the circle watch with a mixture of amusement and fascination.

"It's not up to me to say," I stammer.

Silence. Perspiration leaks into the hollow of my back, weaving between the bumps of my vertebrae.

De Souza is waiting. He leans close, his face only inches from mine. His bottom teeth are brittle and jagged, yellowing like faded newsprint. It is not such a perfect face after all.

"You can offer me nothing," he says dismissively.

I can feel the situation slipping away from me. He is not going to help me.

The anger fermenting inside me, fueled by hostile thoughts and by images of Zala, suddenly finds an escape valve. Words tumble out. "I think you're a criminal and a misogynist but you're not an evil man. You don't exploit children or sell babies to the highest bidder." I point to Sunday's wife who has come to collect our plates. "You would not ask this woman, the wife of a friend, to give up one of her children or force her to have another woman's baby. You support asylum seekers and illegal immigrants; you give them jobs and find them homes. They respect and admire you. We can stop this trade. I can stop it. Help me."

Sunday's wife is embarrassed at having been singled out. She continues collecting the plates, eager to get away. The tension in the room is amplified by the stillness. Every man's eyes are upon me. Oscar makes a choking noise. He would slit my throat in a heartbeat.

De Souza stands abruptly. The meeting is finished. Oscar takes a step toward me. De Souza signals for him to stop. Alone, he walks me to the front door and takes my hand. Pressed between his fingers is a small scrap of paper.

The door closes. I do not look at the message. It's too dark to read it. The taxi is waiting. I slide into the backseat and lean against Ruiz as I close the car door. Hokke tells the driver to go.

The note is rolled into a tube, wedged between my thumb and forefinger. My hands are shaking as I unroll it and hold it up to the inside light.

Five words. Handwritten. "She leaves tonight from Rotterdam."

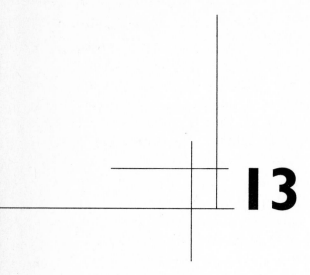

13

Our taxi driver takes an entry ramp onto a motorway.

"How far is it?"

"Seventy-five kilometers."

"What about the port?"

"Longer."

I look at my watch. It's 8:00 p.m.

"The Port of Rotterdam is forty kilometers long," says Hokke. "There are tens of thousands of containers, hundreds of ships. How are you going to find her?"

"We need a ship's name," says Ruiz.

"Or a sailing time," echoes Hokke.

I stare at the slip of paper. It's not enough. We can't phone ahead and alert Customs or the police. What would we tell them?

"Most likely they want to smuggle her into the U.K.," I say. "They've used Harwich before."

"They might choose an alternative port this time."

"Or stick to what they know."

Hokke shakes his head. It is a wild impossible chase. Rotterdam is the biggest container port in Europe. He has an idea. A friend, a former police officer, works for a private security firm that patrols some of the terminals.

Hokke calls him. They chat to each other gruffly, in stern sentences full of Dutch consonants. Meanwhile, I follow the brightly lit motorway signs, counting down the kilometers and the minutes. In the moonlight I can make out wind turbines like ghostly giants marching across the fields.

Trucks and semis are nose-to-tail in the outside lane. I wonder if Samira could be inside one of them. What must it be like? Deafening. Black. Lonely.

Hokke finishes the call and outlines the possibilities. Security is tight around the terminals and docks with CCTV cameras on the fences and regular dog patrols. Once inside there are Customs checks, heat-seeking scanners and more dogs. More than six and a half million shipping containers pass through the port every year. These have to be specially sealed. Empty containers awaiting transfer are a different story but even if someone breached the security and reached the containers, they wouldn't know which ship it was meant to be loaded on unless they had inside information.

"Which means they're more likely to target a truck *before* it reaches the port," says Ruiz. "One they know is traveling to the U.K."

Hokke nods. "We're probably looking at roll-on, roll-off ferries. There are two major ferry operators doing North Sea crossings. Stena Line has a terminal on the Hook of Holland. P&O operates from a dock fifteen kilometers farther east, closer to the city."

We're still twenty miles away and it's nearly eight thirty.

Hokke makes another call, getting a timetable of departures, calling out the details. A P&O ferry sails for Hull at nine o'clock. The Stena Line night ferry to Harwich leaves at eleven. Both arrive in the U.K. in the early hours of tomorrow morning.

"Are you carrying a passport, grasshopper?"

"Yes, sir."

"You want to take the first ferry or the second?"

"I'll take the second."

Ruiz nods in agreement. "Anyone know the weather forecast?"

Hokke is on the mobile to P&O seeing if they will hold the passenger gates open. They're supposed to close fifteen minutes before departure, which means we won't make it.

We're basing our assumptions on a ratio of about 2 percent detail and 98 percent desire. Even if Samira is on board one of the ferries, she won't be mingling with other passengers. They'll keep her hidden. How are we going to find her?

My mind aches when I think about her. I made promises. I said I would find Zala and keep her safe. What am I going to say to her?

De Souza asked if I wanted the babies for myself. It was a ridiculous suggestion. Why would he say that? I'm doing this for Cate and for Samira. For the twins.

The docks are lit up for miles. Cranes and gantries act as massive lighting towers, painting the hulls of ships and rows of stacked containers. The water is dark and solid in between, and the waves are hardly waves at all, they're wrinkles on a sluggish river.

The taxi pulls up outside the P&O terminal. Ruiz is out the door before we stop moving. A week of maddening pain and morphine won't slow him down.

"Good luck," he yells without turning back. "I'm going to find her first."

"Yeah, right. You'll spend your entire time throwing up."

His hand rises. One finger extends.

The Stena Line terminal is at the western edge of the port where the Hook of Holland reaches out into the North Sea. The taxi drops me and I say goodbye to Hokke.

"I can never repay you."

"But you will," he laughs, pointing to the meter.

I give him all my remaining Euros for he still has to get home.

He kisses me three times—left cheek, right cheek and left cheek again.

"Be careful."

"I will."

I have an hour until the *Stena Britannica* leaves. The ship dominates the skyline, towering over the surrounding structures. It is the length of two football fields and the height of a fifteen-story building, with twin stacks that slope backward and give the impression, although not the conviction, of speed.

Seagulls circle and swoop for insects in the beam of the spotlights. They appear so graceful in flight yet they squabble like fishwives on the ground. And they always sound so desperately sad, wailing in misery like creatures already condemned to hell.

Many trucks and trailers are already on board. I can see them lined up on the open decks, a few feet apart, buttressed hard against the stern railings. More trucks are queuing on the loading ramp. Meanwhile cars and vans are being marshaled in a different parking area, waiting their turn.

A young woman in the ticket office wears a light blue skirt and matching jacket, like a maritime stewardess. "You will need to write down the details of your vehicle," she says.

"I don't have a vehicle."

"I'm sorry but there is no pedestrian footbridge on this service. We cannot board foot passengers."

"But I have to catch this ferry."

"That is not possible." She glances over my shoulder. "Perhaps . . . ?"

An elderly couple has just pulled up in an early-model Range Rover towing an old-fashioned caravan that looks like a Cinderella pumpkin carriage. The driver is bald with a small goatee that could be a shaving oversight. His wife is twice his size, wearing acres of denim across her hips. They look Welsh and sound Welsh.

"What is it, pet?" she asks, as I interrupt their cup of thermos tea.

"They won't let me onto the ferry as a foot passenger. I really need to get back to England. I was wondering if I could ride with you."

Husband and wife look at each other.

"Are you a terrorist?" he asks.

"No."

"Are you carrying drugs?"

"No."

"Do you vote Tory?"

"No."

"Are you a Catholic?"

"No."

He winks at his wife. "Clear on all counts."

"Welcome aboard," she announces, thrusting out her hand. "I'm Bridget Jones. Not the fat one from the movies—the fatter one from Cardiff. This is Bryce, my husband."

The Range Rover is packed to the gunwales with suitcases, shopping bags and duty-free: Dutch cheeses, French sausage, two cases of Stella Artois, a bottle of Baileys Irish Cream and assorted souvenirs.

They are very cute. A twee couple, with matching lumbar cushions and traveling mugs. Mr. Jones is wearing driving gloves with cut-off fingers and she has road maps, color-coded in a pocket on the dashboard.

"We've been to Poland," she announces.

"Really?"

"Nobody we know has ever been to Poland. Not even our friends Hettie and Jack from the caravanning club, who think they've been everywhere."

"And to Estonia," her husband adds. "We've done 3,264 miles since we left home on August 28." He strokes the steering wheel. "She's managed eighteen mile to the gallon, which is pretty bloody good for an old girl, especially after that bad batch of diesel in Gdansk."

"Gdansk was very dodgy," agrees his wife.

"It must be cold to be caravanning."

"Oh, we don't mind," she giggles. "A spouse is better than a hot water bottle."

Mr. Jones nods. "I get pretty good mileage out of this old girl."

I don't know if he's referring to his wife or still talking about the car.

Ahead of us the traffic is moving. Vehicles pull onto the ramp and disappear inside, maneuvered into marked lanes barely wide enough for their axles. Engines are turned off. The caravan is strapped down. Men in fluorescent vests direct us to the air-lock doors, which lead to stairs and lifts.

"Don't dawdle, pet," says Mrs. Jones. "The buffet is included in the price. You want to beat the queue."

Mr. Jones nods. "They do a fine apple crumble and custard."

A key card is included with my ticket. It corresponds to a cabin on one of the accommodation decks. Deck 8 has signs asking passengers to be quiet because truck drivers are sleeping. Some of them must have boarded hours ago. How am I going to find Samira?

I don't bother visiting my cabin. I have no luggage to stow. Instead I study the ship's floor plan, which is bolted to the wall near an emergency exit. There are four vehicle decks which are restricted to authorized personnel during the voyage. Deck 10 is crew only. It must be the bridge.

The corridors between the cabins are just wide enough for two people to pass. I search them, looking for the familiar or the unfamiliar. This used to be my job when I worked for the Diplomatic Protection Group—looking for small changes, trying to sense the presence of someone in a crowd or notice their absence in the instant of looking. It could be a person who doesn't belong or who tries too hard to belong or who draws the eye for some other reason.

The ship's engines have started. I can feel the faint vibrations through my feet and they seem to transfer to my nerve endings.

The buffet is being served in the Globetrotter Restaurant. Most of the passengers seem to be truck drivers, dressed in jeans and T-shirts. Food is piled high on their plates—congealed curries, cottage pie, vegetarian lasagna. Big engines need refueling.

The Dutch drivers are playing cards, while the British drivers smoke and read tabloids. The ferry has slipped its moorings and pulled out into the river. As the shore lights slide past the window, it feels as though the land is moving and not the ferry. England is five hours away.

Hokke was right. This haystack is too big. I could search the ferry for weeks and not find Samira. She could be locked in a truck or in one of the cabins. She might not even be on board. Perhaps de Souza had no intention of letting me find her and was simply getting me out of the Netherlands.

The cavernous vehicle decks are below me. Some are open to the elements while others are enclosed. I have to search them. How? Do I hammer on the side of each truck, calling her name? Will she answer?

If there's any chance at all that she's on board, I have to find her. Running along the gangways and up the stairs, I stop people and show them Samira's photograph. I'm doubling back on myself, lost in a maze. Have I been down this corridor before? Is that the same passenger I asked earlier? Most of them are in their cabins now, lying down to sleep.

I turn another corner and suddenly I feel it. A shiver in the air. It's an uncanny sensation, as if I'm prescient. Along a long corridor, a figure with his back to me pauses to unlock a cabin door. I see a quarter profile and suddenly flatten myself against a wall. My phantoms are following me.

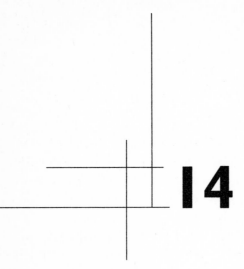

14

The ferry shifts and I brace myself. We must have reached open water, or maybe it's my heart lurching. I am sure it was *him*. Brendan Pearl. He is here because *she* is here.

My first reaction is to retreat. I pull back and take a few deep breaths on the stairwell, while contemplating what to do. Taking out my mobile, I check the signal. Nothing. The ferry has moved out of range. I should talk to the captain. He can radio ahead and get a message to Forbes.

A member of the crew is climbing the stairs. Although dressed in dark trousers and a white shirt with epaulettes, he looks too young to be at sea. He has a name tag on his chest. Raoul Jakobson.

"Do you have keys to all the cabins?" I ask.

"Is there a problem?"

"There is a man on board who is wanted by the British police. He is staying in cabin 8021." I point along the passage. His gaze follows my outstretched hand. "I am a British police officer. A detective constable. Is there a passenger list?" I show him my badge.

"Yes, of course."

He opens a door marked AUTHORIZED PERSONNEL ONLY and retrieves a clipboard, running his finger down the page until he finds the cabin number.

"That cabin is occupied by a Patrick Norris. He is a British driver."

Pearl has a new identity.

Is it possible to find out what vehicle he drove on board?"

Raoul consults the list again. "V743 LFB. On Deck 5."

"I need to check this vehicle."

"Passengers are not authorized to be on that deck."

"I'm looking for an illegal passenger. She could be locked inside the truck."

"Perhaps you should talk to the captain."

"Yes, of course, but there isn't time right now. *You* go to the captain. I need him to send a message to this man," I scribble a phone number on the clipboard. "His name is Detective Inspector Robert Forbes. Mention my name. Tell him that Brendan Pearl is on this ferry."

"Is that it?"

"He'll understand."

Raoul looks at the phone number and glances down the passage toward Pearl's cabin.

"Is he dangerous, this man?"

"Yes, but nobody is to panic. Let him sleep." I look at my watch. "We'll be in Harwich in four hours." Moving toward the stairwell, I nod goodbye. "Tell the captain. I have to go."

Taking the stairs two at a time, I swing through the landings and reach Deck 5. Hitting the red button, I hear the air hiss out as the seal is broken. The metal door slides open. The noise of the ship's engines is amplified in the cavernous space and transfers through the floor in pulsing vibrations.

Stepping over the lip of the door, I begin walking down the first line of vehicles. The trucks are parked seven abreast and nose-to-tail, so close together there is just enough room to squeeze between them. I wish I had a torch. The strip lighting can barely cut through the gloom and I have difficulty reading the vehicle numbers.

I walk the length of the deck and back again, following the lanes. When the ferry pitches and rolls in the swell, I brace my hand against a wheel arch or trailer. My imagination puts me inside them. I can picture Hassan and the others, trapped, suffocating. I want to hammer on the metal sides and fling open the doors, filling them with air.

I'm in the second lane on the starboard side when I find it. The rig has a maroon Mercedes cab and a white box trailer. Stepping onto the running board, I grip the side mirror and pull myself up to peer into the cab. Takeaway coffee cups and food wrappers litter the floor.

Stepping down, I slowly circle the trailer. Pressing my ear against the steel skin I listen for a sneeze or a cough or a whisper, any sound at all. Nothing. The rear doors are sealed with a metal rod and cam lock. The barrel is closed and padlocked.

Someone holding a torch is walking toward me. The beam swings from side to side, blinding me momentarily. I edge away from the trailer. Darkness feathers around me.

"You're not supposed to be down here," says a voice.

At that same moment a hand snakes around my face, cupping my mouth. Smothering all sound away.

I can't breathe. My feet are off the ground. His fingers are digging into my cheek, tearing at my gums. His other forearm wraps around my neck, searching for my windpipe. I brace my hands against it and kick backward, trying to find his instep or his knee. The blow barely touches him.

He lifts me higher. My toes scrabble at the floor, unable to get leverage. I can hear blood pulsing in my ears. I need to breathe.

Karate training taught me about pressure points. There is one in the soft flesh between the thumb and forefinger, above the webbing. I find the spot. He grunts in pain, releasing his grip on my mouth and nose. I still can't breathe. My windpipe is being crushed. I keep driving my thumb into his flesh.

A knee snaps into my kidneys. The pain is like a blast of heat. I don't let go of his right hand but at the same time I can't see his left fist cocking. The punch is like a punctuation mark. Darkness sweeps away the pain and the memories. I am free of the ferry and the incessant noise of the engines. Free of Cate and Samira. Free of the unborn twins. Free at last.

———————

Slowly the world becomes wider. Lighter. I am suspended for a moment a few inches above my body, staring down at a strange scene.

My hands are bound with electrical tape behind my back. Another piece of tape covers my mouth, wrapped around my head like a mask, pulling at my split and swollen lip.

There is a weak light from a torch, lying on the floor near my feet. My head is on Samira's lap. She leans forward and whispers something in my ear. She wants me to lie still. Light catches her pupils. Her fingers are like ice.

My head is pressed to her womb. I feel her babies moving. I can hear the sough and gurgle of the fluid, the melody of their heartbeats. Blood slides back and forth beneath her skin, squeezing into smaller and smaller channels, circulating oxygen.

I wonder if twins are aware of each other's existence. Do they hear the other's heartbeat? Do they hold each other or communicate by touch?

Bit by bit the confusion and darkness work their way into some semblance of order. If I stay relaxed, I can breathe through the tape.

Samira's body suddenly spasms and jackknifes from the waist, squeezing my head against her thighs. Regaining control, she leans back and breathes deeply. I try to lift my head. She wants me to lie still.

I can't talk with the gag. She hooks her fingers beneath the plastic tape and lifts it away from my lips just enough for me to speak.

"Where are we?"

"In a truck."

Our whispers are magnified by the hollowness.

"Are you all right?"

She shakes her head. Tears form at the edge of her eyes. Her body convulses again. She's in labor.

"Who brought me here?"

"Yanus."

He and Pearl must be working together.

"You have to untie me."

Her eyes sweep to the closed rear doors and she shakes her head.

"Please."

"They will kill you."

They will kill me anyway.

"Help me to sit up."

She lifts my head and shoulders until I'm leaning with my back against a wall. My inner gyroscope is totally messed up. I may have ruptured an eardrum.

The trailer appears to be full of pallets and crates. Through a square narrow opening I see a crawl space with a mattress and three plastic bottles. Someone has built a false wall to create a secret compartment in the trailer. Customs officers wouldn't notice the difference unless they measured the outside and inside of the truck.

"When did the contractions start?"

She looks at me helplessly. She has no way of judging time.

"How far are they apart?"

"A minute."

How long was I unconscious? Raoul will have gone to the ferry's captain by now. They will telephone Forbes and come looking for me. Forbes will tell them to be careful.

"Undo my hands."

Samira shakes her head.

Letting go of the tape, she tugs a blanket around my shoulders. She is more worried about me than herself.

"You should not have come."

I can't reply. Another contraction contorts her face. Her entire body seems to lock up.

The rear doors swing open. I feel the draft and hear the intake of Samira's breath.

"I told you not to touch her," says Yanus, springing into the trailer. He seizes her, smearing his hands over her face as if covering her with filth. Then he peels back her lips, forcing her jaw open and spits into her mouth. She gags and tries to turn away.

Then he confronts me, ripping off the gag. It feels like half my face is torn off with it.

"Who knows you're here?"

My voice is slurred: "The captain. The crew . . . they're radioing ahead."

"Liar!"

Another figure is standing in the open end of the trailer. Brendan Pearl. He can't have been there for more than a few seconds yet I have the sensation that he's been watching me for a long time.

The light behind him washes out his features, but I can see how he's changed his appearance since I saw him last. His hair is shorter and he's wearing glasses. The walking stick is a nice touch. He's holding it upside down. Why? It's not a walking stick. It has a curved hook like a fishing gaff or a marlin spike. I remember what Ruiz called him—the Shankhill Fisherman.

Yanus kicks me in the stomach. I roll once and he places a shoe on my neck, forcing it down, concentrating his weight on the point where my spine joins my skull. Surely it must snap.

Samira cries out, her body wracked by another contraction. Pearl says something and Yanus lifts his foot. I can breathe. He circles the empty trailer and returns, putting his heel on my neck again.

I force my arms out, pointing toward Samira. She is staring at her hands in horror. Liquid stains her skirt and pools beneath her knees.

Pearl pushes Yanus aside.

"Her water has broken." Desperately, I choke the words out.

"She pissed herself," sneers Yanus.

"No. She's having the babies."

"Make them stop," says Pearl.

"I can't. She needs a doctor."

Another contraction arrives, stronger than before. Her scream echoes from the metal walls. Pearl loops the barbed hook around her neck. "She makes another sound like that and I'll take out her throat."

Samira shakes her head, covering her mouth with her hands.

Pearl pulls me into a sitting position and cuts the electrical tape away from my wrists. He pauses for a moment, chewing at his cheek like a cud.

"She don't look so healthy does she?" he says, in an Irish lilt.

"She needs a doctor."

"Can't have no doctors."

"But she's having twins!"

"I don't care if she's having *puppies*. You'll have to deliver them."

"I don't know how to deliver a baby!"

"Then you better learn quick."

"Don't be stupid—"

The stave of the marlin spike strikes my jaw. When the pain passes, I count teeth with my tongue. "Why should I help you?"

"Because I'll kill you if you don't."

"You're going to kill me anyway."

"Know that, do you?"

Samira's hand shoots out and grips my wrist. Her knuckles are white and the pain is etched on her face. She wants help. She wants the pain to go away. I glance at Pearl and nod.

"That's grand as grand can be." He stands and stretches, twirling the spike in his fist.

"We can't do it here," I say. "We need to get her to a cabin. I need light. Clean sheets. Water."

"No."

"Look at this place!"

"She stays here."

"Then she dies! And her babies die! And whoever is paying you will get nothing."

I think Pearl is going to hit me again. Instead he weighs the wooden stave in both hands before swinging it down until the metal hook touches the floor and he leans on it like a walking stick. He and Yanus converse in whispers. Decisions have to be made. Their plan is unraveling.

"You have to try to hold on," I tell Samira. "It's going to be OK."

She nods, far calmer than I am.

Why hasn't anyone come looking for me? Surely they will have called Forbes by now. He'll tell them what to do.

Pearl comes back.

"OK, we move her." He raises his shirt to show me a pistol tucked into his belt. "No fuckin' tricks. You escape and Yanus here will cut the babies out of her. He's a frustrated fuckin' surgeon."

The Irishman collects Samira's things—a small cotton bag and a spare blanket. Then he helps her to stand. She cups her hands beneath her pregnancy as though taking the weight. I wrap the blanket around her shoulders. Her damp gray skirt sticks to her thighs.

Yanus has gone ahead to check the stairs. I can picture crew members waiting for him. He'll be overpowered. Pearl will have no choice but to surrender.

He lifts Samira down from the trailer. I follow, stumbling slightly as I land. Pearl pushes me out of the way and closes the rear doors, sliding the barrel lock into place. Something is different about the truck. The color. It's not the same.

My stomach turns over. There are two trucks. Yanus and Pearl must have each driven a vehicle on board. Glancing toward the nearest stairwell, I see the glowing exit sign. We're on a different deck. They don't know where to look for me.

Samira goes first. Her chin is drawn down to her clavicle and she seems to be whispering a prayer. A contraction stops her suddenly and her knees buckle. Pearl puts his arm around her waist. Although in his late forties, he has the upper-body strength of someone who has bulked up in prison weight rooms. You don't work a regular job and have a physique like his.

We move quickly up the stairs and along empty passageways. Yanus has found a cabin on Deck 9, where there are fewer passengers. He takes Samira from Pearl and I glance at them, fleetingly, sidelong. Surely they can't expect to get away with this.

The two-berth cabin is oppressively neat. It has a narrow single bunk about a foot from the floor and another directly above it, hinged and folded flat against the wall. There is a square porthole with rounded corners. The window is dark. Land has ceased to exist and I can only imagine the emptiness of the North Sea. I look at my watch. It's twelve thirty. Harwich is another three and a half hours away. If Samira can stay calm and the contractions are steady, we may reach Harwich in time. In time for what?

Her eyes are wide and her forehead is beaded with perspiration. At the same time she is shivering. I sit on the bed, with my back to the bulkhead, pulling her against me with my arms wrapped around her, trying to keep her warm. Her belly balloons between her knees and her entire body jolts with each contraction.

I am running on instinct. Trying my best not to panic or show fear. The first-aid course I did when I joined the Met was comprehensive but it didn't include childbirth. I remember something my mama said to my sisters-in-law: "Doctors don't deliver babies, women do."

Yanus and Pearl take turns guarding the door. There isn't enough room in the cabin for both of them. One will watch the passageway.

Yanus leans against the narrow cabin counter, watching with listless curiosity. Taking an orange from his pocket, he peels it expertly and separates it into segments that he lines up along the bench. Each piece is finally crushed between his teeth and he sucks the juices down his throat before spitting out the pith and seeds onto the floor.

I have never believed that people could be wholly evil. Psychopaths are made not born. Yanus could be the exception. I try to picture him as a youngster and cling to the hope that there might be some warmth inside him. He must have loved someone, something—a pet, a parent, a friend. I see no trace of it.

One or twice Samira can't stifle her cries. He tosses a roll of masking tape into my lap. "Shut her up!"

"No! She has to tell me when the contractions are coming."

"Then keep her quiet."

Where does he keep his knife? Strapped to his chest on his left side, next to his heart. He seems to read my mind and taps his jacket.

"I can cut them out of her, you know. I've done it before with animals. I start cutting just here." He puts his finger just above his belt buckle and draws it upward over his navel and beyond. "Then I peel back her skin."

Samira shudders.

"Just shut up, will you?"

He gives me his shark's smile.

Night presses against the porthole. There might be five hundred passengers on board the ferry, but right now it feels as though the cabin light is burning in a cold hostile wasteland.

Samira tilts her head back until she can look into my eyes.

"Zala?" she asks.

I wish I could lie to her but she reads the truth on my face. I can almost see her slipping backward into blackness, disappearing. It is the look of someone who knows that fate has abandoned them to a sadness so deep that nothing can touch it.

"I should never have let her go," she whispers.

"It's not your fault."

Her chest rises and falls in a silent sob. She has turned her eyes away. It is a gesture that says everything. I vowed to find Zala and keep her safe. I broke my promise.

The contractions seem to have eased. Her breathing steadies and she sleeps.

Pearl has replaced Yanus.

"How is she?"

"Exhausted."

He braces his back against the door, sliding down until he settles on his haunches, draping his arms over his knees. In such a small space he appears larger, overgrown, with big hands. Yanus has feminine hands, shapely and delicate, fast with a blade. Pearl's are like blunt instruments.

"You'll never get away with this, you know that."

He smiles. "There are many things I know and many more things I don't know."

"Listen to me. You're only making this worse. If she dies or the babies die they'll charge you with murder."

"They won't die."

"She needs a doctor."

"Enough talk."

"The police know I'm here. I saw you earlier. I told the captain to radio ahead. There will be a hundred police officers waiting at Harwich. You can't get away. Let me take Samira. There could be a doctor on board or a nurse. They'll have medical supplies."

Pearl doesn't seem to care. Is that what happens when you spend most of your life in prison or committing acts that should put you there?

My scalp tingles. "Why did you kill my friend Cate and her husband?"

"Who?"

"The Beaumonts."

His eyes, not quite level with each other, give the impression of lopsidedness until he talks and his features suddenly line up. "She was greedy."

"How?"

"She could only pay for one baby but wanted both of them."

"You asked her to *choose*?"

"Not me."

"Someone else did?"

He doesn't have to answer.

"That's obscene."

He shrugs. "Pitter or Patter—seems simple enough. Life is about choices."

That's what Cate meant—at the reunion—when she said they were trying to take her baby. They wanted her to pay double. Her bank account was empty. She had to choose: the boy or the girl.

How can a mother make a decision like that and live for the rest of her life gazing into the eyes of one child and seeing a reflection of another that she never knew?

Pearl is still talking. "She threatened to go to the police. We warned her. She ignored it. That's the problem with folks nowadays. Nobody takes responsibility for their actions. Make a mistake and you pay for it. That's life."

"Have you paid for your mistakes?"

"All my life." His eyes are closed. He wants to go back to ignoring me.

A knock. Pearl slides the pistol from his belt and points it toward me while holding a finger to his lips. He opens the door a fraction. I can't see a face. Someone is asking about a missing passenger. They're looking for me.

Pearl yawns. "Is that why you woke me?"

A second voice: "Sorry, sir."

"What does she look like?"

I can't hear the description.

"Well, I ain't seen her. Maybe she went for a swim."

"I hope not, sir."

"Yeah, well, I got to sleep."

"Sorry, sir, you won't be disturbed again."

The door closes. Pearl waits for a moment, pressing his ear to the door. Satisfied, he tucks the pistol back in his belt.

There's another knock on the door. Yanus.

"Where the fuck were you?" demands Pearl.

"Watching," replies Yanus.

"You were supposed to fucking warn me."

"Would have made no difference. They're knocking on every door. They won't come back now."

Samira sits bolt upright screaming. The contraction is brutal and I scissor my legs around her, holding her still. An unseen force possesses her, racking her body in spasms. I find myself drawn to her pain. Caught up in it. Breathing when she breathes.

Another contraction comes almost immediately. Her back arches and her knees rise up.

"I have to push now."

"No!"

"I have to."

This is it. I can't stop her. Sliding out from behind her, I lie her down and take off her underwear.

Pearl is unsure of what to do. "Take deep breaths, that's a good girl. Good deep breaths. You thirsty? I'll get you a drink of water."

He fills a glass in the small bathroom and returns.

"Shouldn't you be checking the cervix?" he asks.

"And I suppose you know all about it."

"I seen movies."

"Take over anytime you want."

His tone softens. "What can I do?"

"Run some hot water in the sink. I need to wash my hands."

Samira unclenches her teeth as the pain eases. Short panting breaths become longer. She focuses on Pearl and begins issuing instructions. She needs things—scissors and string, clips and towels. For a moment I think she's delirious but soon realize that she knows more about childbirth than any of us.

He opens the door and passes on the instructions to Yanus. They argue. Pearl threatens him.

Samira has another instruction. Men cannot be present at the birth. I expect Pearl to say no but I see him wavering.

I tell him: "Look at this place. We can't go anywhere. There's one door and a porthole fifty feet above the water."

He accepts this and glances at his watch. It's after two. "An hour from now she has to be back in the truck." His hand is on the door handle. He turns and addresses me.

"My ma is a good Catholic. Pro-life, you understand? She'd say there were already five people in this room, babies included. When I come back I expect to see the same number. Keep them alive."

He closes the door and Samira relaxes a little. She asks me to fetch a flannel from the bathroom. She folds it several times and wedges it between her teeth when she feels a contraction coming.

"How do you know so much?"

"I have seen babies born," she explains. "Women would sometimes come to the orphanage to give birth. They left the babies with us because they could not take them home."

Her contractions are coming forty seconds apart. Her eyes bulge and she bites down hard on the flannel. The pain passes.

"I need you to see if I'm ready," she whispers.

"How?"

"Put two fingers inside me to measure."

"How do I tell?"

"Look at your fingers," she says. "See how long they are. Measure with them."

Opening her legs, I do as she asks. I have never touched a woman so intimately or been so terrified.

"I think you're ready."

She nods, clenching the flannel between her teeth through the first part of the contraction and then breathing in short bursts, trying to ease the pain. Tears squeeze from her eyes and mingle with her sweat. I smell her exertions.

"I have to get to the floor," she says.

"Are you going to pray?"

"No. I'm going to have a baby."

She squats with her legs apart, bracing her arms between the bunk and the bench table. Gravity is going to help her.

"You must feel for the baby's head," she says.

My hand is inside her, turning and dipping. I feel a baby's head. It's crowning. Should there be blood?

"They will kill you after the babies are born," whispers Samira. "You must get out of here."

"Later."

"You must go now."

"Don't worry about me."

There's a knock on the door. I undo the latch and Pearl hands me scissors, a ball of string and a rusty clip. Yanus hisses from behind him. "Keep the bitch quiet."

"Fuck you! She's having a baby."

Yanus makes a lunge for me. Pearl pushes him back and closes the door.

Samira is pushing now, three times with each contraction. She has long slender lemurlike feet, roughly calloused along the outer edges. Her chin is tucked to her throat and oily coils of her hair fall over her eyes.

"If I pass out, you must make sure you get the babies out. Don't leave them inside me." Teeth pull at her bottom lip. "Do whatever you have to."

"Shhh."

"Promise me."

"I promise."

"Am I bleeding a lot?"

"You're bleeding. I don't know if it's too much. I can see the baby's head."

"It hurts."

"I know."

Existence narrows to just breathing, pain and pushing. I brush hair from her eyes and crouch between her legs. Her face contorts. She screams into the flannel. The baby's head is out. I hold it in my cupped hand, feeling the dips and hollows of the skull. The shoulders are trapped. Gently I put my finger beneath its chin and the tiny body rotates within her. On the next contraction the right shoulder appears, then the left, and the baby slides into my hands.

A boy.

"Rub your finger down his nose," gasps Samira.

It takes only a fingertip to perform the task. There is a soft, shocked sob, a rattle and a breath.

Samira issues more instructions. I am to use the string and tie off the umbilical cord in two places, cutting between the knots. My hands are shaking.

She is crying. Spent. I help her back onto the bunk and she leans against the bulkhead wall. Wrapping the baby in a towel, I hold him close, smelling his warm breath, letting his nose brush against my cheek. Which one are you, I wonder, Pitter or Patter?

I look at my watch and make a mental note of the time: 2:55 a.m. What is the date? October 29. Where will they say he was born? In the Netherlands or Britain? And who will be his true mother? What a mixed-up way to start a life.

The contractions have started again. Samira kneads her stomach, trying to feel the unborn twin.

"What's wrong?"

"She is facing the wrong way. You must turn her."

"I don't know how."

Each new contraction brings a groan of resignation. Samira is almost too exhausted to cry out; too tired to push. I have to hold her up this time. She squats. Her thighs part still further.

Reaching inside her, I try to push the baby back, turning her body, fighting gravity and the contractions. My hands are slick. I'm frightened of hurting her.

"It's coming."

"Push now."

The head arrives with a gush of blood. I glimpse something white with blue streaks wrapped around its neck.

"Stop! Don't push!"

My hand slides along the baby's face until my fingers reach beneath her chin and untangle the umbilical cord.

"Samira you *really* need to push the next time. It's very important."

The contraction begins. She pushes once, twice . . . nothing.

"Push."

"I can't."

"Yes, you can. One last time, I promise."

She throws back her head and muffles a scream. Her body stiffens and bucks. A baby girl emerges, blue, slick, wrinkled, cupped in both my hands. I rub her nose. Nothing. I hold her on her side, sweeping my index finger round her mouth and throat, trying to clear the dripping goo.

I drape her over my hand, with her arms and legs dangling and slap her back hard. Why won't she breathe?

Putting her on a towel I begin chest compressions with the tips of my index and middle fingers. At the same time I lower my lips and puff into the baby's mouth and nose.

I know about resuscitation. I have done the training and I have witnessed paramedics do it dozens of times. Now I am breathing into a body that has never taken a breath. Come on, little one. Come on.

Samira is half on the bunk and half on the floor. Her eyes are closed. The first twin is swaddled and lying between her arm and her side.

I continue the compressions and breathing. It is like a mantra, a physical prayer. Almost without noticing, the narrowest of chests rises and eyelids flutter. Blue has become pink. She's alive. Beautiful.

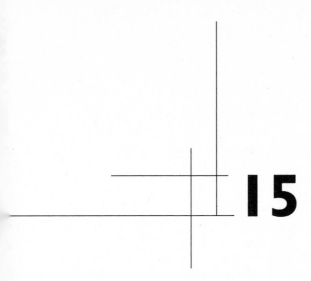

15

A girl and a boy—Pitter and Patter—each with ten fingers and ten toes, squashed-up noses, tiny ears. Rocking back on my heels, I feel like laughing with relief, until I catch my reflection in the mirror. I am smeared with blood and tears yet have a look of complete wonderment on my face.

Samira groans softly.

"You're bleeding."

"It will stop when I feed them."

How does she know so much? She is massaging her belly, which ripples and sways in its emptiness. I swaddle the baby girl and tuck her next to Samira.

"Go now!"

"I can't leave you."

"Please!"

An extraordinary calmness washes through me. I have only two options—to fight or to fall. I take the scissors, weighing them in my hand. Maybe there is a way.

I open the door. Pearl is in the passage.

"Quickly! I need a drinking straw. The girl. Her lungs are full of fluid."

"What if I can't?"

"A ballpoint pen, a tube, anything like that. Hurry!"

I close the door. He will leave Yanus to watch the passage.

Taking the babies from Samira, I lie them side by side on the floor of the bathroom, tucked between the sink and the toilet. Cupping my hands beneath the running water, I wash away the blood and clean my face.

I have been trained to use a firearm. I can shoot a perfect score with a pistol from thirty yards on an indoor range. What good is that now? My hand-to-hand skills are defensive but I know the vital organs. I glance again at the scissors.

It is a plan I can only try once. Lying on the bathroom floor, I face the bedroom, holding the scissors like an ice pick with a reverse grip. My thumb hooks through the handle. If I look toward my toes, I can see the babies.

Taking a deep breath I open my lungs, screaming for help. How long will it take?

Yanus shoulders the door open, shattering the lock. He charges inside, holding the knife ahead of him. In mid-stride he looks down. Beneath his raised foot is the afterbirth, purple slick and glistening. I don't know what he imagines it to be, but the possibilities are too much for him to comprehend. He rears back and I drive the scissors into the soft flesh behind his right knee, aiming for the artery and the tendons that work his leg. The knee buckles and he swings his arm down in an arc trying to stab me but I'm too low and the blade sweeps past my ear.

I grab his arm and lock it straight, spearing the scissors into the inside of his elbow, severing another artery. The knife slips from his fingers.

He tries to spin and grab me, but I am already out of reach. Leaping to my feet, I jump onto his back and send him down. I could kill him if I wanted. I could drive the blade into his kidneys.

Instead, I reach into his pocket and find the masking tape. His right leg is flapping like the wooden limb of a marionette. Pulling his good arm behind his back, I tape it in a reverse sling around his neck. Another piece covers his mouth.

Yanus is groaning. I grab his face. "Listen to me. I have severed the popliteal artery in your leg and the brachial artery in your arm. You know this already because you're a knife man. You also know that you will bleed to death unless you keep pressure on these wounds. You will have to squat on your haunches and keep this arm bent. I will send someone to help you. If you do as I suggest, you might still be alive when they get here."

Samira has been watching all this with a curious detachment. Crawling off the bed, she takes several painful steps toward Yanus before leaning down and spitting in his face.

"We have to go."

"You go. Take the babies."

"Not without you."

I take the smallest twin, the girl, whose eyes are open, watching me. Samira takes the sleeping boy. Cautiously, I peer into the passageway. Pearl will be coming back soon.

Samira has a towel pressed between her thighs. We head toward the stairs moving as quickly as she can. The passage is so narrow that I bounce off the wall as I try to keep hold of Samira's arm. People are asleep. I don't know which cabins are occupied.

There is a service lift. I can't open the door. Samira's legs buckle. I stop her falling. This is Deck 9. The bridge is on Deck 10. She isn't strong enough to climb the stairs. I have to get her away from the cabin and hide her.

There is a linen room with shelves on either side, stacked with folded sheets and towels. I could leave her here and go for help. No, she shouldn't be left alone.

I hear movement. Someone is awake. Hammering on the cabin door, it opens hurriedly. A middle-aged man, wearing pajamas and gray socks looks irritated. A fuzz of red hair spills from the V of his shirt and makes it seem like his stuffing is coming out.

I push Samira ahead of me. "Help her! I have to find a doctor!"

He says something in German. Then he spies the bloody towel between her thighs. I hand him the baby girl.

"Who are you?"

"Police. There's no time to explain. Help her."

Samira curls up on the bunk, her arms around the other twin.

"Don't open the door. Don't let anyone know she's here."

Before he can protest, I step back into the passage and run toward the stairs. The passenger lounge is deserted apart from two rough-looking men at the bar, hunched over pints. A woman files her nails at a cash register.

I yell for the captain. It isn't the desperation in my voice that affects them most. It's the blood on my clothes. I have come from a nightmare place, another dimension.

People are running. Members of the crew appear, yelling orders and ushering me farther upstairs. Sentences stream out of me, between snorting sobs. They're not listening to me. They have to get Samira and the twins.

The captain is a large man with shaggy eyebrows and a semicircle of hair clinging to the scalp above his ears and neck. His uniform is white and blue, matching his eyes.

He stands in the middle of the bridge, his head thrust forward, listening without any hint of skepticism. The state of my clothes is proof enough. The chief engineer is a medic. He wants to examine me. We don't have time. The captain is on the radio, using emergency frequencies, talking to HM Coast Guard, customs and mainland police. A cutter has been sent from Felixstowe to intercept and a Royal Navy helicopter is being scrambled from Prestwick in Scotland.

Pearl is somewhere on board. Yanus is bleeding to death. This is taking too long.

"You have to get Samira," I hear myself say. My voice sounds shrill and frightened. "She needs medical help."

The captain won't be rushed. He is following the protocols and procedures set down for piracy or violent incidents at sea. He wants to know how many there are. Are they armed? Will they take hostages?

The information is relayed to the coast guard and police. We are twenty minutes from port. Huge glass windows frame the approaching coastline, which is still blanketed in darkness. The bridge is high up, overlooking the bow. Nothing approximates a steering wheel. Instead there are computer screens, buttons and keyboards.

I confront the captain, demanding that he listen to me.

"I understand that you're a British police officer," he says abruptly, "but this is a Dutch vessel and you have no authority here. My responsibility is to my passengers and crew. I will not endanger their safety."

"A woman has just given birth. She's bleeding. She needs medical help."

"We are twenty minutes from docking."

"So you'll do nothing?"

"I am waiting for my instructions."

"What about the passengers downstairs? They're waking up."

"I don't believe they should be panicked. We have contingency plans to evacuate passengers to the Globetrotter Lounge, where most of them are due to have breakfast."

The chief engineer is a neat little man with a college-boy haircut.

"Will you come with me?" I ask.

He hesitates. I pick up the first-aid box from the bench and turn to leave. The engineer looks at the captain, seeking permission. I don't know what passes between them but he's ready to follow me.

"Are there any weapons on board?"

"No."

God, they make it hard! This time we use a service lift to reach Deck 9. The doors open. The passage is empty. The deck below has the freight drivers who are due to disembark first.

At every corner I expect to see Pearl. He is a natural at this. Even my presence on the ferry didn't fluster him. He simply adjusted his sights and made a new plan. Yanus is the more unpredictable but Pearl is the more dangerous because he can adapt. I can picture him, waylaid for a moment by the loss of Samira and the twins, but still calculating his chances of escape.

Even before I reach the cabin I can see that something is wrong. A handful of passengers crowd the passage, craning to look over one another's heads. Among them is the Welsh couple. Mrs. Jones looks naked without her lipstick and is squeezed into a gray tracksuit that struggles to encompass her buttocks.

"You can't escape them," she says to the others. "Thugs and criminals. And what do the police do? Nothing. Too busy giving out speeding tickets. Even if they do get charged, some judge or magistrate will let them off on account of their drug addiction or deprived childhood. What about the bloody victims, eh? Nobody cares about them."

The cabin door is open, the lock broken. Sitting on his bunk, the German truck driver holds his head back to stop his nose bleeding. There is no sign of Samira or the twins.

"Where are they?" I grab his shoulder. "Where?"

The worst thing is not the anger. It is the murderous desire behind the anger.

My mobile phone is ringing. We must be in range of a signal. I don't recognize the number.

"Hello."

"And hello to you," says Pearl. "Have you ever seen that TV commercial about the Energizer bunny that keeps going and going and going? You're like that fucking bunny. You just don't quit."

His voice has an echo. He's on the vehicle deck. "Where is she?"

"I found her, bunny."

"Yes."

"Do you know how? The blood. You left a trail of it." A baby is crying in the background. "I also found Yanus. You cut him pretty good, but I patched him up."

"He'll bleed to death."

"Don't you worry about that, bunny. I don't leave *my* friends behind."

I'm already on the move, running along the passage to the first cabin. The chief engineer struggles to keep up with me. Yanus has gone. The floor is polished red with blood and dozens of footprints stain the passageway.

People are amazing. They will walk past a scene like this and ignore it because it's beyond their ordinary, mundane, workaday comprehension. Pearl is still on the line. "You'll never get off the ferry," I yell. "Give them back. Please."

"I need to talk to the captain."

"He won't negotiate."

"I don't wanna fuckin' negotiate! We have a mutual interest."

"What's that?"

"We both want me off this ferry."

My head is clearer now. Others are making decisions for me. It is three hours before dawn and the Essex coast is somewhere ahead of us in the darkness. I can't hear the engines from the bridge and without any points of reference the ferry doesn't appear to be moving. Two coast guard launches have joined the *Stena Britannica*, escorting us into port. The captain is communicating directly with his superiors in Rotterdam.

I am being kept away, at arm's length, as though I'm a liability or worse, a hysterical woman. What could I have done differently? Hindsight is a cruel teacher. I should never have left Samira or the twins. I should have stayed with them. Perhaps I could have fought Pearl off.

My mind goes further back. I should never have gone to Amsterdam looking for her. I have made things worse rather than better. That's the story of my life—good intentions. And being a hundredth of a second too slow—close enough to touch victory in a contest where first and last were separated by the width of a chest.

How can they negotiate with Pearl? He can't be trusted. The chief engineer hands me something hot to drink.

"Not long to go now," he says, motioning to the windows. The lights of Harwich appear and disappear as we ride the swell. Massive cranes with four legs and oblong torsos seem to stand guard at the gates of the town. I stay at the window watching it approach.

The captain and navigator stare at screens, using external cameras to maneuver the ferry, edging it against the dock. We are so high up that the stevedores look like Lilliputians trying to tie down a giant.

DI Forbes is first on board, pausing just long enough to look at my clothes with a mixture of awe and disgust. He takes the phone from the captain.

"Don't trust him," I yell across the bridge. It is all I have a chance to say before the DI introduces himself to Pearl. I can only hear one side of their conversation but Forbes repeats each demand as it is made. The clicks in his throat are like punctuation marks.

Pearl wants the main ferry doors opened and vehicles moved to clear a path for his truck. Nobody is to approach. If he sees a police officer on the deck, or if he hears a fire alarm, or if anything is different or untoward, he will kill Samira and the twins.

"You have to give me more time," says Forbes. "I'll need at least an hour . . . That's not long enough. I can't do it in fifteen minutes . . . Let me talk to Samira . . . Yes, that's why I want to talk to her . . . No, I don't want that. Nobody has to get hurt."

In the background one of the babies is crying—perhaps both of them. Do twins sound the same? Do they harmonize when they cry?

There are CCTV cameras on the vehicle decks. One of them is

trained on the truck. Yanus can be seen clearly behind the wheel. Samira is in the passenger seat.

The rest of the passengers are being evacuated down gangways to the main terminal building. The port area has been closed and sealed off by armed response teams in black body armor. There are sharpshooters on surrounding rooftops.

The anguish of the past hours has swelled up inside me, making it hard to breathe. I can feel myself sinking into the background.

Forbes has agreed to take a limited number of vehicles off the ferry, clearing a path for the truck. I follow the detective down the footbridge to the dock as he supervises the evacuation. Men in yellow reflective vests wave the first of the rigs down the ramp.

Forbes has put Pearl onto a speakerphone. The Irishman sounds calm. Confident. Perhaps it's bravado. He is talking over the sound of engines, telling Forbes to hurry. Slowly a clear lane emerges on the vehicle deck. The Mercedes truck is at the far end, with its headlights blazing and engine running.

I still can't understand how he hopes to get away. There are unmarked police cars waiting outside and helicopters in the air. He can't outrun them.

Yanus is bleeding to death. Even with a bandaged leg and forearm his blood pressure will be dropping. How long before he loses consciousness?

"You definitely saw a gun?" asks Forbes, addressing me directly for the first time.

"Yes."

"Could he have other firearms?"

"Yes."

"What is the truck carrying?"

"This one is empty. There's another on Deck 5. I didn't see inside." I give him the vehicle number.

"So it could be a trafficking run. There might be illegals on board."

"It's possible."

The last of the rigs has been moved. Yanus has a clear path to the ramp. Pearl is still issuing instructions. The twins are silent.

In a beat of flushed silence I realize something is wrong. Pearl is too calm, too confident. His plan doesn't make sense. As the notion occurs to me, I'm moving, pushing past Forbes and sprinting up the ramp. A hundred meters is not my favorite distance but I can cover it in less time than it takes most people to tie their shoes.

Forbes is yelling at me to stop. He's too late. Reacting to the new development, he orders his teams to move. Heavy boots thunder up the ramp after me, sweeping between the outer rows of trucks.

Yanus is still behind the wheel, staring out through the wind-screen, unperturbed by my approach. His eyes seem to follow me as I swing on the door handle and wrench it open. His hands are taped to the steering wheel. Blood has drained onto the floor at his feet. I press my hand to his neck. He's dead.

Samira's hands are also taped. I lean across Yanus and touch her shoulder. Her eyes open.

"Where are they?"

She shakes her head.

I swing down and run to the rear of the truck. A sledgehammer pulverizes the lock and the doors swing open. Guns sweep from side to side. The trailer is empty.

Forbes reaches us, puffing and wheezing, still clogged with his cold. I snatch the phone from him. The line is dead.

Amid the commotion of the next few minutes I see things at half speed and struggle to find saliva to push around my mouth. Forbes is bellowing orders and kicking angrily at the truck tires. Someone will have to pop him with a tranquilizer gun if he doesn't calm down.

Teams of police have secured the ferry. Nobody is being allowed on or off. Passengers are being screened and interviewed in the ter-minal. Floodlights on the dock make it appear like a massive stage or film set, ready for the cameras to roll.

Yanus watches and waits, as though expecting his cue. My heart jolts on the reality of having killed him. Yes, he deserved it, but *I did this*. I took his life. His blood still stains my clothes, along with Samira's.

Paramedics are lifting her onto a stretcher. The towel is still wedged between her thighs. The medics gently shunt me to one side when I approach. She can't talk to me now. I want to say I'm sorry, it was my fault. I should never have left her. I should have stayed with them. Perhaps I could have stopped Pearl.

Some time later Forbes comes looking for me.

"Let's walk," he says.

Instinctively, I take his arm. I'm frightened my legs might fail.

"What time is it?" I ask.

"Five thirty."

"My watch says five fifteen."

"It's slow."

"How do you know yours isn't fast?"

"Because the ferry company has those big fucking clocks on the wall that say *your* watch is wrong in four different time zones."

We walk down the ramp, along the dock, away from the ferry. Refinery tanks and shipping containers create silhouettes against the brightening sky. Wind and smoke and scudding clouds are streaming over us.

"You don't think he's on the ferry, do you?" asks Forbes.

"No."

There is another long pause. "We found a life buoy missing from the starboard railing. He could have gone over the side."

"Someone would have seen him."

"We were distracted."

"Even so."

I can still smell the twins and feel the smoothness of their skin. We're both thinking the same thing. What happened to them?

"You should never have put yourself on that ferry," he says.

"I couldn't be sure she was on board."

Taking a packet of cigarettes from his pockets, he counts the contents.

"You shouldn't smoke with a cold."

"I shouldn't smoke at all. My wife thinks men and women can have precisely the same ailment with the same symptoms but it's always the man who is sicker."

"That's because men are hypochondriacs."

"I got a different theory. I think it's because no matter how sick a woman is there's always a small part of her brain thinking about shoes."

"I bet you didn't tell her that."

"I'm sick, not stupid."

His demeanor is different now. Instead of sarcasm and cynicism, I sense anxiety and a hardening resolve.

"Who's behind this?"

"Samira mentioned an Englishman who called himself 'Brother.'

She said he had a cross on his neck. There's someone you should look at. His name is Paul Donavon. He went to school with Cate Beaumont—and with me. He was there on the night she was run down."

"You think he's behind this?"

"Samira met 'Brother' at an orphanage in Kabul. Donavon was in Afghanistan with the British Army. The traffickers targeted orphans because it meant fewer complications. There were no families to search for them or ask questions. Some were trafficked for sex. Others were given the option of becoming surrogates."

"The pregnant illegals you asked about. Both claimed to be orphans."

Forbes still hasn't lit his cigarette. It rests between his lips, wagging up and down as he talks. He glances over his shoulder at the ferry.

"About the other night."

"What night?"

"When we had dinner."

"Yeah?"

"Did I conduct myself in a proper fashion? I mean, did I behave?"

"You were a perfect gentleman."

"That's good," he mumbles. "I mean, I thought so." After a pause. "You took something that didn't belong to you."

"I prefer to think that we shared information."

He nods. "You might want to reconsider your career choice, DC Barba. I don't know if you're what I'd call a team player."

He can't stay. There is a debriefing to attend, which is going to be rough. His superiors are going to want to know how he let Pearl get away. And once the media get hold of this story it's going to run and run.

Forbes looks at my clothes. "If he's not on the ferry, how did he get off?"

"He could still be on board."

"You don't believe that."

"No. What about the crew?"

"You think he took a uniform?"

"It's possible."

He turns abruptly and strides back toward the waiting police cars. The CCTV footage will most likely provide the answer. There are cameras on every corner of the dock and every deck of the ship. One of them will have recorded Pearl.

"Eat bananas," I yell after him.

"Pardon?"

"My mother's remedy for a cold."

"You said you never listened to her."

"I said almost never."

———————

There have been too many hospitals lately. Too many long waits on uncomfortable chairs, eating machine snacks and drinking powdered coffee and whitener. This one smells of boiled food and feces and has grim checked tiles in the corridors, worn smooth by the trolleys.

Ruiz called me from Hull, after his ferry docked. He wanted to come and get me but I told him to go home and rest. He's done enough.

"Are they looking after you?"

"I'm fine."

"Samira?"

"She's going to be OK."

I hope I'm right. She's been asleep for ten hours and didn't even wake when they lifted her from the ambulance and wheeled her to a private room. I have been waiting here, dozing in my plastic chair, with my head on the bed near her shoulder.

It is mid-afternoon when she finally wakes. I feel the mattress shift and open my eyes to see her looking at me.

"I need the bathroom," she whispers.

I take her by the elbow and help her to the en suite.

"Where am I?"

"In a hospital."

"What country?"

"England."

There is a nod of acceptance but no hint of a journey completed or sense of achievement.

Samira washes her face, ears, hands and feet, talking softly to herself. I take her arm again, leading her back to bed.

Motioning to the window, she wants to look outside. The North

Sea is just visible over the rooftops and between buildings. It is the color of brushed steel.

"As a child I used to wonder what the sea looked like," she says. "I had only ever seen pictures in books and on TV." She gazes at the horizon.

"What do you think now?"

"I think it looks higher than the land. Why doesn't the water rush in and sweep us away?"

"Sometimes it does."

I notice a towel in her hand. She wants to use it as a prayer mat but doesn't know which direction to face toward Mecca. She turns slowly round and round like a cat trying to settle.

There are tears in her eyes and her lips tremble, struggling to form the words.

"They will be hungry soon. Who will feed them?"

BOOK THREE

Love and pain are not the same.
Love is put to the test—pain is not.
You do not say of pain, as you do of
love, "That was not true pain or it
would not have disappeared so
quickly."

—WILLIAM BOYD,
"The Blue Afternoon"

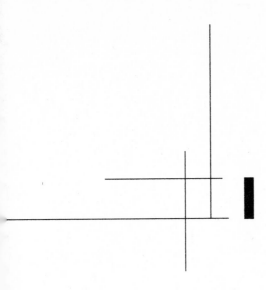

In the nights since the twins were born I have drowned countless times, twitching and kicking at the bedclothes. I see tiny bodies floating in fields of kelp or washed up on beaches. My lungs give out before I can reach them, leaving me choking and numb with an obscure anguish. I wonder if there's such a thing as a swollen heart?

Samira is also awake. She walks through the house at 3:00 a.m. moving as though her feet have an agreement with the ground that she will always tread lightly in return for never encountering another path that is too steep.

It has been five days since the twins went missing. Pearl has soaked through the cracks of the world and vanished. We know how he got off the ferry. A CCTV camera on Deck 3 picked up a man in a hard hat and reflective jacket who couldn't be identified as one of the crew. The footage didn't show his face clearly but he was seen carrying a pet traveling cage. The square gray plastic box was supposed to contain two Siamese cats but they were found wandering in a stairwell.

Another camera in the Customs area picked up the clearest images of the unidentified man. In the foreground trucks are being scanned with heat-seeking equipment designed to find illegals. But in the background, at the edge of the frame, a pumpkin-shaped caravan attached to an early-model Range Rover can be seen. Mr. and Mrs. Jones of Cardiff are seen repacking their duty-frees and souvenirs after being searched. As the car and caravan pull away, a square gray pet cage is visible on the tarmac next to where they were parked.

The Welsh couple were pulled over a little after midday Sunday on the M4 just east of Reading. The caravan was empty but Pearl's fingerprints were lifted from the table and the aluminum door. The couple had stopped for petrol at a motorway service center on the M25. A cashier remembered Pearl buying bottles and baby formula. Shortly afterward, at 10:42 a.m., a car was reported stolen from an adjacent parking area. It still hasn't been found.

Forbes is running the investigation, liaising with Spijker in Amsterdam, combining resources, pitting their wills against the problem. They are cross-checking names from the IVF clinic with the U.K. immigration records.

There has been a news blackout about the missing twins. DI Forbes made the decision. Stolen children make dramatic headlines and he wants to avoid creating panic. A year ago a newborn was snatched from a hospital in Harrogate and there were 1,200 alleged sightings in the first two days. Mothers were accosted in the street and treated like kidnappers. Homes were raided needlessly. Innocent families suffered.

The only public statement has been about Pearl, who has a warrant out for his arrest. Another one. I have taken to carrying my gun again. As long as he's out there, I'm going to keep it with me. I am not going to lose Samira again.

She has been staying with me since leaving hospital on Wednesday. Hari has moved out of the spare room and is sleeping downstairs on a sofa bed. He seems quite taken by our lodger. He has started wearing a shirt around the house because he senses that she disapproves.

I am to face a Police Disciplinary Tribunal. Neglect of duty, deliberate falsehood and abuse of authority are just three of the charges. Failing to show up at Hendon is the least of my worries. Barnaby Elliot has accused me of harassment and arson. The investigation is being supervised by the Police Complaints Authority. I am guilty until proven innocent.

A toilet flushes along the hallway. A light switch clicks off. A few minutes later comes the hum of a machine and the rhythmic suction of a breast pump. Samira's milk has come in and she has to express every six hours. The sound of the pump is strangely soporific. I close my eyes again.

She hasn't said anything about the twins. I keep wondering when she is going to crack, fragmented by the loss. Even when she identified Hassan's body at Westminster Mortuary she held it all inside.

"It's OK to cry," I told her.

"That is why Allah gave us tears," she answered.

"You think God played a part in this?"

"He would not give me this suffering if he did not think I could endure it."

How can she be so wise, yet so accepting? Can she really believe this is part of some grand master plan or that Allah would test her so cruelly?

Such faith seems positively medieval, yet she has an appetite for learning. Things that I take for granted she finds fascinating, like central heating, dual flush toilets and my washer/dryer. In Kabul she had to carry water upstairs to their flat and the power failed almost daily. London has lights along every street, burning through the night. Samira asked me if perhaps we British are scared of the dark. She didn't understand why I laughed.

I took her shopping for clothes at Canary Wharf yesterday. "There is not so much glass in all of Afghanistan," she said, pointing to the office towers that shone in the morning sun. I could see her studying the office workers queuing for coffee and "skinny" muffins: the women dressed in narrow skirts, tight tops and jackets, flicking their short hair, chatting on mobile phones.

The clothing boutiques intimidated her. The shop assistants were dressed like mourners and the shops felt like funeral parlors. I told Samira there was a better place to find clothes. We left and went to Commercial Road where garments were crammed on racks and spilling from bins. She chose two skirts, a long-sleeved blouse and a cardigan. It came to less than sixty pounds.

She studied the twenty-pound notes.

"Is this your Queen?"

"Yes."

"She looks like she has been dipped in plaster."

I laughed. "I guess she does."

The Christmas decorations were up. Even the bagel bakery and halal butcher had fairy lights and fake snow. Samira stopped and peered into a lobster tank in the window of a restaurant.

"I am never going to swim in the sea."

"Why?"

"I don't want to meet one of them."

I think she had visions of lobsters crawling over one another in the same density as in the tank.

"This must be like science fiction to you."

"Science? Fiction?"

"It means like a fantasy. Unreal."

"Yes, unreal."

Seeing London through Samira's eyes has given me a different perspective on the city. Even the most mundane scene takes on a new life. When I took her underground to catch the Tube, she clutched my hand as an approaching train roared through the tunnel, sounding like a "monster in a cave" she said.

The casual wealth on display is embarrassing. There are more vets in the East End than there were doctors in Kabul. And the animals are better fed than the orphans.

The breast pump has stopped. She had turned on Hari's TV and is flicking between channels. Slipping out of bed, I tiptoe along the hall and knock on her door. She's wearing my old dressing gown, the one with an owl sewn onto the pocket.

"Can't you sleep?"

"No."

"I'll make us a sleeping potion."

Her eyes widen.

She follows me down the stairs, along the hall into the kitchen. I close the door and take a bottle of milk from the fridge, pouring it into mugs. Two minutes in the microwave and they're steaming. Breaking up pieces of dark chocolate, I drop them in the liquid, watching them melt. Samira uses a spoon to catch the melting shards, licking it clean.

"Tell me about your family."

"Most of them are dead."

She licks the spoon. I break off more pieces of chocolate and add them to her mug.

"Did you have a big family?"

"Not so big. In Afghanistan people exaggerate what their family has done. Mine is no different. One of my ancestors traveled to China with Marco Polo they say, but I don't believe it. I think he was a smuggler, who brought the black powder from India to Afghanistan. The king heard of the magic and asked to see a demonstration. According to my father, a thousand rockets streamed back and forth across the sky. Bamboo castles dripped with fire. Fireworks became our family business. The formulas were passed down from father to son—and to me."

I remember the photograph among Hassan's possessions showing a factory with workers lined up outside, most of them missing limbs or eyes, or incomplete in other ways. Hassan had burn scars on his arms.

"It must have been dangerous work."

Samira holds up her hands, showing her fingers. "I am one of the lucky ones." She sounds almost disappointed. "My father lost both his thumbs when a shell exploded. Uncle Yousuf lost his right arm and his wife lost her left arm. They helped each other to cook and sew and drive a car. My aunt changed gears and my uncle steered. My father's other brother, Fahad, lost his fingers during a display. He was a very good gambler but he began to lose when he couldn't shuffle the cards.

"I didn't meet my grandfather. He was killed in a factory explosion before I was born. Twelve others died in the same fire, including two of his brothers. My father said it was a sacrifice that only our family could make. One hand is enough to sin, he said. One hand is enough to save."

She glances at the dark square of the window. "It was our calling—to paint the sky. My father believed that one day our family would make a rocket that would light the way to Heaven. In the meantime, we would make rockets that drew the gaze of Allah in the hope that he would bless our family and bring us happiness and good health." She pauses and considers the irony of such a statement. Perfectly still, she is canted forward over the table, firm yet fragile. Her stare seems to originate at the back of her eyes.

"What happened to the factory?"

"The Talibs closed it down. Fireworks were sinful, they said. People celebrated when they arrived. They were going to stop the warlords and end the corruption. Things changed but not in a good way.

Girls could not go to school. Windows were painted over so women could not be seen. There was no music or TV or videos, no card games or kites. I was ten years old and they made me wear a burka. I could not buy things from male shopkeepers. I could not talk to men. I could not laugh in public. Women had to be ordinary. Invisible. Ignorant. My mother educated us in secret. Books were hidden each night and homework had to be destroyed.

"Men with beards and black turbans patrolled the streets, listening for music and videos. They beat people with whips soaked in water and with chains. Some were taken away and didn't come back.

"My father took us to Pakistan. We lived in a camp. My mother died there and my father blamed himself. One day he announced that we were going home. He said he would rather starve in Kabul than live like a beggar."

She falls silent, shifting in her chair. The motor of the refrigerator rattles to life and I feel the same shudder pass through me.

"The Americans dropped leaflets from the sky saying they were coming to liberate us but there was nothing left to free us from. Still we cheered because the Talibs were gone, running, like frightened dogs. But the Northern Alliance was not so different. We had learned not to expect too much. In Afghanistan we sleep with the thorns and not the flowers."

The effort of remembering has made her sleepy. I wash the mugs and follow her upstairs. She pauses at my door, wanting to ask me something.

"I am not used to the quiet."

"You think London is quiet?"

She hesitates. "Would it be all right if I slept in your room?"

"Is there something wrong? Is it the bed?"

"No."

"Are you frightened?"

"No."

"What is it then?"

"At the orphanage we slept on the floor in the same room. I am not used to being alone."

My heart twists. "You should have said something earlier. Of course you can sleep with me."

She collects a blanket and spreads it on the floor beside my wardrobe.

"My bed is big enough. We can share."

"No, this is better."

She curls up on the floor and breathes so quietly that I want to make sure she's still there.

"Good night," I whisper. "May you sleep amid the flowers, not the thorns."

———

DI Forbes arrives in the morning, early as usual. Dressed in a charcoal suit and yellow tie, he is ready to front a news conference. The media blackout is being lifted. He needs help to find the twins.

I show him to the kitchen. "Your cold sounds better."

"I can't stomach another bloody banana."

Hari is with Samira in the sitting room. He is showing her his old Xbox and trying to explain what it does.

"You can shoot people."

"Why?"

"For fun."

"Why would you shoot people for *fun*?"

I can almost hear Hari's heart sinking. Poor boy. The two of them have something in common. Hari is studying chemical engineering and Samira knows more about chemical reactions than any of his lecturers, he says.

"She's an odd little thing," says Forbes, whispering.

"How do you mean?"

"She doesn't say much."

"Most people talk too much and have nothing to say."

"What is she going to do?" he asks.

"I don't know."

What would I do in her shoes? I have never been without friends or family or stranded in a foreign country (unless you count Wolverhampton, which is pretty bloody foreign).

Hari walks into the kitchen looking pleased with himself.

"Samira is going teach me to make fireworks," he announces, taking a biscuit from Forbes's plate.

"So you can blow yourself up," I say.

"I'm very careful."

"Oh yes. Like the time you filled that copper pipe with black powder and blew a hole in the wooden siding."

"I was fifteen."

"Old enough to know better."

"Sunday is Guy Fawkes Night. We're going to make a whistling chaser."

"Which is?"

"A rocket that whistles and has white-and-red stars with a salute at the end."

"A salute?"

"A big bang."

Hari has already compiled a list of ingredients: potassium nitrate, sulfur, barium chlorate and copper powder. I have no idea what this stuff does but I can almost see the fireworks exploding in his eyes.

Forbes looks at the list. "Is this stuff legal?"

"We're only making three-inch shells."

It doesn't answer the question but the detective lets it pass.

Although Samira doesn't mention the twins, I know she must think about them, just as I do. Rarely does a minute pass when my mind doesn't drift back to them. I can feel their skin against my lips and see their narrow rib cages moving with each breath. The baby girl had trouble breathing. Perhaps her lungs weren't fully developed. We have to find her.

Forbes has opened the car door and waits for Samira to sit in the rear seat. She is wearing her new clothes—a long woolen skirt and white blouse. She looks so composed. Still. There is a landscape inside her that I will never reach.

"You won't have to answer questions," the DI explains. "I'll help you prepare a statement."

He drives hunched over the wheel, frowning at the road, as if he hates city traffic. At the same time he talks. With the help of Spijker, he has managed to trace five asylum seekers impregnated at the fertility clinic in Amsterdam who subsequently turned up in the U.K.

"All admit to giving birth and claim the babies were taken from them. They were each given £500 and told their debt had been repaid."

"Where did they give birth?"

"A private address. They couldn't give an exact location. They were taken there in the back of a transit van with blacked-out windows. Two of them talked of planes coming in to land."

"It's under a flight path?"

"That's what I figure."

"Births have to be registered. Surely we can find the babies that way."

"It's not as easy as you think. Normally, the hospital or health authority informs the registrar of a birth but not when it happens in a private home or outside of the NHS. Then it's up to the parents. And how's this? Mum and Dad don't even have to turn up at the registry office. They can send along someone else—a witness to the birth or even just the owner of the house."

"Is that it? What about doctor's certificates or medical records?"

"Don't need them. You need more paperwork to register a car than a baby."

We're passing the Royal Chelsea Hospital on the Embankment before turning left over Albert Bridge and circling Battersea Park.

"What about Dr. Banerjee?"

"He admits to providing Cate Beaumont with her surplus embryos but claims to have no knowledge of the surrogacy plan. She told him she was transferring to a different fertility clinic with a higher success rate."

"And you believe him?"

Forbes shrugs. "The embryos belonged to her. She had every right to take them."

This still doesn't explain why Banerjee lied to me. Or why he turned up at my father's birthday party.

"What about Paul Donavon?"

"He did two tours of Afghanistan and six months in Iraq. Won the Queen's Gallantry Medal. The guy is a bona fide fucking hero."

Samira hasn't said a word. Sometimes I feel as if she has turned off or tuned out, or is listening to different voices.

"We are contacting the orphanage in Kabul as well as one in Albania and another in Russia," says Forbes. "Hopefully they can give us more than just a nickname."

———————

The conference room is a stark, windowless place, with vinyl chairs and globe lights full of scorched moths. This used to be the old National Criminal Intelligence Service building, now refitted and rebranded to suit the new crime-fighting agency with new initials. Despite the headlines and high-tech equipment, SOCA still strikes me as being rather more Loch Ness than Eliot Ness—chasing shadowy monsters who live in dark places.

Radio reporters have taken up the front row, taping their station logos to the microphones. Press reporters slouch in the middle rows and their TV counterparts are at the rear with whiter teeth and better clothes.

When I did my detective training at Bramshill they sent us in groups to see an autopsy. I watched a pathologist working on the body of a hiker who had been dead for a fortnight.

Holding up a jar, he said, "This little fellow is a sarcophagid fly, but I like to refer to him as a crime reporter. Notice the red boozer eyes and his gray-checked abdomen, which is perfect for hiding food stains. More important, he's always first to find a corpse . . ."

Forbes looks at his watch. It's eleven o'clock. He straightens his tie and tugs at the sleeves of his suit.

"You ready?"

Samira nods.

Flashguns explode and render me blind as I follow Samira to the conference table. Photographers are fighting for position, holding cameras above their heads in a strange jiggling dance.

Forbes holds a chair for Samira, then reaches across the table to a jug of water and pours her a glass. His slightly pockmarked face is bleached by the brightness of the TV lights.

Clearing his throat he begins. "We are investigating the abduction of two newborn babies, a twin boy and girl, born in the early hours of Sunday morning on board a ferry between the Hook of Holland and Harwich. The *Stena Britannica* docked at 3:36 a.m. GMT and the babies were last seen thirty minutes earlier."

Flashguns fire in his eyes.

Forbes makes no mention of baby broking or illegal surrogacy. Instead he concentrates on the details of the voyage and abduction. An image of Brendan Pearl is projected onto the screen behind him, along with a detailed description.

"DC Barba was returning from a short stay in Amsterdam when

she stumbled upon a people-trafficking operation. She helped deliver the twins but was unable to prevent the babies being taken.

"I want to stress that this is not a domestic dispute and Brendan Pearl is not related to the missing infants. Pearl is on parole after being released as a result of the Good Friday Agreement. He is considered dangerous. We are advising people not to approach him under any circumstances and to call the police if they know his whereabouts. Miss Khan will now make a brief statement."

He slides the microphone toward Samira. She looks at it suspiciously and unfolds a piece of paper. The flashguns create a wall of light and she stumbles over the first words. Someone shouts for her to speak up. She begins again.

"I wish to thank everyone who has looked after me these past few days, especially Miss Barba for helping me on the ferry when I was having the babies. I am also grateful to the police for all they have done. I ask the man who took the twins to give them back. They are very small and need medical care. Please take them to a hospital or leave them somewhere safe."

Samira looks up from the page. She's departing from the script. "I forgive you for this but I do not forgive you for Zala. For this I hope you will suffer eternal agony for every second of every day for the rest of your life."

Forbes cups his hand over the microphone, trying to stop her. Samira stands to leave. Questions are yelled from the floor.

"Who is Zala?"

"Did you know Brendan Pearl?"

"Why did he take your babies?"

The story has more holes than a Florida ballot card. The reporters sense a bigger story. Decorum breaks down.

"Has there been a ransom demand?"

"How did Pearl get off the ferry with the twins?"

"Do you believe they're still alive?"

Samira flinches. She's almost at the door.

"What about names?"

She turns to the questioner, blinking into the flashguns. "A maiden can leave things nameless; a mother must name her children."

The answer silences the room. People look at one another, wondering what she means. Mothers. Maidens. What does that have to do with anything?

Forbes's shoulders are knotted with rage.

"That was a fucking disaster," he mutters as I chase him down the corridor.

"It wasn't so bad."

"God knows what they're going to write tomorrow."

"They're going to write about the twins. That's what we want. We're going to find them."

He suddenly stops and turns. "That's only the beginning."

"What do you mean?"

"I want you to meet someone."

"When?"

"Now."

"The funerals are today."

"It won't take long." He glances ahead of us. Samira is waiting near the lift. "I'll make sure she gets home."

Twenty minutes later we pull up outside a Victorian mansion block in Battersea, overlooking the park. Twisting branches of Wisteria, naked and gray, frame the downstairs windows. The main door is open. An empty pram is poised, ready for an excursion. I can hear the mother coming down the stairs. She is attractive, in her early forties. A baby—too old to be one of the twins—rests on her hip.

"Excuse me, Mrs. Piper."

"Yes?"

"I'm Detective Inspector Forbes. This is DC Barba."

The woman's smile fades. Almost imperceptibly she tightens her hold on the child. A boy.

"How old is he?" I ask.

"Eight months."

"Aren't you beautiful." I lean forward. The mother leans away.

"What's his name?"

"Jack."

"He looks like you."

"He's more like his father."

Forbes interrupts. "We were hoping to have a brief word."

"I'm just going out. I have to meet someone."

"It won't take long."

Her gaze flicks from his face to mine. "I think I should call my husband." Pointedly she adds, "He works for the Home Office."

"Where did you have your baby?" Forbes asks.

She stutters nervously. "It was a home birth. I'm going upstairs to ring my husband."

"Why?" asks Forbes. "We haven't even told you why we're here, yet you're anxious about something. Why do you need your husband's permission to talk to us?"

There is a flaw in the moment, a ripple of disquiet.

Forbes continues: "Have you ever been to Amsterdam, Mrs. Piper? Did you visit a fertility clinic there?"

Backing away toward the stairs, she shakes her head, less in denial than in the vain hope that he'll stop asking her questions. She is on the stairs. Forbes moves toward her. He's holding a business card. She won't take it from him. Instead he leaves it in the pram.

"Please ask you husband to phone me."

I can hear myself apologizing for bothering her. At the same time I want to know if she paid for a baby. Who did she pay? Who arranged it? Forbes has hold of my arm, leading me down the steps. I imagine Mrs. Piper upstairs on the phone, the tears and the turmoil.

"Their names came up among the files Spijker sent me," Forbes explains. "They used a surrogate. A girl from Bosnia."

"Then it's *not* their baby."

"How do we prove that? You saw the kid. Paternity tests, DNA tests, blood samples—every one of them will show that young Jack belongs to the Pipers. And there isn't a judge in this country who would give us permission to take samples in the first place."

"We can prove they visited an IVF clinic in the Netherlands. We can prove their embryos were implanted in a surrogate. We can prove that it resulted in a pregnancy and a successful birth. Surely that's enough."

"It doesn't prove that money changed hands. We need one of these couples to give evidence."

He hands me a list of names and addresses:

Robert & Helena Piper
Alan & Jessica Case
Trevor & Toni Jury
Anaan & Lola Singh
Nicholas & Karin Pederson

"I have interviewed the other four couples. In each case they have called a lawyer and stuck to their story. None of them are going to cooperate—not if it means losing their child."

"They broke the law!"

"Maybe you're right, but how many juries are going to convict? If that was your friend back there, holding her baby, would *you* take it away from her?"

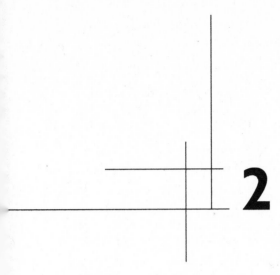

2

The funerals are at two o'clock. I am dressed in a black vest, black jacket, black trousers and black shoes. The only splash of color is my lipstick.

Samira uses the bathroom after me. It's hard to believe that she's just given birth. There are stretch marks across her belly but elsewhere her skin is flawless. Occasionally, I notice a tic or twitch of pain when she moves, but nothing else betrays her discomfort.

She is laying out her clothes on the bed, taking care not to crease her blouse.

"You don't have to come," I tell her, but she has already decided. She met Cate only twice. They spoke through Yanus in stilted sentences rather than having a proper conversation. Yet they shared a bond like no other. Unborn twins.

We sit side by side in the cab. She is tense, restless, as if at any moment she might unfurl a set of hidden wings and take flight. In the distance a chimney belches a column of white smoke like a steam train going nowhere.

"The police are going to find the twins," I announce, as if we're deep in conversation.

She doesn't answer.

I try again. "You do *want* to find them?"

"My debt is paid," she whispers, chewing at her lower lip.

"You *owe* these people nothing."

Again she doesn't answer. How can I make her understand? Without warning she offers an answer, placing her words in careful sentences.

"I have tried not to love them. I thought it would be easier to give them up if I did not love them. I have even tried to *blame* them for what happened to Hassan and Zala. This is unfair, yes? What else can I do? My breasts leak for them. I hear them crying in my dreams. I want the sound to stop."

Twin hearses are parked outside the chapel at the West London Crematorium. A carpet of artificial grass leads to a ramp where a small black sign with movable white letters spells out Felix and Cate's names.

Samira walks with surprising grace along the gravel path—not an easy thing to do. She pauses to look at the marble and stone crypts. Gardeners lean on their shovels and watch her. She seems almost alien. Otherworldly.

Barnaby Elliot is welcoming people and accepting condolences. Ruth Elliot is next to him in her wheelchair, dressed in mourning clothes that make her skin seem bloodless and brittle.

She sees me first. Her mouth twists around my name. Barnaby turns and walks toward me. He kisses me on each cheek and I smell the sharp alcohol scent of his aftershave.

"Who did you see in Amsterdam?" he asks.

"A detective. Why did you lie about Cate's computer?"

He doesn't answer. Instead he raises his eyes to the trees, some of which are clinging to the yellow-and-gold remnants of autumn.

"I feel you should know that I have instructed a lawyer to gain custody of the twins. I want both of them."

I look at him incredulously.

"What about Samira?"

"They're *our* grandchildren. They belong with us."

"Not according to the law."

"The law is an ass."

I glance across at Samira, who is hanging back, perhaps sensing trouble. Barnaby shows no such discretion. "Does she even *want* them?" he says, too loudly.

I have to unclench my jaw to speak. "You stay away from her."

"Listen to me—"

"No! *You* listen! She has been through enough. She has lost *everything.*"

Glaring at me with a sudden crazed energy, he lashes out at a hedge with his fist. His coat sleeve snags and he jerks it violently, tearing the fabric, which billows and flaps. Just as quickly he regains his composure. It's like watching a deep-breathing exercise for anger management. Reaching into his pocket, he takes out a business card.

"The trustee of Felix and Cate's will is having a meeting in chambers at Gray's Inn on Monday afternoon at three. He wants you there."

"Why?"

"He didn't say. This is the address."

I take the card and watch Barnaby return to his wife. Reaching for his hand, she cocks her head into his palm, holding it against her cheek. I have never seen them share a moment—not like this. Maybe it takes one tragedy to mend another.

The chapel is softly lit with red lights flickering behind glass. Flowers cover the coffins and spill out down the center aisle almost to Ruth Elliot's wheelchair. Barnaby is beside her, alongside Jarrod. All three of them are holding hands, as if steeling one another.

I recognize other family and friends. The only person missing is Yvonne. Perhaps she didn't think she could cope with a day like this. It must be like losing a daughter.

On the other side of the church are Felix's family, who look far more Polish than Felix ever did. The women are short and square, with veils on their heads and rosary beads in their fingers.

The funeral director is holding his top hat across his folded arm. His son, dressed identically, mimics his pose, although I notice a wad of chewing gum behind his ear.

A hymn strikes up, "Come Let Us Join Our Friends Above," which is not really Cate's cup of tea. Then again, it must be hard to find something appropriate for a person who once pledged her undying love to a photograph of Kurt Cobain.

Reading from the Bible, Reverend Lunn intones something about the Resurrection and how we're all going to rise together on the same day and live as God's children. At the same time, he rubs a finger along the edge of Cate's coffin as if admiring the workmanship.

"Love and pain are not the same," he says, "but sometimes it feels like they should be. Love is put to the test every day. Pain is not. Yet the two of them are inseparable because true love cannot bear separation."

His voice sounds far away. I have been in a state of suspended mourning for Cate for the past eight years. Trivial, sentimental, everyday sounds and smells bring back memories—lost causes, jazz shoes, cola slushies, Simply Red songs, a teenager singing into a hairbrush, purple eye shadow . . . These things make me want to smile or swell painfully in my chest. There it is again—love and pain.

I don't see the coffins disappear. During the final hymn I slip outside, needing fresh air. On the far side of the parking lot, in the shadows of an arch, I see a familiar silhouette, waiting, tranquil. He's wearing an overcoat and red muffler. Donavon.

Samira is walking through the rose garden at the side of the chapel. She is going to see him when she clears the corner.

Instinctively, I close the gap. Any witness would say that my body language borders on violence. I grab Donavon's arm, twisting it behind his back, before shoving him against a wall, pressing his face to the bricks.

"Where are they? What have you done with them?"

"I don't know what you're talking about."

I want him to struggle. I want to hurt him. Samira is behind me, hanging back.

"Do you know this man?"

"No."

"The Englishman you met at the orphanage. You said he had a cross on his neck." I pull aside Donavon's muffler, revealing his tattoo.

She shakes her head. "A gold cross. Here." She traces the outline on her collar.

Donavon laughs. "Wonderful detective work, yindoo."

I want to hit him.

"You were in Afghanistan."

"Serving Queen and country."

"Spare me the patriotic who-dares-wins crap. You lied to me. You saw Cate before the reunion."

"Yes."

"Why?"

"You wouldn't understand."

"Try me."

I let him go and he turns, blinking slowly, his pale eyes a little more bloodshot than I remember. Mourners are leaving the chapel. He glances at the crowd with a mixture of embarrassment and concern. "Not here. Let's talk somewhere else."

I let him lead the way. Leaving the cemetery, we walk east along the Harrow Road, which is choked with traffic and a conga line of buses. Sneaking sidelong glances at Donavon, I watch how he regards Samira. He doesn't seem to recognize her. Instead he keeps his eyes lowered in a penitent's demeanor, framing answers to the questions that he knows are coming. More lies.

We choose a café with stools at the window and tables inside. Donavon glances at the menu, buying time. Samira slips off her chair and kneels at the magazine rack, turning the pages quickly, as though expecting someone to stop her.

"The magazines are free to read," I explain. "You're allowed to look at them."

Donavon twists the skin on his wrist, leaving a white weal. Blood rushes back to the slackened skin.

"I met Cate again three years ago," he announces. "It was just before my first tour of Afghanistan. It took me a while to find her. I didn't know her married name."

"Why?"

"I wanted to see her."

I wait for something more. He changes the subject. "Have you ever been skydiving?"

"No."

"What a rush. There's no feeling like it—standing in the doorway of a plane at 10,000 feet, heart pounding, charged up. Take that last big step and the slipstream sucks you away. Falling—only it doesn't feel like falling at all. It's flying. Air presses hollows in your cheeks and screams past your ears. I've jumped high altitude, low opening, with oxygen from 25,000 feet. I swear I could open my arms and embrace the entire planet."

His eyes are shining. I don't know why he's telling me this but I let him continue.

"The best thing that ever happened to me was getting booted out of school and joining the Paras. Up until then I was drifting. Angry. I didn't have any ambition. It changed my life.

"I got a little girl now. She's three. Her mother doesn't live with me anymore, they're in Scotland, but I send 'em money every month and presents on her birthday and at Christmas. I guess what I'm trying to say is that I'm a different person."

"Why are you telling me this?"

"Because I want you to understand. You think I'm a thug and a bully but I changed. What I did to Cate was unforgivable but *she* forgave me. That's why I went looking for her. I wanted to find out how things turned out for her. I didn't want to think I screwed up her life because of what I did to her."

I don't want to believe him. I want to keep hating him because that's the world according to me. *My* recorded history.

"Why would Cate agree to see you?"

"She was curious I guess."

"Where did you meet?"

"We had a coffee in Soho."

"And?"

"We talked. I said I was sorry. She said it was OK. I wrote her a few letters from Afghanistan. Whenever I was home on leave we used to get together for lunch or a coffee."

"Why didn't you tell me this before?"

"Like I said, you wouldn't understand."

It's not a good enough reason. How could Cate forgive *Donavon* before she forgave me?

"What do you know about the New Life Adoption Center?"

"Cate took me there. She knew Carla couldn't decide what to do about the baby."

"How did Cate know about the adoption center?"

He shrugs. "Her fertility specialist is on the adoption panel."

"Dr. Banerjee. Are you sure?"

"Yeah."

Julian Shawcroft and Dr. Banerjee *know* each other. More lies.

"Did Cate tell you why she went to Amsterdam?"

"She said she was going to have another round of IVF."

I glance toward Samira. "She paid for a surrogate."

"I don't understand."

"There are twins."

Donavon looks dumbfounded. Speechless.

"Where?"

"They're missing."

I can see the knowledge register in his mind and match up with other details. News of the twins is already on the radio and in the early editions of the *Evening Standard*. I have shaken him more than I thought possible.

"What Cate did was illegal," I explain. "She was going to blow the whistle. That's why she wanted to talk to me."

Donavon has regained a semblance of composure. "Is that why they killed her?"

"Yes. Cate didn't accidentally find Samira. Someone put them together. I'm looking for a man called "Brother"—an Englishman, who came to Samira's orphanage in Kabul."

"Julian Shawcroft has been to Afghanistan."

"How do you know?"

"It came up in conversation. He was asking where I served."

I flip open my mobile and punch the speed dial. "New Boy" Dave answers on the second ring. I haven't talked to him since Amsterdam. He hasn't called. I haven't called. Inertia. Fear.

"Hello, sweet boy."

He sounds hesitant. I don't have time to ask why.

"When you did the background check on Julian Shawcroft, what did you find?"

"He used to be executive director of a Planned Parenthood clinic in Manchester."

"Before that."

"He studied theology at Oxford and then joined some sort of religious order."

"A religious order?"

"He became a Catholic brother."

There's the link! Cate, Banerjee, Shawcroft and Samira—I can tie them together.

Dave is no longer on the phone. I can't remember saying goodbye.

Donavon has been talking to me, asking questions. I haven't been listening.

"Did they look like Cate?" he asks.

"Who?"

"The twins."

I don't know how to answer. I'm not good at describing newborn babies. They all look like Winston Churchill. Why should he care?

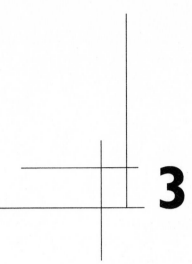

3

A silver-colored Lexus pulls into the driveway of a detached house in Wimbledon, South London. It has a personalized number plate: BABYDOC. Sohan Banerjee collects his things from the backseat and triggers the central locking. Lights flash. If only everything in life could be achieved with the press of a button.

"The penalty for people trafficking is fourteen years," I say.

The doctor wheels around, clutching his briefcase to his stomach like a shield. "I don't know what you're talking about."

"I don't know the penalty for commercial surrogacy but when you add medical rape and kidnapping I'm sure you'll be in prison long enough to make new friends."

"I've done nothing wrong."

"And I almost forgot murder. An automatic life sentence."

"You're trespassing," he blusters.

"Call the police."

He looks toward his house and then at the houses nearby perhaps conscious of what his neighbors might think.

"You *knew* Cate Beaumont was going to Amsterdam. You gave her a liquid nitrogen canister with her remaining embryos. You told her about the Dutch clinic."

"No. No." His chins are wobbling.

"Were you going to deliver the twins?"

"I don't know what you're talking about."

"How well do you know Julian Shawcroft?"

"We have a professional relationship."

"You were at Oxford together. He was studying theology. You were studying medicine. See how much I know, Dr. Banerjee? Not bad for some uppity Sikh girl who can't get a husband."

His briefcase is still resting on the shelf of his stomach. My skin prickles with something more physical than loathing.

"You're on his adoption panel."

"An independent body."

"You told Cate about the New Life Adoption Center. You introduced her to Shawcroft. What did you imagine you were doing? This wasn't some humanitarian crusade to help the childless. You got into bed with sex traffickers and murderers. Young women have been raped and exploited. People have died."

"You've got it all wrong. I had nothing to do with any of that. What motive would I have?"

Motive? I still don't understand why Banerjee would get mixed up in something like this. It can't be the money. Maybe he was trapped or tricked into doing a "favor." It takes only one mistake and the hooks are planted.

He looks toward the house again. There is no wife waiting for him inside. No children at the door.

"It's personal isn't it?"

He doesn't answer.

Forbes showed me a list of names. They were couples who provided embryos to the IVF clinic in Amsterdam. A surname suddenly stands out—Anaan and Lola Singh from Birmingham.

"Do you have family in the U.K., Dr. Banerjee? A sister, perhaps? Any nieces or nephews?"

He wants to deny it but the truth is imprinted on his features like fingerprints in putty. Mama mentioned that he had a nephew. The good doctor was so proud he told stories about him over Sunday lunch. I take a stab at the rest of the story. His sister couldn't get pregnant. And not even her very clever brother—a fertility specialist—could help her.

Julian Shawcroft suggested there might be another way. He organized a surrogate mother in the Netherlands and Banerjee delivered the baby. He thought it was a one-off—a family matter—but Shawcroft wanted him to deliver other babies. He couldn't say no.

"What do you want from me?"

"Give me Julian Shawcroft."

"I can't do that."

"Are you worried about your career, your reputation?"

Banerjee smiles wryly—a defeated gesture. "I have lived in this country for two-thirds of my life, Alisha. I hold master's and doctoral degrees from Oxford and Harvard. I have published papers, lectured and been a visiting fellow at the University of Toronto." He glances again at his house, the drawn curtains and empty rooms beyond. "My reputation is *all* I have."

"You broke the law."

"Is it so very wrong? I thought we were helping the childless and offering a new life to asylum seekers."

"You exploited them."

"We saved them from orphanages."

"And forced some of them into brothels."

His dense eyebrows are knitted together.

"Give me Shawcroft. Make a statement."

"I must protect my sister and her child."

"By protecting *him*?"

"We protect each other."

"I could have you arrested."

"I will deny everything."

"At least tell me where the twins are."

"I don't meet the families. Julian arranges that side of things." His voice changes. "I beg you, leave this alone. Only bad things can come of it."

"For whom?"

"For everyone. My nephew is a beautiful boy. He's nearly one."

"When he grows up are you going to tell him about the medical rape that led to his conception?"

"I'm sorry."

Everyone is sorry. It must be the times.

4

Forbes shuffles a stack of photographs and lays them out on a desk in three rows as if he's playing solitaire. Julian Shawcroft's picture is on the right edge. He looks like a charity boss straight from central casting: warm, smiling, avuncular . . .

"If you recognize someone I want you to point to the photograph," the detective says.

Samira hesitates.

"Don't worry about getting anyone in trouble—just tell me if there is someone here who you've met before."

Her eyes travel over the photographs and suddenly stop. She points to Shawcroft.

"This one."

"Who is he?"

"Brother."

"Do you know his real name?"

She shakes her head.

"How do you know him?"

"He came to the orphanage."

"In Kabul."

She nods.

"What was he doing there?"

"He brought blankets and food."

"Did you talk to him?"

"He couldn't speak Afghani. I translated for him."

"What did you translate?"

"He had meetings with Mr. Jamal, the director. He said he could arrange jobs for some of the orphans. He wanted only girls. I told him I could not leave without Hassan. He said it would cost more money but I could repay him."

"How much?"

"Five thousand American dollars for each of us."

"How were you supposed to repay this money?"

"He said God would find a way for me to pay."

"Did he say anything about having a baby?"

"No."

Forbes takes a sheet of paper from a folder. "This is a list of names. I want you to tell me if you recognize any of them."

Samira's finger dips down the page and stops. "This girl, Allegra, she was at the orphanage."

"Where did she go?"

"She left before me. Brother had a job for her."

The detective smiles tightly. "He certainly did."

Forbes's office is on the second floor, opposite a large open-plan incident room. There is a photograph of his wife on a filing cabinet. She looks like a no-nonsense country girl, who has never quite managed to shed the baby pounds.

He asks Samira to wait outside. There's a drink machine near the lift. He gives her change. We watch her walk away. She looks so young—a woman in progress.

"We have enough for a warrant," I say. "She identified Shawcroft."

Forbes doesn't answer. What is he waiting for? He stacks the photographs, lining up the edges.

"We can't link him with the surrogacy plot. It's her word against his."

"But the other orphans—"

"Have talked about a saintly man who offered to help them. We can't *prove* Shawcroft arranged for them to be trafficked. And we can't *prove* he blackmailed them into getting pregnant. We need one of the buyers to give evidence, which means incriminating themselves."

"Could we indemnify them from prosecution?"

"Yes, but we can't indemnify them against a civil lawsuit. Once they admit to paying for a surrogate baby, the birth mother could reclaim her child."

I can hear it in his voice—resignation. The task is proving too hard. He won't give up but neither will he go the extra yard, make the extra call, knock on one more door. He thinks I'm clutching at straws, that I haven't thought this through. I have never been more certain.

"Samira should meet him."

"What?"

"She could wear a wire."

Forbes sucks air through his teeth. "You gotta be kidding! Shawcroft would see right through it. He *knows* we have her."

"Yes, but investigations are about building pressure. Right now he thinks we can't touch him. He's comfortable. We have to shake him up—take him out of his comfort zone."

There are strict rules governing the bugging of phones and properties. The surveillance commissioner has to grant permission. But a wire is different—as long as she stays in a public place.

"What would she say?"

"He promised her a job."

"Is that it?"

"She doesn't *have* to say anything. Let's see what *he* says."

Forbes crunches a throat lozenge between his teeth. His breath smells of lemons.

"Is she up for it?"

"I think so."

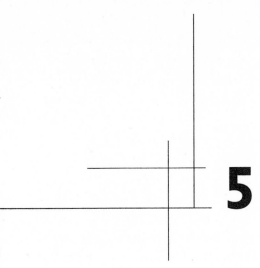

5

Any sport can be made to sound ridiculous if you break it down to its basics—stick, ball, hole—but I have never really understood the appeal of golf. The courses are pretty in an artificial sort of way, like Japanese gardens planned down to the last pebble and shrub.

Julian Shawcroft plays every Sunday morning in the same four-some, with a town planner, a car dealer and a local businessman. They tee off just after ten.

Their club is on the border of Sussex and Surrey, somewhere in the greenbelt and the white stockbroker belt. Brown is a color rarely seen out here unless you take a big divot.

Samira has a battery the size of a matchbox taped to the small of her back and a thin red fiber threaded under her right armpit to a button-sized microphone taped between her breasts.

Adjusting her blouse, I lift my eyes to hers and smile reassuringly. "You don't have to go through with this."

She nods.

"Do you know what you're going to say?"

Another nod.

"If you get frightened, walk away. If you feel threatened, walk away. Any sign of trouble, you understand?"

"Yes."

Groups of golfers are milling outside the locker room and on the practice green, waiting for the starter to call their names. Shawcroft has the loudest laugh but not the loudest trousers, which belong to one of his playing partners. He takes a practice swing beside the first tee and looks up to see Samira standing at the top of a set of stone steps with the sun behind her. He shields his eyes.

Without hesitation, she moves toward him, stopping six feet away.

"Can I help you?" asks one of the other golfers.

"I've come to see Brother."

Shawcroft hesitates, looking past her. He is searching for us.

"Nobody called Brother here, lass," says the car dealer.

Samira points. They turn to Shawcroft, who stutters a denial. "I don't know who she is."

Forbes adjusts the volume on the digital recording equipment. We're watching from eighty yards away, parked beneath the branches of a plane tree, opposite the pro shop.

Samira is a foot shorter than any of the men. Her long skirt flares out in the breeze.

"Maybe she can caddy for you, Julian?" one of them jokes.

"You remember me, Brother," says Samira. "You told me to come. You said you had a job for me."

Shawcroft looks at his playing partners apologetically. Suspicion is turning to anger. "Just ignore her. Let's play."

Turning his back, he takes a hurried practice swing and then sprays his opening drive wildly to the right where it disappears into trees. He tosses his club to the ground in disgust.

The others tee off. Shawcroft is already at the wheel of a golf cart. It jerks forward and accelerates away.

"I told you he wouldn't fall for this," says Forbes.

"Wait. Look."

Samira floats down the fairway after them, the hem of her skirt growing dark with dew. The carts have separated. Shawcroft is looking for his wayward drive in the rough. He glances up and sees her coming. I hear him yelling to his partner. "Lost ball. I'll hit another."

"You haven't even looked for this one."

"It doesn't matter."

He drops another ball and hacks it out, looking more like a woodchopper than a golfer. The cart takes off again. Samira doesn't break stride.

I feel a lump in my throat. This girl never ceases to amaze me. She follows them all the way to the green, skirting the bunkers and crossing a small wooden bridge over a brook. Constantly looking over his shoulder, Shawcroft thrashes at the ball and hurries forward.

"She's going to walk out of range," says Forbes. "We have to stop her."

"Wait. Just a little longer."

The foursome are more than 300 yards away but I can see them clearly enough through binoculars. Samira is standing on the edge of the green, watching and waiting.

Shawcroft finally snaps. "Get off this golf course or I'll have you arrested."

Waving his club, he storms toward her. She doesn't flinch.

"Steady on, old boy," someone suggests.

"Who is she, Julian?" asks another.

"Nobody."

"She's a pretty thing. She could be your ball washer."

"Shut up! Just shut up!"

Samira hasn't moved. "I paid my debt, Brother."

"I don't know what you're talking about."

"You said God would find a way for me to pay. I paid it twice. Twins. I paid for Hassan and for me, but he's dead. Zala didn't make it either."

Shawcroft grabs her roughly by the arm and hisses, "I don't know who sent you here. I don't know what you want, but I can't help you."

"What about the job?"

He is walking her away from the group. One of his partners yells, "Where are you off to, Julian?"

"I'm going to have her thrown off the course."

"What about the round?"

"I'll catch up."

The car dealer mutters, "Not again."

Another foursome is already halfway down the fairway. Shawcroft marches past them still holding Samira by the arm. She has to run to keep from falling.

"You're hurting me."

"Shut up you stupid slut. I don't know what you're playing at but it won't work. Who sent you here?"

"I paid my debt."

"Fuck the debt! There is no job! This is harassment. You come near me again and I'll have you arrested."

Samira doesn't give up. God, she's good.

"Why did Hassan die?"

"It's called life. Stuff happens."

I don't believe it. He's quoting Donald Rumsfeld. Why doesn't stuff happen to people like Shawcroft?

"It took me a long while to find you, Brother. We waited in Amsterdam for you to come or to send word. In the end we couldn't wait any longer. They were going to send us back to Kabul. Hassan came alone. I wanted to go with him but he said I should wait." Her voice is breaking. "He was going to find you. He said you had forgotten your promise. I told him you were honorable and kind. You brought us food and blankets at the orphanage. You wore the cross . . ."

Shawcroft twists her wrist, trying to make her stop.

"I had the babies. I paid my debt."

"Will you shut up!"

"Someone killed Zala—"

"I don't know what you're talking about."

They're nearing the clubhouse. Forbes is out of the car, moving toward them. I hang back. Shawcroft flings Samira into a flower bed. She bangs her knee and cries out.

"That qualifies as assault."

Shawcroft looks up and sees the detective. Then he looks past him and spies me.

"You have no right! My lawyer will hear about this."

Forbes hands him an arrest warrant. "Fine. For your sake I hope he's not playing golf today."

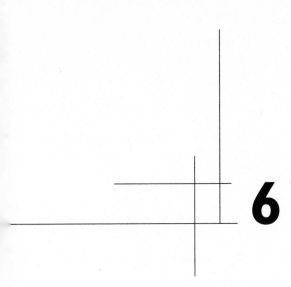

6

Shawcroft regards himself as an intellectual and a textbook lawyer, although he seems to have mixed up the Crimes Act and the Geneva convention as he yells accusations of inhuman treatment from his holding cell.

Intellectuals show off too much and wise people are just plain boring. (My mother is forever telling me to save money, go to bed early and not to lend things.) I prefer clever people who hide their talents and don't take themselves too seriously.

A dozen officers are going through the files and computer records of the New Life Adoption Center. Others are at Shawcroft's house in Hayward's Heath. I don't expect them to find a paper trail leading to the twins. He's too careful for that.

There is, however, a chance that prospective buyers initially came to the center looking to adopt legally. At our first meeting I asked him about the brochure I found at Cate's house, which advertised a baby boy born to a prostitute. Shawcroft was adamant that all adopting parents were properly screened. This should mean interviews, psych reports and criminal background checks. If he was telling me the truth then whoever has the twins could once have been on a waiting list at the adoption center.

It is four hours since we arrested him. Forbes arranged to bring him through the front door, past the public waiting area. He wanted to cause maximum discomfort and embarrassment. Although experienced, I sense that Forbes is not quite in the same league as Ruiz, who knows exactly when to be hard-nosed and when to let someone sweat for another hour in a holding cell, alone with their demons.

Shawcroft is waiting for his lawyer, Eddie Barrett. I could have guessed he would summon the "Bulldog," an old-fashioned ambulance chaser with a reputation for courting the media and getting right up police noses. He and Ruiz are old adversaries, sharing a mutual loathing and grudging respect.

Wolf whistles and howls of laughter erupt in the corridor. Barrett has arrived, dressed in jeans, cowboy boots, a plaid shirt and a ten-gallon hat.

"Look it's Willie Nelson!" someone calls.

"Is that a six-shooter in your pocket, Eddie, or are you just dawg-gone pleased to see me?"

Someone breaks into a hoedown. Eddie tucks his thumbs into his belt and gives them a few boot-scootin' moves. He doesn't seem to mind them taking the mickey out of him. Normally it's the other way round and he makes police look foolish during interviews or in court.

Barrett is a strange-looking man with an upside-down body (short legs and a long torso), and he walks just like George W. Bush with his arms held away from his body, his back unnaturally straight and his chin in the air. Maybe it's a cowboy thing.

One of the uniforms escorts him to an interview room. Shawcroft is brought upstairs. Forbes slips a plastic plug into his ear—a receiver that will allow us to talk to him during the interrogation. He takes a bundle of files and a list of questions. This is about *looking* prepared as much as *being* prepared.

I don't know if the DI is nervous but I can feel the tension. This is about the twins. Unless Shawcroft cracks or cooperates we may never find them.

The charity boss is still wearing his golfing clothes. Barrett sits next to him, placing his cowboy hat on the table. The formalities are dispensed with—names, the location and time of interview. Forbes then places five photographs on the table. Shawcroft doesn't bother looking at them.

"These five asylum seekers allege that you convinced them to leave their homelands and illegally enter the U.K."

"No."

"You deny knowing them?"

"I may have met them. I don't recall."

"Perhaps if you looked at their faces."

Barrett interrupts. "My client has answered your question."

"Where might you have met them?"

"My charities raised more than half a million pounds last year. I visited orphanages in Afghanistan, Iraq, Albania and Kosovo."

"How do you know these women are orphans? I didn't mention that."

Shawcroft stiffens. I can almost see him silently admonish himself for slipping up.

"So you *do* know these women?"

"Perhaps."

"And you know Samira Khan?"

"Yes."

"Where did you meet her?"

"At an orphanage in Kabul."

"Did you talk about her coming to the U.K.?"

"No."

"Did you offer her a job here?"

"No." He smiles his blameless smile.

"You introduced her to a man who smuggled her to the Netherlands and then to Britain."

"No."

"The cost was five thousand U.S. dollars but it rose to ten thousand by the time she reached Turkey. You told her that God would find a way for her to repay this money."

"I meet many orphans on my travels, Detective, and I don't think there has ever been one of them who didn't want to leave. It's what they dream about. They tell one another bedtime stories of escaping to the West where even beggars drive cars and dogs are put on diets because there is so much food."

Forbes places a photograph of Brendan Pearl on the table. "Do you know this man?"

"I can't recall."

"He is a convicted killer."

"I'll pray for him."

"What about his victims—will you pray for them?" Forbes is holding a photograph of Cate. "Do you know this woman?"

"She might have visited the adoption center. I can't be sure."

"She wanted to adopt?"

Shawcroft shrugs.

"You will have to answer verbally for the tape," says Forbes.

"I *can't* recall."

"Take a closer look."

"There's nothing wrong with my eyesight, Detective."

"What about your memory?"

Barrett interrupts. "Listen, Dr. Phil, it's Sunday. I got better things to do than listen to you stroke your pole. How about you tell us what my client is supposed to have done?"

Forbes shows admirable restraint. He places another photograph on the table, this one of Yanus. The questions continue. The answers are the same: "I cannot recall. I do not remember."

Julian Shawcroft is not a pathological liar (why tell a lie when the truth can serve you better?) but he is a natural deceiver and it comes as easily to him as breathing. Whenever Forbes has him under pressure, he carefully unfurls a patchwork of lies, tissue-thin yet carefully wrought, repairing any flaw in the fabric before it becomes a major tear. He doesn't lose his temper or show any anxiety. Instead he projects a disquieting calmness and a firm, fixed gaze.

Among the files at the adoption center are the names of at least twelve couples that also appear on paperwork from the IVF clinic in Amsterdam. I relay the information to Forbes via a transmitter. He touches his ear in acknowledgment.

"Have you ever been to Amsterdam, Mr. Shawcroft?" he asks.

I speak it here, it comes out there—like magic.

"Several times."

"Have you visited a fertility clinic in Amersfoort?"

"I don't recall."

"Surely you would remember this clinic." Forbes relates the name and address. "I doubt if you visit so many."

"I am a busy man."

"Which is why I'm sure you keep diaries and appointment calendars."

"Yes."

"Why haven't we found any?"

"I don't keep my schedule more than a few weeks before throwing it out. I deplore clutter."

"Can you explain how couples who were screened by your adoption center also appear in the files of an IVF clinic in Amsterdam?"

"Perhaps they were getting IVF treatment. People who want to adopt often try IVF first."

Barrett is gazing at the ceiling. He's in danger of getting bored.

"These couples didn't have IVF treatment," says Forbes. "They provided embryos that were implanted in the wombs of asylum seekers who were forced to carry pregnancies to term before the babies were taken from them."

Forbes points to the five photographs on the table. "These women, Mr. Shawcroft, the same women you met at different orphanages, the same women you encouraged to leave. They have identified you. They have provided statements to the police. And each one of them remembers you telling them the same thing: 'God will find a way for you to repay your debt.' "

Barrett takes hold of Shawcroft's arm. "My client wishes to exercise his right to silence."

Forbes gives the textbook reply. "I hope your client is aware that negative inferences can be drawn by the courts if he fails to mention facts that he later relies upon in his defense."

"My client is aware of this."

"Your client should also be aware that he has to remain here and listen to my questions, whether he answers them or not."

Barrett's small dark eyes are glittering. "You do what you have to, Detective Inspector. All we've heard so far is a bunch of fanciful stories masquerading as facts. So what if my client talked to these women? You have no evidence that he organized their illegal entry into this country. And no evidence that he was involved in this Goebbels-like fairy tale about forced pregnancies and stolen babies."

Barrett is perfectly motionless, poised. "It seems to me, Detective, that your entire case rests on the testimony of five illegal immigrants who would say anything to stay in this country. You want to make a case based on that—bring it on."

The lawyer gets to his feet, smooths his boot-cut jeans and adjusts his buffalo-skull belt buckle. He glances at Shawcroft. "My advice to you is to remain silent." He opens the door and swaggers down the corridor, hat in hand. There's that walk again.

7

"Penny for the Guy."

A group of boys with spiky haircuts are loitering on the corner. The smallest one has been dressed up as a tramp in oversize clothes. He looks like he's fallen victim to a shrinking ray.

One of the other boys nudges him. "Show 'em yer teef, Lachie."

Lachie opens his mouth sullenly. Two of them are blacked out.

"Penny for the Guy," they chorus again.

"You're not going to throw him on a bonfire I hope."

"No, ma'am."

"Good." I give them a pound.

Samira has been watching. "What are they doing?"

"Collecting money for fireworks."

"By begging?"

"Not exactly."

Hari has explained to her about Guy Fawkes Night. That's why the two of them have spent the past two days in my garden shed, dressed like mad scientists in cotton clothes, stripped of anything that might create static electricity or cause a spark.

"So this Guy Fawkes, he was a terrorist?"

"Yes, I suppose he was. He tried to blow up the Houses of Parliament with barrels of gunpowder."

"To kill the King?"

"Yes."

"Why?"

"He and his coconspirators weren't happy with the way the King was treating Catholics."

"So it was about religion."

"I guess."

She looks at the boys. "And they celebrate this?"

"When the plot failed, people set off fireworks in celebration and burned effigies of Guy Fawkes. They still do." Never let anyone tell you that Protestants don't hold a grudge.

Samira silently contemplates this as we make our way toward Bethnal Green. It's almost six o'clock and the air is already heavy with the smell of smoke and sulfur. Bonfires are dotted across the grass with families clustered around them, rugged up against the cold.

My entire family has come to see the fireworks. Hari is in his element, having emerged from the back shed carrying an old ammunition box containing the fruits of his labor and Samira's expertise. I don't know how he managed to source what she needed: the various chemicals, special salts and metallic powders. The most important ingredient, black powder, came from a hobby shop in Notting Hill, or more specifically from model rocket motors that were carefully disassembled to obtain the solid fuel propellant.

Torches dance across the grass and small fireworks are being lit: stick rockets, Roman candles, flying snakes, crackle dragons and bags of gold. Children are drawing in the air with sparklers and every dog in London is barking, keeping every baby awake. I wonder if the twins are among them. Perhaps they are too young to be frightened by the noise.

I hook my arm through Bada's and we watch Samira and Hari plant a heavy plastic tube in the earth. Samira has pulled her skirt between her legs and wrapped it tightly around her thighs. Her headscarf is tucked beneath the collar of her coat.

"Who would give him such knowledge?" says Bada. "He'll blow himself up."

"He'll be fine."

Hari has always been a favorite among equals. As the youngest, he has had my parents to himself for the past six years. I sometimes think he's their last link to middle age.

Shielding a pale tapered candle in the palm of her hand, Samira crouches close to the ground. One or two seconds elapses. A rocket whizzes into the air and disappears. One, two, three seconds pass until it suddenly explodes high above us, dripping stars that melt into the darkness. Compared with the fireworks that have come before, it is higher, brighter and louder. People stop their own displays to watch.

Hari sings out the names—dragon's breath, golden phoenix, glitter palm, exploding apples—while Samira moves without fuss between the launch tubes. Meanwhile, ground shells shoot columns of sparks around her and the explosions of color are mirrored in her eyes.

The finale is Hari's whistling chaser. Samira lets him light the fuse. It screams upward until little more than a speck of light detonates into a huge circle of white like a dandelion. Just when it seems about to fade, a red ball of light explodes within the first. The final salute is a loud bang that rattles the neighboring windows, setting off car alarms. The crowd applauds. Hari takes a bow. Samira is already cleaning up the scorched cardboard tubes and shredded paper, which she packs into the old ammunition box.

Hari is buzzing. "We should celebrate," he says to Samira. "I'll take you out."

"Out?"

"Yes."

"Where is out?"

"I don't know. We could have a drink or see a band."

"I do not drink."

"You could have a juice or a soft drink."

"I cannot go out with you. It's not good for a girl to be alone with a boy."

"We wouldn't be alone. The pub is always packed."

"She means without a chaperone," I tell him.

"Oh. Right."

I sometimes wonder why Hari is considered the brightest among my brothers. He looks crestfallen.

"It's a religious thing, Hari."

"But I'm not religious."

I give him a clip round the ear.

I still haven't told Samira about what happened at Shawcroft's interview or, more important, what *didn't* happen. The charity boss gave us nothing. Forbes had to let him go.

How do I explain the rules of evidence and the notion of burden of proof to someone who has never been afforded the luxury of justice or fairness?

On the walk home we drop behind the others, and I hook my arm in Samira's.

"But he did these things," she says, turning to face me. "None of this would have happened without him. Hassan and Zala would still be here. So many people are dead." She lowers her gaze. "Perhaps they are the lucky ones."

"You mustn't think such a thing."

"Why not?"

"Because the twins are going to need a mother."

She cuts me off with a slash of her hand. "I will *never* be their mother!"

Her face has changed. Twisted. I am looking at another face beneath the first, a dangerous one. It lasts only a fraction of a second— long enough to unsettle me. She blinks and it's gone. I have her back again.

We are almost home. A car has slowed about fifty yards behind us, edging forward without closing the gap. Fear crawls down my throat. I reach behind my back and untuck my shirt. The Glock is holstered at the base of my spine.

Hari has already turned into Hanbury Street. Mama and Bada have gone home. Opposite the next streetlight is a footpath between houses. Samira has noticed the car.

"Don't look back," I tell her.

As we pass under the streetlight, I push her toward the footpath, yelling at her to run. She obeys without question. I spin to face the car. The driver is in shadow. I aim the pistol at his head and he raises his hands, palms open like a mime artist pressing against a glass wall.

A rear window lowers. The interior light blinks on. I swing my gun into the opening. Julian Shawcroft has one hand on the door and the other holding what could be a prayer book.

"I want to show you something," he says.

"Am I going to disappear?"

He looks disappointed. "Trust in God to protect you."

"Will you take me to the twins?"

"I will help you understand."

A gust of wind, a splatter of raindrops, the night is growing blustery and bad-tempered. Across London people are heading home and bonfires are burning down. We cross the river and head south through Bermondsey. The glowing dome of St. Paul's is visible between buildings and above the treetops.

Shawcroft is silent. I can see his face in the passing beams of headlights as I nurse my gun and he nurses his book. I should be frightened. Instead I feel a curious calmness. My only phone call has been to home—checking to make sure that Samira made it safely.

The car pulls off the road into a driveway and stops in a rear courtyard.

I step out and see the driver's face for the first time across the vehicle's glistening roof. It's not Brendan Pearl. I didn't expect it to be. Shawcroft isn't foolish enough to be seen with a known killer.

A woman dressed in a French peasant skirt and oversize sweater appears at Shawcroft's side. Her hair is pinned back so tightly it raises her eyebrows.

"This is Delia," he says. "She runs one of my charities."

I shake a smooth dry hand.

Delia leads us through double doors and up a narrow staircase. There are posters on the walls with confronting images of hunger and neglect. Among them is a photograph of an African child with a distended stomach and begging bowl eyes. In the bottom corner there is a logo, a clock with letters instead of numbers spelling out O.R.P.H.A.N.W.A.T.C.H.!

Reaching behind me, I slide the gun into its holster.

We arrive at an office with desks and filing cabinets. A computer screen, dark and asleep, is silhouetted against the window. Shawcroft turns to Delia: "Is it open?"

She nods.

I follow him into a second room, which is fitted out as a small home theater with a screen and a projector. There are more posters on the walls, along with newspaper clippings, some dog-eared, torn or frayed at the edges. A small girl in a dirty white dress peers at the camera; a young boy with his arms folded eyes me defiantly. There are other images, dozens of them, papering the walls beneath display lights that have turned them into tragic works of art.

"These are the ones we could save," he says, his pale priestly hands clasped before him.

The wall panels are concertinaed. He expands them, revealing yet more photographs.

"Remember the orphans from the Asian tsunami? Nobody knows their true number but some estimates put it at 20,000. Homeless. Destitute. Traumatized. Families were queuing up to adopt them; governments were besieged with offers; but almost every one of them was refused."

His gaze slides over me. "Shall I tell you what happened to the tsunami orphans? In Sri Lanka the Tamil Tigers recruited them as soldiers, boys as young as seven. In India greedy relatives fought over the children because of the relief money being offered by the government and abandoned them once the money was paid.

"In Indonesia the authorities refused adoption to any couple who weren't Muslim. Troops dragged 300 orphans from a rescue flight because it was organized by a Christian charity. They were left with nowhere to go and nothing to eat. Even countries like Thailand and India that allow foreign adoptions suddenly closed their borders— spooked by unconfirmed stories of orphans being trafficked out of the country by gangs of pedophiles. It was ridiculous. If someone robs a bank you don't shut down the international banking system. You catch the robber. You prosecute them. Unfortunately, each time a child is trafficked they want to shut down the international adoption system, making things worse for millions of orphans.

"People don't understand the sheer scale of this problem. Two million children are forced into prostitution every year—a million of them in Asia. And more children are orphaned every *week* in Africa than were orphaned by the Asian tsunami. There are thirteen million in sub-Saharan Africa alone.

"The so-called experts say children shouldn't be treated as commodities. Why not? Isn't it better to be treated as a commodity than to be treated like a dog? Hungry. Cold. Living in squalor. Sold into slavery. Raped. They say it shouldn't be about money. What else is it going to be about? How else are we going to save them?"

"You think the end justifies the means."

"I think it *should* be a factor."

"You can't treat people like a resource."

"Of course I can. Economists do it all the time. I'm a pragmatist."

"You're a monster."

"At least I give a damn. The world needs people like me. Realists. Men of action. What do you do? Sponsor a child in Burundi or pledge to Comic Relief. You try to save one, while ten thousand others starve."

"And what's the alternative?"

"Sacrifice one and save ten thousand."

"Who chooses?"

"Pardon?"

"Who chooses the one you're going to sacrifice?"

"I choose. I don't ask others to do it for me."

I hate him then. For all his dark charm and elegant intensity, Shawcroft is a bully and a zealot. I prefer Brendan Pearl's motives. At least he doesn't try to justify his killings.

"What happens if the odds change?" I ask. "Would you sacrifice five lives to save five hundred? What about ten lives to save eleven?"

"Let's ask the people, shall we?" he replies sarcastically. "I get eleven votes. You only get ten. I win."

Fleetingly, unnervingly, I understand what he's saying but cannot accept a world that is so brutally black and white. Murder, rape and torture are the apparatus of terrorists, not of civilized societies. If we become like them, what hope do we have?

Shawcroft thinks he's a moral man, a charitable man, a saintly man, but he's not. He's been corrupted. He has become part of the problem instead of the solution—trafficking women, selling babies, exploiting the vulnerable.

"Nothing gives you the right to choose," I tell him.

"I accepted the role."

"You think you're God!"

"Yes. And do you know why? Because someone has to be. Bleeding hearts like you only pay lip service to the poor and destitute. You wear colored bands on your wrists and claim that you want to make poverty history. How?"

"This isn't about me."

"Yes it is."

"Where are the twins?"

"Being loved."

"Where?"

"Where they belong."

The pistol is resting against the small of my back, warm as blood. My fingers close around it. In a single motion I swing it toward him, pressing the muzzle against his forehead.

I expect to see fear. Instead he blinks at me sadly. "This is like a war, Alisha. I know we use that term too readily, but sometimes it is justified and some wars are just. The war on poverty. The war on hunger. Even pacifists cannot be opposed to wars such as these. Innocent people get hurt in conflict. Your friend was a casualty."

"You sacrificed her."

"To protect others."

"Yourself."

My finger tightens on the trigger. Another half pound of pressure and it's over. He is watching me along the barrel—still not frightened. For a brief moment I think he's prepared to die, having said his piece and made his peace.

He doesn't close his eyes. He *knows* I can't do it. Without him I might never find the twins.

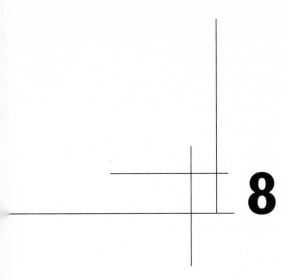

8

A large portrait above the fireplace shows a patrician man in legal robes with a horsehair wig that looks surprisingly like a shih tzu resting on his forearm. He gazes sternly down at a polished table that is surrounded by high-backed chairs.

Felix's mother is dressed in a tweed jacket and black slacks, clutching her handbag as though someone might steal it. Beside her, another of her sons rattles his fingers on the table, already bored.

Barnaby is at the window, studying the small courtyard outside. I don't notice Jarrod as he crosses the room. He touches my shoulder.

"Is it true? Am I an uncle?"

His hair is brushed back from his temples and beginning to thin.

"I'm not sure what you are, technically."

"My father says there are twins."

"They don't belong to Cate. A girl was forced to have them."

His eyes don't understand. "Biologically they belong to Cate. That makes me an uncle."

"Perhaps. I really don't know."

The solicitor enters the conference room and takes a seat. In his mid-fifties, dressed in a three-piece pinstriped suit, he introduces himself as William Grove and stretches his face into a tight smile.

His whole demeanor is one of contained speed. Time is money. Every fifteen minutes is billable.

Chairs scrape backward. People are seated. Mr. Grove glances at his instructions.

"Ladies and gentlemen, a codicil was added to this will six weeks ago and it appears to be predicated on the likelihood that the Beaumonts would become parents."

A frisson disturbs the atmosphere like a sudden change in the air pressure. The solicitor glances up, tugging at his shirt cuffs. "Am I to understand this marriage produced children?"

Silence.

Finally, Barnaby clears his throat. "It does seem likely."

"What do you mean? Please explain."

"We have reason to believe that Cate and Felix arranged a surrogacy. Twins were born eight days ago."

The next minute is one of exclamation and disbelief. Felix's mother makes a choking noise at the back of her throat. Barnaby is looking at his hands, rubbing his fingertips. Jarrod hasn't taken his eyes off me.

Unsure of how to proceed Mr. Grove takes a moment to compose himself. He decides to continue. The estate consists of a heavily mortgaged family home in Willesden Green, North London, which was recently damaged in a fire. Insurance will cover the cost of rebuilding. Felix also had a life insurance policy provided by his employer.

"If there is no objection, I shall read from the wills, which are each ostensibly the same." He takes a sip of water.

"This is the last will and testament of me, Cate Elizabeth Beaumont (née Elliot), made on the 14th day of September 2006. I hereby revoke all wills heretofore made by me and declare this to be my last will and testament. I appoint William Grove of Sadler, Grove and Buffett to be executor and trustee of this, my will. I give, devise and bequeath to my husband, Felix Beaumont (formerly known as Felix Buczkowski), the whole of my estate provided that he survives me by thirty days and, if not, then I give the whole of my estate to my child or children to be shared equally as tenants in common.

"I appoint Alisha Kaur Barba as guardian of my infant children and I direct her to love and care for them and to expend so much as is necessary from the estate of the children to raise, educate and advance their life."

Barnaby is on his feet, his jaw flapping in protest. For a moment I think he might be having a heart attack.

"This is preposterous! I will not have my grandchildren raised by a bloody stranger." He stabs a finger at me. "You knew about this!"

"No."

"You knew all along."

"I didn't."

Mr. Grove tries to calm him down. "I can assure you, sir, that everything has been properly signed and witnessed."

"What sort of idiot do you take me for? This is bullshit! I won't let anyone take my grandchildren away."

The outburst has silenced the room. The only sounds are from the air-conditioning and distant water pipes filling and disgorging. For a moment I think Barnaby might actually strike me. Instead he kicks back his chair and storms out, followed by Jarrod. People turn to look at me. The back of my neck grows warm.

Mr. Grove has a letter for me. As I take it from him, I have to keep my hand steady. Why would Cate do this? Why choose me? Already the sense of responsibility is pressing against my lungs.

The envelope is creased in my fist as I leave the conference room and cross the lobby, pushing through heavy glass doors. I have no idea where I'm going. Is this it? One poxy letter is supposed to explain things? Will it make up for eight years of silence?

Another notion suddenly haunts my confusion. Maybe I'm being given a chance to redeem myself. To account for my neglect, my failures, the things left unsaid, all those sins of omission and commission. I am being asked to safeguard Cate's most precious legacy and to do a better job than I managed with our friendship.

I stop in the doorway of an off-licence and slide my finger beneath the flap of the envelope.

Dear Ali,

It is a weird thing writing a letter that will only be opened and read upon one's death. It's hard to get too sad about it though. And if I am dead, it's a bit late to fret about spilling that particular pint of white.

My only real concern is you. You're my one regret. I have wanted to be friends with you ever since we met at Oaklands and you fought Paul Donavon to defend my honor and lost your front tooth. You were the real thing, Ali, not one of the plastics.

I know you're sorry about what happened with my father. I know it was more his fault than yours. I forgave you a long time ago. I forgave him because, well, you know how it is with fathers. You weren't the first of his infidelities, by the way, but I guess you worked that out.

The reason I could never tell you this is because of a promise I made to my mother. It was the worst sort of promise. She found out about you and my father. He told her because he thought I would tell her.

My mother made me promise never to see you again; never to talk to you; never to invite you to the house; never to mention your name.

I know I should have ignored her. I should have called. Many times I almost did. I got as far as picking up the phone. Sometimes I even dialed your parents' number but then I wondered what I'd say to you. We had left it too long. How would we ever get around the silence, which was like an elephant sitting in the room?

I have never stopped thinking about you. I followed your career as best I could, picking up stories from other people. Poor old Felix has been bored silly listening to me talk about our exploits and adventures. He's heard so much about you that he probably feels like he's been married to both of us.

Six weeks from now, God willing, I will become a mother after six years of trying. If something happens to me and to Felix—if we die in a flaming plane crash or should suicide bombers ever target Tesco at Willesden Green—we want you to be the guardian of our children.

My mother is going to pass a cow when she learns this but I have kept my promise to her, which didn't include any clause covering posthumous contact with you.

There are no strings attached. I'm not going to write provisos or instructions. If you want the job it's yours. I know you'll love my children as much as I do. And I know you'll teach them to look after each other. You'll say the things I would have said to them and tell them about me and about Felix. The good stuff, naturally.

I don't know what else to tell you. I often think how different my life would have been—how much happier—if you'd been a part of it. One day.

Love, Cate

It is just after five o'clock. The streetlights are smudged with my tears. Faces drift past me. Heads turn away. Nobody asks after a crying woman anymore—not in London. I'm just another of the crazies to be avoided.

On the cab ride to West Acton I catch my reflection in the window. I will be thirty years old on Thursday—closer to sixty than I am to birth. I still look young yet exhausted and feverish, like a child who has stayed up too late at an adult party.

There is a FOR SALE sign outside "New Boy" Dave's flat. He's serious about this; he's going to quit the force and start teaching kids how to sail.

I debate whether to go up. I walk to the front door, stare at the bell and walk back to the road. I don't want to explain things. I just want to open a bottle of wine, order a pizza and curl up on the sofa with his legs beneath mine and his hands rubbing my toes, which are freezing.

I haven't seen Dave since Amsterdam. He used to phone me every day, sometimes twice. When I called him after the funerals he sounded hesitant, almost nervous.

The elephant in the room. It can't be talked about. It can't be ignored. My patched-up pelvis is like that. People suddenly want to give me children. Is that ironic? I'm never sure with irony; the term is so misused.

I go back to the door. It takes a long while for anyone to answer. It's a woman's voice on the intercom. Apologetic. She was in the shower.

"Dave's not here."

"It's my fault. I should have phoned."

"He's on his way home. Do you want to come in and wait?"

"No, that's OK."

Who is she? What's she doing here?

"I'll tell him you dropped by."

"OK."

A pause.

"You need to give me your name."

"Of course. Sorry. Don't worry about it. I'll call him."

I walk back to the road, telling myself I don't care.

Shit! Shit! Shit!

The house is strangely quiet. The TV in the front room is turned down and lights are on upstairs. I slip along the side path and through the back door. Hari is in the kitchen.

"You have to stop her."

"Who?"

"Samira. She's leaving. She's upstairs packing."

"Why? What did you do to her?"

"Nothing."

"Did you leave *her* alone?"

"For twenty minutes, I swear. That's all. I had to drop off a mate's car."

Samira is in my bedroom. Her clothes are folded on the bed—a few simple skirts, blouses, a frayed jumper . . . Hassan's biscuit tin sits on top of the pile.

"Where are you going?"

She seems to hold her breath. "I am leaving. You do not want me here."

"What makes you say that? Did Hari do something? Did he say something he shouldn't have said?"

She won't look at me, but I see the bruise forming on her cheek, a rough circle beneath her right eye.

"Who did this?"

She whispers, "A man came."

"What man?"

"The man who talked to you at the church."

"Donavon?"

"No, the other man."

She means Barnaby. He came here, spoiling for a fight.

"He was hitting the door—making so much noise. He said you lied to me and you lied to him."

"I have never lied to you."

"He said you wanted the babies for yourself and he would fight you and he would fight me."

"Don't listen to him."

"He said I wasn't welcome in this country. I should go back where I came from—among the terrorists."

"No."

I reach toward her. She pulls away.

"Did he hit you?"

"I tried to shut the door. He pushed it." She touches her cheek.

"He had no right to say those things."

"Is it true? Do *you* want the babies?"

"Cate wrote a will—a legal document. She nominated me as the guardian if she had children."

"What does guardian mean? Do the twins belong to you now?"

"No. You gave birth to them. They might have Cate's eyes and Felix's nose, but they grew inside your body. And no matter what anyone says they belong to you."

"What if I don't want them?"

My mouth opens but I don't answer. Something has lodged in my throat, a choking lump of desire and doubt. No matter what Cate wanted, they're not my babies. My motives are pure.

I put my arm around Samira's shoulders and pull her close to me. Her breath is warm against my neck and her first sob thuds like a spade hitting wet dirt. Something breaks inside her. She has found her tears.

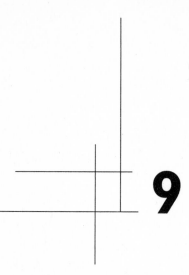

9

The digital numbers of my alarm clock glow in the darkness. It has just gone four. I won't sleep again. Samira is curled up next to me, breathing softly.

I am a collector of elephants. Some are soft toys; others are figurines made from cut glass, porcelain, jade or crystal. My favorite is six inches high and made from heavy glass, inlaid with mirrors. Normally it sits beneath my reading light, throwing colored stars on the walls. It's not there now. I wonder what could have happened to it.

Slipping out of bed quietly, I dress in my running gear and step outside into the darkness of Hanbury Street. There is an edge to the breeze. Seasons changing.

Cate used to help me train after school. She rode her bicycle alongside me, speeding up before we reached the hills because she knew I could outrun her on the climbs. When I ran at the national age championships in Cardiff she begged her parents to let her come. She was the only student from Oaklands to see me win. I ran like the wind that day. Fast enough to blur at the edges.

I couldn't see Cate in the stands but I could pick out my mother who wore a bright crimson sari like a splash of paint against the blue seats and gray spectators.

My father never saw me compete. He didn't approve.

"Running is not ladylike. It makes a woman sweat," he told me.

"Mama sweats all the time in the kitchen."

"It is a different sort of sweat."

"I didn't know there were different kinds of sweat."

"Yes, it is a well-known scientific fact. The sweat of hard work and of food preparation is sweeter than the sweat of vigorous exercise."

I didn't laugh. A good daughter respects her father.

Later I heard my parents arguing.

"How is a boy supposed to catch her if she runs so fast?"

"I don't want boys catching her."

"Have you seen her room? She has weights. My daughter is lifting barbells."

"She's in training."

"Weights are not feminine. And do you see what she wears? Those brief shorts are like underwear. She's running in her underwear."

In darkness I run two circuits of Victoria Park, sticking to the tarmac paths, using the streetlights to navigate.

My mother used to tell me a folktale about a village donkey that was always mocked for being stupid and ugly. One day a guru took pity on the animal. "If you had the roar of a tiger they would not laugh," he thought. So he took a tiger skin and laid it across the donkey's back. The donkey returned to the village and suddenly everything changed. Women and children ran screaming. Men cowered in corners. Soon the donkey was alone in the market and feasted on the lovely apples and carrots.

The villagers were terrified and had to be rid of the dangerous "tiger." A meeting was called and they decided to drive the tiger back to the forest. Drumbeats echoed through the market and the poor bewildered donkey turned this way and that. He ran into the forest but the hunters tracked him down.

"That's no tiger," one of them shouted. "Surely it's only the donkey from the market."

The guru appeared and calmly lifted the tiger skin from the terrified beast. "Remember this animal," he said to the people. "He has the skin of a tiger but the soul of a donkey."

I feel like that now—a donkey not a tiger.

I am just passing Smithfield Market when a realization washes over me. At first it is no more than an inkling. I wonder what prompts such a reaction. Maybe it's a pattern of footsteps or a sound that is out of place or a movement that triggers a thought. It comes to me now. I know how to find the twins!

Forbes has been concentrating on couples who succeeded in obtaining a child by using a genetic surrogate. They cannot give evidence against Shawcroft without incriminating themselves. Why would they? Science supports them. Nobody can prove they're not the birth parents.

But whoever has the twins doesn't have a genetic safety net. DNA tests will expose rather than sustain them. They haven't had time to fake a pregnancy or set up an elaborate deceit. Right now they must be feeling vulnerable.

At this hour of the morning it isn't difficult to find a parking spot in Kennington, close to Forbes's office. Most of the detectives start work at nine, which means the incident room is deserted except for a detective constable who has been working the graveyard shift. He's about my age and quite handsome in a sulky sort of way. Perhaps I woke him up.

"Forbes asked me to come." I lie.

He looks at me doubtfully. "The boss has a meeting at the Home Office this morning. He won't be in the office until later."

"He wants me to follow up a lead."

"What sort of lead?"

"Just an idea, that's all."

He doesn't believe me. I call Forbes to get approval.

"This better be fucking important," he grumbles.

"Good morning, sir."

"Who's this?"

"DC Barba."

"Don't good morning me."

"Sorry, sir."

I can hear Mrs. Forbes in the background telling him to be quiet. Pillow talk.

"I need access to Shawcroft's phone records."

"It's six in the morning."

"Yes, sir."

He's about to say no. He doesn't trust me. I'm bad news or bad luck. Everything I've touched has turned to shit. I sense another reason. A nervousness. Ever since he released Shawcroft, the DI has backtracked and made excuses. He must have copped some heat, but that goes with the territory.

"I want you to go home, DC Barba."

"I have a lead."

"Give it to the night detective. You're not part of this investigation." His voice softens. "Look after Samira."

Why is he being so negative? And why the briefing at the Home Office? It must be about Shawcroft.

"How is your wife, sir?" I ask.

Forbes hesitates. She's lying next to him. What can he say?

There is a long pause. I whisper, "We're on the same side, sir. You didn't screw me that night so don't screw me now."

"Fine. Yes, I can't see a problem," he answers. I hand the phone over to the night detective and listen to their yes-sir, no-sir exchange. The phone is handed back to me. Forbes wants a final word.

"Anything you find, you give to me."

"Yes, sir."

The call ends. The night detective looks at me and we smile in unison. Waking up a senior officer is one of life's small pleasures.

The DC's name is Rod Beckley but everyone calls him Becks. "On account of me being crap at football," he jokes.

After clearing a desk and finding me a chair, he delivers a dozen ring-bound folders. Every incoming and outgoing call from the New Life Adoption Center is listed, including the numbers, the duration of each call, the time and the date they were made. There are six voice lines and two fax lines, as well as a direct-dial number into Shawcroft's office.

Further folders cover his mobile phone and home line. Text messages and e-mails have been printed out and stapled together in chronological order.

Taking a marker pen, I begin to group the calls.

Rather than concentrate on the phone numbers, I look at the times. The ferry arrived in Harwich at 3:36 a.m. on Sunday morning. We know that Pearl walked off the ferry just after four. At 10:25 a.m. he bought nappies and baby formula from a motorway service station on the M25 before stealing a car.

I look down the list of calls to Shawcroft's mobile. There was an incoming call at 10:18 a.m. that lasted less than thirty seconds. I check the number. It appears only once. It could be a wrong number.

DC Beckley is flicking at a keyboard across the office, trying to look busy. I sit on the edge of his desk until he looks up.

"Can we find out who this number belongs to?"

He accesses the Police National Computer and types in the digits. A map of Hertfordshire appears. The details are listed on a separate window. The phone number belongs to a public phone box at Potter's Bar—a motorway service area near junction 24 on the M25. It's the same service area where Brendan Pearl was last sighted. He must have phoned Shawcroft for instructions about where to deliver the twins. It is the closest I've come to linking the two men, although it's not conclusive.

Going back to the folders, I strike a dead end. Shawcroft didn't use his mobile for the next three hours. Surely if his plan was coming apart, he would have called someone.

I try to picture last Sunday morning. Shawcroft was on the golf course. His foursome teed off at 10:05. One of his playing partners said something when Samira interrupted their game and Shawcroft tried to drag her off the course: "Not again."

It had happened before—a week earlier. After the phone call from Pearl, Shawcroft must have abandoned his round. Where did he go? He needed to let the buyer or buyers know that the twins had arrived. He had to bring the pickup forward. It was too risky using his own mobile so he looked for another phone—one that he thought couldn't be traced.

I go back to Becks. "Is it possible to find out if there is a public phone located at a golf club in Surrey?"

"Maybe. You got a name?"

"Yes. Twin Bridges Country Club. It could be in a locker room or lounge. Somewhere quiet. I'm interested in outgoing calls timed between 9:20 a.m. and 10:30 a.m. on Sunday, October 29."

"Is that all?" he asks facetiously.

"No. Then we have to cross-check them with the adoption waiting list at the New Life Adoption Center."

He doesn't understand, but he begins the search anyway. "You think we'll find a match."

"If we're lucky."

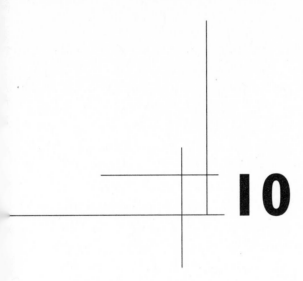

10

"New Boy" Dave hears my voice on the intercom and pauses for a moment before pressing the buzzer to unlock the front door. When I reach his flat the door is propped open. He is in the kitchen stirring paint.

"So you're definitely selling."

"Yep."

"Any offers?"

"Not yet."

There are two cups in the drainer and two cold tea bags solidifying in the sink, alongside a paint roller and a couple of brushes. The ceilings are to be a stowe white. I helped him choose the color. The walls are a misty green, cut back by 50 percent and the skirting boards and frames are full strength.

I follow Dave into the living room. His few pieces of furniture have been pushed to the center and covered in old sheets.

"How is Samira?" he asks.

The question is unexpected. Dave has never met her, but he will have seen the TV bulletins and read the papers.

"I'm worried about her. I'm worried about the twins."

He fills the roller from the tray.

"Will you help me?"

"It's not our case."

"I might have found them. Please help me."

Climbing the ladder he runs the roller across the ceiling creating long ribbons of paint.

"What does it matter, Dave? You've resigned. You're leaving. My career is finished. It doesn't matter what toes we tread on or who we piss off. There's something wrong with this case. People are tiptoeing around it, playing softly softly, while the real culprits are shredding files and covering their tracks."

The roller is gliding across the ceiling. I know he's listening.

"You're acting like these kids belong to *you*."

I have to catch myself before my head snaps up. He looks down at me from the top of the ladder. Why do people keep questioning my motives? Eduardo de Souza, Barnaby, now Dave. Is it me who can't see the truth? No, they're wrong. I don't want the twins for myself.

"I'm doing this because a friend of mine—my best friend—entrusted to me what she loved most, the most precious thing she had. I couldn't save Cate and I couldn't save Zala, but I *can* save the twins."

There is a long silence. Only one of us feels uncomfortable. "New Boy" has always been defined more by what he dislikes than by what he likes. He doesn't like cats, for instance, or hypocrites. He also loathes reality TV shows, Welsh rugby fans and tattooed women who scream at their kids in supermarkets. I can live with a man like that. His silences are another matter. He seems comfortable with them but I want to know what he's thinking. Is he angry that I didn't leave Amsterdam with him? Is he upset at how we left things? We both have questions. I want to know who answered the intercom last night, fresh from his shower.

I turn toward his bedroom. The door is open. I notice a suitcase against the wall and a blouse hanging on the back of the open door. I don't realize I'm staring and I don't notice Dave climb down the ladder and take the roller to the kitchen. He wraps it carefully in cling film, leaving it on the sink. Peeling off his shirt, he tosses it in a corner.

"Give me five minutes. I need to shower." He scratches his unshaven chin. "Better make it ten."

Two addresses: one just across the river in Barnes and the other in Finsbury Park, North London. The first address belongs to a couple whose names also appear on a waiting list at the New Life Adoption Center. The Finsbury Park address doesn't appear on the files.

Sunday week ago—just after ten o'clock—both addresses received a call from a public phone in the locker room of the Twin Bridges Country Club in Surrey. Shawcroft was there when those calls were made.

It's a hunch. It's too many things happening at the same time to be coincidental. It's worth a look.

Dave is dressed in light cords, a shirt and a leather jacket. "What do you want to do?"

"Check them out."

"What about Forbes?"

"He won't make this sort of leap. He might get there in the end by ticking off the boxes, methodically, mechanically, but what if we don't have time for that?"

I picture the smallest twin, struggling to breathe. My own throat closes. She should be in hospital. We should have found her by now.

"OK, so you have two addresses. I still don't know what you expect to do," says Dave.

"Maybe I'm just going to knock on the front door and say, 'Do you have twins that don't belong to you?' I can tell you what I *won't* do. I won't sit back and wait for them to disappear."

Brown leaves swirl from a park onto the pavement and back to the grass, as if unwilling to cross the road. The temperature hasn't strayed above single figures and the wind is driving it lower.

We're parked in a typical street in Barnes: flanked by tall, gabled houses and plane trees that have been so savagely pruned they look almost deformed.

This is a stockbroker suburb, full of affluent middle-class families who move here for the schools and the parks and the proximity to the city. Despite the cold, half a dozen mothers or nannies are in the playground, watching over preschoolers who are dressed in so many clothes they look like junior Michelin Men.

Dave watches the yummy mummies, while I watch the house, No. 85. Robert and Noelene Gallagher drive a Volvo Estate, pay their TV license fee on time and vote Liberal Democrat. I'm guessing, of course, but it strikes me as that sort of area, that sort of house.

Dave rakes his fingers through his lopsided bramble of hair. "Can I ask you something?"

"Sure."

"Have you ever loved me?"

I didn't see this coming.

"What makes you think I don't love you now?"

"You've never said."

"What do you mean?"

"You might have used the word, but not in a sentence with my name in it. You've never said, 'I love you, Dave.' "

I think back, wanting to deny it, but he seems so sure. The nights we lay together with his arms around me, I felt so safe, so happy. Didn't I ever tell him? I remember my philosophical debates and arguments about the nature of love and how debilitating it can be. Were they all internal? I was trying to talk myself *out* of loving him. I lost, but he had no way of knowing that.

I should tell him now. How? It's going to sound contrived or forced. It's too late. I can try to make excuses; I can blame my inability to have children but the truth is that I'm driving him away. There's another woman living in his flat.

He's doing it again—not saying anything. Waiting.

"You're seeing someone," I blurt out, making it sound like an accusation.

"What makes you say that?"

"I met her."

He turns his whole body in the driver's seat to face me, looking surprised rather than guilty.

"I came to see you yesterday. You weren't home. She answered the intercom."

"Jacquie?"

"I didn't take down her name." *I sound so bloody jealous.*

"My sister."

"You don't have a sister."

"My sister-in-law. My brother's wife, Jacquie."

"They're in San Diego."

"They're staying with me. Simon is my new business partner. I told you."

Could this get any worse? "You must think I'm such an idiot," I say. "I'm sorry. I mean, I'm not the jealous type, not usually. It's just that after what happened in Amsterdam, when you didn't call me and I didn't call you, I just thought—it's so stupid—that you'd found someone else who wasn't so crippled, or troublesome or such hard work. Please don't laugh at me."

"I'm not laughing."

"What are you doing?"

"I'm looking at that car."

I follow his gaze. A Volvo Estate is parked near the front gate of No. 85. There is a sunshade on the nearside rear window and what looks like a baby seat.

Dave is giving me a way out. He's like a chivalrous gentleman spreading his coat over a muddy puddle.

"I should check it out," I say, opening the car door. "You stay here."

Dave watches me leave. He knows I'm dodging the issue yet again. I have underestimated him. He's smarter than I am. Nicer, too.

Crossing the street, I walk along the pavement, pausing at the Volvo and bending as if to tie my shoelaces. The windows are tinted but I can make out small handprints inside the glass and a Garfield sticker on the back window.

I glance across at Dave and make a knocking motion with my fist. He shakes his head. Ignoring the signal, I open the front gate and climb the steps to the house.

I press the buzzer. The front door opens a crack. A girl aged about five regards me very seriously. Her hands are stained with paint and a pink blot has dried on her forehead like a misplaced bindi.

"Hello, what's your name?"

"Molly."

"That's a pretty name."

"I know."

"Is your mummy home?"

"She's upstairs."

I hear a yell from that direction. "If that's the boiler man, the boiler is straight down the hall in the kitchen."

"It's not the boiler man," I call back.

"It's an Indian lady," says Molly.

Mrs. Gallagher appears at the top of the stairs. In her early forties, she's wearing a corduroy skirt with a wide belt slung low on her hips.

"I'm sorry to trouble you. My husband and I are moving into the street and I was hoping to ask about local schools and doctors, that sort of thing."

I can see her mentally deciding what to do. It's more than natural caution.

"What beautiful curls," I say, stroking Molly's hair.

"That's what everyone says," the youngster replies.

Why would someone who already has a child buy a baby?

"I'm rather busy at the moment," says Mrs. Gallagher, brushing back her fringe.

"I understand completely. I'm sorry." I turn to leave.

"Which place are you buying?" she asks, not wanting to be impolite.

"Oh, we're not buying. Not yet. We're renting No. 68." I point down the street in the direction of a TO LET sign. We've moved from North London. My husband has a new job. We're both working. But we want to start a family soon."

Mrs. Gallagher is at the bottom of the stairs now. It's too cold to leave the front door open. She either invites me inside or tells me to go.

"Now's not the best time," she says. "Perhaps if I had a phone number I could call you later."

"Thank you very much." I fumble for a pen. "Do you have a piece of paper?"

She looks on the radiator shelf. "I'll get you one."

Molly waits in the hallway, still holding the door. "Do you want to see one of my paintings?"

"I'd love to."

"I'll get one." She dashes upstairs. Mrs. Gallagher is in the kitchen. She finds an old envelope and returns, looking for Molly.

"She's gone upstairs to get one of her paintings," I explain. "A budding artist."

"She gets more paint on her clothes than on the paper."

"I have a boyfriend like that."

"I thought you said you were married." She fixes me with a stare. There's steel behind it.

"We're engaged. We've been together so long It feels like we're married."

She doesn't believe me. Molly yells from the top of the stairs.

"Mummy, Jasper is crying."

"Oh, you have another one."

Mrs. Gallagher reaches for the door. My foot is faster. My shoulder follows. I have no right to enter. I need a warrant or I need proper cause.

I'm at the bottom of the stairs. Mrs. Gallagher yells at me to get out. She grabs my arm. I shrug it away. Above the noise, behind it, in spite of it, I hear a baby crying.

Taking the stairs two at a time, I follow the sound. The first door I come to is the main bedroom. The second door is Molly's room. She has set up a painting easel on an old sheet. I try a third door. Brightly colored fish spin slowly above a white cot. Within it, swaddled tightly, a baby is unhappy at creation.

Mrs. Gallagher pushes past me, scooping up the boy. "Get out of my house!"

"Is he yours, Mrs. Gallagher?"

"Yes."

"Did you give birth to him?"

"Get out! Get out! I'll call the police."

"I *am* the police."

Wordlessly, she shakes her head from side to side. The baby has gone quiet. Molly is tugging at her skirt.

Suddenly her shoulders sag and she seems to deflate in front of me, folding from the knees and then the waist. Still cradling the baby, refusing to let go, she lands in my arms and I maneuver her to a chair.

"We adopted him," she whispers. "He's *ours*."

"He was never available for adoption. You know that."

Mrs. Gallagher shakes her head. I look around the room. Where is she? The girl. My heart skips between beats. Slow then fast.

"There was a baby girl. A twin."

She looks toward the cot. "He's the only one."

Worst case scenarios haunt me now. The baby girl was so small. She struggled to breathe. Please God, let her be safe!

Mrs. Gallagher has found a tissue in the sleeve of her cardigan. She blows her nose and sniffles. "We were told he wasn't wanted. I swear I didn't know—not about the missing twins. It wasn't until I saw the TV news. Then I began to wonder . . ."

"Who gave him to you?"

"A man brought him."

"What did he look like?"

"Mid-fifties, short hair—he had an Irish accent."

"When?"

"The Sunday before last." She wipes her eyes. "It came as a shock. We weren't expecting him for another fortnight."

"Who arranged the adoption?"

"Mr. Shawcroft said a teenage girl was pregnant with twins but couldn't afford to look after both of them. She wanted to put one of them up for adoption. We could jump the queue for fifty thousand pounds."

"You knew it was against the law."

"Mr. Shawcroft said that twins couldn't legally be split. We had to do everything in secret."

"You pretended to be pregnant."

"There wasn't time."

I look at Molly who is playing with a box of shells, arranging them in patterns.

"Is Molly . . . ?" I don't finish the question.

"She's mine," she says fiercely. "I couldn't have any more. There were complications. Medical problems. They told us we were too old to adopt. My husband is fifty-five, you see." She wipes her eyes. "I should phone him."

I hear my name being called from downstairs. "New Boy" must have witnessed the doorstep confrontation. He couldn't stay put.

"Up here."

"Are you OK?"

"Yeah."

He appears at the door, taking in the scene. Mrs. Gallagher. Molly. The baby.

"It's one of the twins," I say.

"One?"

"The boy."

He peers into the cot. "Are you sure?"

I follow his gaze. It's amazing how much a newborn can change in under ten days, but I'm sure.

"What about the girl?" he asks.

"She's not here."

Shawcroft made *two* phone calls from the golf club. The second was to the Finsbury Park address of a Mrs. Y. Moncrieffe, which doesn't cross-reference with any of the names from the New Life Adoption Center files.

I can't leave. I have to stay and talk to Forbes (and no doubt peel him off the ceiling).

"Can you check out the other address?"

Dave weighs up the implications and ramifications. He's not worried about himself. I'm the one facing a disciplinary hearing. He kisses my cheek.

"You make it hard sometimes, you know that?"

"I know."

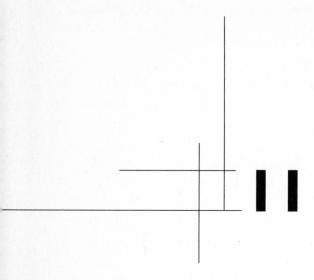

DI Forbes storms through the house, his face hardened into a mask of fury and cold hatred. Ordering me into the rear garden, he ignores the muddy lawn and paces back and forth.

"You had no right!" he yells. "It was an illegal search."

"I had reason to believe—"

"What reason?"

"I was following a lead."

"Which you should have told *me* about. This is *my* fucking investigation!"

His rectangular glasses bobble on his nose. I wonder if it annoys him.

"In my professional judgment I made a necessary choice, sir."

"You don't even *know* if it's one of the twins. There are no birth records or adoption papers."

"Mrs. Gallagher has confirmed that she is not the biological mother. The baby was delivered to her by a man matching Brendan Pearl's description."

"You should have waited."

"With all due respect, sir, you were taking too long. Shawcroft is free. He's shredding files, covering his tracks. You don't *want* to prosecute him."

I think he might explode. His voice carries across the neighborhood gardens and mud sucks at his shoes.

"I should have reported you to the PCA when you went to Amsterdam. You have harassed witnesses, abused your authority and disobeyed the orders of a senior officer. You have failed at almost every opportunity to conduct yourself in a professional manner . . ."

His foot lifts and his shoe remains behind. A sock squelches into the mud up to his ankle. We both pretend it hasn't happened.

"You're suspended from duty. Do you understand me? I'm going to personally see that your career is over."

Social Services have been summoned, a big woman with a backside so large that she appears to be wearing a bustle. Mr. and Mrs. Gallagher are talking to her in the sitting room. They look almost relieved that it's over. The past few days must have been unbearable, wondering and waiting for a knock on the door. Being frightened of falling in love with a child that might never truly be theirs.

Molly is in her bedroom showing a policewoman how she paints flowers and rests them on the radiator to dry. The baby is sleeping. They called him Jasper. He has a name now.

Forbes has peeled off his sock and thrown it into the rubbish bin. Sitting on the back step, he uses a screwdriver to scrape mud from his shoes.

"How did you know?" he asks, having calmed down.

I explain about the phone calls from the golf club and cross-checking the numbers with the adoption files, looking for a match.

"That's how I found the Gallaghers."

"Did he make any other calls?"

"One."

Forbes waits. "Have I got to *arrest* you to get any cooperation?"

Any remaining vestiges of comradeship have gone. We're no longer on the same team.

"I had an interesting conversation with a lawyer this morning," he says. "He was representing Barnaby Elliot and he alleged that you had a conflict of interest concerning this case."

"There's no conflict, sir."

"Mr. Elliot is contesting his late daughter's will."

"He has no legal claim over the twins."

"And neither do you!"

"I know that, sir," I whisper.

"If Samira Khan decides that she doesn't want the babies, they will be taken into care and placed with foster parents."

"I know. I'm not doing this for me."

"Are you sure of that?"

It's an accusation not a question. My motives are under fire again. Perhaps I'm deluding myself. I can't afford to believe that. I won't.

My mobile phone is vibrating in my pocket. I flip it open.

"I might have found her," says Dave. "But there's a problem."

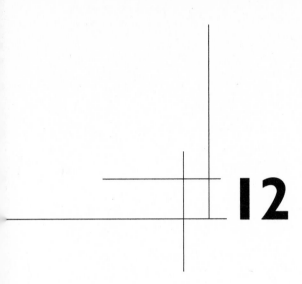

12

The Neonatal Intensive Care Unit (NICU) at Queen Charlotte's Hospital is on the third floor above the delivery suites and maternity ward. Amid low lights, soft footsteps and the hum of machines there are fifteen high-domed incubators.

The unit manager is two paces ahead of me and Dave two paces behind. Our hands are washed with disinfectant and mobile phones have been turned off.

Passing the nearest crib, I look down. It appears to be empty except for a pink blanket and a teddy bear sitting in the corner. Then I notice an arm, no thicker than a fountain pen, emerge from beneath the blanket. Fingers curl and uncurl. Eyes remain shut. Tubes are squashed into a tiny nose, pushing rapid puffs of air into immature lungs.

The manager pauses and waits. Perhaps people do that a lot—stop, stare and pray. It's only then that I notice the faces on the far side of the crib, distorted by the glass.

I look around. There are other parents sitting in the semidarkness, watching and waiting; talking in whispers. I wonder what they say to each other. Do they look at other cribs and wonder if that baby is stronger or sicker or more premature. Not all of the newborns can possibly survive. Do their parents secretly pray, "Save mine! Save mine!"

We have reached the far end of the NICU. Chairs beside the crib are empty. A nurse sits on a high stool at a control screen, monitoring the machines that monitor a child.

At the center of a plain white sheet is a baby girl, wearing just a nappy. She is smaller than I remember, yet compared to some of the premature babies in the NICU she is twice their size. Small pads are stuck to her chest, picking up her heartbeat and her breathing.

"Claudia was brought in last night," explains the ward manager. "She has a serious lung infection. We're giving her antibiotics and feeding her intravenously. The device on her leg is a blood gas monitor. It shines light through her skin to see how much oxygen is in her blood."

"Is she going to be all right?"

She takes a moment to choose her words. The delay is enough to terrify me. "She's stable. The next twenty-four hours are very important."

"You called her Claudia."

"That's the name we were given."

"Who gave it to you?"

"The woman who came in with her in the ambulance."

"I need to see the admission form."

"Of course. If you come to the office I'll print you a copy."

Dave is staring through the glass. I can almost see his lips moving, breathing as the baby breathes. Claudia has captured his attention, even though her eyes are fused shut by sleep.

"Do you mind if I stay for a while?" he asks, directing the question as much to me as to the ward manager. Every other patient in the unit has someone sitting alongside them. Claudia is alone. It doesn't seem right to him.

Retracing our steps, I follow the manager to her office.

"I called Social Services this morning," she says. "I didn't expect the police."

"What made you call?"

"I wasn't happy with some of the answers we were getting. Claudia arrived just after midnight. At first the woman said she was the baby's nanny. She gave the mother's name as Cate Beaumont.

Then she changed her story and said that Claudia had been adopted, but she couldn't give me any details of the adoption agency."

She hands me the admission form. Claudia's date of birth is listed as Sunday, October 29. The mother's name is written down as Cate Elizabeth Beaumont. The address is Cate's fire-damaged house.

Why give Cate's name? How did she even know about her?

"Where is this woman now?"

"One of our consultants wanted to talk to her. I guess she panicked."

"She ran?"

"She made a phone call. Then she walked out."

"What time was that?"

"About 6:00 a.m."

"Do you know who she called?"

"No, but she used my phone."

She points to her desk. The phone console is a command unit, with a memory of the most recently dialed numbers. A small LCD screen displays the call register. The ward manager identifies the number and I hit the redial button.

A woman answers.

"Hello?"

"This is Queen Charlotte's Hospital," I say. "Someone called your home from this number early this morning."

She doesn't answer but in the silence I recognize a sound. I've heard it before—the squeak of wheels on parquetry floor.

I don't have Ruiz's photographic memory or his mother's gifts for telling fortunes. I don't even know if I have a particular methodology. I put facts together randomly. Sometimes leaping ahead or trying things out for size. It's not very efficient and it can't be taught but it works for me.

The woman speaks again. Nervously. "You must have the wrong number."

It's an officious voice, precise, not quite public school. I have heard it often enough, albeit a decade ago, berating her husband for coming home late smelling of shampoo and shower gel.

The line has gone dead. Ruth Elliot has hung up. Simultaneously, there is a knock on the door. A nurse smiles apologetically and whispers something to the ward manager, who looks at me.

"You asked about the woman who brought in Claudia. She didn't run away. She's downstairs in the cafeteria."

A pressure pad opens the doors automatically. The cafeteria is small and bright with white-flecked tables to hide the crumbs. Trays are stacked near the doors. Steam rises from the warming pans.

A handful of nurses are picking up sandwiches and cups of tea—healthy options in a menu where everything else comes with chips.

Yvonne is squeezed into a booth, with her head resting on her forearms. For a moment I think she might be asleep, but her head lifts and she blinks at me wetly. A low moan escapes and she lowers her head. The pale brown of her scalp is visible where her gray hair has started to thin.

"What happened?"

"I did a foolish, foolish thing, cookie," she says, talking into the crook of her arm. "I thought I could make her better, but she kept getting sicker and sicker."

A shuddering breath vibrates through her frame. "I should have taken her to a doctor but Mr. and Mrs. Elliot said that nobody could ever know about Cate's baby. They said people wanted to take Claudia away and give her to someone she don't belong to. I don't know why people would do something like that. Mr. and Mrs. Elliot didn't explain it so good, not sufficient for me to understand, you know."

She draws back, hoping I might comprehend. Her eyes are wet and crumbs have stuck to her cheek.

"I knew Cate weren't having no baby," she explains. "She didn't have no baby inside her. I know when a woman is with child. I can see it in her eyes and on her skin. I can smell it. Sometimes I can even tell when a woman's having another man's baby, on account of the skin around her eyes, which is darker 'cos she's frightened her husband might find out.

"I tried to say something to Mrs. Elliot but she called me crazy and laughed. She must have told young Cate 'cos she avoided me after that. She wouldn't come to the house if I was working."

Details shiver and shift, finding their places. Events are no longer figments or mysteries, no longer part of my imagining. Barnaby *knew* I was in Amsterdam. And even before I mentioned Samira he *knew* she was having twins. He read Cate's e-mails and began covering her tracks.

At first he probably intended to protect his precious reputation.

Later he and his wife came up with another plan. They would finish what Cate started. Barnaby contacted Shawcroft with a message: "Cate and Felix are dead but the deal isn't."

Why would Shawcroft agree? He had to. Barnaby had the e-mails. He could go to the police and expose the illegal adoptions and baby broking. Blackmail is an ugly word. So is kidnapping.

At the funeral Barnaby told me he was going to fight for the twins. "I want *both* of them," he said. I didn't realize what he meant. He already had one—Claudia. He wanted the boy. And his tirade at the lawyer's office and the scene at my house weren't just for show. He was frightened that he might be denied, if not by Samira, then by me.

The Elliots swore Yvonne to secrecy. They charged her with looking after Claudia and hopefully her brother if they could unite the twins. If the scandal unraveled and Shawcroft was exposed, they could play the grieving parents, trying to protect their daughter's precious legacy, their grandchildren.

Yvonne accepted the heaviest burden. She couldn't risk taking Claudia to a doctor. She tried her own remedies: running hot taps, filling the bathroom with steam, trying to help her breathe. She dosed her with droplets of paracetamol, rubbed her with warm flannels, lay awake beside her through the night, listening to her lungs fill with fluid.

Barnaby came to see the baby, his thumbs hitched in his belt and his feet splayed. He peered over the cot with a fixed smile, looking vaguely disappointed. Perhaps he wanted the boy—the healthy twin.

Meanwhile, Claudia grew sicker and Yvonne more desperate.

"I couldn't take it anymore," she whispers, lifting her gaze to the ceiling. "She was dying. Every time she coughed her body shook until she didn't have the strength to cough. That's when I called the ambulance."

She blinks at me. "She's going to die, isn't she?"

"We don't know that."

"It's going to be my fault. Arrest me. Lock me up. I deserve it."

I want to stop her talking about death. "Who chose the name?"

"It's Mrs. Elliot's name."

"Her first name is Ruth."

"Her middle name. I know you don't have much time for Mrs. Elliot but she's harder on herself than she is on anyone else."

What I feel most is resentment. Maybe that's part of the process of grieving. Cate doesn't feel as though she's gone. I keep thinking that she's just walked off in the middle of things and will come back presently and sort this mess out.

I have spent weeks delving into her life, investigating her movements and motives and I still don't understand how she could have risked so much and endangered so many. I keep entertaining the hope that I'll stumble upon the answer in some cache of her papers or a dusty bundle of letters. But I know it's not going to happen. One half of the truth is lying upstairs, pinned like an insect to a glass display case. The other half is being looked after by Social Services.

It sounds preposterous but I'm still trying to justify Cate's actions, trying to conjure up a friendship from the afterlife. She was an inept thief, a childless wife and a foolish dreamer. I don't want to think about her anymore. She has spoiled her own memory.

"The police are going to need a statement," I say.

Yvonne nods, wiping her cheeks.

She doesn't stand as I leave. And although her face is turned to the window, I know she's watching me.

"New Boy" Dave is still beside Claudia in the NICU, sitting forward on a chair, peering through the glass. We sit together. He takes my hand. I don't know for how long. The clock on the wall doesn't seem to change. Not even for a second. Perhaps that's what happens in a place like this: time slows down. Every second is made to count.

You are a very lucky little girl, Claudia. Do you know why? You have *two* mothers. One of them you'll never meet but that's OK, I'll tell you about her. She made some mistakes but I'm sure you won't judge her too harshly. Your other mother is also very special. Young. Beautiful. Sad. Sometimes life can turn on the length of an eyelash, even one as small as yours.

The ward manager touches my shoulder. A police officer wants to talk to me on the phone.

Forbes sounds far away. "The Gallaghers have given a statement. I'm on my way to arrest Julian Shawcroft."

"That's good. I found the girl. She's very sick."

He doesn't rant this time. "Who should we be talking to?"

"Barnaby Elliot and his wife, along with their housekeeper, Yvonne Moncrieffe."

Behind me a door opens and I hear the sound of an electronic alarm. Through an observation window I notice curtains being drawn around Claudia's crib.

The phone is no longer in my hand. Like everyone else I seem to be moving. I push through the curtains. Someone pushes me back and I stumble.

"What's wrong? What are they doing?"

A doctor is issuing instructions. A hand covers Claudia's face, holding a mask. A bag is squeezed and squeezed again. The mask is lifted briefly and a tube is slipped into her nose before being slowly fed into her lungs. White tape crosses her cheeks.

Dave has hold of my arm, trying to pull me away.

"What's happening?"

"We have to wait outside."

"They're hurting her."

"Let them do their job."

This is my fault. My mistake. If I had been stronger, fitter, faster, I would have saved Claudia from Pearl. She would have gone straight to hospital instead of being smuggled off the ferry. She would never have gone to Yvonne or caught a lung infection.

Thoughts like this plague me as I count down the minutes—fifteen of them, stretched and deformed by my imagination. The door swings open. A young doctor emerges.

"What happened?"

"The blood gas monitor triggered the alarm. Her oxygen levels had fallen too low. She's too weak to breathe on her own so we've put her on a ventilator. We'll help her breathe for a while and see how strong she is tomorrow."

The sense of relief saps what energy I have left and I feel suddenly dizzy. My eyes are sticky and I can't get rid of the coppery taste in my mouth. I still haven't told Samira and already my heart has been shredded.

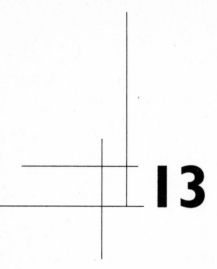

13

Sometimes London is a parody of itself. Today is like that. The sky is fat and heavy and the wind is cold, although not cold enough to snow. Ladbrokes is offering 3 to 1 on a white Christmas in London. All it takes is a single snowflake to fall on the rooftop of the Met Office.

The bail hearing is today. I'm wearing my court clothes: a red pencil skirt, cream blouse and a short jacket that is cut well enough to have an expensive label but has no label at all.

Shawcroft has been charged with people trafficking, forced pregnancy and offenses under the Child Protection Act. The penalty for trafficking alone is up to fourteen years. More charges are pending, as well as possible extradition to the Netherlands.

Samira is sitting on the bed watching me apply my makeup. An overcoat lies across her lap. She has been dressed for hours, after waking early and praying. She won't have to give evidence until the trial, which could be a year away, but she wants to come along for today's hearing.

"Shawcroft is still only a suspect," I say. "Under our legal system a suspect is innocent until *proven* guilty."

"But we know he *is* guilty."

"Yes but a jury has to decide that after hearing all the evidence."

"What is bail?"

"A judge will sometimes let a defendant out of prison just until the trial if he or she promises not to run away or approach any of the witnesses. As a way of guaranteeing this, the judge will ask for a large amount of money, which the defendant won't get back if he breaks the law or doesn't show up for the trial."

She looks astonished. "He will pay the judge money?"

"The money is like a security deposit."

"A bribe."

"No, not a bribe."

"So you are saying Brother could pay money and get out of jail."

"Well, yes, but it's not what you think."

The conversation keeps going round in circles. I'm not explaining it very well.

"I'm sure it won't happen," I reassure her. "He won't be able to hurt anyone again."

It has been three weeks since Claudia left hospital. I still worry about her—she seems so small compared to her brother—but the infection has gone and she's putting on weight.

The twins have become tabloid celebrities, Baby X and Baby Y, without first names or surnames. The judge deciding custody has ordered DNA tests on the twins and medical reports from Amsterdam. Samira will have to prove she is their mother and then decide what she wants to do.

Despite being under investigation, Barnaby has maintained his campaign for custody, hiring and sacking lawyers on a weekly basis. During the first custody hearing, Judge Freyne threatened to jail him for contempt for continually interjecting and making accusations of bias.

I have had my own hearing to deal with—a disciplinary tribunal in front of three senior officers. I tendered my resignation on the first day. The chairman refused to accept it.

"I thought I was making it easier for them," I told Ruiz.

"They can't sack you and they don't want to let you go," he explained. "Imagine the headlines."

"So what do they want?"

"To lock you away in an office somewhere—where you can't cause any trouble."

Samira adjusts her breast pads and buttons her blouse. Four

times a day she expresses milk for the twins, which is couriered to the foster family. She gets to see them every afternoon for three hours under supervision. I have watched her carefully, looking for some sign that she is drawing closer to them. She feeds, bathes and nurses them, giving the impression that she is far more accomplished and comfortable with motherhood than I could ever imagine myself being. At the same time her movements are almost mechanical, as though she is doing what's expected of her rather than what she wants.

She has developed a strange affectation around the twins. Whether expressing milk, changing nappies or dressing them, she uses only her right hand. When she picks one of them up, she slides the hand between their legs, along their spine and scoops them in a single motion, supporting the head with the palm of her hand. And when she feeds them, she tucks a bottle under her chin or lays the baby along her thighs.

I thought for a while that it might be a Muslim thing, like only eating with the right hand. When I asked her, she raised her eyes dismissively. "One hand is enough to sin. One hand is enough to save."

"What does that mean?"

"What it says."

Hari is downstairs. "Are you sure you don't want me to come with you?"

"I'm sure."

"I could hold up an umbrella."

"It's not raining."

"They do it for the film stars who don't want to be photographed— hold up umbrellas. Their bodyguards do it."

"You're not a bodyguard."

He's a lovesick puppy. University has broken up for Christmas and he's supposed to be helping his brothers at the garage but he keeps finding excuses to spend time with Samira. She'll even be alone with him, but only in the garden shed when they're working on some pyrotechnic project. The fireworks on Guy Fawkes Night were supposed to be a one-off but Hari has kept that particular fuse burning, for obvious reasons.

"New Boy" Dave is waiting outside for us.

"You're not wearing black?"

"Strange, isn't it?"

"You look good in red."

I whisper, "You should see my underwear."

Samira pulls on her overcoat, which has toggles instead of buttons. It used to belong to Hari and the cuffs have to be folded twice because the sleeves are so long. Her hands find the pockets and hibernate there.

The day is growing brighter, climbing toward noon. Dave negotiates the traffic and parks a block away from Southwark Crown Court, ready to run the gauntlet. Ahead of us, on the pavement, TV cameras and photographers are waiting.

The charges against Julian Shawcroft are merely a sideshow to the main event—the custody battle for the twins—which has everything the tabloids crave: sex, a beautiful "virgin" and stolen babies.

Flashguns fire around us. Samira lowers her head and keeps her hands in her pockets. Dave pushes a path through the scrum, not afraid to drop his shoulder into someone who won't move out of the way. These are tactics from the rugby field, not a sailing school.

Southwark Crown Court is a soulless modern precinct with less charm than the Old Bailey. We pass through the metal detectors and make our way upstairs. I recognize some of the people holding meetings in the corridors, discussing last-minute tactics with counsel. Dr. Sohan Banerjee has hired his own Queen's Counsel in expectation of being charged. He and Shawcroft still haven't turned on each other but the finger-pointing is only a matter of time according to Forbes.

Shawcroft's barrister is a woman, five foot ten in two-inch dagger heels, with white-blond hair and drop pearl earrings that swing back and forth as she talks.

The prosecutor, Francis Hague, QC, is older and grayer, with glasses perched on top of his head. He is talking to Forbes, making notes on a long pad. DS Softell has also turned up, perhaps hoping for some clue in the search for Brendan Pearl, who seems to have vanished completely. I wonder how many different identities he's stolen.

Samira is nervous. She knows that people are looking at her, court staff and reporters. I have tried to reassure her that the publicity will stop once the twins are home. Nobody will be allowed to identify them.

We take a seat in the public gallery at the rear of the courtroom with Samira sitting in between us. She shrinks inside her overcoat, keeping her hands in the pockets. I spy Donavon slipping into the row behind us. His eyes scan the courtroom and rest on mine for a moment before moving on.

Soon the press box is full and there are no seats in the public gallery. The court clerk, an Asian woman of indeterminate age, enters and takes a seat, tapping at a keyboard.

Feet shuffle and everyone stands for the judge, who is surprisingly young and quite handsome in a stuffy sort of way. Within minutes, Shawcroft emerges via a stairway leading directly into the dock. Dressed in a neat suit, speckled tie and polished shoes, he turns and smiles at the gallery, soaking up the atmosphere as though this were a performance being laid on for his benefit.

"You wish to make an application for bail?" asks the judge.

Shawcroft's QC, Margaret Curillo, is already on her feet, introducing herself in plummy obsequious tones. Francis Hague, QC, plants his hands on the table and raises his buttocks several inches from his chair, mumbling an introduction. Perhaps he feels that everyone knows him already or at least should.

The door of the court opens quietly and a man enters. Tall and thin, with an effeminate air, he nods distractedly at the bench and barely raises his polished shoes from the carpet as he glides toward the bar table. Bending, he whispers something to Hague, who cocks his head.

Mrs. Curillo has begun her submission, outlining the many "outstanding achievements" of her client in a "lifetime of service to the community."

The prosecutor rises fully to his feet this time.

"Your Honor, I must apologize for interrupting my learned friend but I wish to request a short adjournment."

"We've only just started."

"I need to seek further instructions, Your Honor. Apparently, the director of public prosecutions is reviewing details of the case."

"With what aim?"

"I'm not in a position to say at this point."

"How long do you require?"

"If it pleases, Your Honor, perhaps we could re-list this matter for three o'clock this afternoon."

The judge stands abruptly, causing a chain reaction in the courtroom. Shawcroft is already being led back downstairs. I look at Dave, who shrugs. Samira is watching us, waiting for an explanation. Outside, in the corridor, I look for Forbes, who seems to have disappeared, along with Softell. What on earth is happening?

For the next two hours we wait. Cases are called for different courts. Lawyers have meetings. People come and go. Samira is sitting with her shoulders hunched, still wearing her overcoat.

"Do you believe in Heaven?" she asks.

It is such an unexpected question that I feel my mouth fall open. Consciously, I close it again. "Why do you ask?"

"Do you think Hassan and Zala are in Heaven?"

"I don't know."

"My father believed we should live our lives over and over, getting better each time. Only when we're completely happy should we get into Heaven."

"I don't know whether I'd like to live the same life over and over."

"Why?"

"It would diminish the consequences. I already put things off until another day. Imagine putting them off until another life."

Samira wraps her arms around herself. "Afghanistan is leaving me."

"What do you mean?"

"I am forgetting things. I cannot remember what sort of flowers I planted on my father's grave. I once pressed the same flowers between the pages of his Koran and made him very angry. He said I was dishonoring Allah. I said I was praising Allah with flowers. He laughed at that. My father could never stay angry with me."

We have afternoon tea in the cafeteria, avoiding the reporters whose ranks are starting to thin. Francis Hague and Shawcroft's barrister still haven't surfaced and neither has Forbes. Perhaps they've gone Christmas shopping.

Shortly before three, a Crown Solicitor finds us. Counsel wants to talk to Samira. I should come too.

"I'll wait for you here," says Dave.

We climb a flight of stairs and are shown through a door marked COURT STAFF ONLY. A long corridor is flanked by offices. A lone potted palm sits at one end alongside a rather annoyed-looking woman waiting on a chair. Her black-stockinged legs are like burned matchsticks sticking out from beneath a fur coat.

The solicitor knocks gently on a door. It opens. The first person I see is Spijker, who looks depressingly somber even by his standards. He takes my hand, kissing my cheeks three times, before bowing slightly to Samira.

Shawcroft's barrister is at the far end of the table, sitting opposite Francis Hague. Beside them is another man, who seems pressed for time. It could be his wife waiting outside, expecting to be somewhere else.

"My name is Adam Greenburg, QC," he says, standing and shaking Samira's hand. "I am the deputy director of public prosecutions at the Crown Prosecution Service."

He apologizes for the stuffiness of the room and almost makes a running gag of his Jewishness, dabbing his forehead with a handkerchief.

"Let me explain my job to you, Miss Khan. When someone is arrested for a criminal offense, they don't automatically go to court and then to prison. The police first have to gather evidence and the job of the Crown Prosecution Service is to examine that evidence and to make sure that the right person is prosecuted for the right offense and that all relevant facts are given to the court. Do you understand?"

Samira looks at me and back to Greenburg. An elephant is sitting on my chest.

The only person who hasn't introduced himself is the man who entered the courtroom and interrupted the bail hearing. Standing by the window in a Savile Row suit, he has a raptor's profile and oddly inexpressive eyes, yet something about his attitude suggests he knows a secret about everyone in the room.

Mr. Greenburg continues: "There are two stages in the decision to prosecute. The first stage is the evidential test. Crown prosecutors must be satisfied there is enough evidence to provide a realistic prospect of conviction against each defendant on each charge.

"The second stage is the public-interest test. We must be satisfied there is a public interest to be served in prosecuting. The CPS will only start or continue a prosecution when a case has passed both these tests no matter how important or serious it might be."

Mr. Greenburg is about to cut to the chase. Spijker won't look at me. Everyone's eyes are fixed on the table.

"The CPS has decided not to proceed with the prosecution of Mr. Shawcroft because it does not pass the public-interest test and because he has agreed to cooperate fully with the police and has given certain assurances about his future conduct."

For a moment the shock takes my breath away and I can't respond. I look at Spijker, hoping for support. He stares at his hands.

"A case such as this raises serious moral and ethical issues," explains Greenburg. "Fourteen infants, born as a result of illegal surrogacy, have been identified. These children are now living with their biological parents in stable loving families.

"If we prosecute Mr. Shawcroft these families will be torn apart. Parents will be charged as co-conspirators and their children will be taken into care, perhaps permanently. In prosecuting one individual, we risk destroying the lives of many many more.

"The Dutch authorities face a similar dilemma involving six children from surrogate mothers. The German authorities have identified four births and the French could have as many as thirteen.

"I am as shocked and appalled by this evil trade as anyone else, but we have to make decisions here today that will decide what legacy remains afterward."

I find my voice. "You don't have to charge the couples."

"If we choose to proceed, Mr. Shawcroft's counsel has indicated that she will subpoena all the couples involved who are legally and ethically raising children who belong to someone else.

"That is the situation we face. And the question we have to answer is this: Do we draw a line beneath this, or do we proceed and upset the lives of innocent children?"

Samira sits passively in her overcoat. She hasn't stirred. Everything is done with such politeness and decorum that there is a sense of unreality about it all.

"He murdered innocent people." My voice sounds hollow.

Mrs. Curillo protests. "My client denies all involvement in any such crimes and has not been charged in relation to any such event."

"What about Cate and Felix Beaumont? What about Hassan Khan and Zala?"

Greenburg raises his hand, wanting me to be silent.

"In return for the dropping of all charges, Mr. Shawcroft has provided police with the whereabouts of Brendan Pearl, an alleged people trafficker and wanted felon, who is still on parole for offenses committed in Northern Ireland. Mr. Shawcroft has given a statement saying that he had no involvement in the deaths of the Beaumonts, alleging that Brendan Pearl acted alone. He also maintains that he played no part in the trafficking operation that led to the unfortunate deaths at Harwich International Port in October. A criminal gang took advantage of his naïveté. He admits to commercial surrogacy, but says that Brendan Pearl and his associates took over the scheme and blackmailed him into participating."

"This is ridiculous! He's the architect! He forced women to get pregnant! He took their babies!" I can't hear myself yelling, but no other voices are raised. Focusing my anger on Greenburg, I use words like "justice" and "fairness" while he counters with terms like "common sense" and "public interest."

My language is disintegrating. I call him gutless and corrupt. Growing tired of my tantrum, he threatens to have me removed.

"Mr. Pearl will be extradited to the Netherlands where he will face charges related to prostitution, people smuggling and murder," he explains. "In addition, Mr. Shawcroft has agreed to relinquish all involvement in his charities, including the New Life Adoption Center—effective immediately. The center's license to oversee adoptions has been revoked. The Charities Commission is drafting a press release. Early retirement seems to be the agreed terminology. The CPS will also make a statement saying the charges are being dropped due to lack of evidence."

There is a tone of finality to the sentence. Greenburg's job is done. Getting to his feet, he straightens his jacket. "I promised my wife lunch. Now it will have to be dinner. Thank you for your cooperation."

Samira shrugs me away, pushing past people, stumbling toward the lift.

"I'm sorry, Alisha," says Spijker.

I can't answer him. He warned me about this. We were sitting in his office in Amsterdam and he talked about Pandora's box. Some lids are best kept closed, glued, nailed, screwed down and buried under six feet of earth.

"There is a logic to it, you know. There is no point punishing the guilty if we punish the innocent," he says.

"Someone has to pay."

"Someone will."

I gaze across the paved courtyard where pigeons have coated the statues with mouse-gray excrement. The wind has sprung up again, driving needles of sleet against the glass.

I phone Forbes. Gusts of wind snag at his words.

"When did you know?"

"Midday."

"Do you have Pearl?"

"Not my show anymore."

"Are you off the case?"

"I'm not a high-enough grade of public servant to handle this one."

Suddenly I picture the quiet man, standing by the window, tugging at his cuff links. He was MI5. The security services want Pearl. Forbes has been told to take a backseat.

"Where are you now?"

"Armed-response teams have surrounded a boarding house in Southend-on-Sea."

"Is Pearl inside?"

"Standing at the window, watching."

"He's not going to run."

"Too late for that."

Another image comes to me. This one shows Brendan Pearl strolling out of the boarding house with a pistol tucked into the waistband of his trousers, ready to fight or to flee. Either way, he's not going back to prison.

Samira. What am I going to say to her? How can I possibly explain? She heard what Greenburg said. Her silence spoke volumes. It was as if she had known all along it would come to this. Betrayal. Broken promises. Duplicity. She has been here before, visited this place. "Some people are born to suffer," that's what Lena Caspar said. "It never stops for them, not for a second."

I can see Samira now, smudged by the wet glass, standing by the statue, wearing Hari's overcoat. I want to teach her about the future. I want to show her the Christmas lights in Regent Street, tell her about the daffodils in spring, show her real things, true things, happiness.

A dark-colored car has pulled up, waiting at the curb. Photographers and cameramen spill out of the court building walking backward, jostling for space. Julian Shawcroft emerges flanked by his barrister and Eddie Barrett. His silver hair shines in the TV lights.

He laughs with the reporters, relaxed, jovial, a master of the moment.

I spy Samira walking toward him in a zigzag pattern. Her hands are buried deep in the pockets of her coat.

I am moving now, swerving left and right past people in the corridor. I hammer the lift button and choose the stairs instead, swinging through each landing and out the double fire doors on the ground floor.

I'm on the wrong side of the building. Which way? Left.

Some track athletes are good at running bends. They lean into the corner, shifting their center of balance rather than fighting the g-forces that want to fling them off. The trick is not to fight the force, but to work with it by shortening your stride and hugging the inside line.

A Russian coach once told me that I was the best bend runner he had ever seen. He even had a video of me that he used to train his young runners at the academy in Moscow.

Right now I don't have a cambered track and the paving stones are slick with rain, but I run this bend as if my life depends upon it. I tell myself to hold the turn, hold the turn and then explode out. Kick. Kick. Everything is burning, my legs and lungs, but I'm flying.

The 200 meters was my trademark event. I don't have the lungs for middle distance.

The media scrum is ahead of me. Samira stands on the outside, rocking from foot to foot like an anxious child. Finally she burrows inside, pushing between shoulders. A reporter spies her and pulls back. Another follows. More people peel off, sensing a story.

Samira's overcoat is open. There is something in her hand that catches the light—a glass elephant with tiny mirrors. My elephant.

Shawcroft is too busy talking to notice her. She embraces him from behind, wrapping her arms around his waist, pressing her left fist against his heart and her head against the middle of his back. He tries to shake her loose, but she won't let go. A wisp of smoke curls from her fingers.

Someone yells and people dive away. They're saying it's a bomb! How?

The sound of my scream disappears beneath the crack of an explosion that snaps at the air, making it shudder. Shawcroft spins slowly, until he faces me, looking puzzled. The hole in his chest is the size of a dinner plate. I can see right inside.

Samira falls in the opposite direction, with her knees splayed apart. Her face hits the ground first because her left arm can't break her fall. Her eyes are open. A hand reaches out to me. There are no fingers. There is no *hand*.

People are running and yelling, screaming like the damned; their faces peppered with shards of glass.

"She's a terrorist," someone shouts. "Be careful."

"She's not a terrorist," I reply.

"There could be more bombs."

"There are *no* more bombs."

Pieces of mirror and glass are embedded along Samira's arms, but her face and torso escaped the force of the blast, shielded behind Shawcroft.

I should have realized. I should have seen it coming. How long ago did she plan this? Weeks, maybe longer. She took my elephant from my bedside table. Hari unwittingly helped her by buying the model rocket engines full of black powder. The fuse must have been taped down her forearm, which is why she didn't take off her overcoat. The glass and mirrors of the elephant didn't trigger the metal detectors.

The frayed lining of her coat sleeve is still smoldering, but there's surprisingly little blood. The exploding powder seems to have cauterized her flesh around a jagged section of bone.

She turns her head. "Is he dead?"

"Yes."

Satisfied, she closes her eyes. Two paramedics gently take her from me, placing her on a stretcher. I try to stand but fall backward. I want to keep falling.

I thought I knew everything about friendship and family; the happiness, simplicity and joy within them. But there is another side to devotion, which Samira understands. She is her father's daughter after all.

One hand is enough to sin. One hand is enough to save.

Epilogue

I had a dream last night that I got married in a white dress, not a sari. My father came storming up the aisle haranguing me and the congregation burst into spontaneous applause thinking it was some sort of Sikh floor show.

Samira was there, holding up Jasper, who kicked and giggled and waved his arms excitedly. Hari held Claudia above his head to watch. She was far more serious and looked ready to cry. My mother was shedding buckets, of course. She could cry for two countries.

I am having a lot of dreams like this lately. Perfect-life fantasies, full of ideal matches and soap opera endings. See how wet I've become. I used to be a girl who didn't cry at sad endings or get mushy over babies. Nowadays I have to bite my lip to hold back the tears and I want to float through the ceiling I love them so much.

Jasper is always happy and laughs for no apparent reason, while Claudia watches the world with troubled eyes and sometimes, when you least expect it, she produces tears of abject sorrow and I know that she's crying for those who can't.

Their names have stayed. That happens sometimes; something is given a name and it just doesn't seem right to change it. I won't be changing mine when I get married, but other things are already different. It used to be *me*; now it's *we* and *us*.

Rolling over on my side, I run my fingers across the sheet until they touch Dave's chest. The duvet is wrapped around us and it feels safe, cocooned, shielded from the world.

He's letting his hair grow longer now. It suits his new lifestyle. I never thought I'd fall in love with a man who wears Aran sweaters and waterproof trousers. His hand is lying between us. There are calluses forming on his palms from working the sheets and raising sails.

There is a snuffled cry from the next room. After a pause, I hear it again.

"It's your turn," I whisper, tickling Dave's ear.

"You're getting up anyway," he mumbles.

"That makes no difference."

"It's the girl."

"How do you know?"

"She has a whiny cry."

I jab him hard in the ribs. "Girls do *not* whine. And since when has there been any demarcation?"

He rolls out of bed and looks for his boxer shorts.

"You just keep the bed warm."

"Always."

Although it was only three weeks ago, the events of those days have become a surreal blur. There was no custody battle. Barnaby Elliot withdrew gracelessly when faced with charges of withholding information from the police and being an accessory after the fact.

Judge Freyne found Samira to be the mother of the twins, however the DNA test threw up another twist to the story. The twins were brother and sister and the eggs came from Cate, as expected, but they had been fertilized by some third party, someone other than Felix. More than a ripple went round the courtroom when that little piece of information became public.

How was it possible? Dr. Banerjee harvested twelve viable embryos and implanted ten of them in IVF procedures. Cate took the remaining pair to Amsterdam.

There could have been a mix-up, of course, and someone else's sperm may have contaminated the process. According to Dr. Banerjee, the primary reason why Felix and Cate couldn't conceive was because her womb treated his sperm like cancerous cells and destroyed them. In another womb, with stronger sperm, who knows? But there was another issue: the recessive gene carried by Cate and Felix that caused a rare genetic disorder, a lethal form of dwarfism. Should she conceive, there was a 25 percent chance that the fetus would be affected.

Cate would never have cheated on Felix in the bedroom or in her heart, but she desperately wanted a child and having waited for so long and taken such risks she couldn't afford to be disappointed again. Perhaps she found someone she trusted, someone Felix would never meet, someone who looked a lot like him, someone who *owed* her.

It is just a theory of course. Nothing but speculation. It first occurred to me as I watched the twins sleeping and glanced at the dream catcher above their heads, letting my fingers brush the feathers and beads.

I doubt if Donavon had any idea what Cate planned. And even if he is the father, he has kept his promise to her and never revealed the fact. It's better that way.

I slip out of bed, shivering as I pull on my track pants and a fleece-lined top. By the time I step outside the cottage, it is beginning to grow light over the Solent and the Isle of Wight. Taking Sea Road past Smuggler's Inn, I turn left through the car park and arrive at a long shingle spit that reaches out into the Solent almost halfway to the island.

Wading birds lift off from the marshes as I pass and the beam from the lighthouse flashes every few seconds, growing fainter against the brightening sky. The sound of my shoes on the compacted shingle is reassuring as I cover the final mile to Hurst Castle, which guards the western approach to the Solent. Some days when southeasters have whipped the sea into a foaming monster, I don't reach the castle. Great white-tipped rollers arc upward and smash against the seawall, exploding into a mist that blurs the air and turns it solid. I can barely walk against the wind, bent double, blinking away the salt.

The weather is kind today. There are skiffs on the water already and, to my left, a father and son are hunting for cockles in the shallows. The sailing school will reopen in May. The skiffs are ready and

I've become a dab hand at repairing sails. (Those years of watching Mama at her sewing machine weren't entirely wasted.)

My life has changed so much in the past three months. The twins don't let me sleep beyond 6:00 a.m. and some nights I bring them into bed, which all the experts say I shouldn't. They have pushed me around, robbed me of sleep, filled me up and made me laugh. I am besotted. Spellbound. My heart has doubled in size to make room for them.

As I near the coastal end of the spit, I notice a figure sitting on an upturned rowboat with his boots planted in the shingle and hands in his pockets. Beside him is a canvas fishing bag and a rod.

"I know you don't sleep, sir, but this is ridiculous."

Ruiz raises his battered cap. "You have to get up early to catch a fish, grasshopper."

"So why aren't you fishing?"

"I've decided to give them a head start."

He slings the bag over his shoulder and climbs the rocky slope, falling into step beside me.

"Have you ever actually caught a fish, sir?"

"You being cheeky?"

"You don't seem to use any bait."

"Well that means we start as equals. I don't believe in having an unfair advantage."

We walk in silence, our breath steaming the air. Almost home, I stop opposite Milford Green and get a newspaper and muffins.

Samira is in the kitchen, wearing pajamas and my old dressing gown with the owl stitched on the pocket. Jasper is nestled in the crook of her left arm, nuzzling her right breast. Claudia is in the bassinet by the stove, frowning slightly as if she disapproves of having to wait her turn.

"Good morning, Mr. Ruiz."

"Good morning." Ruiz takes off his cap and leans over the bassinet. Claudia gives him her most beatific smile.

Samira turns to me. "How were they last night?"

"Angels."

"You always say that. Even when they wake you five times."

"Yes."

She laughs. "Thank you for letting me sleep."

"What time is your exam?"

"Ten."

Ruiz offers to drive her into Southampton where she's studying for her A-levels at the City College. Her exams aren't until June and the big question is whether she'll sit them at Her Majesty's pleasure or in a normal classroom with other students.

Her lawyers seem confident that they can argue a case of diminished responsibility or temporary insanity. Given what she's been through, nobody is very enthusiastic about sending her to prison, not even Mr. Greenburg, who had to choke back his emotions when he told her the CPS was pressing ahead with the murder charge.

"What about the public interest?" I demanded, acidly.

"The public saw it happen on the BBC, prime time. She killed a man. I have to let it go to a jury."

Samira posted bail thanks to Ruiz and my parents. The DI has become like a grandfather to the twins, who seem enthralled by his craggy face and by the low rumble of his voice. Perhaps it's his Gypsy blood but he seems to understand what it's like to enter the world violently, clinging on to life.

My mother is the other one who is besotted. She phones four times a day wanting updates on how they're sleeping and feeding and growing.

I take Jasper from Samira and hold him over my shoulder, gently rubbing his back. She scoops up Claudia with her right hand and offers her a breast, which she nuzzles anxiously until her mouth finds the nipple.

A missing hand doesn't even seem like a disability when you watch her with the twins, loving them completely; doing everyday chores like washing and feeding and changing nappies. She is a bright, pretty teenage mother of baby twins.

Samira doesn't talk about the future. She doesn't talk about the past. Today matters. The twins matter.

I don't know how long we're going to have them or what's going to happen next, but I've come to realize that we can never know something like that. There are no certainties in life or in death. The end of one story is merely the beginning of the next.